Siddhartha

Hermann Hesse

A Dual-Language Book

Translation, Introduction, and Glossary of Indian Terms by
STANLEY APPELBAUM

DOVER PUBLICATIONS, INC.
Mineola, New York

Copyright

Copyright © 1998 by Dover Publications, Inc.
All rights reserved under Pan American and International Copyright Conventions.

Published in Canada by General Publishing Company, Ltd., 30 Lesmill Road, Don Mills, Toronto, Ontario.
Published in the United Kingdom by Constable and Company, Ltd., 3 The Lanchesters, 162–164 Fulham Palace Road, London W6 9ER.

Bibliographical Note

The present edition, first published by Dover in 1998, contains the full German text of the work originally published by S. Fischer, Berlin, in 1922, along with a new English translation by Stanley Appelbaum, who also wrote the Introduction, footnotes, and Glossary of Indian Terms, and added a table of contents.

Library of Congress Cataloging-in-Publication Data

Hesse, Hermann, 1877–1962.
    [Siddhartha. English & German]
    Siddhartha : a dual-language book / Hermann Hesse ; translation, introduction, and glossary of Indian terms by Stanley Appelbaum.
       p. cm.
    ISBN 0-486-40437-4 (pbk.)
    I. Appelbaum, Stanley. II. Title.
PT2617.E85S513 1998
833'.912—dc21   98-30250
                                                                    CIP

Manufactured in the United States of America
Dover Publications, Inc., 31 East 2nd Street, Mineola, N.Y. 11501

Contents

INTRODUCTION

The Author

Hermann Hesse was born in 1877 in Calw, in the Black Forest region of southwestern Germany. Calw was a center of missionary publishing to which his father, a North German, had been posted after becoming ill while a missionary in India. In Calw the author's father married the daughter of his superior, a prominent linguist; she herself had been born in India when her father was a missionary there. Thus, young Hermann grew up in an atmosphere that was unusually cultured and cosmopolitan for a small town.

But it was also an atmosphere of piety and duty; the boy was expected to become a minister. Although extremely bright, however, and gifted at writing and drawing, Hermann was surprisingly rebellious and difficult. His school record was not brilliant, and, finally, at the age of fifteen, he even ran away from his seminary. A breakdown ensued, the beginning of a lifelong series of visits to sanatoria, spas, and psychiatrists. Formal schooling, and with it a career in the clergy, was eventually called off, and Hesse thenceforth educated himself on his own time—but so successfully that he became one of the best-read of all German writers, and was able to publish a famous reading list of "best books" for people aspiring to culture.

After uncongenial work in a church-clock factory, he concentrated on learning the bookseller's trade, which he had looked into earlier. After four years with a book dealer in the tradition-rich university town of Tübingen, a period in which he began writing seriously, he joined another firm in Basel, and from then on usually resided in Switzerland, although he did not change his citizenship until 1924. In 1899, the year of the move to Basel, his first book was published: *Romantische Lieder,* a book of verse. Hesse continued to write verse all his life, becoming one of the most prolific and respected German poets of the century. His poems were to appeal to a number of major

song composers; three of Richard Strauss's famous Four Last Songs are to texts by Hesse.

Hesse's novels, however, are undoubtedly his best work (although eventually he was also to write many, many volumes' worth of short stories, travel accounts, essays, book reviews, translations, introductions to new editions of classics, articles for periodicals, and a vast correspondence). His first novel, the important *Peter Camenzind* of 1903, was a breakthrough for Hesse in several ways: it began his association with the great Berlin publisher S. [Samuel] Fischer; it brought him enough money and fame to live off his writings from then on, giving up bookselling; and this financial stability allowed him to marry. His first wife, older than he, was to present him with three sons; unfortunately, she was neurotically reclusive, and he was compelled to divorce her in 1923. From 1904 to 1912 they lived on a farm near Lake Constance; farm life was one of several dreams that went sour on Hesse when put into practice.

Another dream that failed to stand up to reality was Hesse's quest in 1911 for some sort of roots in India, a country where both of his parents had lived and whose literature, religions, and philosophies were dear to him. The steamer he sailed on touched at ports in Ceylon, the Malayan island of Penang, Singapore, and Sumatra. Hesse suffered from the heat and from dysentery. He was away only a few months and never set foot in what we call India; English-language reference books that speak of a stay in India are carelessly mistranslating the German word *Indien,* which can also be an overall term covering *Vorderindien* (Hither India; i.e., our "India") and *Hinterindien* (Farther India; i.e., Southeast Asia). Hesse himself referred to his destination variously as *Indien,* Asia, or Malaya. On his return he expressed disappointment, claiming that colonial rule had denatured the territory; he seems to have been more comfortable with the Chinese merchants he met than with the largely impoverished Hindu and Muslim population. (For Hesse's literary works involving India, see the section "The Novel," below.)

From 1912 to 1919 Hesse lived in Berne. Unable to serve in the First World War because of his bad eyes, he worked for organizations that supplied reading matter to German prisoners of war. Though not a militant pacifist, he had pacifist leanings and thus became associated with the like-minded French author Romain Rolland, to whom he would later dedicate Part One of *Siddhartha.*

Hesse had been writing excellent novels and stories all this time, but his real blossoming out came after the war. In 1919 he published pseudonymously (fooling all but a few canny readers) the novel some

critics believe to be his best, *Demian* (actually written in 1917). Always concerned with the problems of children and young people (and later encouraged in this by his psychoanalytic sessions with Jung), from *Demian* on he became a recognized mentor of German intellectual and avant-garde youth. During the same year, 1919, he wrote some major short stories, began writing *Siddhartha* (not published until 1922; see "The Novel," below), and moved to the Ticino, the Italian-speaking part of Switzerland. From 1919 to 1931 he rented a villa in the village of Montagnola, near Lugano; it was there that he wrote his weirdest and most experimental novel, *Der Steppenwolf* (1927). In 1931 a wealthy patron built a new, isolated house for Hesse in the same village and gave him free use of it for his lifetime. There the writer lived happily with his third wife (they married in 1931; Hesse's unsuccessful second marriage in 1924 had been extremely brief); he happily tended an extensive garden, received visits from friends and admirers, and continued his writing career.

In the early years of the Nazi Reich, Hesse spoke out against Swiss intolerance toward the numerous German emigrants seeking refuge in his adopted country. Even during the Second World War, however, he still tried to get his new works published in Germany, and he gave hospitality to German writers who had stayed at home. The great product of those years was his long novel *Das Glasperlenspiel* (*The Glass Bead Game*, a.k.a. *Magister Ludi*), published in Zurich in 1943 (the composition had taken eleven years). Although some critics prefer *Demian, Siddhartha, Der Steppenwolf*, or the 1930 novel *Narziss und Goldmund*, there is no doubt that *Das Glasperlenspiel* is Hesse's most ambitious work, in construction, in imagination, and in style, the one with most breadth, depth, and scope. It was largely on the basis of that novel that Hesse was awarded the Nobel Prize in literature in 1946 (his friend Thomas Mann, the laureate in 1929, had already been canvassing for him for years).

Das Glasperlenspiel was the last major work. Active to the end, though suffering from leukemia, Hesse died of a cerebral hemorrhage in 1962.

The Novel

Part One of *Siddhartha* was written in the fall and winter of 1919. Then, after that amazingly productive year, Hesse experienced a lengthy fit of depression and was unable to continue for a year and a half. He was finally able to finish the book in the spring of 1922, and

it was published by S. Fischer, Berlin, later that year. (Various sections of Part One had already been published in several magazines and newspapers.) Part One was originally dedicated to Romain Rolland; Part Two, to Wilhelm Gundert, a cousin of Hesse's on his mother's side, an expert on Japan whose visit had helped clarify the author's thoughts about Part Two.[1] In a 1950 reprinting, Hesse dropped these dedications, substituting one to his third wife, Ninon Dolbin.

In German editions, the novel (sometimes called a novella) carries the subtitle *Eine indische Dichtung* (*An Indian Literary Work*). Though this can also mean "a work about India," the connotation "a work originating in India" is strong. This connotation is consonant with the book's style, which simulates that of an old pious legend. Hesse's style, although generally lucid and classical, avoiding syntactic or other extremes, was nevertheless very malleable and could change drastically to suit varied narrative situations (it should be recalled that almost no one identified him as the author of *Demian*, although he had been an established author for twenty years). For *Siddhartha* he chose a highly poetic style reminiscent of ancient scriptures, particularly the sermons attributed to the Buddha (available to him in excellent German translations), with their parallelism of simple clauses and their incantatory repetitions. He uses a number of archaic words, unusual forms, and rarer secondary meanings of everyday words. (This style is imitated in the present translation, not by using archaisms, but by retaining the repetitions, avoiding contractions, using "dignified" word choices, and very occasionally wrenching the syntax where the German does this very conspicuously.)

Hesse's relationship to India through his family has already been mentioned, as has his journey to Southeast Asia. *Siddhartha* was the most important product of that relationship, but far from the only one. In 1913, for example, Hesse had published the volume *Aus Indien,* which consisted chiefly of an account of his trip, but also included, among other items, the short story "Robert Aghion," about a young missionary in India who balks at becoming part of the colonial establishment and who loses his calling when no longer convinced that the religion he came to impose was necessarily superior to that of the local population. Another journey to the East, although this time very un-

---

[1] Although the novel is formally divided into these two parts, it actually falls naturally into three parts of four chapters each. One ingenious critic laboriously attempted to equate the four chapters of Part One with the Four Great Truths of Buddhism, and the eight chapters of Part Two with the Buddhist Eightfold Path!

realistic and much more of a fantasy than even in *Siddhartha,* is the basis of Hesse's important novella of 1931 *Die Morgenlandfahrt (The Journey to the Orient).* And, significantly, one of the previous incarnations of the hero of *Das Glasperlenspiel* takes place in ancient India.

In *Siddhartha* the historical situation is very specific. The sixty or so years of the hero's life can be dated to around 540 to 480 B.C. on the basis of the traditional dates for the Buddha (roughly 560 to 480). This was a period of great intellectual and spiritual upheaval. The older Vedic religion, or Brahmanism, which, at least as far as written records show, was based on strict ritual observances in the worship of old Indo-European deities—observances requiring the participation of the Brahmans, the highest, priestly caste—was coming to an end. The new Vedic writings of the time were the Upanishads, which reinterpreted the religion philosophically and mystically, preaching the oneness of the universe. Brahmanism was slowly developing into Hinduism, which was still polytheistic, but largely characterized by almost exclusive devotion to a single supreme god chosen from among a small number; the most popular gods now proved to be the gods of the common people, who had played only a minor role in the Vedas, Shiva and Vishnu (Vishnu also being worshipped in various of his incarnations, especially Rama and Krishna).

Another contemporary result of the fundamental questioning of the established religion at this time was a number of sects or heresies, particularly Buddhism, which looked on earthly life as mere suffering and whose adherents sought release from the eternal round of reincarnation that was universally believed in at the time. Whereas the Hindu hoped that good works in this life would lead to a loftier and more comfortable position in his next existence, the Buddhist saw no good in living at all, and sought total extinction (*nirvana*). The historical Buddha, Siddhartha[2] Gautama of the Sakya clan, preached Four Great Truths: all existence is suffering; suffering is caused by desires; to stop suffering, one must cease to desire; this is achieved by the Eightfold Path. That path consisted of: correct opinions, correct

---

[2] It is hard to say why Hesse gave his hero the same given name as the Buddha's (the Buddha is never called by that name in the book); it is a source of confusion at first for anyone familiar with Buddhism—and Hesse expected some familiarity, because he uses a number of Buddhist terms and concepts without further explanation. The similarity of names certainly confused the writer of the short article on Hesse in a prominent encyclopedia; one edition after another has transmitted the notion that the novel is about the early life of the Buddha. (It is rather unnerving to reflect that the author of the article obviously never read the book!)

thoughts, correct speech, correct actions, correct way of living, correct effort, correct attention, and correct concentration.

This original (or "primitive") Buddhism, specifically intended to save those who took a vow of poverty and became monks, renouncing all worldly ties, ignored the gods and included little in the way of worship; it has been called a philosophy or a therapy rather than a religion. Much later, however, by the beginning of the Christian era, Buddhism developed in India into the Mahayana ("great vehicle") school, which became a religion for the masses, with an extensive pantheon, a multiplicity of Buddhas, the possibility of instant salvation without great efforts, and an active corps of "guardian angels" (bodhisattvas). In this form, Buddhism (which was to disappear in India) conquered Tibet, China, Mongolia, Korea, Japan, and Vietnam. A form of Buddhism closer to the original survives only in Ceylon, Burma, Thailand, Cambodia, and Laos. (For the technical Indian terms in the novel, as well as a brief analysis of the names of the characters, see the Glossary that follows this Introduction.)

Hesse was interested in Chinese philosophy, as well, and even stated that Taoism was a greater influence on *Siddhartha* than Indian philosophies were. Some typical Taoist elements are the praise of quietism, seclusion, and an austerely simple life-style; and the belief that softness is stronger than hardness.

Almost all of Hesse's novels are philosophical and allegorical to some extent; they are not character studies, like Stendhal's, for instance; or depictions of society, like Balzac's; or vivid tableaux of real people interacting with one another and with their circumstances, like Tolstoy's. But *Siddhartha* is by far the most schematic; the incidents can readily be plotted on a graph, and the characters have no more individuality than those in such medieval allegories as *The Romance of the Rose*. *Siddhartha* is a long preachment, quite literally offering us "books in the running brooks, / Sermons in stones, and good in everything." The philosophy, however, is much more emotional and imagistic than systematic or really thought out.

The novel's vitality and connection to reality are due to its genuine sources in Hesse's own life. Siddhartha (minus, perhaps, some of the virtues he acquires at the end, such as unstinting love) *is* Hesse. The struggles of Siddhartha against his priestly father, and those of his own son against him, reflect Hesse's defiance of authority as a child. Siddhartha's conclusion that teachings are useless reflects Hesse's interrupted schooling and his pride in his self-education. Siddhartha's self-doubts and attempt at suicide have real echoes in Hesse's life.

Even small details are relevant: the raft Siddhartha builds with Vasudeva may very well refer to Hesse's rides on loggers' rafts when a boy in Calw. Like Peter Camenzind, like Demian, like the *Steppenwolf,* like the Magister Ludi, Siddhartha is an outsider choosing his own path, no matter how disturbing it may be to society (although a fundamentally antisocial life-style, such as a criminal's, is rarely a choice for Hesse's heroes).

Aside from its verbal charm, the book is also enlivened by a series of remarkably insightful touches with a ring of psychological veracity, as when the love-starved Siddhartha dreams he is embracing his friend Govinda and the figure dissolves into that of a nurturing woman.

The book was immediately successful in Germany, and is still regarded by some as Hesse's greatest; there is a vast body of critical literature in German concerning it. It was translated into Hungarian in 1923; into Russian in 1924; into French and Japanese in 1925; into Dutch in 1928; into Polish in 1932; and into Czech in 1935. Translations into two dozen other languages, including over a dozen spoken in India, date from after the Second World War. It was Henry Miller, another kind of influential outsider, who, becoming enamored of the novel, urged his publishers, New Directions, to commission an English translation. Although this pioneering effort, first published in 1951, did not meet high standards of accuracy, completeness, fidelity to the tone of the original, or even proper English, it did yeoman service in introducing *Siddhartha* to the English-speaking world. This novel has remained Hesse's most popular in the United States.

It must remain a matter of personal opinion whether the best possible use was made of the novel in the first decade or two after its English translation; that is, whether Hesse had ever envisioned the book as a side dish to LSD, a hippie handbook, or a bible for the dropout and the draft dodger. Although the unguarded and unqualified terms in which he sometimes praises the rejection of conventional wisdom and morality, inviting the reader to "do his own thing," make him partly responsible for any results whatsoever, only a hasty, superficial reading could have produced the most unfortunate results that did ensue (in some people's opinion).

Today, in a substantially calmer period, we can recognize that this outcry against oppressive social forces, this plea for self-fulfillment despite the expectations of others, was that of a mature, responsible man; a friend of writers, composers, and artists (himself a violinist and painter, as well); a highly educated and sophisticated intellectual aristocrat—and that it was intended for his peers.

GLOSSARY OF INDIAN TERMS

Preliminary Remarks

The lore of Buddhism in India has been chiefly handed down in two different languages: Sanskrit (Saṁskṛta), a direct outgrowth of the Vedic language, and the classical language of Hindu India par excellence (like Latin for medieval and Renaissance Europe; it is mainly the later, Mahāyāna, Buddhist writings that use a form of Sanskrit), and Pali (Pāli), a later, but closely related, language exhibiting significant phonetic simplification vis-à-vis Sanskrit. Pali is the chief language in which the oldest Buddhist writings have come down to us and is the sacred tongue of the conservative Theravādin sect of Buddhism still prevalent in Ceylon, Burma, Thailand, Cambodia, and Laos. (See the discussion of Buddhism in the Introduction.)

Hesse, though a voracious reader deeply imbued with Asian thought, was not a scholar, and in this novel he indiscriminately mixed Sanskrit and Pali terms (as well as nomenclature from different periods); in fact, some commentators on *Siddhartha* have seen him as basically a name-dropper. Moreover, he never used any of the standard diacritical marks (such as a horizontal rule [or a circumflex] over vowels to indicate length, a dot beneath certain consonants to indicate their pronunciation with the tongue tip placed behind the upper teeth ridge, etc.). Quite naturally, for a few words he used a German spelling that has become standard (just as we do, for example, with "Upanishad"): "Nirwana," "Vischnu," "Krischna," etc.

In the present translation, to avoid confusion and pedantry, the English uses a Pali form where the German does, and a Sanskrit form where the German does (usually in the same form, except where the German has an outright error, as in "Savathi"); at the request of the publisher, the translation (like the Introduction) also omits the (really useful, if not essential) diacritical marks (the ignorance of which, as well as general linguistic carelessness, has led a few commentators on

Siddhartha into ludicrous errors). Here and there, it would have been foolish not to use a few standard English spellings, analogous to the German ones mentioned at the end of the foregoing paragraph.

This glossary, however, *does* use a scholarly transliteration, including diacritical marks, and, where necessary, distinguishes Pali from Sanskrit terms. All the terms and proper names are historical and not invented by Hesse, except those preceded by an asterisk (*), which are those of his fictional characters. Two terms in the glossary are not from the text itself, but from the translator's footnotes; they are preceded by a dagger (†).

Agni. God of fire and burnt offerings in the Vedic and Brahmanic religion.

Anāthapiṇḍika. Rich banker who bought the park Jetavana and donated it to the Buddha.

Atharva Veda. The Veda principally concerned with magic spells. See "Vedas."

Ātman. The self; one's own nature; the individual soul. In some of the Upanishads, this is equated with the *Brahman,* or universal soul. The term is Sanskrit, the Pali equivalent being *attan.*

Bo tree. The tree (in Buddhagayā [Bodh Gaya]) beneath which the Buddha was sitting when he attained enlightenment (*bodhi*). It was a pipal, or sacred fig, tree (*Ficus religiosa*). The specific form *bo* is neither Sanskrit nor Pali, but Singhalese (Ceylonese).

"Brahma, Brahman." For the purposes of the novel, three terms have to be distinguished: (1) Brahmā is either the supreme god, or one of the three supreme gods, of the Brahmanic/Hindu tradition (the creator of the world; in the novel he is alluded to only twice, and the other two terms are far more significant); (2) *Brahman* (a neuter noun) is the absolute, the world soul, the highest being, the unifying principle of the universe (always italicized in the present English translation); (3) "Brahman" (*brāhmaṇa*) is a member of the highest caste, the priests, who guard the Vedic tradition and officiate at numerous rites and sacrifices (this term appears in German as "der Brahmane," in the present translation as "Brahman"; the alternate English spelling "Brahmin" is now chiefly used figuratively and pejoratively). (In this entry, to avoid counterproductive complications, some niceties of Sanskrit linguistics have been intentionally overlooked.)

Chandogya Upanishad. In Sanskrit, *Chāndogya Upaniṣad* ("the Upanishad concerning the chanter of the *Sāma* melodies"), this Upanishad (see that term) is part of the *Sāma Veda* (see that term).

Among its chief topics are the mystical meanings of certain sounds, especially the syllable *om* (see that term), and the oneness of the individual and world souls.

Gotama. This is the Pali form equivalent to the Sanskrit Gautama. It was the family name of the man who became the Buddha (see Introduction).

***Govinda.** Siddhārtha's boyhood friend in the novel. Hesse probably derived the name from later literature about Krishna (see that entry), where it is a title of Krishna, and sometimes of Vishnu (see that entry), of whom Krishna is considered an avatar (incarnation). The name appears to mean "cow-seeker," and is appropriate to Krishna's life as a herdsman.

Jetavana. A park ("[Prince] Jeta's forest") in Sāvatthi (see that entry), donated to the Buddha by Anāthapiṇḍika (see that entry), who bought it at a vast price from Jeta.

***Kamalā.** A courtesan loved by Siddhārtha in the novel. The name means "lotus blossom." The first *a* is short, and the word has nothing to do with *kāma* (love, desire, passion) despite the opinion of careless commentators. That Hesse himself knew what the name meant is indicated, if not proved, by the reference to a lotus blossom in the poem that Siddhārtha addresses to the courtesan; whether even Hesse connected it with *kāma,* as well, is hard to say. Kamalā is also a title of the goddess Lakṣmī.

†*Kāmasūtra.* "Treatise on Love"; written in the early centuries of the Christian era, thus hundreds of years after the events of the novel (although its teachings may have been common knowledge at an earlier date).

***Kamaswami.** In the novel, a merchant who takes Siddhārtha in as his assistant. Hesse probably invented the name, which is seemingly compounded of *kāma* (love, desire, passion) and *svāmin* (owner of, master of).

Krishna (Kṛṣṇa). As referred to in the novel, a Hindu herdsman-god of northern India, considered to be an avatar (incarnation) of the major god Vishnu. (Krishna is also a character in the epic poem *Mahābhārata,* in which he utters the sublime *Bhagavadgītā*.)

Lakshmi (Lakṣmī). A goddess, the consort of the great Hindu god Vishnu (Viṣṇu).

Magadha. A large region, part of the present-day Indian state of Bihār. Gayā, where Gautama became the Buddha, was a district within Magadha.

Māra. A demon who unsuccessfully assailed Gautama with magi-

cal illusions during the *bo*-tree meditations that led to Gautama's Buddhahood.

Māyā. Illusion; used in different contexts—for instance, the illusion that what our senses perceive is reality; the Buddha strove to dispel illusion.

Nirvana. In Sanskrit, *nirvāṇa*; in Pali, *nibbānaṃ*. Literally, "extinction, blowing out." Used to refer to a death no longer subject to rebirths; the goal of the original Buddhists.

Om (also, *aum*). The untranslatable syllable uttered before every recitation from the Vedas. This prominence led mystics, in the Upanishads and elsewhere, to elevate *om* to the greatest heights—indeed, to the position of the Supreme in the universe.

†Parinirvāṇa. "Ultimate extinction"; a term applied to the death of the Buddha.

Prajāpati. "Lord of engendered beings"; an abstract creator divinity often mentioned in the Upanishads.

Rig Veda (*Ṛg-Veda*). The most famous Veda, an anthology of hymns to the gods to be performed at sacrifices.

Śākya. The clan to which Gautama's family belonged.

Śākyamuni. The wise man (or, seer; or, ascetic) of the Śākya clan; a title of the Buddha.

Samana. In Pali, *samaṇa*; in Sanskrit, *śramaṇa*. In general, a wandering ascetic; this is how the word is used through most of the novel. But, in Buddhism in particular, it refers to a mendicant monk, and Hesse uses it in this way at times. From the root *śram-*, indicating heavy labor and exhaustion; some commentators have given incredibly fanciful etymologies. (This term is intentionally not italicized in the translation, since it is such an integral part of the narrative.)

Sāma Veda. The Veda concerned with the chanting of the ritual hymns; it includes some musical notation.

Saṃsāra. Only in the final chapter does Hesse use this term in its primary meaning of reincarnation, the round of rebirths from which Buddhists wished to escape. Everywhere else, he uses it in the secondary sense of "this world we live in, in which we are subject to reincarnation." In this usage, it is reminiscent of *karma* (the actions that inevitably lead to reincarnation), a term that Hesse never uses in the novel. Generally speaking, *saṃsāra* is largely secularized in *Siddhartha,* at times practically reduced to "the annoyances (or monotony) of life."

Satyam (Sanskrit; in Pali, *saccaṃ*). The truth (both literally and as a philosophical principle).

Sāvatthi (Pali; in Sanskrit, *Śrāvastī*). A city in the Kosala region, northwest of Magadha (in the present state of Uttar Pradesh). Location of Jetavana (see that term). Hesse's form "Savathi" is incorrect in any language.

*   **Siddhārtha.** Hesse's hero, "one who has achieved his goal" in Sanskrit (in Pali, Siddhattha). This was also the personal name of the man who became the Buddha (see the Introduction for a discussion of Hesse's unusual choice of this very name).

Upanishads (Upaniṣad). The most recent writings within each Veda (see "Vedas"); mystical and/or philosophical reflections on elements in the Vedas (or on religion in general). Influential in all later Indian thought and, eventually, on European thought. Some of the Upanishads are gems of literature as well.

*   **Vasudeva.** The ferryman in the novel. The name was probably borrowed by Hesse from that of the foster father of the herdsman-god Krishna in later mythology (see "Krishna").

Vedas. The basic holy books of Brahmanism and Hinduism, probably composed gradually between about 1500 and 500 B.C. The four Vedas are the *Rig* (*Ṛg*) *Veda* (ritual hymns), the *Sāma Veda* (instructions on chanting the hymns), the *Yajur Veda* (a collection of ritual formulas), and the *Atharva Veda* (a collection of magic spells). In addition to the fundamental elements briefly characterized in the foregoing sentence, the Vedas also contain a vast amount of supplementary material, both mythological and theological, including the mystical and philosophical Upanishads (see that entry).

Vishnu (Viṣṇu). A relatively minor god in Vedic times, Vishnu ultimately became one of the chief gods of India, not only in the "trinity" Brahma-Vishnu-Shiva (Śiva), but also—for many millions—the supreme, practically the only, god (but one with many manifestations or incarnations, the two most famous being Krishna and Rāma).

Yoga Veda. There is no such thing, strictly speaking, but there is a group of Upanishads known as Yoga Upanishads, and there is a *Yogasūtra*. Yoga, of course, is the special set of methods of concentration and meditation intended to result in enlightenment or the acquisition of supernatural powers; it is present in some form in almost every area of Indian religion. (Could Hesse have been thinking of the *Yajur Veda*?)

Siddhartha

boot · boat
fluss · river
ufer · bank
wald · wood/forest
bad · bath
opfer - sacrifice
hain - grove
Knabe - boy
gesang - song
lehre - teaching, lesson

teil - part
rede - speech, word
versenkung - sinking, contemplation

ERSTER TEIL

DER SOHN DES BRAHMANEN

Im Schatten des Hauses, in der Sonne des Flußufers bei den
Booten, im Schatten des Salwaldes, im Schatten des Feigenbaumes
wuchs Siddhartha auf, der schöne Sohn des Brahmanen, der junge
Falke, zusammen mit Govinda, seinem Freunde, dem Brahman-
ensohn. Sonne bräunte seine lichten Schultern am Flußufer, beim
Bade, bei den heiligen Waschungen, bei den heiligen Opfern.
Schatten floß in seine schwarzen Augen im Mangohain, bei den
Knabenspielen, beim Gesang der Mutter, bei den heiligen Opfern,
bei den Lehren seines Vaters, des Gelehrten, beim Gespräch der
Weisen. Lange schon nahm Siddhartha am Gespräch der Weisen
teil, übte sich mit Govinda im Redekampf, übte sich mit Govinda in
der Kunst der Betrachtung, im Dienst der Versenkung. Schon verstand er, lautlos das Om zu sprechen, das Wort der Worte, es lautlos
in sich hinein zu sprechen mit dem Einhauch, es lautlos aus sich heraus zu sprechen mit dem Aushauch, mit gesammelter Seele, die
Stirn umgeben vom Glanz des klardenkenden Geistes. Schon verstand er, im Innern seines Wesens Atman zu wissen, unzerstörbar,
eins mit dem Weltall.

Freude sprang in seines Vaters Herzen über den Sohn, den
Gelehrigen, den Wissensdurstigen, einen großen Weisen und Priester
sah er in ihm heranwachsen, einen Fürsten unter den Brahmanen.

Wonne sprang in seiner Mutter Brust, wenn sie ihn sah, wenn sie
ihn schreiten, wenn sie ihn niedersitzen und aufstehen sah,

PART ONE

THE SON OF THE BRAHMAN

In the shadow of the house, in the sunshine of the riverbank by the boats, in the shadow of the *sal*-tree forest,[1] in the shadow of the fig tree, Siddhartha[2] grew up, the handsome son of the Brahman,[2] the young falcon, together with Govinda his friend, the Brahman's son. Sunshine tanned his fair shoulders at the riverbank, when he bathed, during the holy ablutions, during the holy sacrifices. Shadow flowed into his dark eyes in the mango grove, during his boyish games, while his mother sang, during the holy sacrifices, when he was taught by his father, the learned man, when he conversed with the sages. For some time now, Siddhartha had taken part in the conversations of the sages, had practiced oratorical contests with Govinda, had practiced with Govinda the art of contemplation, the duty of total concentration. He already understood how to utter the *om* silently, that word of words, how to utter it silently into himself as he inhaled, how to utter it silently forth from himself as he exhaled, his psychic powers concentrated, his brow encircled with the glow of the clear-thinking mind. He already understood how to recognize *Atman* within his being, indestructible, at one with the universe.

Joy leapt in his father's heart at that son, so quick to learn, so eager for knowledge; he saw a great sage and priest developing in him, a prince among the Brahmans.

Bliss leapt in his mother's bosom whenever she saw him, when she saw him walking, sitting down, and standing up, Siddhartha the

---

[1] A timber tree (*Shorea robusta*) with wood nearly as hard as teak. Buddha was born while his mother clutched a *sal* tree.

[2] Siddhartha; Brahman: see the Glossary for all proper names and Indian terms. The English translation basically uses the linguistic versions chosen by Hesse; diacritical marks appear only in the Glossary (see explanations there).

Siddhartha, den Starken, den Schönen, den auf schlanken Beinen
Schreitenden, den mit vollkommenem Anstand sie Begrüßenden.

Liebe rührte sich in den Herzen der jungen Brahmanentöchter,
wenn Siddhartha durch die Gassen der Stadt ging, mit der leuchten-
den Stirn, mit dem Königsauge, mit den schmalen Hüften.

Mehr als sie alle aber liebte ihn Govinda, sein Freund, der
Brahmanensohn. Er liebte Siddharthas Auge und holde Stimme, er
liebte seinen Gang und den vollkommenen Anstand seiner Bewegun-
gen, er liebte alles, was Siddhartha tat und sagte, und am meisten
liebte er seinen Geist, seine hohen, feurigen Gedanken, seinen glühenden Willen, seine hohe Berufung. Govinda wußte: dieser wird
kein gemeiner Brahmane werden, kein fauler Opferbeamter, kein
habgieriger Händler mit Zaubersprüchen, kein eitler, leerer Redner,
kein böser, hinterlistiger Priester, und auch kein gutes, dummes Schaf
in der Herde der Vielen. Nein, und auch er, Govinda, wollte kein
solcher werden, kein Brahmane, wie es zehntausend gibt. Er wollte
Siddhartha folgen, dem Geliebten, dem Herrlichen. Und wenn Siddhartha einstmals ein Gott würde, wenn er einstmals eingehen würde
zu den Strahlenden, dann wollte Govinda ihm folgen, als sein Freund,
als sein Begleiter, als sein Diener, als sein Speerträger, sein Schatten.

So liebten den Siddhartha alle. Allen schuf er Freude, allen war er
zur Lust.

Er aber, Siddhartha, schuf sich nicht Freude, er war sich nicht zur
Lust. Wandelnd auf den rosigen Wegen des Feigengartens, sitzend im
bläulichen Schatten des Hains der Betrachtung, waschend seine
Glieder im täglichen Sühnebad, opfernd im tiefschattigen
Mangowald, von vollkommenem Anstand der Gebärden, von allen
geliebt, aller Freude, trug er doch keine Freude im Herzen. Träume
kamen ihm und rastlose Gedanken aus dem Wasser des Flusses
geflossen, aus den Sternen der Nacht gefunkelt, aus den Strahlen der
Sonne geschmolzen, Träume kamen ihm und Ruhelosigkeit der
Seele, aus den Opfern geraucht, aus den Versen der Rig-Veda
gehaucht, aus den Lehren der alten Brahmanen geträufelt.

Siddhartha hatte begonnen, Unzufriedenheit in sich zu nähren. Er
hatte begonnen zu fühlen, daß die Liebe seines Vaters, und die Liebe
seiner Mutter, und auch die Liebe seines Freundes, Govindas, nicht
immer und für alle Zeiten ihn beglücken, ihn stillen, ihn sättigen,
ihm genügen werde. Er hatte begonnen zu ahnen, daß sein

strong, the handsome, walking on slender legs, greeting her with perfect propriety.

Love stirred in the hearts of the young Brahman daughters whenever Siddhartha passed through the lanes of the town, with his gleaming brow, with his kingly eyes, with his narrow hips.

But, more than by all of these, he was loved by Govinda his friend, the Brahman's son. He loved Siddhartha's eyes and pleasant voice, he loved his gait and the perfect propriety of his movements, he loved everything Siddhartha did and said; and, above all, he loved his intelligence, his lofty and fiery thoughts, his burning will, his high vocation. Govinda knew: this man will not become any ordinary Brahman, no lazy functionary at sacrifices, no avaricious merchant of magic charms, no vain, empty speechmaker, no malicious, crafty priest, but also no kindly, stupid sheep in the flock of the multitude. No, and he, too, Govinda, did not wish to become one of those, a Brahman like ten thousand others. He wanted to follow Siddhartha, the loved one, the splendid one. And if Siddhartha should ever become a god,[3] if he should ever enter the company of the Radiant Ones, then Govinda wished to follow him, as his friend, as his companion, as his servant, as his spear bearer, his shadow.

Thus did everyone love Siddhartha. He gave joy to all, he was a pleasure to all.

But he, Siddhartha, did not give himself joy, he was no pleasure to himself. Strolling on the pinkish walks of the fig orchard, sitting in the bluish shade of the grove of contemplation, washing his limbs in the daily expiatory bath, sacrificing in the deep shade of the mango forest, with gestures of perfect propriety, loved by all, the joy of all, nevertheless he bore no joy in his heart. Dreams came to him, and uneasy thoughts, flowing to him from the water of the river, sparkling from the night stars, molten in the rays of the sun; dreams came to him, and restlessness of the soul, smoking to him out of the sacrifices, uttered from the verses of the *Rig Veda,* trickling from the teachings of the old Brahmans.

Siddhartha had begun to nurture dissatisfaction within himself. He had begun to feel that his father's love, and his mother's love, and also the love of his friend Govinda, would not always and for all time make him happy, content him, sate him, suffice him. He had begun to foresee that his venerable father and his other teachers, that the Brahman

---

[3] Presumably, in a future reincarnation, as a reward for his exemplary mortal life.

ehrwürdiger Vater und seine anderen Lehrer, daß die weisen Brahmanen ihm von ihrer Weisheit das meiste und beste schon mitgeteilt, daß sie ihre Fülle schon in sein wartendes Gefäß gegossen hätten, und das Gefäß war nicht voll, der Geist war nicht begnügt, die Seele war nicht ruhig, das Herz nicht gestillt. Die Waschungen waren gut, aber sie waren Wasser, sie wuschen nicht Sünde ab, sie heilten nicht Geistesdurst, sie lösten nicht Herzensangst. Vortrefflich waren die Opfer und die Anrufung der Götter – aber war dies alles? Gaben die Opfer Glück? Und wie war das mit den Göttern? War es wirklich Prajapati, der die Welt erschaffen hat? War es nicht der Atman, Er, der Einzige, der All-Eine? Waren nicht die Götter Gestaltungen, erschaffen wie ich und du, der Zeit untertan, vergänglich? War es also gut, war es richtig, war es ein sinnvolles und höchstes Tun, den Göttern zu opfern? Wem anders war zu opfern, wem anders war Verehrung darzubringen als Ihm, dem Einzigen, dem Atman? Und wo war Atman zu finden, wo wohnte Er, wo schlug Sein ewiges Herz, wo anders als im eigenen Ich, im Innersten, im Unzerstörbaren, das ein jeder in sich trug? Aber wo, wo war dies Ich, dies Innerste, dies Letzte? Es war nicht Fleisch und Bein, es war nicht Denken noch Bewußtsein, so lehrten die Weisesten. Wo, wo also war es? Dorthin zu dringen, zum Ich, zu mir, zum Atman, – gab es einen andern Weg, den zu suchen sich lohnte? Ach, und niemand zeigte diesen Weg, niemand wußte ihn, nicht der Vater, nicht die Lehrer und Weisen, nicht die heiligen Opfergesänge! Alles wußten sie, die Brahmanen und ihre heiligen Bücher, alles wußten sie, um alles hatten sie sich gekümmert und um mehr als alles, die Erschaffung der Welt, das Entstehen der Rede, der Speise, des Einatmens, des Ausatmens, die Ordnungen der Sinne, die Taten der Götter – unendlich vieles wußten sie – aber war es wertvoll, dies alles zu wissen, wenn man das Eine und Einzige nicht wußte, das Wichtigste, das allein Wichtige?

Gewiß, viele Verse der heiligen Bücher, zumal in den Upanishaden des Samaveda, sprachen von diesem Innersten und Letzten, herrliche Verse. »Deine Seele ist die ganze Welt«, stand da geschrieben, und geschrieben stand, daß der Mensch im Schlafe, im Tiefschlaf, zu seinem Innersten eingehe und im Atman wohne. Wunderbare Weisheit stand in diesen Versen, alles Wissen der Weisesten stand

sages, had already imparted to him the greatest part and the best part
of their wisdom, that they had already poured their abundance into
his expectant vessel; and the vessel was not full, his mind was not satisfied, his soul was not at ease, his heart was not contented. The ablutions were good, but they were water, they did not wash away sin, they
did not heal the mind's thirst, they did not dispel the heart's anguish.
Excellent were the sacrifices and the invocation of the gods—but was
that everything? Did the sacrifices offer happiness? And what was all
that talk about the gods? Was it really Prajapati who had created the
world? Was it not the *Atman,* He, the Only One, the All-One?[4] Were
not the gods beings that had been formed, created just as you and I,
subject to time, mortal? And so, was it good, was it correct, was it a
meaningful and supreme activity, to sacrifice to the gods? To whom
else should one sacrifice, to whom else was reverence to be offered,
but to Him, the Only One, the *Atman*? And where was *Atman* to be
found, where did He dwell, where did His eternal heart beat, where
else but in one's own self, deep within oneself, in that indestructible
something that each man bore inside him? But where, where was this
self, this innermost thing, this ultimate thing? It was not flesh and
bone, it was not thought or consciousness: thus the sages taught.
Where, where then was it? To reach that far, to attain the ego, the self,
the *Atman*—was there another path that was profitably to be sought?
Ah! But no one pointed out that path, no one knew it, not his father,
not his teachers or the sages, not the holy sacrificial chants! They
knew everything, the Brahmans and their sacred books; they knew
everything, they had troubled their minds over everything, and more
than everything: the creation of the world, the origin of speech, of
food, of inhalation, of exhalation, the categories of the senses, the ex-
ploits of the gods—they knew an infinite amount—but was it of any
value to know all this when they did not know the one and only thing,
the most important thing, the only important thing?

To be sure, many verses of the sacred books, especially in the
Upanishads of the *Sama Veda,* spoke of this innermost, ultimate
thing—splendid verses. "Your soul is the whole world" was written
there, and it was written there that in sleep, in deep sleep, men
entered their innermost being and dwelt in the *Atman.* Marvelous
wisdom was contained in those verses, all the knowledge of the

---

[4] An untranslatable word play on *all* (everything, universe), *ein* (one), and *allein* (alone, unique).

hier in magischen Worten gesammelt, rein wie von Bienen gesammelter Honig. Nein, nicht gering zu achten war das Ungeheure an Erkenntnis, das hier von unzählbaren Geschlechterfolgen weiser Brahmanen gesammelt und bewahrt lag. – Aber wo waren die Brahmanen, wo die Priester, wo die Weisen oder Büßer, denen es gelungen war, dieses tiefste Wissen nicht bloß zu wissen, sondern zu leben? Wo war der Kundige, der das Daheimsein im Atman aus dem Schlafe herüberzauberte ins Wachsein, in das Leben, in Schritt und Tritt, in Wort und Tat? Viele ehrwürdige Brahmanen kannte Siddhartha, seinen Vater vor allen, den Reinen, den Gelehrten, den höchst Ehrwürdigen. Zu bewundern war sein Vater, still und edel war sein Gehaben, rein sein Leben, weise sein Wort, feine und adlige Gedanken wohnten in seiner Stirn – aber auch er, der so viel Wissende, lebte er denn in Seligkeit, hatte er Frieden, war er nicht auch nur ein Suchender, ein Dürstender? Mußte er nicht immer und immer wieder an heiligen Quellen, ein Durstender, trinken, am Opfer, an den Büchern, an der Wechselrede der Brahmanen? Warum mußte er, der Untadelige, jeden Tag Sünde abwaschen, jeden Tag sich um Reinigung mühen, jeden Tag von neuem? War denn nicht Atman in ihm, floß denn nicht in seinem eigenen Herzen der Urquell? Ihn mußte man finden, den Urquell im eigenen Ich, ihn mußte man zu eigen haben! Alles andre war Suchen, war Umweg, war Verirrung.

So waren Siddharthas Gedanken, dies war sein Durst, dies sein Leiden.

Oft sprach er aus einem Chandogya-Upanishad sich die Worte vor: »Fürwahr, der Name des Brahman ist Satyam – wahrlich, wer solches weiß, der geht täglich ein in die himmlische Welt.« Oft schien sie nahe, die himmlische Welt, aber niemals hatte er sie ganz erreicht, nie den letzten Durst gelöscht. Und von allen Weisen und Weisesten, die er kannte und deren Belehrung er genoß, von ihnen allen war keiner, der sie ganz erreicht hatte, die himmlische Welt, der ihn ganz gelöscht hatte, den ewigen Durst.

»Govinda«, sprach Siddhartha zu seinem Freunde, »Govinda, Lieber, komm mit mir unter den Banyanenbaum, wir wollen der Versenkung pflegen.«

Sie gingen zum Banyanenbaum, sie setzten sich nieder, hier Siddhartha, zwanzig Schritte weiter Govinda. Indem er sich niedersetzte, bereit, das Om zu sprechen, wiederholte Siddhartha murmelnd den Vers:

greatest sages was gathered together there in magical words, pure as honey gathered by bees. No, one should not hold lightly the immense store of knowledge that had been gathered and preserved there by countless generations of Brahman sages.—But where were those Brahmans, where were those priests, where were those sages or penitents, who had succeeded not merely in knowing this most profound knowledge, but in living it? Where was the expert who could magically transfer his sojourn in the *Atman* from the sleeping to the waking state, to real life, to every step he took, to words and deeds? Siddhartha knew many venerable Brahmans, his father especially: a pure man, a learned man, a man most highly to be revered. His father was admirable; his demeanor was calm and noble, his life pure, his words wise; subtle and noble thoughts resided in his brow—but even he, who knew so much, did he, then, live in bliss, was he at peace, was not he, too, merely a seeker, a man athirst? Was it not necessary for him, a long-parched man, to drink again and again at sacred springs, at the sacrifice, at the books, at the dialogues of the Brahmans? Why was it necessary for him, the faultless one, to wash away his sins every day, to strive for purification every day, all over again every day? Was *Atman* not in him, then? Did the wellspring not flow, then, in his own heart? It had to be found, the wellspring in one's own self, it had to be securely possessed! All else was a mere quest, a detour, an aberration.

Thus ran Siddhartha's thoughts, this was his thirst, this his sorrow.

Often he recited to himself the words from the *Chandogya Upanishad:* "Verily, the name of the *Brahman* is *satyam*—truly, he who knows this enters daily into the heavenly world." It often seemed near, that heavenly world, but he had never fully attained it, he had never quenched his ultimate thirst. And among all the wise and wisest men whom he knew, and whose instruction he enjoyed, there was none of them who had fully attained it, that heavenly world; who had fully quenched it, that eternal thirst.

"Govinda," Siddhartha said to his friend, "my dear Govinda, come with me under the banyan tree; we shall practice concentration."

They went to the banyan tree, they sat down, Siddhartha here, Govinda twenty paces further. As he was sitting down, ready to utter the *om*, Siddhartha repeated in a murmur the verse:

>»Om ist Bogen, der Pfeil ist Seele,
Das Brahman ist des Pfeiles Ziel,
Das soll man unentwegt treffen.«

Als die gewohnte Zeit der Versenkungsübung hingegangen war, erhob sich Govinda. Der Abend war gekommen, Zeit war es, die Waschung der Abendstunde vorzunehmen. Er rief Siddharthas Namen. Siddhartha gab nicht Antwort. Siddhartha saß versunken, seine Augen standen starr auf ein sehr fernes Ziel gerichtet, seine Zungenspitze stand ein wenig zwischen den Zähnen hervor, er schien nicht zu atmen. So saß er, in Versenkung gehüllt, Om denkend, seine Seele als Pfeil nach dem Brahman ausgesandt.

Einst waren Samanas durch Siddharthas Stadt gezogen, pilgernde Asketen, drei dürre, erloschene Männer, nicht alt noch jung, mit staubigen und blutigen Schultern, nahezu nackt, von der Sonne versengt, von Einsamkeit umgeben, fremd und feind der Welt, Fremdlinge und hagere Schakale im Reich der Menschen. Hinter ihnen her wehte heiß ein Duft von stiller Leidenschaft, von zerstörendem Dienst, von mitleidloser Entselbstung.

Am Abend, nach der Stunde der Betrachtung, sprach Siddhartha zu Govinda: »Morgen in der Frühe, mein Freund, wird Siddhartha zu den Samanas gehen. Er wird ein Samana werden.«

Govinda erbleichte, da er die Worte hörte und im unbewegten Gesicht seines Freundes den Entschluß las, unablenkbar wie der vom Bogen losgeschnellte Pfeil. Alsbald und beim ersten Blick erkannte Govinda: nun beginnt es, nun geht Siddhartha seinen Weg, nun beginnt sein Schickzal zu sprossen, und mit seinem das meine. Und er wurde bleich wie eine trockene Bananenschale.

»O Siddhartha«, rief er, »wird das dein Vater dir erlauben?«

Siddhartha blickte herüber wie ein Erwachender. Pfeilschnell las er in Govindas Seele, las die Angst, las die Ergebung.

»O Govinda«, sprach er leise, »wir wollen nicht Worte verschwenden. Morgen mit Tagesanbruch werde ich das Leben der Samanas beginnen. Rede nicht mehr davon.«

Siddhartha trat in die Kammer, wo sein Vater auf einer Matte aus Bast saß, und trat hinter seinen Vater und blieb da stehen, bis sein Vater fühlte, daß einer hinter ihm stehe. Sprach der Brahmane: »Bist du es, Siddhartha? So sage, was zu sagen du gekommen bist.«

Sprach Siddhartha: »Mit deiner Erlaubnis, mein Vater. Ich bin gekommen, dir zu sagen, daß mich verlangt, morgen dein Haus zu

"*Om* is the bow, the arrow is the soul,
The *Brahman* is the arrow's goal,
Which should be hit unswervingly."

When the customary period of the concentration practice had passed, Govinda arose. Evening had come; it was time to perform the ablution of the evening hour. He called Siddhartha's name. Siddhartha made no reply. Siddhartha sat in concentration; his eyes were fixed on a very distant goal; the tip of his tongue protruded slightly between his teeth; he seemed not to be breathing. Thus he sat, shrouded in concentration, thinking of *om*, his soul having been shot like an arrow at the *Brahman*.

Once, samanas had passed through Siddhartha's town, itinerant ascetics, three dried-up, burnt-out men, neither old nor young, with dusty and bloody shoulders, nearly nude, scorched by the sun, surrounded by solitude, strangers and enemies to the world, outsiders and emaciated jackals in the realm of human beings. Behind them wafted a hot smell of silent passion, of destructive duty, of pitiless liberation from the self.

In the evening, after the hour of contemplation, Siddhartha said to Govinda: "Tomorrow morning, my friend, Siddhartha will go to the samanas. He will become a samana."

Govinda turned pale when he heard those words and read the resolve in his friend's motionless features, a resolve as impossible to deflect as an arrow loosed from a bow. Immediately, at the first glance, Govinda realized: now it is beginning, now Siddhartha is going his way, now his destiny is beginning to germinate, and mine along with his. And he became as pale as a dry plantain peel.

"O Siddhartha," he called, "will your father allow you to?"

Siddhartha glanced over at him like a man awakening. With the speed of an arrow he read in Govinda's soul, he read the anguish there, he read the devotion.

"O Govinda," he said softly, "let us not waste words. Tomorrow at daybreak I shall begin the life of the samanas. Speak no more of it."

Siddhartha stepped into the room where his father was sitting on a palm-fiber mat, and stepped behind his father, and remained standing there until his father felt someone standing behind him. The Brahman said: "Is it you, Siddhartha? If so, say what you have come to say."

Siddhartha said: "With your permission, Father. I have come to tell you that I desire to leave your house tomorrow and to go to the as-

verlassen und zu den Asketen zu gehen. Ein Samana zu werden, ist
mein Verlangen. Möge mein Vater dem nicht entgegen sein.«

Der Brahmane schwieg, und schwieg so lange, daß im kleinen
Fenster die Sterne wanderten und ihre Figur veränderten, ehe das
Schweigen in der Kammer ein Ende fand. Stumm und regungslos
stand mit gekreuzten Armen der Sohn, stumm und regungslos saß auf
der Matte der Vater, und die Sterne zogen am Himmel. Da sprach der
Vater: »Nicht ziemt es dem Brahmanen, heftige und zornige Worte zu
reden. Aber Unwille bewegt mein Herz. Nicht möchte ich diese Bitte
zum zweiten Male aus deinem Munde hören.«

Langsam erhob sich der Brahmane, Siddhartha stand stumm mit
gekreuzten Armen.

»Worauf wartest du?« fragte der Vater.

Sprach Siddhartha: »Du weißt es.«

Unwillig ging der Vater aus der Kammer, unwillig suchte er sein
Lager auf und legte sich nieder.

Nach einer Stunde, da kein Schlaf in seine Augen kam, stand der
Brahmane auf, tat Schritte hin und her, trat aus dem Hause. Durch
das kleine Fenster der Kammer blickte er hinein, da sah er Siddhartha stehen, mit gekreuzten Armen, unverrückt. Bleich schimmerte sein helles Obergewand. Unruhe im Herzen, kehrte der Vater
zu seinem Lager zurück.

Nach einer Stunde, da kein Schlaf in seine Augen kam, stand der
Brahmane von neuem auf, tat Schritte hin und her, trat vor das Haus,
sah den Mond aufgegangen. Durch das Fenster der Kammer blickte
er hinein, da stand Siddhartha, unverrückt, mit gekreuzten Armen, an
seinen bloßen Schienbeinen spiegelte das Mondlicht. Besorgnis im
Herzen, suchte der Vater sein Lager auf.

Und er kam wieder nach einer Stunde, und kam wieder nach
zweien Stunden, blickte durchs kleine Fenster, sah Siddhartha stehen, im Mond, im Sternenschein, in der Finsternis. Und kam wieder
von Stunde zu Stunde, schweigend, blickte in die Kammer, sah den
unverrückt Stehenden, füllte sein Herz mit Zorn, füllte sein Herz mit
Unruhe, füllte sein Herz mit Zagen, füllte es mit Leid.

Und in der letzten Nachtstunde, ehe der Tag begann, kehrte er
wieder, trat in die Kammer sah den Jüngling stehen, der ihm groß
und wie fremd erschien.

»Siddhartha«, sprach er, »worauf wartest du?«

»Du weißt es.«

»Wirst du immer so stehen und warten, bis es Tag wird, Mittag
wird, Abend wird?«

cetics. To become a samana is my desire. I hope my father will not oppose this."

The Brahman was silent, and for so long that in the small window the stars progressed and altered their configuration before the silence in the room came to an end. Mute and motionless stood the son, with arms crossed; mute and motionless sat the father on his mat, and the stars moved across the sky. Then the father said: "It is unseemly for a Brahman to speak violent and angry words. But indignation stirs my heart. I should not like to hear that request from your lips a second time."

Slowly the Brahman rose; Siddhartha stood mute, with arms crossed.

"What are you waiting for?" asked the father.

Siddhartha said: "You know what for."

Indignantly the father left the room; indignantly he sought his bed and lay down.

An hour later, since no sleep visited his eyes, the Brahman got up, paced to and fro, stepped out of the house. He looked in through the small window of the room, where he saw Siddhartha standing, with arms crossed, on the same spot. His light-colored outer garment glimmered palely. Uneasy at heart, his father returned to his bed.

An hour later, since no sleep visited his eyes, the Brahman got up again, paced to and fro, stepped in front of the house, saw that the moon had risen. He looked in through the window of the room, where Siddhartha was standing on the same spot, with arms crossed, the moonlight reflected on his bare shins. Anxious at heart, his father sought his bed.

And he came again an hour later, and came again two hours later, looked in through the small window, saw Siddhartha standing in the moonlight, in the starshine, in the darkness. And he came again from hour to hour, in silence, looked into the room, saw his son standing motionless, filled his heart with anger, filled his heart with unrest, filled his heart with fearfulness, filled it with sorrow.

And in the last hour of the night, before the day began, he returned, stepped into the room, saw the young man standing there, looking tall and seemingly a stranger.

"Siddhartha," he said, "what are you waiting for?"

"You know what for."

"Will you keep on standing and waiting like this until it is day, noon, evening?"

»Ich werde stehen und warten.«

»Du wirst müde werden, Siddhartha.«

»Ich werde müde werden.«

»Du wirst einschlafen, Siddhartha.«

»Ich werde nicht einschlafen.«

»Du wirst sterben, Siddhartha.«

»Ich werde sterben.«

»Und willst lieber sterben, als deinem Vater gehorchen?«

»Siddhartha hat immer seinem Vater gehorcht.«

»So willst du dein Vorhaben aufgeben?«

»Siddhartha wird tun, was sein Vater ihm sagen wird.«

Der erste Schein des Tages fiel in die Kammer. Der Brahmane sah, daß Siddhartha in den Knien leise zitterte. In Siddharthas Gesicht sah er kein Zittern, fernhin blickten die Augen. Da erkannte der Vater, daß Siddhartha schon jetzt nicht mehr bei ihm und in der Heimat weile, daß er ihn schon jetzt verlassen habe.

Der Vater berührte Siddharthas Schulter.

»Du wirst«, sprach er, »in den Wald gehen und ein Samana sein. Hast du Seligkeit gefunden im Walde, so komm und lehre mich Seligkeit. Findest du Enttäuschung, dann kehre wieder und laß uns wieder gemeinsam den Göttern opfern. Nun gehe und küsse deine Mutter, sage ihr, wohin du gehst. Für mich aber ist es Zeit, an den Fluß zu gehen und die erste Waschung vorzunehmen.«

Er nahm die Hand von der Schulter seines Sohnes und ging hinaus. Siddhartha schwankte zur Seite, als er zu gehen versuchte. Er bezwang seine Glieder, verneigte sich vor seinem Vater und ging zur Mutter, um zu tun, wie der Vater gesagt hatte.

Als er im ersten Tageslicht langsam auf erstarrten Beinen die noch stille Stadt verließ, erhob sich bei der letzten Hütte ein Schatten, der dort gekauert war, und schloß sich dem Pilgernden an – Govinda.

»Du bist gekommen«, sagte Siddhartha und lächelte.

»Ich bin gekommen«, sagte Govinda.

BEI DEN SAMANAS

Am Abend dieses Tages holten sie die Asketen ein, die dürren Samanas, und boten ihnen Begleitschaft und Gehorsam an. Sie wurden angenommen.

Siddhartha schenkte sein Gewand einem armen Brahmanen auf der Straße. Er trug nur noch die Schambinde und den erdfarbenen

"I shall stand and wait."

"You will grow weary, Siddhartha."

"I shall grow weary."

"You will fall asleep, Siddhartha."

"I shall not fall asleep."

"You will die, Siddhartha."

"I shall die."

"And you would rather die than obey your father?"

"Siddhartha has always obeyed his father."

"And so you will give up your plan?"

"Siddhartha will do what his father tells him to."

The first light of day entered the room. The Brahman saw that Siddhartha's knees were trembling slightly. In Siddhartha's face he saw no trembling; his eyes were looking into the distance. Then his father realized that by now Siddhartha was no longer with him and at home, that he had already left him.

Siddhartha's father touched his shoulder.

He said: "You will go to the forest and be a samana. If you find salvation in the forest, come and teach me salvation. If you find disappointment, then come back and let us once more sacrifice to the gods together. Now go and kiss your mother; tell her where you are going. But, for me, it is time to go to the river and perform the first ablution."

He lifted his hand from his son's shoulder and went out. Siddhartha swayed to one side when he tried to walk. He brought his limbs under control, bowed to his father, and went to his mother to do as his father had said.

When, at the first daylight, he was slowly leaving the still-silent town on his stiff legs, near the last cottage there arose a shadow that had been crouching there; it joined the wanderer—it was Govinda.

"You have come," said Siddhartha, and smiled.

"I have come," said Govinda.

WITH THE SAMANAS

On the evening of that day they overtook the ascetics, the dried-out ascetics, and offered to accompany them and obey them. They were accepted.

Siddhartha gave away his robe to a poor Brahman on the road. All he still wore was a loincloth and an untailored, earth-colored wrap. He

ungenähten Überwurf. Er aß nur einmal am Tage, und niemals
Gekochtes. Er fastete fünfzehn Tage. Er fastete achtundzwanzig
Tage. Das Fleisch schwand ihm von Schenkeln und Wangen. Heiße
Träume flackerten aus seinen vergrößerten Augen, an seinen dorren-
den Fingern wuchsen lang die Nägel und am Kinn der trockne, strup-
pige Bart. Eisig wurde sein Blick, wenn er Weibern begegnete; sein
Mund zuckte Verachtung, wenn er durch eine Stadt mit schön ge-
kleideten Menschen ging. Er sah Händler handeln, Fürsten zur Jagd
gehen, Leidtragende ihre Toten beweinen, Huren sich anbieten,
Ärzte sich um Kranke bemühen, Priester den Tag für die Aussaat be-
stimmen, Liebende lieben, Mütter ihre Kinder stillen – und alles war
nicht den Blick seines Auges wert, alles log, alles stank, alles stank
nach Lüge, alles täuschte Sinn und Glück und Schönheit vor, und
alles war uneingestandene Verwesung. Bitter schmeckte die Welt.
Qual war das Leben.

Ein Ziel stand vor Siddhartha, ein einziges: leer werden, leer von
Durst, leer von Wunsch, leer von Traum, leer von Freude und Leid.
Von sich selbst wegsterben, nicht mehr Ich sein, entleerten Herzens
Ruhe zu finden, im entselbsteten Denken dem Wunder offen zu ste-
hen, das war sein Ziel. Wenn alles Ich überwunden und gestorben
war, wenn jede Sucht und jeder Trieb im Herzen schwieg, dann
mußte das Letzte erwachen, das Innerste im Wesen, das nicht mehr
Ich ist, das große Geheimnis.

Schweigend stand Siddhartha im senkrechten Sonnenbrand,
glühend vor Schmerz, glühend vor Durst, und stand, bis er nicht
Schmerz noch Durst mehr fühlte. Schweigend stand er in der
Regenzeit, aus seinem Haare troff das Wasser über frierende
Schultern, über frierende Hüften und Beine, und der Büßer stand,
bis Schultern und Beine nicht mehr froren, bis sie schwiegen, bis sie
still waren. Schweigend kauerte er im Dorngerank, aus der brennenden Haut tropfte das Blut, aus Schwären der Eiter, und Siddhartha
verweilte starr, verweilte regungslos, bis kein Blut mehr floß, bis
nichts mehr stach, bis nichts mehr brannte.

Siddhartha saß aufrecht und lernte den Atem sparen, lernte mit
wenig Atem auskommen, lernte den Atem abzustellen. Er lernte, mit
dem Atem beginnend, seinen Herzschlag beruhigen, lernte die
Schläge seines Herzens vermindern, bis es wenige und fast keine
mehr waren.

Vom Ältesten der Samanas belehrt, übte Siddhartha Entselbstung,
übte Versenkung, nach neuen Samanaregeln. Ein Reiher flog überm
Bambuswald – und Siddhartha nahm den Reiher in seine Seele auf,

ate only once a day, and the food was never cooked. He fasted for fifteen days. He fasted for twenty-eight days. The flesh wasted away from his thighs and cheeks. Dreams flickered hotly from his widened eyes, on his shriveling fingers the nails grew long, as did the dry, stubbly beard on his chin. His gaze became icy when he met women; his mouth twitched in contempt when he passed through a town with well-dressed people. He saw merchants doing business, princes leaving for the hunt, mourners lamenting their dead, whores offering their services, doctors busy with patients, priests determining the proper day to begin sowing, lovers in love, mothers nursing their children—and none of it was worth the trouble of a glance, it was all a lie, it all stank, it all stank of lies, it all gave the illusion of meaning and happiness and beauty, and it was all unacknowledged decay. The world had a bitter taste. Life was torment.

One goal was Siddhartha's and only one: to become empty, empty of thirst, empty of wishes, empty of dreams, empty of joy and sorrow. To die away from himself, no longer to be "I," to find repose with an emptied heart, to be ready for a miracle with thought liberated from ego: that was his goal. When all ego was overcome and dead, when every yearning and every impulse in the heart was silent, then the Ultimate had to awaken, that innermost part of his being which is no longer the self—the great mystery.

Silently Siddhartha stood beneath the fierce vertical rays of the sun, burning with pain, burning with thirst, and he stood there until he no longer felt either pain or thirst. Silently he stood in the rainy season, the water dripping from his hair onto his chilled shoulders, onto his chilled hips and legs; and the penitent stood there until shoulders and legs no longer felt cold, until they were silent, until they were still. Silently he crouched in the brambles, blood oozing from his prickling skin, and pus from his abscesses; and Siddhartha remained there rigidly, remained there motionlessly, until no more blood flowed, until there was no more pricking, until there was no more burning.

Siddhartha sat up straight and learned to conserve his breath, learned how to make do with just a little breath, learned how to cut off his breath. He learned how to slacken his heartbeat, beginning with the breath; he learned how to diminish the number of his heartbeats until there were only a few, and practically none.

Instructed by the samana elder, Siddhartha practiced denial of self; he practiced concentration in accordance with new samana rules. A heron flew over the bamboo forest—and Siddhartha absorbed the

flog über Wald und Gebirg, war Reiher, fraß Fische, hungerte
Reiherhunger, sprach Reihergekrächz, starb Reihertod. Ein toter
Schakal lag am Sandufer, und Siddharthas Seele schlüpfte in den
Leichnam hinein, war toter Schakal, lag am Strande, blähte sich,
stank, verweste, ward von Hyänen zerstückt, ward von Geiern ent-
häutet, ward Gerippe, ward Staub, wehte ins Gefild. Und Siddharthas Seele kehrte zurück, war gestorben, war verwest, war zer-
stäubt, hatte den trüben Rausch des Kreislaufs geschmeckt, harrte in
neuem Durst wie ein Jäger auf die Lücke, wo dem Kreislauf zu ent-
rinnen wäre, wo das Ende der Ursachen, wo leidlose Ewigkeit
begänne. Er tötete seine Sinne, er tötete seine Erinnerung, er
schlüpfte aus seinem Ich in tausend fremde Gestaltungen, war Tier,
war Aas, war Stein, war Holz, war Wasser, und fand sich jedesmal
erwachend wieder, Sonne schien oder Mond, war wieder Ich,
schwang im Kreislauf, fühlte Durst, überwand den Durst, fühlte
neuen Durst.

Vieles lernte Siddhartha bei den Samanas, viele Wege vom Ich
hinweg lernte er gehen. Er ging den Weg der Entselbstung durch
den Schmerz, durch das freiwillige Erleiden und Überwinden des
Schmerzes, des Hungers, des Durstes, der Müdigkeit. Er ging den
Weg der Entselbstung durch Meditation, durch das Leerdenken des
Sinnes von allen Vorstellungen. Diese und andere Wege lernte er
gehen, tausendmal verließ er sein Ich, stundenlang und tagelang ver-
harrte er im Nicht-Ich. Aber ob auch die Wege vom Ich hinweg-
führten, ihr Ende führte doch immer zum Ich zurück. Ob Siddhartha
tausendmal dem Ich entfloh, im Nichts verweilte, im Tier, im Stein
verweilte, unvermeidlich war die Rückkehr, unentrinnbar die
Stunde, da er sich wiederfand, im Sonnenschein oder im
Mondschein, im Schatten oder im Regen, und wieder Ich und
Siddhartha war, und wieder die Qual des auferlegten Kreislaufes
empfand.

Neben ihm lebte Govinda, sein Schatten, ging dieselben Wege, un-
terzog sich denselben Bemühungen. Selten sprachen sie anderes
miteinander, als der Dienst und die Übungen erforderten. Zuweilen
gingen sie zu zweien durch die Dörfer, um Nahrung für sich und ihre
Lehrer zu betteln.

»Wie denkst du, Govinda«, sprach einst auf diesem Bettelgang
Siddhartha, »wie denkst du, sind wir weiter gekommen? Haben wir
Ziele erreicht?«

Antwortete Govinda: »Wir haben gelernt, und wir lernen weiter.
Du wirst ein großer Samana sein, Siddhartha. Schnell hast du jede

heron into his soul; he flew over forest and mountain, he was the heron, he ate fish, he hungered with a heron's hunger, he spoke with a heron's croaking, he died a heron's death. A dead jackal lay on the sandy riverbank, and Siddhartha's soul slipped into the carcass; he was a dead jackal, he lay on the sand, he swelled up, stank, rotted, was torn apart by hyenas, was skinned by vultures, became a skeleton, turned to dust, blew away into the fields. And Siddhartha's soul returned; it had died, it had rotted, it had fallen into dust, it had tasted the dismal intoxication of the cycle of existences; filled with fresh thirst, like a hunter it was awaiting the gap through which it might escape the cycle, where causation would come to an end, where sorrowless eternity began. He mortified his senses, he mortified his power to remember, he stole out of his ego and into a thousand unfamiliar forms of creation; he was an animal, he was a carcass, he was stone, he was wood, he was water; and each time, upon awakening, he found himself again; the sun or the moon was shining; he was himself once again, he was moving through the cycle; he felt thirst, overcame his thirst, felt fresh thirst.

Many things did Siddhartha learn from the samanas; he learned how to take many paths away from self. He took the path of liberation from self through pain, through voluntary suffering and conquest of the pain, of hunger, thirst, fatigue. He took the path of liberation from self through meditation, by consciously emptying his mind of all ideas. He learned to take these and other paths; a thousand times he left his self behind, for hours and days at a time he remained in a state of nonself. But even though the paths led away from self, at the end they always led back to self. Even though Siddhartha escaped from self a thousand times, sojourning in the void, sojourning as an animal, as a stone, the return was unavoidable, inescapable the hour in which he found himself again, in sunlight or in moonlight, in shadow or in rain, and was once again "I" and Siddhartha, and once again felt the torment of the cycle that was imposed on him.

Alongside him lived Govinda, his shadow, taking the same paths, subjecting himself to the same efforts. Seldom did they say to each other any more than their duty and exercises required. At times they walked through the villages together to beg for food for themselves and their teachers.

"What do you think, Govinda?" Siddhartha said on one of these mendicant rounds, "What do you think? Have we made any progress? Have we reached any goals?"

Govinda answered: "We have learned, and we are continuing to learn. You will be a great samana, Siddhartha. You have learned every

Übung gelernt, oft haben die alten Samanas dich bewundert. Du
wirst einst ein Heiliger sein, o Siddhartha.«

Sprach Siddhartha: »Mir will es nicht so erscheinen, mein Freund.
Was ich bis zu diesem Tage bei den Samanas gelernt habe, das, o
Govinda, hätte ich schneller und einfacher lernen können. In jeder
Kneipe eines Hurenviertels, mein Freund, unter den Fuhrleuten und
Würfelspielern hätte ich es lernen können.«

Sprach Govinda: »Siddhartha macht sich einen Scherz mit mir. Wie
hättest du Versenkung, wie hättest du Anhalten des Atems, wie
hättest du Unempfindsamkeit gegen Hunger und Schmerz dort bei
jenen Elenden lernen sollen?«

Und Siddhartha sagte leise, als spräche er zu sich selber: »Was ist
Versenkung? Was ist Verlassen des Körpers? Was ist Fasten? Was ist
Anhalten des Atems? Es ist Flucht vor dem Ich, es ist ein kurzes Ent-
rinnen aus der Qual des Ichseins, es ist eine kurze Betäubung gegen
den Schmerz und die Unsinnigkeit des Lebens. Dieselbe Flucht,
dieselbe kurze Betäubung findet der Ochsentreiber in der Herberge,
wenn er einige Schalen Reiswein trinkt oder gegorene Kokosmilch.
Dann fühlt er sein Selbst nicht mehr, dann fühlt er die Schmerzen des
Lebens nicht mehr, dann findet er kurze Betäubung. Er findet, über
seiner Schale mit Reiswein eingeschlummert, dasselbe, was Siddhartha und Govinda finden, wenn sie in langen Übungen aus ihrem
Körper entweichen, im Nicht-Ich verweilen. So ist es, o Govinda.«

Sprach Govinda: »So sagst du, o Freund, und weißt doch, daß
Siddhartha kein Ochsentreiber ist und ein Samana kein Trunkenbold.
Wohl findet der Trinker Betäubung, wohl findet er kurze Flucht und
Rast, aber er kehrt zurück aus dem Wahn und findet alles beim alten,
ist nicht weiser geworden, hat nicht Erkenntnis gesammelt, ist nicht
um Stufen höher gestiegen.«

Und Siddhartha sprach mit Lächeln: »Ich weiß es nicht, ich bin nie
ein Trinker gewesen. Aber daß ich, Siddhartha, in meinen Übungen
und Versenkungen nur kurze Betäubung finde und ebenso weit von
der Weisheit, von der Erlösung entfernt bin wie als Kind im
Mutterleibe, das weiß ich, o Govinda, das weiß ich.«

Und wieder ein anderes Mal, da Siddhartha mit Govinda den Wald
verließ, um im Dorfe etwas Nahrung für ihre Brüder und Lehrer zu
betteln, begann Siddhartha zu sprechen und sagte: »Wie nun, o
Govinda, sind wir wohl auf dem rechten Wege? Nähern wir uns wohl
der Erkenntnis? Nähern wir uns wohl der Erlösung? Oder gehen wir
nicht vielleicht im Kreise – wir, die wir doch dem Kreislauf zu entrin-
nen dachten?«

exercise quickly, the old samanas have admired you often. Some day you will be a saint, O Siddhartha."

Siddhartha said: "It just does not seem so to me, my friend. What I have learned from the samanas up to this day, O Govinda, I could have learned more quickly and more simply. I could have learned it in any tavern in a prostitutes' district, my friend, among the teamsters and the dice players."

Govinda said: "Siddhartha is joking with me. How could you have learned concentration, retention of breath, insensibility to hunger and pain, there among those miserable creatures?"

And Siddhartha said softly, as if speaking to himself: "What is concentration? What is the ability to leave one's body? What is fasting? What is retention of breath? It is a flight from the self, it is a brief escape from the torment of being 'I,' it is a brief numbing of the mind to counter pain and the senselessness of life. The same escape, the same brief numbing is found by the ox drover in his inn when he drinks a few bowls of rice wine or fermented coconut milk. Then he no longer feels his self, then he no longer feels the pains of life, then he finds a brief numbing of the mind. When he has dozed off over his bowl of rice wine, he finds the same thing that Siddhartha and Govinda find when, in lengthy exercises, they are released from their bodies and dwell in the nonself. It is thus, O Govinda."

Govinda said: "You speak thus, O friend, and yet you know that Siddhartha is not a drover, and a samana is not a drunkard. Yes, the drinker is numbed for a while; yes, he finds a brief escape and rest, but he comes out of his delusion and finds that everything is still the same; he has not grown wiser, he has not gathered knowledge, he has not risen a few steps higher."

And Siddhartha said with a smile: "I do not know, I have never been a drinker. But that I, Siddhartha, find only a brief numbing in my exercises and bouts of concentration, and that I am just as far removed from wisdom and salvation as a child in the womb: this I know, O Govinda, this I know."

And on another occasion, when Siddhartha left the forest with Govinda to beg some food in the village for their brothers and teachers, Siddhartha began to speak, saying: "Well, now, O Govinda, are we on the right path? Are we perhaps approaching knowledge? Are we perhaps approaching salvation? Or are we not rather going around in a circle—we, who after all thought we could escape the cycle of existences?"

Sprach Govinda: »Viel haben wir gelernt, Siddhartha, viel bleibt noch zu lernen. Wir gehen nicht im Kreise, wir gehen nach oben, der Kreis ist eine Spirale, manche Stufe sind wir schon gestiegen.«

Antwortete Siddhartha: »Wie alt wohl, meinst du, ist unser ältester Samana, unser ehrwürdiger Lehrer?«

Sprach Govinda: »Vielleicht sechzig Jahre mag unser Ältester zählen.«

Und Siddhartha: »Sechzig Jahre ist er alt geworden und hat Nirwana nicht erreicht. Er wird siebzig werden und achtzig, und du und ich, wir werden ebenso alt werden und werden uns üben, und werden fasten und werden meditieren. Aber Nirwana werden wir nicht erreichen, er nicht, wir nicht. O Govinda, ich glaube, von allen Samanas, die es gibt, wird vielleicht nicht einer, nicht einer Nirwana erreichen. Wir finden Tröstungen, wir finden Betäubungen, wir lernen Kunstfertigkeiten, mit denen wir uns täuschen. Das Wesentliche aber, den Weg der Wege, finden wir nicht.«

»Mögest du doch«, sprach Govinda, »nicht so erschreckende Worte aussprechen, Siddhartha! Wie sollte denn unter so vielen gelehrten Männern, unter so viel Brahmanen, unter so vielen strengen und ehrwürdigen Samanas, unter so viel suchenden, so viel innig beflissenen, so viel heiligen Männern keiner den Weg der Wege finden?«

Siddhartha aber sagte mit einer Stimme, welche so viel Trauer wie Spott enthielt, mit einer leisen, einer etwas traurigen, einer etwas spöttischen Stimme: »Bald, Govinda, wird dein Freund diesen Pfad der Samanas verlassen, den er so lang mit dir gegangen ist. Ich leide Durst, o Govinda, und auf diesem langen Samanawege ist mein Durst um nichts kleiner geworden. Immer habe ich nach Erkenntnis gedürstet, immer bin ich voll von Fragen gewesen. Ich habe die Brahmanen befragt, Jahr um Jahr, und habe die heiligen Vedas befragt, Jahr um Jahr. Vielleicht, o Govinda, wäre es ebenso gut, wäre es ebenso klug und ebenso heilsam gewesen, wenn ich den Nashornvogel oder den Schimpansen befragt hätte. Lange Zeit habe ich gebraucht und bin noch nicht damit zu Ende, um dies zu lernen, o Govinda: daß man nichts lernen kann! Es gibt, so glaube ich, in der Tat jenes Ding nicht, das wir ›Lernen‹ nennen. Es gibt, o mein Freund, nur ein Wissen, das ist überall, das ist Atman, das ist in mir und in dir und in jedem Wesen. Und so beginne ich zu glauben: dies Wissen hat keinen ärgeren Feind als das Wissenwollen, als das Lernen.«

Govinda said: "We have learned much, Siddhartha; much still remains to be learned. We are not going around in a circle, we are proceeding upward; the circle is a spiral, and we have already climbed many a step."

Siddhartha answered: "How old do you think our samana elder is, our venerable teacher?"

Govinda said: "Our elder is about sixty years old."

And Siddhartha: "He has become sixty years old and has never attained *nirvana*. He will become seventy and eighty, and you and I shall become just as old, and shall do exercises, and shall fast, and shall meditate. But we shall never attain *nirvana*, not he, not we. O Govinda, I believe that, of all the samanas who exist, perhaps not one, not one, will attain *nirvana*. We find consolations, we find ways to numb the mind, we learn technical skills for deceiving ourselves. But the essential, the path of paths, that we do not find."

Govinda said: "Please do not pronounce such terrifying words, Siddhartha! How could it be that, among so many learned men, among so many Brahmans, among so many severe and venerable samanas, among so many questing men, so many assiduous men, so many holy men, no one will find the path of paths?"

But Siddhartha said, in a voice containing as much sadness as mockery, in a soft, slightly sad, slightly mocking voice: "Soon, Govinda, your friend will abandon this path of the samanas, which he has followed with you for so long. I am suffering from thirst, O Govinda, and on this long samana path my thirst has not diminished one whit. I have always thirsted for knowledge, I have always been full of questions. I have questioned the Brahmans, year after year, and I have questioned the sacred Vedas, year after year. Perhaps, O Govinda, it would have been just as good, it would have been just as clever and just as beneficial if I had questioned the hornbill or the chimpanzee.[5] I have needed a long time, and that time is not yet up, to learn this, O Govinda: that no one can learn a thing! I believe firmly that in reality the thing we call 'learning' does not exist. O my friend, all there is is a knowledge, which is everywhere, which is *Atman*, which is in me and in you and in every being. And so I am beginning to believe that this knowledge has no worse enemy than the desire to know, than learning."

---

[5] An outright error on Hesse's part. Chimpanzees are found only in Africa.

Da blieb Govinda auf dem Wege stehen, erhob die Hände und sprach: »Mögest du, Siddhartha, deinen Freund doch nicht mit solchen Reden beängstigen! Wahrlich, Angst erwecken deine Worte in meinem Herzen. Und denke doch nur: wo bliebe die Heiligkeit der Gebete, wo bliebe die Ehrwürdigkeit des Brahmanenstandes, wo die Heiligkeit der Samanas, wenn es so wäre, wie du sagst, wenn es kein Lernen gäbe?! Was, o Siddhartha, was würde dann aus alledem werden, was auf Erden heilig, was wertvoll, was ehrwürdig ist?!«

Und Govinda murmelte einen Vers vor sich hin, einen Vers aus einer Upanishad:

»Wer nachsinnend, geläuterten Geistes, in Atman sich versenkt,
Unaussprechlich durch Worte ist seines Herzens Seligkeit.«

Siddhartha aber schwieg. Er dachte der Worte, welche Govinda zu ihm gesagt hatte, und dachte die Worte bis an ihr Ende.

Ja, dachte er, gesenkten Hauptes stehend, was bliebe noch übrig von allem, was uns heilig schien? Was bleibt? Was bewährt sich? Und er schüttelte den Kopf.

Einstmals, als die beiden Jünglinge gegen drei Jahre bei den Samanas gelebt und ihre Übungen geteilt hatten, da erreichte sie auf mancherlei Wegen und Umwegen eine Kunde, ein Gerücht, eine Sage: einer sei erschienen, Gotama genannt, der Erhabene, der Buddha, der habe in sich das Leid der Welt überwunden und das Rad der Wiedergeburten zum Stehen gebracht. Lehrend ziehe er, von Jüngern umgeben, durch das Land, besitzlos, heimatlos, weiblos, im gelben Mantel eines Asketen, aber mit heiterer Stirn, ein Seliger, und Brahmanen und Fürsten beugten sich vor ihm und würden seine Schüler.

Diese Sage, dies Gerücht, dies Märchen klang auf, duftete empor, hier und dort, in den Städten sprachen die Brahmanen davon, im Wald die Samanas, immer wieder drang der Name Gotamas, des Buddha, zu den Ohren der Jünglinge, im Guten und im Bösen, in Lobpreisung und in Schmähung.

Wie wenn in einem Lande die Pest herrscht, und es erhebt sich die Kunde, da und dort sei ein Mann, ein Weiser, ein Kundiger, dessen Wort und Anhauch genüge, um jeden von der Seuche Befallenen zu heilen, und wie dann diese Kunde das Land durchläuft und jedermann davon spricht, viele glauben, viele zweifeln, viele aber sich alsbald auf den Weg machen, um den Weisen, den Helfer aufzusuchen, so durchlief das Land jene Sage, jene duftende Sage von Gotama,

At that point Govinda stopped short on their path, raised his hands, and said: "Siddhartha, please do not alarm your friend with such talk! Truly, your words awaken anxiety in my heart. And just think: where would the sacredness of prayers be, where would the venerableness of the Brahman class be, or the holiness of the samanas, if things were as you say, if there were no such thing as learning?! What, O Siddhartha, what would then become of everything on earth that is holy, valuable, and venerable?!"

And Govinda murmured a verse to himself, a verse from an Upanishad:

"He who in contemplation, with purified mind, immerses himself in *Atman*, Inexpressible in words is his heart's bliss."

But Siddhartha was silent. He was thinking about the words Govinda had spoken to him, and thought the words through to their very end.

"Yes," he thought, standing there with lowered head, "what would still be left of everything that seemed holy to us? What is left? What stands up to the test?" And he shook his head.

On one occasion, when the two young men had lived about three years with the samanas, participating in their exercises, there came to them by many direct and indirect routes a notice, a rumor, a legend: that a man had appeared, Gotama by name, the Sublime One, the Buddha, who had overcome the sorrow of the world within himself, bringing the wheel of rebirths to a halt. He was said to be traveling through the land, surrounded by disciples, without possessions, without a home, without a wife, in the yellow mantle of an ascetic, but with a serene brow, a beatified man before whom Brahmans and princes were bowing, becoming his pupils.

This legend, this rumor, this tale, made itself heard, rose upward like a fragrance, here and there. In the towns the Brahmans were talking about it; in the forest, the samanas. Again and again the name of Gotama, the Buddha, reached the young men's ears, for good and for bad, in praise and in revilement.

Just as when the plague reigns in a land and the news arises that, in this place or that, there is a man, a sage, a knowledgeable one, whose mere words or insufflation are able to cure every victim of the epidemic; just as that news then spreads through the land, and everyone talks about it, many believing, many doubting, but many immediately setting out to seek the sage, the helper: so did that legend spread through the land, that fragrant legend of Gotama, the Buddha, the

dem Buddha, dem Weisen aus dem Geschlecht der Sakya. Ihm war, so sprachen die Gläubigen, höchste Erkenntnis zu eigen, er erinnerte sich seiner vormaligen Leben, er hatte Nirwana erreicht und kehrte nie mehr in den Kreislauf zurück, tauchte nie mehr in den trüben Strom der Gestaltungen unter. Vieles Herrliche und Unglaubliche wurde von ihm berichtet, er hatte Wunder getan, hatte den Teufel überwunden, hatte mit den Göttern gesprochen. Seine Feinde und Ungläubige aber sagten, dieser Gotama sei ein eitler Verführer, er bringe seine Tage in Wohlleben hin, verachte die Opfer, sei ohne Gelehrsamkeit und kenne weder Übung noch Kasteiung.

Süß klang die Sage von Buddha, Zauber duftete aus diesen Berichten. Krank war ja die Welt, schwer zu ertragen war das Leben – und siehe, hier schien eine Quelle zu springen, hier schien ein Botenruf zu tönen, trostvoll, mild, edler Versprechungen voll. Überall, wohin das Gerücht vom Buddha erscholl, überall in den Ländern Indiens horchten die Jünglinge auf, fühlten Sehnsucht, fühlten Hoffnung, und unter den Brahmanensöhnen der Städte und Dörfer war jeder Pilger und Fremdling willkommen, wenn er Kunde von ihm, dem Erhabenen, dem Sakyamuni, brachte.

Auch zu den Samanas im Walde, auch zu Siddhartha, auch zu Govinda war die Sage gedrungen, langsam, in Tropfen, jeder Tropfen schwer von Hoffnung, jeder Tropfen schwer von Zweifel. Sie sprachen wenig davon, denn der Älteste der Samanas war kein Freund dieser Sage. Er hatte vernommen, daß jener angebliche Buddha vormals Asket gewesen und im Walde gelebt, sich dann aber zu Wohlleben und Weltlust zurückgewendet habe, und er hielt nichts von diesem Gotama.

»O Siddhartha«, sprach einst Govinda zu seinem Freunde. »Heute war ich im Dorf, und ein Brahmane lud mich ein, in sein Haus zu treten, und in seinem Hause war ein Brahmanensohn aus Magadha, dieser hat mit seinen eigenen Augen den Buddha gesehen und hat ihn lehren hören. Wahrlich, da schmerzte mich der Atem in der Brust, und ich dachte bei mir: möchte doch auch ich, möchten doch auch wir beide, Siddhartha und ich, die Stunde erleben, da wir die Lehre aus dem Munde jenes Vollendeten vernehmen! Sprich, Freund, wollen wir nicht auch dorthin gehen und die Lehre aus dem Munde des Buddha anhören?«

Sprach Siddhartha: »Immer, o Govinda, hatte ich gedacht, Govinda würde bei den Samanas bleiben, immer hatte ich geglaubt, es wäre sein Ziel, sechzig und siebzig Jahre alt zu werden und immer weiter die Künste und Übungen zu treiben, welche den Samana zieren. Aber sieh, ich hatte Govinda zu wenig gekannt, wenig wußte ich von

sage from the clan of the Sakyas. The believers said that he possessed the loftiest knowledge, that he remembered his previous lives, that he had attained *nirvana* and would never return to the cycle of existences, would never again sink into the troubled current of created forms. Many splendid and unbelievable things were reported of him; he had performed miracles, he had conquered the Devil, he had conversed with the gods. But his enemies and the unbelievers said that this Gotama was a vain seducer, that he spent his days in luxury, looked down on sacrifices, lacked scholarly attainments, and was unfamiliar with either ascetic exercises or castigation.

Sweet-sounding was the legend of Buddha; a magical fragrance emanated from these reports. The world was indeed ill, life was hard to bear—and, behold, here a spring seemed to be welling up, here a messenger's call seemed to be sounding, consoling, mild, full of noble promises. Wherever the rumor about the Buddha was heard, throughout the Indian realms, the young men hearkened, felt a longing, felt a hope; and among the Brahman's sons of the towns and villages every wanderer and stranger was welcome if he brought word of him, the Sublime One, the Sakyamuni.

To the samanas in the forest as well, to Siddhartha as well, to Govinda as well, the legend had made its way, slowly, drop by drop, each drop laden with hope, each drop laden with doubt. They spoke of it little, for the samana elder was no friend of this legend. He had heard that that alleged Buddha had formerly been an ascetic and had lived in the forest, but had then returned to luxuries and secular pleasures; and he had a low opinion of this Gotama.

"O Siddhartha," Govinda said to his friend on one occasion, "today I was in the village, and a Brahman invited me to come into his house; in his house there was a Brahman's son from Magadha, who has seen the Buddha with his own eyes and has heard him preaching. Truly, the breath in my chest ached me then, and I thought to myself: 'If only I too, if only both of us, Siddhartha and I, might live to see that hour in which we hear the doctrine from the very lips of that Perfect One.' Tell me, friend, shall we not go there, too, and listen to the doctrine from the Buddha's lips?"

Siddhartha said: "O Govinda, I had always thought that Govinda would stay with the samanas; I had always thought his goal was to become sixty and seventy years old, continuing all the while to practice the arts and exercises that adorn a samana. But see, I had known too little of Govinda, I had known too little about his heart. So, best of

seinem Herzen. Nun also willst du, Teuerster, einen Pfad einschlagen und dorthin gehen, wo der Buddha seine Lehre verkündet.«

Sprach Govinda: »Dir beliebt es zu spotten. Mögest du immerhin spotten, Siddhartha! Ist aber nicht auch in dir ein Verlangen, eine Lust erwacht, diese Lehre zu hören? Und hast du nicht einst zu mir gesagt, nicht lange mehr werdest du den Weg der Samanas gehen?«

Da lachte Siddhartha auf seine Weise, wobei der Ton seiner Stimme einen Schatten von Trauer und einen Schatten von Spott annahm, und sagte: »Wohl, Govinda, wohl hast du gesprochen, richtig hast du dich erinnert. Mögest du doch auch des andern dich erinnern, das du von mir gehört hast, daß ich nämlich mißtrauisch und müde gegen Lehre und Lernen geworden bin, und daß mein Glaube klein ist an Worte, die von Lehrern zu uns kommen. Aber wohlan, Lieber, ich bin bereit, jene Lehre zu hören – obschon ich im Herzen glaube, daß wir die beste Frucht jener Lehre schon gekostet haben.«

Sprach Govinda: »Deine Bereitschaft erfreut mein Herz. Aber sage, wie sollte das möglich sein? Wie sollte die Lehre des Gotama, noch ehe wir sie vernommen, uns schon ihre beste Frucht erschlossen haben?«

Sprach Siddhartha: »Laß diese Frucht uns genießen und das Weitere abwarten, o Govinda! Diese Frucht aber, die wir schon jetzt dem Gotama verdanken, besteht darin, daß er uns von den Samanas hinwegruft! Ob er uns noch anderes und Besseres zu geben hat, o Freund, darauf laß uns ruhigen Herzens warten.«

An diesem selben Tage gab Siddhartha dem Ältesten der Samanas seinen Entschluß zu wissen, daß er ihn verlassen wollte. Er gab ihn dem Ältesten zu wissen mit der Höflichkeit und Bescheidenheit, welche dem Jüngeren und Schüler ziemt. Der Samana aber geriet in Zorn, daß die beiden Jünglinge ihn verlassen wollten, und redete laut und brauchte grobe Schimpfworte.

Govinda erschrak und kam in Verlegenheit, Siddhartha aber neigte den Mund zu Govindas Ohr und flüsterte ihm zu: »Nun will ich dem Alten zeigen, daß ich etwas bei ihm gelernt habe.«

Indem er sich nahe vor dem Samana aufstellte, mit gesammelter Seele, fing er den Blick des Alten mit seinen Blicken ein, bannte ihn, machte ihn stumm, machte ihn willenlos, unterwarf ihn seinem Willen, befahl ihm, lautlos zu tun, was er von ihm verlangte. Der alte Mann wurde stumm, sein Auge wurde starr, sein Wille gelähmt, seine Arme hingen herab, machtlos war er Siddharthas Bezauberung erlegen. Siddharthas Gedanken aber bemächtigten sich des Samana, er mußte vollführen, was sie befahlen. Und so verneigte sich der Alte

friends, you now wish to make a journey and go where the Buddha is proclaiming his doctrine!"

Govinda said: "You are pleased to mock me. May you go on mocking all the same, Siddhartha! But has no desire, no inclination, awakened in you, as well, to hear this teaching? And did you not once tell me you would not follow the path of the samanas much longer?"

Then Siddhartha laughed after his manner, the tone of his voice taking on a shade of sadness and a shade of mockery, and he said: "Well, Govinda, you have spoken well, your recollection was correct. But please also recollect that other thing you heard me say, that I have become distrustful and weary of teaching and learning, and that I have little faith in words that come to us from teachers. But, all right, my dear friend, I am prepared to hear that doctrine—although I believe in my heart that we have already tasted the finest fruits of that doctrine."

Govinda said: "Your preparedness pleases my heart. But tell me, how could that be possible? How could Gotama's doctrine, which we have not yet heard, already have disclosed its finest fruits to us?"

Siddhartha said: "Let us enjoy those fruits and wait for the rest, O Govinda! But these fruits, for which we are already obliged to Gotama, consist in his calling us away from the samanas! Whether he has other and better things to give us, O friend, let us wait and see with a calm heart."

On that same day Siddhartha informed the samana elder of his decision to leave him. He informed the elder of this with the courtesy and modesty befitting a younger man and a pupil. But the samana flew into a rage because the two young men wished to leave him; he raised his voice and indulged in coarse insults.

Govinda was frightened and became embarrassed, but Siddhartha inclined his lips to Govinda's ear and whispered to him: "Now I am going to show the old man that I have learned something from him."

Placing himself right in front of the samana, with concentrated psychic powers, he caught the old man's gaze with his own, spellbound him, reduced him to silence, robbed him of his will, subjected him to his own will, and commanded him to perform in silence whatever he desired him to. The old man became mute, his eyes grew rigid, his will was paralyzed, his arms hung down limply; powerless, he had succumbed to Siddhartha's enchantment. But Siddhartha's thoughts took control of the samana, who had to carry out their orders. And so the old man bowed several times, executed gestures of blessing, and stam-

mehrmals, vollzog segnende Gebärden, sprach stammelnd einen frommen Reisewunsch. Und die Jünglinge erwiderten dankend die Verneigungen, erwiderten den Wunsch, zogen grüßend von dannen.

Unterwegs sagte Govinda: »O Siddhartha, du hast bei den Samanas mehr gelernt, als ich wußte. Es ist schwer, es ist sehr schwer, einen alten Samana zu bezaubern. Wahrlich, wärest du dort geblieben, du hättest bald gelernt, auf dem Wasser zu gehen.«

»Ich begehre nicht, auf dem Wasser zu gehen«, sagte Siddhartha. »Mögen alte Samanas mit solchen Künsten sich zufriedengeben.«

GOTAMA

In der Stadt Savathi kannte jedes Kind den Namen des Erhabenen Buddha, und jedes Haus war gerüstet, den Jüngern Gotamas, den schweigend Bittenden, die Almosenschale zu füllen. Nahe bei der Stadt lag Gotamas liebster Aufenthalt, der Hain Jetavana, welchen der reiche Kaufherr Anathapindika, ein ergebener Verehrer des Erhabenen, ihm und den Seinen zum Geschenk gemacht hatte.

Nach dieser Gegend hatten die Erzählungen und Antworten hingewiesen, welche den beiden jungen Asketen auf der Suche nach Gotamas Aufenthalt zuteil wurden. Und da sie in Savathi ankamen, ward ihnen gleich im ersten Hause, vor dessen Tür sie bittend stehenblieben, Speise angeboten, und sie nahmen Speise an, und Siddhartha fragte die Frau, welche ihnen die Speise reichte:

»Gerne, du Mildtätige, gerne möchten wir erfahren, wo der Buddha weilt, der Ehrwürdigste, denn wir sind zwei Samanas aus dem Walde und sind gekommen, um ihn, den Vollendeten, zu sehen und die Lehre aus seinem Munde zu vernehmen.«

Sprach die Frau: »Am richtigen Orte wahrlich seid ihr hier abgestiegen, ihr Samanas aus dem Walde. Wisset, in Jetavana, im Garten Anathapindikas, weilt der Erhabene. Dort möget ihr, Pilger, die Nacht verbringen, denn genug Raum ist daselbst für die Unzähligen, die herbeiströmen, um aus seinem Munde die Lehre zu hören.«

Da freute sich Govinda, und voll Freude rief er: »Wohl denn, so ist unser Ziel erreicht und unser Weg zu Ende! Aber sage uns, du Mutter

mered out a pious wish for a good journey. And the young men returned his bows, giving thanks, returned his good wishes, and left, saying farewell.

On the way Govinda said: "O Siddhartha, you learned more from the samanas than I knew. It is difficult, it is very difficult, to cast a spell on an old samana. Truly, had you remained there, you would soon have learned how to walk on water."

"I do not desire to walk on water," said Siddhartha. "Let old samanas content themselves with arts of that kind."

GOTAMA

In the town of Savatthi[6] every child knew the name of Buddha the Sublime One, and every household was prepared to fill the alms bowl of Gotama's disciples, who begged in silence. Just outside the town lay the place where Gotama most liked to stay, the Jetavana grove, which the wealthy merchant Anathapindika, a devoted worshipper of the Sublime One, had presented as a gift to him and his followers.

It was this neighborhood that had been indicated in the stories and replies that were communicated to the two young ascetics during their quest for the place where Gotama abode. And when they arrived in Savatthi, at the very first house before whose door they remained standing in supplication, they were offered food; they accepted the food, and Siddhartha asked the woman who handed them the food:

"Gladly, you charitable woman, gladly would we learn where the Buddha abides, the Most Venerable One, for we are two samanas from the forest, and we have come to see him, the Perfect One, and hear the doctrine from his own lips."

The woman said: "Truly, you have stopped at the right place, you samanas from the forest. Let me tell you that the Sublime One abides in Jetavana, in Anathapindika's garden. There, wanderers, you can spend the night, for there is enough room there for the countless people who come flocking to hear the doctrine from his lips."

Thereupon Govinda rejoiced and, full of joy, he called: "Well, then, so our goal is attained and our journey at an end! But tell us, mother

---

[6] The form "Savati" in the German text is incorrect either in Pali or in Sanskrit. See the Glossary under "Savatthi."

der Pilgernden, kennst du ihn, den Buddha, hast du ihn mit deinen Augen gesehen?«

Sprach die Frau: »Viele Male habe ich ihn gesehen, den Erhabenen. An vielen Tagen habe ich ihn gesehen, wie er durch die Gassen geht, schweigend, im gelben Mantel, wie er schweigend an den Haustüren seine Almosenschale darreicht, wie er die gefüllte Schale von dannen trägt.«

Entzückt lauschte Govinda und wollte noch vieles fragen und hören. Aber Siddhartha mahnte zum Weitergehen. Sie sagten Dank und gingen und brauchten kaum nach dem Wege zu fragen, denn nicht wenige Pilger und Mönche aus Gotamas Gemeinschaft waren nach dem Jetavana unterwegs. Und da sie in der Nacht dort anlangten, war daselbst ein beständiges Ankommen, Rufen und Reden von solchen, welche Herberge heischten und bekamen. Die beiden Samanas, des Lebens im Walde gewohnt, fanden schnell und geräuschlos einen Unterschlupf und ruhten da bis zum Morgen.

Beim Aufgang der Sonne sahen sie mit Erstaunen, welch große Schar, Gläubige und Neugierige, hier genächtigt hatte. In allen Wegen des herrlichen Haines wandelten Mönche im gelben Gewand, unter den Bäumen saßen sie hier und dort, in Betrachtung versenkt oder im geistlichen Gespräch, wie eine Stadt waren die schattigen Gärten zu sehen, voll von Menschen wimmelnd wie Bienen. Die Mehrzahl der Mönche zog mit der Almosenschale aus, um in der Stadt Nahrung für die Mittagsmahlzeit, die einzige des Tages, zu sammeln. Auch der Buddha selbst, der Erleuchtete, pflegte am Morgen den Bettelgang zu tun.

Siddhartha sah ihn, und er erkannte ihn alsbald, als hätte ihm ein Gott ihn gezeigt. Er sah ihn, einen schlichten Mann in gelber Kutte, die Almosenschale in der Hand tragend, still dahin gehen.

»Sieh hier!« sagte Siddhartha leise zu Govinda. »Dieser hier ist der Buddha.«

Aufmerksam blickte Govinda den Mönch in der gelben Kutte an, der sich in nichts von den Hunderten der Mönche zu unterscheiden schien. Und bald erkannte auch Govinda: dieser ist es. Und sie folgten ihm nach und betrachteten ihn.

Der Buddha ging seines Weges bescheiden und in Gedanken versunken, sein stilles Gesicht war weder fröhlich noch traurig, es schien leise nach innen zu lächeln. Mit einem verborgenen Lächeln, still, ruhig, einem gesunden Kinde nicht unähnlich, wandelte der Buddha, trug das Gewand und setzte den Fuß gleich wie alle seine Mönche, nach genauer Vorschrift. Aber sein Gesicht und sein Schritt, sein still gesenkter Blick, seine still herabhängende Hand, und noch jeder Finger an seiner still

of wanderers, do you know him, the Buddha, have you seen him with your own eyes?"

The woman said: "Many times have I seen him, the Sublime One. Many days I have seen him walking through the lanes, silently, in his yellow robe, silently holding out his alms bowl at the house doors, and bearing away the filled bowl."

Govinda listened in delight, and wanted to ask and hear much more. But Siddhartha urged him to continue the journey. They gave thanks, left, and hardly needed to ask the way, because a large number of pilgrims and monks from Gotama's community were on their way to Jetavana. And when they reached it at night, there were constant new arrivals, calling out and speaking as they sought and received lodging. The two samanas, accustomed to life in the forest, found shelter quickly and noiselessly, and rested there till morning.

At sunrise they saw in amazement how great a throng of believers and the idly curious had spent the night there. On every path in the splendid grove yellow-robed monks were walking, they were sitting here and there under the trees, immersed in contemplation or in spiritual conversation; the shady gardens looked like a town full of people swarming like bees. Most of the monks set out with their alms bowls to gather food in town for the midday meal, the only one of the day. Even the Buddha himself, the Enlightened One, used to make his mendicant rounds in the morning.

Siddhartha saw him, and recognized him at once, as if a god had pointed him out to him. He saw him, a simple man in a yellow monk's robe, carrying his alms bowl in his hand as he walked calmly onward.

"Look!" said Siddhartha softly to Govinda. "This man is the Buddha."

Govinda looked attentively at the monk in the yellow robe, who seemed to differ in no way from the hundreds of other monks. And soon Govinda, too, realized: this is the one. And they followed him and observed him.

The Buddha went his way modestly and lost in thought; his calm face was neither merry nor sad, but seemed to be gently smiling inwardly. With a concealed smile, calmly, peacefully, not unlike a healthy child, the Buddha walked, wore his robe, and planted his feet just like all his monks, in accordance with precise rules. But his face and his step, his calmly lowered gaze, his hands held calmly at his side, and indeed every finger of his calmly held hands, spoke of

herabhängenden Hand sprach Friede, sprach Vollkommenheit, suchte nicht, ahmte nicht nach, atmete sanft in einer unverwelklichen Ruhe, in einem unverwelklichen Licht, einem unantastbaren Frieden.

So wandelte Gotama der Stadt entgegen, um Almosen zu sammeln, und die beiden Samanas erkannten ihn einzig an der Vollkommenheit seiner Ruhe, an der Stille seiner Gestalt, in welcher kein Suchen, kein Wollen, kein Nachahmen, kein Bemühen zu erkennen war, nur Licht und Frieden.

»Heute werden wir die Lehre aus seinem Munde vernehmen«, sagte Govinda.

Siddhartha gab nicht Antwort. Er war wenig neugierig auf die Lehre, er glaubte nicht, daß sie ihn Neues lehren werde, hatte er doch, ebenso wie Govinda, wieder und wieder den Inhalt dieser Buddhalehre vernommen, wenn schon aus Berichten von zweiter und dritter Hand. Aber er blickte aufmerksam auf Gotamas Haupt, auf seine Schultern, auf seine Füße, auf seine still herabhängende Hand, und ihm schien, jedes Glied an jedem Finger dieser Hand war Lehre, sprach, atmete, duftete, glänzte Wahrheit. Dieser Mann, dieser Buddha, war wahrhaftig bis in die Gebärde seines letzten Fingers. Dieser Mann war heilig. Nie hatte Siddhartha einen Menschen so verehrt, nie hatte er einen Menschen so geliebt wie diesen.

Die beiden folgten dem Buddha bis zur Stadt und kehrten schweigend zurück, denn sie selbst gedachten diesen Tag sich der Speise zu enthalten. Sie sahen Gotama wiederkehren, sahen ihn im Kreise seiner Jünger die Mahlzeit einnehmen – was er aß, hätte keinen Vogel satt gemacht – und sahen ihn sich zurückziehen in den Schatten der Mangobäume.

Am Abend aber, als die Hitze sich legte und alles im Lager lebendig ward und sich versammelte, hörten sie den Buddha lehren. Sie hörten seine Stimme, und auch sie war vollkommen, war von vollkommener Ruhe, war voll von Frieden. Gotama lehrte die Lehre vom Leiden, von der Herkunft des Leidens, vom Weg zur Aufhebung des Leidens. Ruhig und klar floß seine stille Rede. Leiden war das Leben, voll Leid war die Welt, aber Erlösung vom Leid war gefunden: Erlösung fand, wer den Weg des Buddha ging.

Mit sanfter, doch fester Stimme sprach der Erhabene, lehrte die vier Hauptsätze, lehrte den achtfachen Pfad, geduldig ging er den gewohnten Weg der Lehre, der Beispiele, der Wiederholungen, hell und still schwebte seine Stimme über den Hörenden, wie ein Licht, wie ein Sternhimmel.

Als der Buddha – es war schon Nacht geworden – seine Rede schloß, traten manche Pilger hervor und baten um Aufnahme in die Gemeinschaft, nahmen ihre Zuflucht zur Lehre. Und Gotama nahm

peace, spoke of perfection, sought nothing, imitated nothing, but breathed softly in unfading repose, in unfading light, in unassailable peace.

Thus Gotama walked toward the town to gather alms, and the two samanas recognized him solely by the perfection of his repose, by the calmness of his figure, in which there was no trace of seeking, desiring, imitating, or striving, only light and peace.

"Today we shall hear the doctrine from his own lips," said Govinda.

Siddhartha made no reply. He was not so curious about the doctrine; he did not believe that it would teach him anything new; after all, both he and Govinda had heard the contents of this Buddhist doctrine time and again, although only from second- and third-hand reports. But he looked attentively at Gotama's head, at his shoulders, at his feet, at his hands held calmly at his side; and it seemed to him as if every joint of every finger of those hands were doctrine, speaking and breathing truth, wafting it abroad like a fragrance, emitting it like light. This man, this Buddha, was filled with truth down to the least movement of his smallest finger. This man was holy. Never had Siddhartha revered any person, never had he loved any person, as he did this man.

The two followed the Buddha all the way to town and returned in silence, for they themselves intended to refrain from eating that day. They saw Gotama returning, they saw him eat his meal in the circle of his disciples—what he ate would not have filled a bird—and they saw him withdraw into the shade of the mango trees.

But in the evening, when the heat abated and all those in the camp became lively and gathered together, they heard the Buddha preach. They heard his voice, and it, too, was perfect, it was perfectly calm, it was full of peace. Gotama preached the doctrine of suffering, the origin of suffering, and the way to abolish suffering. Tranquilly and clearly his calm words flowed. Life meant suffering, the world was full of sorrow, but deliverance from sorrow had been found: he who followed the Buddha's path found deliverance.

In a gentle but firm voice the Sublime One spoke; he taught the Four Basic Truths, he taught the Eightfold Way; patiently he followed the customary path of the doctrine, with its parables, with its repetitions; brightly and calmly his voice hovered over the listeners, like a light, like a starry sky.

When the Buddha—night had already fallen—ended his speech, many pilgrims stepped forward and requested admittance to the community, taking refuge in the Law. And Gotama admitted them, saying:

sie auf, indem er sprach: »Wohl habt ihr die Lehre vernommen, wohl
ist sie verkündigt. Tretet denn herzu und wandelt in Heiligkeit, allem
Leid ein Ende zu bereiten.«

Siehe, da trat auch Govinda hervor, der Schüchterne, und sprach:
»Auch ich nehme meine Zuflucht zum Erhabenen und zu seiner Lehre«,
und bat um Aufnahme in die Jüngerschaft, und ward aufgenommen.

Gleich darauf, da sich der Buddha zur Nachtruhe zurückgezogen
hatte, wendete sich Govinda zu Siddhartha und sprach eifrig:
»Siddhartha, nicht steht es mir zu, dir einen Vorwurf zu machen.
Beide haben wir den Erhabenen gehört, beide haben wir die Lehre
vernommen. Govinda hat die Lehre gehört, er hat seine Zuflucht zu
ihr genommen. Du aber, Verehrter, willst denn nicht auch du den
Pfad der Erlösung gehen? Willst du zögern, willst du noch warten?«

Siddhartha erwachte wie aus einem Schlafe, als er Govindas Worte
vernahm. Lange blickte er in Govindas Gesicht. Dann sprach er leise,
mit einer Stimme ohne Spott: »Govinda, mein Freund, nun hast du
den Schritt getan, nun hast du den Weg erwählt. Immer, o Govinda,
bist du mein Freund gewesen, immer bist du einen Schritt hinter mir
gegangen. Oft habe ich gedacht: Wird Govinda nicht auch einmal
einen Schritt allein tun, ohne mich, aus der eigenen Seele? Siehe, nun
bist du ein Mann geworden und wählst selber deinen Weg. Mögest du
ihn zu Ende gehen, o mein Freund! Mögest du Erlösung finden!«

Govinda, welcher noch nicht völlig verstand, wiederholte mit einem
Ton von Ungeduld seine Frage: »Sprich doch, ich bitte dich, mein Lieber!
Sage mir, wie es ja nicht anders sein kann, daß auch du, mein gelehrter
Freund, deine Zuflucht zum erhabenen Buddha nehmen wirst!«

Siddhartha legte seine Hand auf die Schulter Govindas: »Du hast
meinen Segenswunsch überhört, o Govinda. Ich wiederhole ihn:
Mögest du diesen Weg zu Ende gehen! Mögest du Erlösung finden!«

In diesem Augenblick erkannte Govinda, daß sein Freund ihn verlassen habe, und er begann zu weinen.

»Siddhartha!« rief er klagend.

Siddhartha sprach freundlich zu ihm: »Vergiß nicht, Govinda, daß
du nun zu den Samanas des Buddha gehörst! Abgesagt hast du
Heimat und Eltern, abgesagt Herkunft und Eigentum, abgesagt
deinem eigenen Willen, abgesagt der Freundschaft. So will es die
Lehre, so will es der Erhabene. So hast du selbst es gewollt. Morgen,
o Govinda, werde ich dich verlassen.«

Lange noch wandelten die Freunde im Gehölz, lange lagen sie und
fanden nicht den Schlaf. Und immer von neuem drang Govinda in
seinen Freund, er möge ihm sagen, warum er nicht seine Zuflucht zu

"You have heard the teaching well, it is well proclaimed. So then, step up and walk in holiness, to prepare an end to all sorrow."

Behold, thereupon Govinda, too, the shy one, stepped forth, saying: "I, too, take refuge in the Sublime One and his Law," and requested admittance to the band of disciples, and was admitted.

Immediately afterward, when the Buddha had retired to his night's rest, Govinda turned to Siddhartha, saying earnestly: "Siddhartha, it is not for me to reproach you. We have both listened to the Sublime One, we have both heard the doctrine. Govinda has listened to the doctrine, he has taken refuge in it. But you, whom I honor, will you not also walk the road to salvation? Will you hesitate, will you still wait?"

Siddhartha awoke, as if from slumber, when he heard Govinda's words. For a long while he gazed at Govinda's face. Then he said softly, in a voice free from mockery: "Govinda, my friend, now you have taken the step, now you have chosen the path. O Govinda, you have always been my friend, you have always walked one step behind me. I have often thought: 'Will not Govinda ever take a step on his own, without me, from his own soul?' Behold, now you have become a man and are choosing your path yourself. May you follow it to the end, O my friend! May you find salvation!"

Govinda, who did not yet completely understand, repeated his question in an impatient tone: "But speak, I beg of you, my dear friend! Tell me—and it surely cannot be otherwise—that you, too, my learned friend, will take refuge in the sublime Buddha!"

Siddhartha laid his hand on Govinda's shoulder: "You have failed to hear my words of benediction, O Govinda. I repeat them: May you follow this path to the end! May you find salvation!"

At that moment Govinda realized that his friend had taken leave of him, and he began to weep.

"Siddhartha!" he called lamentingly.

Siddhartha spoke to him like a friend: "Do not forget, Govinda, that you now belong to the samanas of the Buddha! You have renounced home and parents, renounced ancestry and possessions, renounced your own will, renounced friendship. That is what the doctrine desires, that is what the Sublime One desires. You yourself have desired it. Tomorrow, O Govinda, I shall leave you."

For a long while still, the friends walked through the grove, for a long while they lay down but could not fall asleep. And ever anew Govinda urged his friend to tell him why he did not wish to take refuge in Gotama's doctrine, what flaw he could possibly find in that

Gotamas Lehre nehmen wolle, welchen Fehler denn er in dieser Lehre finde. Siddhartha aber wies ihn jedesmal zurück und sagte: »Gib dich zufrieden, Govinda! Sehr gut ist des Erhabenen Lehre, wie sollte ich einen Fehler an ihr finden.«

Am frühesten Morgen ging ein Nachfolger Buddhas, einer seiner ältesten Mönche, durch den Garten und rief alle jene zu sich, welche als Neulinge ihre Zuflucht zur Lehre genommen hatten, um ihnen das gelbe Gewand anzulegen und sie in den ersten Lehren und Pflichten ihres Standes zu unterweisen. Da riß Govinda sich los, umarmte noch einmal den Freund seiner Jugend und schloß sich dem Zuge der Novizen an.

Siddhartha aber wandelte in Gedanken durch den Hain.

Da begegnete ihm Gotama, der Erhabene, und als er ihn mit Ehrfurcht begrüßte und der Blick des Buddha so voll Güte und Stille war, faßte der Jüngling Mut und bat den Ehrwürdigen um Erlaubnis, zu ihm zu sprechen. Schweigend nickte der Erhabene Gewährung.

Sprach Siddhartha: »Gestern, o Erhabener, war es mir vergönnt, deine wundersame Lehre zu hören. Zusammen mit meinem Freund kam ich aus der Ferne her, um die Lehre zu hören. Und nun wird mein Freund bei den Deinen bleiben, zu dir hat er seine Zuflucht genommen. Ich aber trete meine Pilgerschaft aufs neue an.«

»Wie es dir beliebt«, sprach der Ehrwürdige höflich.

»Allzu kühn ist meine Rede«, fuhr Siddhartha fort, »aber ich möchte den Erhabenen nicht verlassen, ohne ihm meine Gedanken in Aufrichtigkeit mitgeteilt zu haben. Will mir der Ehrwürdige noch einen Augenblick Gehör schenken?«

Schweigend nickte der Buddha Gewährung.

Sprach Siddhartha: »Eines, o Ehrwürdigster, habe ich an deiner Lehre vor allem bewundert. Alles in deiner Lehre ist vollkommen klar, ist bewiesen; als eine vollkommene, als eine nie und nirgends unterbrochene Kette zeigst du die Welt, als eine ewige Kette, gefügt aus Ursachen und Wirkungen. Niemals ist dies so klar gesehen, nie so unwiderleglich dargestellt worden; höher wahrlich muß jedem Brahmanen das Herz im Leibe schlagen, wenn er, durch deine Lehre hindurch, die Welt erblickt als vollkommenen Zusammenhang, lückenlos, klar wie ein Kristall, nicht vom Zufall abhängig, nicht von Göttern abhängig. Ob sie gut oder böse, ob das Leben in ihr Leid oder Freude sei, möge dahingestellt bleiben, es mag vielleicht sein, daß dies nicht wesentlich ist – aber die Einheit der Welt, der Zusammenhang alles Geschehens, das Umschlossensein alles Großen und Kleinen vom selben Strome, vom selben Gesetz der Ursachen, des Werdens und

doctrine. But each time Siddhartha refused, saying: "Be contented, Govinda! The Sublime One's doctrine is very good; how should I find a flaw in it?"

Very early in the morning a follower of the Buddha, one of his oldest monks, walked through the garden, calling after all those who had taken refuge in the Law as novices, so he could dress them in the yellow robe and instruct them in the rudimentary teachings and duties of their order. Thereupon Govinda tore himself away, embraced the friend of his youth once more, and joined the group of novices.

But Siddhartha walked through the grove deep in thought.

Then Gotama, the Sublime One, came across him; and when he greeted him respectfully, and the Buddha's eyes were so full of kindness and calm, the young man took heart and asked the Venerable One for permission to speak to him. Silently the Sublime One nodded his consent.

Siddhartha said: "Yesterday, O Sublime One, I was privileged to hear your marvelous teachings. Together with my friend I came here from far off to hear the teachings. And now my friend will remain with your followers; he has taken refuge in you. But I am continuing my wanderings again."

"As you please," said the Venerable One courteously.

"My words are much too bold," Siddhartha went on, "but I would not like to depart from the Sublime One without having told him honestly what I think. Will the Venerable One grant me another moment's audience?"

Silently the Buddha nodded his consent.

Siddhartha said: "One thing above all, O Most Venerable One, I have admired in your teachings. Everything in your teachings is perfectly clear and fully proven; you show the world to be a perfect chain, never and nowhere interrupted, an eternal chain fashioned out of causes and effects. Never before has this been seen so clearly, never so irrefutably presented; truly, every Brahman's heart must beat more jubilantly in his breast when, through your teachings, he sees the world as being perfectly interconnected, without a gap, clear as a crystal, not dependent on chance, not dependent on gods. Whether it is good or evil, whether life in it is sorrow or joy, is not the immediate question—perhaps it is a question of no importance. But the unity of the world, the connectedness of all events, the fact that all things, great and small, are bounded by the same current, by the same law of causality, becoming, and dying—that shines brightly

des Sterbens, dies leuchtet hell aus deiner erhabenen Lehre, o
Vollendeter. Nun aber ist, deiner selben Lehre nach, diese Einheit und
Folgerichtigkeit aller Dinge dennoch an einer Stelle unterbrochen,
durch eine kleine Lücke strömt in diese Welt der Einheit etwas
Fremdes, etwas Neues, etwas, das vorher nicht war, und das nicht
gezeigt und nicht bewiesen werden kann: das ist deine Lehre von der
Überwindung der Welt, von der Erlösung. Mit dieser kleinen Lücke,
mit dieser kleinen Durchbrechung aber ist das ganze ewige und ein-
heitliche Weltgesetz wieder zerbrochen und aufgehoben. Mögest du
mir verzeihen, wenn ich diesen Einwand ausspreche.«

Still hatte Gotama ihm zugehört, unbewegt. Mit seiner gütigen, mit
seiner höflichen und klaren Stimme sprach er nun, der Vollendete:
»Du hast die Lehre gehört, o Brahmanensohn, und wohl dir, daß du
über sie so tief nachgedacht hast. Du hast eine Lücke in ihr gefunden,
einen Fehler. Mögest du weiter darüber nachdenken. Laß dich aber
warnen, du Wißbegieriger, vor dem Dickicht der Meinungen und vor
dem Streit um Worte. Es ist an Meinungen nichts gelegen, sie mögen
schön oder häßlich, klug oder töricht sein, jeder kann ihnen anhängen
oder sie verwerfen. Die Lehre aber, die du von mir gehört hast, ist
nicht meine Meinung, und ihr Ziel ist nicht, die Welt für
Wißbegierige zu erklären. Ihr Ziel ist ein anderes; ihr Ziel ist Erlösung
vom Leiden. Diese ist es, welche Gotama lehrt, nichts anderes.«

»Mögest du mir, o Erhabener, nicht zürnen«, sagte der Jüngling.
»Nicht um Streit mit dir zu suchen, Streit um Worte, habe ich so zu dir
gesprochen. Du hast wahrlich recht, wenig ist an Meinungen gelegen.
Aber laß mich dies eine noch sagen: Nicht einen Augenblick habe ich an
dir gezweifelt. Ich habe nicht einen Augenblick gezweifelt, daß du
Buddha bist, daß du das Ziel erreicht hast, das höchste, nach welchem
so viel tausend Brahmanen und Brahmanensöhne unterwegs sind. Du
hast die Erlösung vom Tode gefunden. Sie ist dir geworden aus deinem
eigenen Suchen, auf deinem eigenen Wege, durch Gedanken, durch
Versenkung, durch Erkenntnis, durch Erleuchtung. Nicht ist sie dir
geworden durch Lehre! Und – so ist mein Gedanke, o Erhabener –
keinem wird Erlösung zuteil durch Lehre! Keinem, o Ehrwürdiger,
wirst du in Worten und durch Lehre mitteilen und sagen können, was
dir geschehen ist in der Stunde deiner Erleuchtung! Vieles enthält die
Lehre des erleuchteten Buddha, viele lehrt sie, rechtschaffen zu leben,
Böses zu meiden. Eines aber enthält die so klare, die so ehrwürdige
Lehre nicht: sie enthält nicht das Geheimnis dessen, was der Erhabene
selbst erlebt hat, er allein unter den Hunderttausenden. Dies ist es, was
ich gedacht und erkannt habe, als ich die Lehre hörte. Dies ist es,

forth from your sublime teachings, O Perfect One. And yet, according to your own doctrine, this unity and consequentiality of all things is interrupted in one place; through a small gap there flows into this unified world something strange to it, something new, something that did not previously exist, and that cannot be shown or proven: it is your doctrine of overcoming the world, of salvation. But by this small gap, by this small breach, the whole eternal and unified world law is once again shattered and canceled. Please forgive me for pointing out this objection."

Gotama had listened to him calmly, unruffled. In his kindly, courteous, and clear voice he now said, the Perfect One: "You have heard the doctrine, O Brahman's son, and you are fortunate in having meditated on it so profoundly. You have found a gap in it, a flaw. I hope you will continue to meditate on it. But let me warn you, you thirster after knowledge, against the jungle of opinions and quarreling over mere words. Opinions are completely unimportant, whether they are beautiful or ugly, clever or foolish; anyone can adhere to them or reject them. But the doctrine you have heard from me is not an opinion of mine; its goal is not to explain the world to thirsters after knowledge. Its goal is different; its goal is deliverance from suffering. This is what Gotama preaches, and nothing else."

"Please, O Sublime One, do not be cross with me," the young man said. "I did not speak to you that way in order to pick a quarrel with you, a quarrel over words. Truly, you are right, opinions are quite unimportant. But let me say just one thing more: Not for a moment have I had doubts about you. I have not doubted for a moment that you are the Buddha, that you have attained the goal, that highest goal which so many thousands of Brahmans and Brahman's sons are seeking. You have found deliverance from death. It has become yours through your own quest, on your own path, by means of thought, concentration, realization, enlightenment. It did not become yours through teachings! And—this is my thought, O Sublime One—no one will achieve salvation through teachings! O Venerable One, you will not be able to inform and tell a single person in words and by means of teachings what happened to you in the hour of your enlightenment! The doctrine of the enlightened Buddha contains a great deal, it teaches many to live righteously, to shun evil. But one thing this doctrine, so clear, so venerable, does not contain: it does not contain the secret of what the Sublime One himself experienced, he alone among the hundreds of thousands. This is what I thought and realized when I heard the doctrine. This is why I am continuing

weswegen ich meine Wanderschaft fortsetze – nicht um eine andere, eine bessere Lehre zu suchen, denn ich weiß, es gibt keine, sondern um alle Lehren und alle Lehrer zu verlassen und allein mein Ziel zu erreichen oder zu sterben. Oftmals aber werde ich dieses Tages gedenken, o Erhabener, und dieser Stunde, da meine Augen einen Heiligen sahen.«

Die Augen des Buddha blickten still zu Boden, still in vollkommenem Gleichmut strahlte sein unerforschliches Gesicht.

»Mögen deine Gedanken«, sprach der Ehrwürdige langsam, »keine Irrtümer sein! Mögest du ans Ziel kommen! Aber sage mir: Hast du die Schar meiner Samanas gesehen, meiner vielen Brüder, welche ihre Zuflucht zur Lehre genommen haben? Und glaubst du, fremder Samana, glaubst du, daß es diesen allen besser wäre, die Lehre zu verlassen und in das Leben der Welt und der Lüste zurückzukehren?«

»Fern ist ein solcher Gedanke von mir«, rief Siddhartha. »Mögen sie alle bei der Lehre bleiben, mögen sie ihr Ziel erreichen! Nicht steht mir zu, über eines andern Leben zu urteilen! Einzig für mich, für mich allein muß ich urteilen, muß ich wählen, muß ich ablehnen. Erlösung vom Ich suchen wir Samanas, o Erhabener. Wäre ich nun einer deiner Jünger, o Ehrwürdiger, so fürchte ich, es möchte mir geschehen, daß nur scheinbar, nur trügerisch mein Ich zur Ruhe käme und erlöst würde, daß es aber in Wahrheit weiterlebte und groß würde, denn ich hätte dann die Lehre, hätte meine Nachfolge, hätte meine Liebe zu dir, hätte die Gemeinschaft der Mönche zu meinem Ich gemacht!«

Mit halbem Lächeln, mit einer unerschütterten Helle und Freundlichkeit sah Gotama dem Fremdling ins Auge und verabschiedete ihn mit einer kaum sichtbaren Gebärde.

»Klug bist du, o Samana«, sprach der Ehrwürdige. »Klug weißt du zu reden, mein Freund. Hüte dich vor allzu großer Klugheit!«

Hinweg wandelte der Buddha, und sein Blick und halbes Lächeln blieb für immer in Siddharthas Gedächtnis eingegraben.

So habe ich noch keinen Menschen blicken und lächeln, sitzen und schreiten sehen, dachte er, so wahrlich wünsche auch ich blicken und lächeln, sitzen und schreiten zu können, so frei, so ehrwürdig, so verborgen, so offen, so kindlich und geheimnisvoll. So wahrlich blickt und schreitet nur der Mensch, der ins Innerste seines Selbst gedrungen ist. Wohl, auch ich werde ins Innerste meines Selbst zu dringen suchen.

Einen Menschen sah ich, dachte Siddhartha, einen einzigen, vor dem ich meine Augen niederschlagen mußte. Vor keinem andern mehr will ich meine Augen niederschlagen, vor keinem mehr. Keine Lehre mehr wird mich verlocken, da dieses Menschen Lehre mich nicht verlockt hat.

my wanderings—not to seek another, better doctrine, because I know there is none, but to leave behind all teachings and all teachers, and either to attain my goal alone or to die. But I shall often remember this day, O Sublime One, and this hour, in which my eyes beheld a saint."

The Buddha's eyes were calmly fixed on the ground; his inscrutable face beamed calmly in perfect equanimity.

The Venerable One said slowly: "May your thoughts not be errors! May you reach your goal! But tell me: have you seen the throng of my samanas, of my many brothers who have taken refuge in the Law? And do you believe, samana stranger, that it would be better for all of them to abandon the Law and return to the life of the world and its pleasures?"

"Far from me is such a thought!" Siddhartha cried. "May they all remain in the Law, may they attain their goal! It is not for me to stand in judgment over another man's life! Solely for myself, for me alone, I must judge, I must choose, I must reject. O Sublime One, we samanas seek deliverance from the self. Now, if I were one of your disciples, O Venerable One, I fear it might occur that my self would find repose and be delivered only seemingly, only deceptively, but that it would actually live on and develop further—because I would then have turned the Law, my adherence to it, my love for you, and the monastic community, into my new self!"

With a half-smile, with unshakable brightness and friendliness, Gotama looked the stranger in the eye and sent him on his way with a barely visible gesture.

"You are clever, O samana," said the Venerable One. "You can speak cleverly, my friend. Beware of too much cleverness!"

The Buddha walked away, and his gaze and half-smile remained engraved in Siddhartha's memory forever.

"I have never seen anyone gaze and smile, sit and walk, that way," he thought; "truly I wish I could also gaze and smile, sit and walk, that way, with such freedom, such venerableness, such concealment, such openness, such childlikeness, and such mystery. Truly, such a gaze and stride belong only to a person who has penetrated into his innermost self. Well, I, too, will strive to penetrate into my innermost self.

"I have seen a person," Siddhartha's thoughts continued, "a single person, in whose presence I had to cast down my eyes. Never again will I cast down my eyes in anyone's presence, not anyone's. From now on, no doctrine will entice me, since this person's doctrine has not enticed me."

Beraubt hat mich der Buddha, dachte Siddhartha, beraubt hat er mich, und mehr noch hat er mich beschenkt. Beraubt hat er mich meines Freundes, dessen, der an mich glaubte und der nun an ihn glaubt, der mein Schatten war und nun Gotamas Schatten ist. Geschenkt aber hat er mir Siddhartha, mich selbst.

ERWACHEN

Als Siddhartha den Hain verließ, in welchem der Buddha, der Vollendete, zurückblieb, in welchem Govinda zurückblieb, da fühlte er, daß in diesem Hain auch sein bisheriges Leben hinter ihm zurückblieb und sich von ihm trennte. Dieser Empfindung, die ihn ganz erfüllte, sann er im langsamen Dahingehen nach. Tief sann er nach, wie durch ein tiefes Wasser ließ er sich bis auf den Boden dieser Empfindung hinab, bis dahin, wo die Ursachen ruhen, denn Ursachen erkennen, so schien ihm, das eben ist Denken, und dadurch allein werden Empfindungen zu Erkenntnissen und gehen nicht verloren, sondern werden wesenhaft und beginnen auszustrahlen, was in ihnen ist.

Im langsamen Dahingehen dachte Siddhartha nach. Er stellte fest, daß er kein Jüngling mehr, sondern ein Mann geworden sei. Er stellte fest, daß eines ihn verlassen hatte, wie die Schlange von ihrer alten Haut verlassen wird, daß eines nicht mehr in ihm vorhanden war, das durch seine ganze Jugend ihn begleitet und zu ihm gehört hatte: der Wunsch, Lehrer zu haben und Lehren zu hören. Den letzten Lehrer, der an seinem Wege ihm erschienen war, auch ihn, den höchsten und weisesten Lehrer, den Heiligsten, Buddha, hatte er verlassen, hatte sich von ihm trennen müssen, hatte seine Lehre nicht annehmen können.

Langsamer ging der Denkende dahin und fragte sich selbst: »Was nun ist es aber, das du aus Lehren und von Lehrern hattest lernen wollen, und was sie, die dich viel gelehrt haben, dich doch nicht lehren konnten?« Und er fand: »Das Ich war es, dessen Sinn und Wesen ich lernen wollte. Das Ich war es, von dem ich loskommen, das ich überwinden wollte. Ich konnte es aber nicht überwinden, konnte es nur täuschen, konnte nur vor ihm fliehen, mich nur vor ihm verstecken. Wahrlich, kein Ding in der Welt hat so viel meine Gedanken beschäftigt wie dieses mein Ich, dies Rätsel, daß ich lebe, daß ich einer und von allen andern getrennt und abgesondert bin, daß ich Siddhartha bin! Und über kein Ding in der Welt weiß ich weniger als über mich, über Siddhartha!«

"The Buddha has robbed me," Siddhartha's thoughts continued, "he has robbed me, but he has bestowed even more on me. He has robbed me of my friend, who used to believe in me and now believes in him, who used to be my shadow and is now Gotama's shadow. But he has bestowed on me Siddhartha, myself."

AWAKENING

When Siddhartha left the grove in which the Buddha, the Perfect One, remained behind, in which Govinda remained behind, he felt that in that grove his previous life, too, had remained behind him and had separated itself from him. As he walked on slowly, he pondered over that feeling, which filled his mind completely. He thought it over profoundly; as if sinking into deep waters, he let himself reach the bottom of that feeling, all the way to where the causes reside; for it seemed to him that to recognize causes is precisely what thinking means, and that only thereby do feelings become firm realizations, which are no longer lost, but become substantial and begin to diffuse their contents.

As he walked on slowly, Siddhartha pondered. He ascertained that he was no longer a youth, but had become a man. He ascertained that something had left him behind, just as a snake is left behind by its old skin, that there was no longer present within him something that had accompanied him throughout his youth and had belonged to him: the wish to have teachers and to hear teachings. The last teacher who had appeared on his path—even him, the loftiest and wisest teacher, the holiest, the Buddha—he had left behind; he had had to part from him, he had been unable to accept his doctrine.

Deep in thought, he walked on more slowly, asking himself: "But what is it, then, that you wanted to learn from teachings and from teachers, but which they—who taught you a lot—were nevertheless unable to teach you?" And he discovered: "It was the self whose meaning and nature I wanted to learn. It was the self that I wanted to be free of, that I wanted to overcome. But I could not overcome it, I could only deceive it, I could only run away from it, I could only hide from it. Truly, nothing in the world has occupied my thoughts as much as this self of mine, this riddle of my living, of my being one person sundered and separated from all the rest, of my being Siddhartha! And there is nothing in the world I know less about than myself, Siddhartha!"

Der im langsamen Dahingehen Denkende blieb stehen, von diesem Gedanken erfaßt, und alsbald sprang aus diesem Gedanken ein anderer hervor, ein neuer Gedanke, der lautete:»Daß ich nichts von mir weiß, daß Siddhartha mir so fremd und unbekannt geblieben ist, das kommt aus einer Ursache, einer einzigen: ich hatte Angst vor mir, ich war auf der Flucht vor mir! Atman suchte ich, Brahman suchte ich, ich war gewillt, mein Ich zu zerstücken und auseinanderzuschälen, um in seinem unbekannten Innersten den Kern aller Schalen zu finden, den Atman, das Leben, das Göttliche, das Letzte. Ich selbst aber ging mir dabei verloren.«

Siddhartha schlug die Augen auf und sah um sich, ein Lächeln erfüllte sein Gesicht, und ein tiefes Gefühl von Erwachen aus langen Träumen durchströmte ihn bis in die Zehen. Und alsbald lief er wieder, lief rasch, wie ein Mann, welcher weiß, was er zu tun hat.

»Oh«, dachte er aufatmend mit tiefem Atemzug,»nun will ich mir den Siddhartha nicht mehr entschlüpfen lassen! Nicht mehr will ich mein Denken und mein Leben beginnen mit Atman und mit dem Leid der Welt. Ich will mich nicht mehr töten und zerstücken, um hinter den Trümmern ein Geheimnis zu finden. Nicht Yoga-Veda mehr soll mich lehren, noch Atharva-Veda, noch die Asketen, noch irgendwelche Lehre. Bei mir selbst will ich lernen, will ich Schüler sein, will ich mich kennenlernen, das Geheimnis Siddhartha.«

Er blickte um sich, als sähe er zum ersten Male die Welt. Schön war die Welt, bunt war die Welt, seltsam und rätselhaft war die Welt! Hier war Blau, hier war Gelb, hier war Grün, Himmel floß und Fluß, Wald starrte und Gebirg, alles schön, alles rätselvoll und magisch, und inmitten er, Siddhartha, der Erwachende, auf dem Wege zu sich selbst. All dieses, all dies Gelb und Blau, Fluß und Wald ging zum erstenmal durchs Auge in Siddhartha ein, war nicht mehr Zauber Maras, war nicht mehr der Schleier der Maja, war nicht mehr sinnlose und zufällige Vielfalt der Erscheinungswelt, verächtlich dem tiefdenkenden Brahmanen, der die Vielfalt verschmäht, der die Einheit sucht. Blau war Blau, Fluß war Fluß, und wenn auch im Blau und Fluß in Siddhartha das Eine und Göttliche verborgen lebte, so war es doch eben des Göttlichen Art und Sinn, hier Gelb, hier Blau, dort Himmel, dort Wald und hier Siddhartha zu sein. Sinn und Wesen waren nicht irgendwo hinter den Dingen, sie waren in ihnen, in allem.

»Wie bin ich taub und stumpf gewesen!« dachte der rasch dahin Wandelnde.»Wenn einer eine Schrift liest, deren Sinn er suchen will, so verachtet er nicht die Zeichen und Buchstaben und nennt sie

He who had been pondering as he slowly walked on now came to a halt, in the clutch of this thought; and at once there emanated from this thought yet another one, a new thought, formulated thus: "That I know nothing of myself, that Siddhartha has remained so strange and unfamiliar to me, has one cause, just one: I was afraid of myself, I was running away from myself! I was seeking *Atman,* I was seeking *Brahman,* I was determined to dismember my self and tear away its layers of husk in order to find in its unknown innermost recess the kernel at the heart of all those layers, the *Atman,* life, the divine principle, the Ultimate. But in so doing I was losing myself."

Siddhartha opened his eyes and looked around him; a smile spread over his face, and a profound sensation of awakening from lengthy dreams flowed through him down to his toes. And at once he was on his way again, walking swiftly, like a man who knows what he must do.

"Oh," he thought, drawing a deep breath of relief, "now I shall not allow Siddhartha to slip away from me again. No longer shall I begin my thinking and my life with *Atman* and the sorrow of the world. No longer shall I mortify and dismember myself in order to find a mystery in back of the ruins. I shall no longer be instructed by the *Yoga Veda,* or the *Atharva Veda,* or the ascetics, or any other doctrine whatsoever. I shall learn from myself, be a pupil of myself; I shall get to know myself, the mystery of Siddhartha."

He looked around as if he were seeing the world for the first time. The world was beautiful, the world was full of variety, the world was strange and puzzling! Here was blue, here was yellow, here was green; sky flowed, and river; forest jutted upward, and mountains; everything beautiful, everything puzzling and magical; and, in the midst of it all, he, Siddhartha, awakening, on the path to himself. All this, all this yellow and blue, river and forest, passed into Siddhartha through his eyes for the first time; it was no longer the sorcery of Mara, it was no longer the veil of *maya,* it was no longer the meaningless, accidental multiplicity of the world of phenomena, contemptible to the philosophical Brahman, who scorns multiplicity and seeks unity. Blue was blue, river was river; and if the One, the divine principle, lay concealed even in the blueness and river within Siddhartha, it was precisely the nature and meaning of that divine principle to be here yellow, here blue, there sky, there forest, and here Siddhartha. Meaning and essence were not somewhere or other in back of things, they were in them, in everything.

"How deaf and obtuse I have been!" he thought as he walked on swiftly. "When someone reads a piece of writing and wants to find out what it means, he does not feel contempt for the written signs and let-

Täuschung, Zufall und wertlose Schale, sondern er liest sie, er studiert und liebt sie, Buchstabe um Buchstabe. Ich aber, der ich das Buch der Welt und das Buch meines eigenen Wesens lesen wollte, ich habe, einem im voraus vermuteten Sinn zuliebe, die Zeichen und Buchstaben verachtet, ich nannte die Welt der Erscheinungen Täuschung, nannte mein Auge und meine Zunge zufällige und wertlose Erscheinungen. Nein, dies ist vorüber, ich bin erwacht, ich bin in der Tat erwacht und heute erst geboren.«

Indem Siddhartha diesen Gedanken dachte, blieb er abermals stehen, plötzlich, als läge eine Schlange vor ihm auf dem Weg.

Denn plötzlich war auch dies ihm klargeworden: er, der in der Tat wie ein Erwachter oder Neugeborener war, er mußte sein Leben neu und völlig von vorn beginnen. Als er an diesem selben Morgen den Hain Jetavana, den Hain jenes Erhabenen, verlassen hatte, schon erwachend, schon auf dem Wege zu sich selbst, da war es seine Absicht gewesen und war ihm natürlich und selbstverständlich erschienen, daß er, nach den Jahren seines Asketentums, in seine Heimat und zu seinem Vater zurückkehre. Jetzt aber, erst in diesem Augenblick, da er stehenblieb, als läge eine Schlange auf seinem Wege, erwachte er auch zu dieser Einsicht: »Ich bin ja nicht mehr, der ich war, ich bin nicht mehr Asket, ich bin nicht mehr Priester, ich bin nicht mehr Brahmane. Was denn soll ich zu Hause und bei meinem Vater tun? Studieren? Opfern? Die Versenkung pflegen? Dies alles ist ja vorüber, dies alles liegt nicht mehr an meinem Wege.«

Regungslos blieb Siddhartha stehen, und einen Augenblick und Atemzug lang fror sein Herz, er fühlte es in der Brust innen frieren wie ein kleines Tier, einen Vogel oder einen Hasen, als er sah, wie allein er sei. Jahrelang war er heimatlos gewesen und hatte es nicht gefühlt. Nun fühlte er es. Immer noch, auch in der fernsten Versenkung, war er seines Vaters Sohn gewesen, war Brahmane gewesen, hohen Standes, ein Geistiger. Jetzt war er nur noch Siddhartha, der Erwachte, sonst nichts mehr. Tief sog er den Atem ein, und einen Augenblick fror er und schauderte. Niemand war so allein wie er. Kein Adliger, der nicht zu den Adligen, kein Handwerker, der nicht zu den Handwerkern gehörte und Zuflucht bei ihnen fand, ihr Leben teilte, ihre Sprache sprach. Kein Brahmane, der nicht zu den Brahmanen zählte und mit ihnen lebte, kein Asket, der nicht im

ters, calling them illusion, chance, and a valueless husk, but he reads them, he studies and loves them, letter by letter. But I, who wanted to read the book of the world and the book of my own nature, I have held the signs and letters in contempt, for the sake of a preassumed interpretation; I called the world of phenomena an illusion, I called my eyes and my tongue an accident, valueless phenomena. No, that is all over; I have awakened, I have really awakened and I have just been born today."

As Siddhartha was thinking that last thought, he came to a halt again, all of a sudden, as if a snake lay on the path before him.

For suddenly this, too, had become clear to him: since he was really like a man who had awakened or had just been born, he had to begin his life afresh, from the very outset. When, on that same morning, he had left the grove of Jetavana, the grove of that Sublime One, already awakening, already on the path to himself, it had been his intention, and had seemed a natural and obvious course to him, to return home to his father after his years of ascetic life. But now, only at the moment when he stopped short as if a snake lay on his path, did he awaken to this insight as well: "Now, I am no longer the man I was, I am no longer an ascetic, I am no longer a priest, I am no longer a Brahman. So, what am I to do at home with my father? Study? Perform sacrifices? Practice concentration? All that is past, all that no longer lies along my path."

Siddhartha stood there motionless, and for the space of a moment and a breath his heart grew chill; he felt it cold in his breast like a little animal, a bird or a hare, when he saw how alone he was. For years he had been homeless and had not felt it. Now he felt it. Up to now, even when lost most fully in ritual concentration,[7] he had been his father's son, he had been a Brahman, a man of high rank, an intellectual. Now he was only Siddhartha, the man who had awakened, and nothing more. He drew a deep breath, and for a moment he was cold and shuddered. No one was so alone as he. There was no nobleman who did not belong to the nobility; no artisan who did not belong among the artisans and could not take refuge with them, sharing their way of life, speaking their language. There was no Brahman who was not numbered among the Brahmans, living with them; no ascetic who did

---

[7] Another possible translation (Hesse possibly had both interpretations in mind) is: "even when he had disappeared from sight in the remotest places."

Stande der Samanas seine Zuflucht fand, und auch der verlorenste
Einsiedler im Walde war nicht einer und allein, auch ihn umgab
Zugehörigkeit, auch er gehörte einem Stande an, der ihm Heimat
war. Govinda war Mönch geworden, und tausend Mönche waren
seine Brüder, trugen sein Kleid, glaubten seinen Glauben, sprachen
seine Sprache. Er aber, Siddhartha, wo war er zugehörig? Wessen
Leben würde er teilen? Wessen Sprache würde er sprechen?

Aus diesem Augenblick, wo die Welt rings von ihm wegschmolz, wo
er allein stand wie ein Stern am Himmel, aus diesem Augenblick
einer Kälte und Verzagtheit tauchte Siddhartha empor, mehr Ich als
zuvor, fester geballt. Er fühlte: dies war der letzte Schauder des
Erwachens gewesen, der letzte Krampf der Geburt. Und alsbald
schritt er wieder aus, begann rasch und ungeduldig zu gehen, nicht
mehr nach Hause, nicht mehr zum Vater, nicht mehr zurück.

not find refuge in his status as a samana. And even the most forlorn hermit in the forest was not solitary and alone; he, too, was sheltered by a sense of belonging; he, too, belonged to a group that meant home to him. Govinda had become a monk, and a thousand monks were his brothers, wore the same garment, shared the same faith, spoke his language. But he, Siddhartha, where did he belong? Whose life would he share? Whose language would he speak?

From that moment, in which the world melted away from him all around, in which he stood alone like a star in the sky—from that moment of chill and despondency—Siddhartha emerged, more himself than before, his powers more firmly compacted. He felt that this had been the final shudder of awakening, the final throe of birth. And at once he set out again, beginning to walk swiftly and impatiently, no longer homeward, no longer to his father, no longer looking back.

ZWEITER TEIL

KAMALA

Siddhartha lernte Neues auf jedem Schritt seines Weges, denn die Welt war verwandelt, und sein Herz war bezaubert. Er sah die Sonne überm Waldgebirge aufgehen und überm fernen Palmenstrande untergehen. Er sah nachts am Himmel die Sterne geordnet, und den Sichelmond wie ein Boot im Blauen schwimmend. Er sah Bäume, Sterne, Tiere, Wolken, Regenbogen, Felsen, Kräuter, Blumen, Bach und Fluß, Taublitz im morgendlichen Gesträuch, ferne hohe Berge blau und bleich, Vögel sangen und Bienen, Wind wehte silbern im Reisfelde. Dies alles, tausendfalt und bunt, war immer dagewesen, immer hatten Sonne und Mond geschienen, immer Flüsse gerauscht und Bienen gesummt, aber es war in den früheren Zeiten für Siddhartha dies alles nichts gewesen als ein flüchtiger und trügerischer Schleier vor seinem Auge, mit Mißtrauen betrachtet, dazu bestimmt, vom Gedanken durchdrungen und vernichtet zu werden, da es nicht Wesen war, da das Wesen jenseits der Sichtbarkeit lag. Nun aber weilte sein befreites Auge diesseits, es sah und erkannte die Sichtbarkeit, suchte Heimat in dieser Welt, suchte nicht das Wesen, zielte in kein Jenseits. Schön war die Welt, wenn man sie so betrachtete, so ohne Suchen, so einfach, so kinderhaft. Schön war Mond und Gestirn, schön war Bach und Ufer, Wald und Fels, Ziege und Goldkäfer, Blume und Schmetterling. Schön und lieblich war es, so durch die Welt zu gehen, so kindlich, so erwacht, so dem Nahen aufgetan, so ohne Mißtrauen. Anders brannte die Sonne aufs Haupt, anders kühlte der Waldschatten, anders schmeckte Bach und Zisterne, anders Kürbis und Banane. Kurz waren die Tage, kurz die Nächte, jede Stunde floh schnell hinweg wie ein Segel auf dem Meere, unterm Segel ein Schiff voll von Schätzen, voll von Freuden. Siddhartha sah ein Affenvolk im hohen Waldgewölbe wandern, hoch im Geäst, und hörte einen wilden, gierigen Gesang. Siddhartha sah

PART TWO

KAMALA

Siddhartha learned something new with every step of his journey, for the world was transformed and his heart was under an enchantment. He saw the sun rise above the wooded mountains and set above the distant palm-bordered beach. At night he saw the stars patterned in the sky, and the moon's sickle floating in the blue like a boat. He saw trees, stars, animals, clouds, rainbows, cliffs, plants, flowers, brook and river, the flashing of dew on the bushes in the morning, distant, tall mountains blue and pale; birds sang and bees buzzed, the wind blew silvery in the rice paddies. All this, multiple and diversified, had always been there, the sun and moon had always shone, rivers had always roared and bees had buzzed; but in earlier days all this had been nothing to Siddhartha but a transitory, deceptive veil before his eyes, looked upon with mistrust, only existing in order to be penetrated and annihilated by thought, since it was not essence, since essence lay beyond the visible, on its far side. But now his liberated eyes tarried on the near side; he saw and appreciated the visible, he sought a home in this world; he did not seek essence or aim for any "beyond." The world was beautiful when looked at in this way, without a quest for the transcendent; it was so simple, so childlike. The moon and stars were beautiful, the brook and its banks were beautiful, forest and crag, goat and rose beetle, flower and butterfly. It was beautiful and lovely to wander through the world this way, so like a child, so wide awake, so open to your surroundings, so free from mistrust. The sun burned down on your head in a different way, the forest shade cooled you in a different way, the brook and the cistern tasted different, and so did the gourd and the plantain. The days were short, the nights were short; every hour sped rapidly by like a sail on the sea, and beneath that sail a ship laden with treasures, laden with joys. Siddhartha saw a tribe of monkeys moving through the lofty forest ceiling, high up in

einen Schafbock ein Schaf verfolgen und begatten. Er sah in einem Schilfsee den Hecht im Abendhunger jagen, vor ihm her schnellten angstvoll, flatternd und blitzend die jungen Fische in Scharen aus dem Wasser, Kraft und Leidenschaft duftete dringlich aus den hastigen Wasserwirbeln, die der ungestüm Jagende zog.

All dieses war immer gewesen, und er hatte es nicht gesehen; er war nicht dabeigewesen. Jetzt war er dabei, er gehörte dazu. Durch sein Auge lief Licht und Schatten, durch sein Herz lief Stern und Mond.

Siddhartha erinnerte sich unterwegs auch alles dessen, was er im Garten Jetavana erlebt hatte, der Lehre, die er dort gehört, des göttlichen Buddha, des Abschiedes von Govinda, des Gespräches mit dem Erhabenen. Seiner eigenen Worte, die er zum Erhabenen gesprochen hatte, erinnerte er sich wieder, jedes Wortes, und mit Erstaunen wurde er dessen inne, daß er da Dinge gesagt hatte, die er damals noch gar nicht eigentlich wußte. Was er zu Gotama gesagt hatte: sein, des Buddha, Schatz und Geheimnis sei nicht die Lehre, sondern das Unaussprechliche und nicht Lehrbare, das er einst zur Stunde seiner Erleuchtung erlebt habe – dies war es ja eben, was zu erleben er jetzt auszog, was zu erleben er jetzt begann. Sich selbst mußte er jetzt erleben. Wohl hatte er schon lange gewußt, daß sein Selbst Atman sei, vom selben ewigen Wesen wie Brahman. Aber nie hatte er dies Selbst wirklich gefunden, weil er es mit dem Netz des Gedankens hatte fangen wollen. War auch gewiß der Körper nicht das Selbst, und nicht das Spiel im Sinne, so war es doch auch das Denken nicht, nicht der Verstand, nicht die erlernte Weisheit, nicht die erlernte Kunst, Schlüsse zu ziehen und aus schon Gedachtem neue Gedanken zu spinnen. Nein, auch diese Gedankenwelt war noch diesseits, und es führte zu keinem Ziele, wenn man das zufällige Ich der Sinne tötete, dafür aber das zufällige Ich der Gedanken und Gelehrsamkeiten mästete. Beide, die Gedanken wie die Sinne, waren hübsche Dinge, hinter beiden lag der letzte Sinn verborgen, beide galt es zu hören, mit beiden zu spielen, beide weder zu verachten noch zu überschätzen, aus beiden die geheimen Stimmen des Innersten zu erlauschen. Nach nichts wollte er trachten, als wonach die Stimme ihm zu trachten befehle, bei nichts verweilen, als wo die Stimme es riete. Warum war Gotama einst, in der Stunde der Stunden, unter dem Bo-Baume niedergesessen, wo die Erleuchtung ihn traf? Er hatte eine Stimme gehört, eine Stimme im eigenen Herzen, die ihm befahl, unter diesem Baume Rast zu suchen, und er hatte nicht Kasteiung, Opfer, Bad oder Gebet, nicht Essen noch Trinken, nicht Schlaf noch Traum vorgezogen, er hatte der

the branches, and heard a wild chant of desire. Siddhartha saw a ram pursue a ewe and mate with her. In a reedy lake he saw a pike hunting as hunger came over it in the evening; before it whole schools of young fish leapt out of the water, fearful, wriggling, flashing; power and passion arose like a penetrating scent from the rushing eddies that the violent hunter created.

All this had always existed, but he had not seen it; he had not been present. Now he was present, he belonged to it all. Through his eyes light and shadow raced, through his heart stars and moon raced.

As he journeyed, Siddhartha also recalled all his experiences in the garden of Jetavana, the teachings he had heard there, the divine Buddha, his leavetaking from Govinda, his conversation with the Sublime One. He recalled once more his own words that he had spoken to the Sublime One, every word, and with amazement he realized that he had said things then that were actually beyond his ken at the time. What he had said to Gotama, that his (the Buddha's) treasure and secret were not his doctrine but the ineffable, unteachable experience he had once had in the hour of his enlightenment—it was this very thing that he was now setting out to experience, that he was now beginning to experience. He now had to experience himself. Of course, he had already long known that his self was *Atman,* of the same eternal essence as *Brahman.* But he had never really found that self, because he had tried to catch it with the net of thought. Even if the body was certainly not the self, and the play of the senses was not it, nevertheless, thought was not the self, either, nor was the intellect, nor acquired wisdom, nor the acquired art of drawing conclusions and spinning new thoughts out of preexisting ones. No, this world of thought was also terrestrial, and you arrived at no goal when you killed the accidental "I" of the senses but instead fattened the accidental "I" of thinking and scholarship. Thoughts and senses were both fine things behind which ultimate meaning lay concealed; both should be listened to, both should be played with, neither of them should be condemned or overrated, by means of both you should try to hear the secret voices of the innermost essence. He decided to strive solely for what the voice commanded him to strive for; to linger over nothing unless the voice advised him to. Why had Gotama once, in the hour of hours, sat down beneath the *bo* tree, where he received enlightenment? He had heard a voice, a voice in his own heart, ordering him to seek repose beneath that tree, and he had preferred neither castigation nor sacrifices, neither bath nor prayer, neither eating nor drinking, neither sleep nor dream, but had obeyed that

Stimme gehorcht. So zu gehorchen, nicht äußerm Befehl, nur der Stimme, so bereit zu sein, das war gut, das war notwendig, nichts anderes war notwendig.

In der Nacht, da er in der strohernen Hütte eines Fährmannes am Flusse schlief, hatte Siddhartha einen Traum: Govinda stand vor ihm, in einem gelben Asketengewand. Traurig sah Govinda aus, traurig fragte er: Warum hast du mich verlassen? Da umarmte er Govinda, schlang seine Arme um ihn, und indem er ihn an seine Brust zog und küßte, war es nicht Govinda mehr, sondern ein Weib, und aus des Weibes Gewand quoll eine volle Brust, an der lag Siddhartha und trank, süß und stark schmeckte die Milch dieser Brust. Sie schmeckte nach Weib und Mann, nach Sonne und Wald, nach Tier und Blume, nach jeder Frucht, nach jeder Lust. Sie machte trunken und bewußtlos. – Als Siddhartha erwachte, schimmerte der bleiche Fluß durch die Tür der Hütte, und im Walde klang tief und wohllaut ein dunkler Eulenruf.

Als der Tag begann, bat Siddhartha seinen Gastgeber, den Fährmann, ihn über den Fluß zu setzen. Der Fährmann setzte ihn auf seinem Bambusfloß über den Fluß, rötlich schimmerte im Morgenschein das breite Wasser.

»Das ist ein schöner Fluß«, sagte er zu seinem Begleiter.

»Ja«, sagte der Fährmann, »ein sehr schöner Fluß, ich liebe ihn über alles. Oft habe ich ihm zugehört, oft in seine Augen gesehen, und immer habe ich von ihm gelernt. Man kann viel von einem Flusse lernen.«

»Ich danke dir, mein Wohltäter«, sprach Siddhartha, da er ans andere Ufer stieg. »Kein Gastgeschenk habe ich dir zu geben, Lieber, und keinen Lohn zu geben. Ein Heimatloser bin ich, ein Brahmanensohn und Samana.«

»Ich sah es wohl«, sprach der Fährmann, »und ich habe keinen Lohn von dir erwartet, und kein Gastgeschenk. Du wirst mir das Geschenk ein anderes Mal geben.«

»Glaubst du?« sagte Siddhartha lustig.

»Gewiß. Auch das habe ich vom Flusse gelernt: alles kommt wieder! Auch du, Samana, wirst wiederkommen. Nun lebe wohl! Möge deine Freundschaft mein Lohn sein. Mögest du meiner gedenken, wenn du den Göttern opferst.«

Lächelnd schieden sie voneinander. Lächelnd freute sich Siddhartha über die Freundschaft und Freundlichkeit des Fährmanns. »Wie Govinda ist er«, dachte er lächelnd, »alle, die ich auf meinem Wege antreffe, sind wie Govinda. Alle sind dankbar, obwohl sie selbst Anspruch auf Dank hätten. Alle sind unterwürfig, alle

voice. To obey in that fashion, not a command from outside but only that voice, to be thus prepared, was good, was necessary; nothing else was necessary.

During the night, while sleeping in the straw hut of a ferryman by the river, Siddhartha had a dream: Govinda stood before him, in a yellow ascetic's robe. Govinda looked sad, sadly he asked: "Why have you deserted me?" Then he embraced Govinda, threw his arms around him, and as he drew him to his breast and kissed him, it was no longer Govinda, but a woman, and from the woman's robe a milk-laden breast was exposed; Siddhartha lay and drank from it; the milk from that breast tasted sweet and strong. It tasted of woman and man, of sun and forest, of animal and flower, of every fruit, of every pleasure. It made him drunk and unconscious.—When Siddhartha awoke, the pale river was glimmering through the door of the hut, and in the forest the dark cry of an owl resounded, deep and melodious.

When the day began, Siddhartha asked his host, the ferryman, to take him across the river. The ferryman took him across the river on his bamboo raft; the wide waters had a red glimmer in the morning light.

"This is a beautiful river," he said to his companion.

"Yes," said the ferryman, "a very beautiful river; I love it above all other things. I have often listened to it, I have often looked into its eyes, and I have always learned from it. You can learn a lot from a river."

"Thank you, my benefactor," said Siddhartha as he climbed onto the other bank. "I have no gift for you, my dear man, such as one gives to one's host, nor can I pay you. I am a homeless man, a Brahman's son and a samana."

"I could see that," said the ferryman, "and I did not expect any payment from you, nor a guest's gift. You will give me the gift another time."

"You think so?" said Siddhartha merrily.

"Absolutely. This, too, I have learned from the river: everything returns! You, too, samana, will return. Now farewell! Let your friendship be my pay. May you think of me when you sacrifice to the gods."

Both smiled as they parted. Siddhartha smiled as he rejoiced over the friendship and friendliness of the ferryman. "He is like Govinda," he thought with a smile; "everyone I meet on my journey is like Govinda. They are all grateful, even though they are the ones who deserve the thanks. They are all ready to serve me, they would all like to

mögen gern Freund sein, gern gehorchen, wenig denken. Kinder sind die Menschen.«

Um die Mittagszeit kam er durch ein Dorf. Vor den Lehmhütten wälzten sich Kinder auf der Gasse, spielten mit kürbiskernen und Muscheln, schrien und balgten sich, flohen aber alle scheu vor dem fremden Samana. Am Ende des Dorfes führte der Weg durch einen Bach, und am Rande des Baches kniete ein junges Weib und wusch Kleider. Als Siddhartha sie grüßte, hob sie den Kopf und blickte mit Lächeln zu ihm auf, daß er das Weiße in ihrem Auge blitzen sah. Er rief einen Segensspruch hinüber, wie er unter Reisenden üblich ist, und fragte, wie weit der Weg bis zur großen Stadt noch sei. Da stand sie auf und trat zu ihm her, schön schimmerte ihr feuchter Mund im jungen Gesicht. Sie tauschte Scherzreden mit ihm, fragte, ob er schon gegessen habe, und ob es wahr sei, daß die Samanas nachts allein im Walde schliefen und keine Frauen bei sich haben dürften. Dabei setzte sie ihren linken Fuß auf seinen rechten und machte eine Bewegung, wie die Frau sie macht, wenn sie den Mann zu jener Art des Liebesgenusses auffordert, welchen die Lehrbücher »das Baumbesteigen« nennen. Siddhartha fühlte sein Blut erwarmen, und da sein Traum ihm in diesem Augenblick wieder einfiel, bückte er sich ein wenig zu dem Weibe herab und küßte mit den Lippen die braune Spitze ihrer Brust. Aufschauend sah er ihr Gesicht voll Verlangen lächeln und die verkleinerten Augen in Sehnsucht flehen.

Auch Siddhartha fühlte Sehnsucht und den Quell des Geschlechts sich bewegen; da er aber noch nie ein Weib berührt hatte, zögerte er einen Augenblick, während seine Hände schon bereit waren, nach ihr zu greifen. Und in diesem Augenblick hörte er, erschauernd, die Stimme seines Innern, und die Stimme sagte nein. Da wich vom lächelnden Gesicht der jungen Frau aller Zauber, er sah nichts mehr als den feuchten Blick eines brünstigen Tierweibchens. Freundlich streichelte er ihre Wange, wandte sich von ihr und verschwand vor der Enttäuschten leichtfüßig in das Bambusgehölze.

An diesem Tage erreichte er vor Abend eine große Stadt, und freute sich, denn er begehrte nach Menschen. Lange hatte er in den Wäldern gelebt, und die stroherne Hütte des Fährmanns, in welcher er diese Nacht geschlafen hatte, war seit langer Zeit das erste Dach, das er über sich gehabt hatte.

Vor der Stadt, bei einem schönen umzäunten Haine, begegnete

be my friends, to obey me without thinking hard about it. People are like children."

About midday he was walking through a village. In front of the clay huts children were tumbling about in the street, playing with gourd seeds and seashells, yelling and scuffling, but they all ran in fright from the strange samana. At the end of the village the path led across a brook, and at the edge of the brook a young woman was kneeling and washing clothes. When Siddhartha greeted her, she raised her head and looked up at him with a smile, so that he saw the gleam from the whites of her eyes. He called out a blessing on her, as is customary with travelers, and asked her how far it still was to the big town. Then she stood up and walked over to him; her moist lips were beautiful, glimmering in her young face. She exchanged jocular words with him, asked him if he had already eaten and if it was true that samanas slept alone at night in the forest and were not allowed to have any women with them. At the same time, she placed her left foot on his right and moved her body like a woman inviting a man to the style of lovemaking that the manuals call "climbing a tree."[8] Siddhartha felt his blood heat up and, since he recalled his dream at that moment, he stooped down slightly to the woman and, with his lips, kissed the brown tip of one breast. Looking up, he saw her face smiling, filled with desire, and her narrowed eyes beseeching him longingly.

Siddhartha, too, felt a longing, and felt the fountain of sex stirring; but, since he had never yet touched a woman, he hesitated for a moment, though his hands were already all set to reach out for her. And at that moment, with a shudder, he heard his inner voice, and the voice said no. Thereupon all the magic vanished from the young woman's smiling face; he no longer saw anything there but the moist eyes of a female animal in heat. In a friendly way he stroked her cheek, turned away from her, and with light steps disappeared from the disappointed woman's view into the bamboo grove.

Before evening of that day he reached a big town, and was happy, for he desired to be among people. For a long time he had lived in the forests, and the ferryman's straw hut, in which he had slept the night before, had been the first roof over his head in a long while.

Just outside town, near a beautiful grove enclosed by a hedge, the

---

[8] A sex position described in the *Kamasutra:* the man stands upright while the woman stands on his feet, hoists herself up, and wraps herself around him. See *"Kamasutra"* in the Glossary.

dem Wandernden ein kleiner Troß von Dienern und Dienerinnen, mit Körben beladen. Inmitten in einer geschmückten Sänfte, von Vieren getragen, saß auf roten Kissen unter einem bunten Sonnendach eine Frau, die Herrin. Siddhartha blieb beim Eingang des Lusthaines stehen und sah dem Aufzuge zu, sah die Diener, die Mägde, die Körbe, sah die Sänfte, und sah in der Sänfte die Dame. Unter hochgetürmten schwarzen Haaren sah er ein sehr helles, sehr zartes, sehr kluges Gesicht, hellroten Mund wie eine frisch aufgebrochene Feige, Augenbrauen gepflegt und gemalt in hohen Bogen, dunkle Augen klug und wachsam, lichten hohen Hals aus grün und goldenem Oberkleide steigend, ruhende helle Hände lang und schmal mit breiten Goldreifen über den Gelenken.

Siddhartha sah, wie schön sie war, und sein Herz lachte. Tief verneigte er sich, als die Sänfte nahe kam, und sich wieder aufrichtend blickte er in das helle holde Gesicht, las einen Augenblick in den klugen hochüberwölbten Augen, atmete einen Hauch von Duft, den er nicht kannte. Lächelnd nickte die schöne Frau, einen Augenblick, und verschwand im Hain, und hinter ihr die Diener.

So betrete ich diese Stadt, dachte Siddhartha, unter einem holden Zeichen. Es zog ihn, sogleich in den Hain zu treten, doch bedachte er sich, und nun erst ward ihm bewußt, wie ihn die Diener und Mägde am Eingang betrachtet hatten, wie verächtlich, wie mißtrauisch, wie abweisend.

Noch bin ich ein Samana, dachte er, noch immer, ein Asket und Bettler. Nicht so werde ich bleiben dürfen, nicht so in den Hain treten. Und er lachte.

Den nächsten Menschen, der des Weges kam, fragte er nach dem Hain und nach dem Namen dieser Frau, und erfuhr, daß dies der Hain der Kamala war, der berühmten Kurtisane, und daß sie außer dem Haine ein Haus in der Stadt besaß.

Dann betrat er die Stadt. Er hatte nun ein Ziel.

Sein Ziel verfolgend, ließ er sich von der Stadt einschlürfen, trieb im Strom der Gassen, stand auf Plätzen still, ruhte auf Steintreppen am Flusse aus. Gegen den Abend befreundete er sich mit einem Barbiergehilfen, den er im Schatten eines Gewölbes hatte arbeiten sehen, den er betend in einem Tempel Vishnus wiederfand, dem er von den Geschichten Vishnus und der Lakschmi erzählte. Bei den Booten am Flusse schlief er die Nacht, und früh am Morgen, ehe die ersten Kunden in seinen Laden kamen, ließ er sich von dem Barbiergehilfen den Bart rasieren und das Haar beschneiden, das Haar kämmen und mit feinem Öle salben. Dann ging er im Flusse baden.

wanderer was met by a small train of male and female servants laden with baskets. In their midst, in a decorated sedan chair carried by four men, a woman, their mistress, sat on red cushions under a colorful canopy. Siddhartha remained standing at the entrance to the pleasure grove, watching the procession; he saw the servants, the maids, the baskets; he saw the sedan chair and saw the lady in the chair. He saw beneath high-piled black hair a very fair, very soft, very clever face, bright-red lips like a newly opened fig, eyebrows well tended and painted in the form of high arches, dark eyes clever and alert, a long, fair neck emerging from the green-and-gold outer garment, fair hands at rest, long and narrow, with wide gold bracelets at the wrists.

Siddhartha saw how beautiful she was, and his heart rejoiced. He made a low bow when the chair came near him, and, straightening up again, he looked at the fair, lovely face; for a moment he read the clever eyes with the high arches above them, inhaled a breath of fragrance that he did not recognize. The beautiful woman, smiling, nodded for a moment, then disappeared into the grove, her servants following.

"And so," Siddhartha thought, "I am entering this town with a favorable omen." He was tempted to walk right into the grove, but he thought it over and only then became aware of how the servants and maids had looked at him at the entrance, how contemptuously, how distrustfully, how distantly.

"I am still a samana," he thought, "still an ascetic and mendicant. I cannot remain this way, this way I shall be unable to enter the grove." And he laughed.

He asked the next person who came his way about the grove and that woman's name, and he learned that it was the grove of Kamala, the renowned courtesan, and that, in addition to the grove, she owned a house in town.

Then he entered the town. Now he had an aim.

Pursuing his aim, he let himself be engulfed by the town; he floated on the current of the lanes; he remained standing on the squares; he rested on the stone steps by the river. Toward evening he made friends with a barber's assistant whom he had seen working in the shade of an archway, whom he ran across again praying in a temple of Vishnu, and whom he told stories concerning Vishnu and Lakshmi. That night he slept near the boats by the river, and early in the morning, before the first customers came to his shop, he had the barber's assistant shave off his beard and cut his hair, then had his hair combed and anointed with fine oil. Next he went to bathe in the river.

Als am Spätnachmittag die schöne Kamala in der Sänfte sich ihrem Haine näherte, stand am Eingang Siddhartha, verbeugte sich und empfing den Gruß der Kurtisane. Demjenigen Diener aber, der zuletzt im Zuge ging, winkte er und bat ihn, der Herrin zu melden, daß ein junger Brahmane mit ihr zu sprechen begehre. Nach einer Weile kam der Diener zurück, forderte den Wartenden auf, ihm zu folgen, führte den ihm Folgenden schweigend in einen Pavillon, wo Kamala auf einem Ruhebette lag, und ließ ihn bei ihr allein.

»Bist du nicht gestern schon da draußen gestanden und hast mich begrüßt?« fragte Kamala.

»Wohl habe ich gestern schon dich gesehen und begrüßt.«

»Aber trugst du nicht gestern einen Bart, und lange Haare, und Staub in den Haaren?«

»Wohl hast du beobachtet, alles hast du gesehen. Du hast Siddhartha gesehen, den Brahmanensohn, welcher seine Heimat verlassen hat, um ein Samana zu werden, und drei Jahre lang ein Samana gewesen ist. Nun aber habe ich jenen Pfad verlassen, und kam in diese Stadt, und die erste, die mir noch vor dem Betreten der Stadt begegnete, warst du. Dies zu sagen, bin ich zu dir gekommen, o Kamala! Du bist die erste Frau, zu welcher Siddhartha anders als mit niedergeschlagenen Augen redet. Nie mehr will ich meine Augen niederschlagen, wenn eine schöne Frau mir begegnet.«

Kamala lächelte und spielte mit ihrem Fächer aus Pfauenfedern. Und fragte: »Und nur um mir dies zu sagen, ist Siddhartha zu mir gekommen?«

»Um dir dies zu sagen, und um dir zu danken, daß du so schön bist. Und wenn es dir nicht mißfällt, Kamala, möchte ich dich bitten, meine Freundin und Lehrerin zu sein, denn ich weiß noch nichts von der Kunst, in welcher du Meisterin bist.«

Da lachte Kamala laut.

»Nie ist mir das geschehen, Freund, daß ein Samana aus dem Walde zu mir kam und von mir lernen wollte! Nie ist mir das geschehen, daß ein Samana mit langen Haaren und in einem alten zerrissenen Schamtuche zu mir kam! Viele Jünglinge kommen zu mir, und auch Brahmanensöhne sind darunter, aber sie kommen in schönen Kleidern, sie kommen in feinen Schuhen, sie haben Wohlgeruch im Haar und Geld in den Beuteln. So, du Samana, sind die Jünglinge beschaffen, welche zu mir kommen.«

Sprach Siddhartha: »Schon fange ich an, von dir zu lernen. Auch gestern schon habe ich gelernt. Schon habe ich den Bart abgelegt, habe das Haar gekämmt, habe Öl im Haare. Weniges ist, das mir noch fehlt, du Vortreffliche: feine Kleider, feine Schuhe, Geld im Beutel. Wisse,

Late in the afternoon, when the beautiful Kamala approached her grove in her sedan chair, Siddhartha was standing at the entrance; he bowed and received the courtesan's greeting. But he beckoned to the servant who was last in line, asking him to announce to his mistress that a young Brahman wished to speak with her. After a while the servant returned, invited the waiting man to follow him, silently led the man following him into a pavilion where Kamala lay on a day bed, and left him alone with her.

"Were you not already standing there yesterday to greet me?" asked Kamala.

"Yes, I already saw you and greeted you yesterday."

"But were you not wearing a beard yesterday, and long hair, and dust in your hair?"

"You observed well, you saw everything. You saw Siddhartha, the Brahman's son, who left his home to become a samana, and was a samana for three years. But now I have abandoned that path and have come to this town; and the first person who met me, even before I entered the town, was you. I have come to tell you that, O Kamala! You are the first woman to whom Siddhartha has spoken without standing with downcast eyes. Never again shall I lower my eyes when a beautiful woman meets me."

Kamala smiled and played with her peacock-feather fan. And she asked: "And Siddhartha has visited me merely to tell me that?"

"To tell you that, and to thank you for being so beautiful. And, if it does not displease you, Kamala, I would like to ask you to be my friend and instructress, for I still know nothing of the art in which you are an expert."

At that point Kamala laughed out loud.

"My friend, I have never had a samana come to me from the forest and want to learn from me! I have never had a samana come to me with long hair and in an old, torn loincloth! Many young men visit me, and there are Brahman's sons among them, too, but they come in fine clothes, they come in elegant shoes, they have perfumed hair and money in their purses. That, samana, is what the young men are like who visit me."

Siddhartha said: "I am already beginning to learn from you. Even yesterday I already learned something. I have already removed my beard, combed my hair, and put oil on my hair. It is only a little that I still lack, excellent woman: elegant clothes, elegant shoes, money in my purse. Let me tell you, Siddhartha has set his mind on things more difficult than such trifles, and has at-

Schwereres hat Siddhartha sich vorgenommen, als solche Kleinigkeiten sind, und hat es erreicht. Wie sollte ich nicht erreichen, was ich gestern mir vorgenommen habe: dein Freund zu sein und die Freuden der Liebe von dir zu lernen! Du wirst mich gelehrig sehen, Kamala, Schwereres habe ich gelernt, als was du mich lehren sollst. Und nun also: Siddhartha genügt dir nicht, so wie er ist, mit Öl im Haar, aber ohne Kleider, ohne Schuhe, ohne Geld?«

Lachend rief Kamala: »Nein, Werter, er genügt noch nicht. Kleider muß er haben, hübsche Kleider, und Schuhe, hübsche Schuhe, und viel Geld im Beutel, und Geschenke für Kamala. Weißt du es nun, Samana aus dem Walde? Hast du es dir gemerkt?«

»Wohl habe ich es mir gemerkt«, rief Siddhartha. »Wie sollte ich mir nicht merken, was aus einem solchen Munde kommt! Dein Mund ist wie eine frisch aufgebrochene Feige, Kamala. Auch mein Mund ist rot und frisch, er wird zu deinem passen, du wirst sehen. – Aber sage, schöne Kamala, hast du gar keine Furcht vor dem Samana aus dem Walde, der gekommen ist, um Liebe zu lernen?«

»Warum sollte ich denn Furcht vor einem Samana haben, einem dummen Samana aus dem Walde, der von den Schakalen kommt und noch gar nicht weiß, was Frauen sind?«

»Oh, er ist stark, der Samana, und er fürchtet nichts. Er könnte dich zwingen, schönes Mädchen. Er könnte dich rauben. Er könnte dir weh tun.«

»Nein, Samana, das fürchte ich nicht. Hat je ein Samana oder ein Brahmane gefürchtet, einer könnte kommen und ihn packen und ihm seine Gelehrsamkeit, und seine Frömmigkeit, und seinen Tiefsinn rauben? Nein, denn die gehören ihm zu eigen, und er gibt davon nur, was er geben will und wem er geben will. So ist es, genau ebenso ist es auch mit Kamala, und mit den Freuden der Liebe. Schön und rot ist Kamalas Mund, aber versuche, ihn gegen Kamalas Willen zu küssen, und nicht einen Tropfen Süßigkeit wirst du von ihm haben, der so viel Süßes zu geben versteht! Du bist gelehrig, Siddhartha, so lerne auch dies: Liebe kann man erbetteln, erkaufen, geschenkt bekommen, auf der Gasse finden, aber rauben kann man sie nicht. Da hast du dir einen falschen Weg ausgedacht. Nein, schade wäre es, wenn ein hübscher Jüngling wie du es so falsch angreifen wollte.«

Siddhartha verneigte sich lächelnd. »Schade wäre es, Kamala, wie sehr hast du recht! Überaus schade wäre es. Nein, von deinem Munde soll mir kein Tropfen Süßigkeit verlorengehen, noch dir von dem meinen! Es bleibt also dabei: Siddhartha wird wiederkommen, wenn

tained them. How should I not attain what I set my mind on yesterday: to be your friend and to learn the joys of love from you!
You will find me a quick learner, Kamala; I have learned more difficult things than what you are to teach me. And so, now:
Siddhartha does not satisfy you as he is, with oil on his hair, but
without clothes, without shoes, without money?"

Laughing, Kamala cried: "No, my good man, he still does not
satisfy me! He must have clothes, handsome clothes, and shoes,
good-looking shoes, and a lot of money in his purse, and gifts for
Kamala. Now do you know, samana from the forest? Have you
paid close attention?"

"Yes, I have paid close attention!" cried Siddhartha. "How could I
fail to pay attention to words from such lips! Your mouth is like a
newly opened fig, Kamala. My lips are red and fresh, too; they will
suit yours, you will see.—But tell me, beautiful Kamala, are you not
at all afraid of the samana from the forest, who has come to learn
love?"

"Why, then, should I be afraid of a samana, a stupid samana from
the forest, who has come from the jackals and does not yet know what
women are?"

"Oh, he is strong, the samana, and afraid of nothing. He could
take you by force, pretty girl. He could rob you. He could hurt
you."

"No, samana, I am not afraid of that. Has a samana or a Brahman
ever been afraid that someone might come, grab him, and rob him of
his scholarship, his piety, and his wisdom? No, because they are his
very own, and he imparts only as much of them as he wishes, and to
whom he wishes. It is the same, exactly the same, with Kamala, too,
and with the joys of love. Kamala's lips are beautiful and red, but try
to kiss them against Kamala's will, and not a drop of sweetness will you
have from them, although they are able to grant so much sweetness!
You are a quick learner, Siddhartha, so learn this as well: Love can be
won by begging, it can be bought, received as a gift, found on the
street, but it cannot be stolen. You have hatched out a useless plan
there. No, it would be a pity if a handsome young man like you wanted
to attack things in such a wrong way."

Siddhartha bowed with a smile. "It would be a pity, Kamala, how
right you are! It would be a terrible pity. No, not a drop of sweetness
shall I lose from your lips, nor you from mine! So this is how it stands:
Siddhartha will return when he has what he now lacks: clothes, shoes,

er hat, was ihm noch fehlt: Kleider, Schuhe, Geld. Aber sprich, holde Kamala, kannst du mir nicht noch einen kleinen Rat geben?«

»Einen Rat? Warum nicht? Wer wollte nicht gerne einem armen, unwissenden Samana, der von den Schakalen aus dem Walde kommt, einen Rat geben?«

»Liebe Kamala, so rate mir: wohin soll ich gehen, daß ich am raschesten jene drei Dinge finde?«

»Freund, das möchten viele wissen. Du mußt tun, was du gelernt hast, und dir dafür Geld geben lassen und Kleider und Schuhe. Anders kommt ein Armer nicht zu Geld. Was kannst du denn?«

»Ich kann denken. Ich kann warten. Ich kann fasten.«

»Nichts sonst?«

»Nichts. Doch, ich kann auch dichten. Willst du mir für ein Gedicht einen Kuß geben?«

»Das will ich tun, wenn dein Gedicht mir gefällt. Wie heißt es denn?«

Siddhartha sprach, nachdem er sich einen Augenblick besonnen hatte, diese Verse:

»In ihren schattigen Hain trat die schöne Kamala,
An Haines Eingang stand der braune Samana.
Tief, da er die Lotusblüte erblickte,
Beugte sich jener, lächelnd dankte Kamala.
Lieblicher, dachte der Jüngling, als Göttern zu opfern,
Lieblicher ist es, zu opfern der schönen Kamala.«

Laut klatschte Kamala in die Hände, daß die goldenen Armringe klangen.

»Schön sind deine Verse, brauner Samana, und wahrlich, ich verliere nichts, wenn ich dir einen Kuß für sie gebe.«

Sie zog ihn mit den Augen zu sich, er beugte sein Gesicht auf ihres, und legte seinen Mund auf den Mund, der wie eine frisch aufgebrochene Feige war. Lange küßte ihn Kamala, und mit tiefem Erstaunen fühlte Siddhartha, wie sie ihn lehrte, wie sie weise war, wie sie ihn beherrschte, ihn zurückwies, ihn lockte, und wie hinter diesem ersten eine lange, eine wohlgeordnete, wohlerprobte Reihe von Küssen stand, jeder vom andern verschieden, die ihn noch erwarteten. Tief atmend blieb er stehen, und war in diesem Augenblick wie ein Kind erstaunt über die Fülle des Wissens und Lernenswerten, die sich vor seinen Augen erschloß.

»Sehr schön sind deine Verse«, rief Kamala, »wenn ich reich wäre, gäbe ich dir Goldstücke dafür. Aber schwer wird es dir werden, mit

money. But tell me, lovely Kamala, can you give me another small piece of advice?"

"Advice? Why not? Who would not be glad to give advice to a poor, ignorant samana who has come from the jackals in the forest?"

"Dear Kamala, then advise me: where should I go to find those three things as quickly as possible?"

"My friend, many people would like to know that. You must do what you have learned, and receive money for it, and clothes and shoes. There is no other way for a poor man to come into money. Well, what can you do?"

"I can think. I can wait. I can fast."

"Nothing else?"

"Nothing. Oh, yes, I can also compose poetry. Will you give me a kiss for a poem?"

"Yes, I will, if I like your poem. How does it go?"

After reflecting for a moment, Siddhartha uttered these verses:

"Into her shady grove stepped Kamala,
  At the entrance to the grove stood the tanned samana.
  When he caught sight of the lotus blossom,
  He made a low bow, and Kamala thanked him with a smile.
  'More lovely,' thought the young man, 'than to sacrifice to the gods,
  'More lovely it is to sacrifice to the beautiful Kamala.'"

Kamala clapped her hands loudly so that her golden arm rings clinked.

"Your verses are beautiful, tan samana, and truly I lose nothing if I give you a kiss for them."

She drew him over to her with her eyes, he lowered his face to hers, and placed his lips on those lips that were like a newly opened fig. Kamala gave him a long kiss, and in deep amazement Siddhartha felt that she was teaching him, that she was wise, that she dominated him, repulsed him, and lured him on; and that, behind this first kiss, there was a long, well-organized, and well-tested series of kisses, each one different, still awaiting him. Breathing deeply, he stood there, at that moment as astonished as a child at the wealth of knowledge and things worth learning that revealed itself to his eyes.

"Your verses are very beautiful!" Kamala cried. "If I were rich, I would give you gold coins for them. But you will find it hard to earn

Versen so viel Geld zu erwerben, wie du brauchst. Denn du brauchst viel Geld, wenn du Kamalas Freund sein willst.«

»Wie kannst du küssen, Kamala« stammelte Siddhartha.

»Ja, das kann ich schon, darum fehlt es mir auch nicht an Kleidern, Schuhen, Armbändern und allen schönen Dingen. Aber was wird aus dir werden? Kannst du nichts als denken, fasten, dichten?«

»Ich kann auch die Opferlieder«, sagte Siddhartha, »aber ich will sie nicht mehr singen. Ich kann auch Zaubersprüche, aber ich will sie nicht mehr sprechen. Ich habe die Schriften gelesen – «

»Halt«, unterbrach ihn Kamala. »Du kannst lesen? Und schreiben?«

»Gewiß kann ich das. Manche können das.«

»Die meisten können es nicht. Auch ich kann es nicht. Es ist sehr gut, daß du lesen und schreiben kannst, sehr gut. Auch die Zaubersprüche wirst du noch brauchen können.«

In diesem Augenblick kam eine Dienerin gelaufen und flüsterte der Herrin eine Nachricht ins Ohr.

»Ich bekomme Besuch«, rief Kamala. »Eile und verschwinde, Siddhartha, niemand darf dich hier sehen, das merke dir! Morgen sehe ich dich wieder.«

Der Magd aber befahl sie, dem frommen Brahmanen ein weißes Obergewand zu geben. Ohne zu wissen, wie ihm geschah, sah sich Siddhartha von der Magd hinweggezogen, auf Umwegen in ein Gartenhaus gebracht, mit einem Oberkleid beschenkt, ins Gebüsch geführt und dringlich ermahnt, sich alsbald ungesehen aus dem Hain zu verlieren.

Zufrieden tat er, wie ihm geheißen war. Des Waldes gewohnt, brachte er sich lautlos aus dem Hain und über die Hecke. Zufrieden kehrte er in die Stadt zurück, das zusammengerollte Kleid unterm Arm tragend. In einer Herberge, wo Reisende einkehrten, stellte er sich an die Tür, bat schweigend um Essen, nahm schweigend ein Stück Reiskuchen an. Vielleicht schon morgen, dachte er, werde ich niemand mehr um Essen bitten.

Stolz flammte plötzlich in ihm auf. Er war kein Samana mehr, nicht mehr stand es ihm an zu betteln. Er gab den Reiskuchen einem Hunde und blieb ohne Speise.

»Einfach ist das Leben, das man in der Welt hier führt«, dachte Siddhartha. »Es hat keine Schwierigkeiten. Schwer war alles, mühsam und am Ende hoffnungslos, als ich noch Samana war. Nun ist alles leicht, leicht wie der Unterricht im Küssen, den mir Kamala gibt. Ich brauche Kleider und Geld, sonst nichts, das sind kleine nahe Ziele, sie stören einem nicht den Schlaf.«

as much money as you need with verses. For you need a lot of money
if you wish to be Kamala's friend."

"The way you can kiss, Kamala!" Siddhartha stammered.

"Yes, I am good at it, and so I have no lack of clothes, shoes, arm-
bands, and every beautiful thing. But what will become of you? Can
you do nothing but think and fast and compose poems?"

"I also know the sacrificial chants," said Siddhartha, "but I shall not
sing them anymore. I also know magic charms, but I shall not pronounce them anymore. I have read the scriptures—"

"Stop there!" Kamala interrupted him. "You can read? And write?"

"Of course I can. Many people can."

"Most people cannot. I cannot, either. It is very good that you can
read and write, very good. You will still be able to use the magic
charms, too."

At that moment a maid came running in and whispered a piece of
news in her mistress' ear.

"I am receiving a visit!" Kamala cried. "Vanish at once, Siddhartha;
no one must see you here, mind that! Tomorrow I shall see you
again."

But she ordered the maid to give the pious Brahman a white outer
garment. Without knowing what was happening to him, Siddhartha
found himself being dragged away by the maid, taken to a garden
house by roundabout paths, presented with an outer garment, led
into the bushes, and urgently admonished to get out of the grove at
once without being seen.

He contentedly did as he was told. Accustomed to the forest, he
made his way out of the grove and over the hedge noiselessly.
Contentedly he returned to town, carrying the rolled-up garment
under his arm. In an inn where travelers stayed, he took up a stand
near the door, silently asked for food, and silently accepted a piece of
rice cake. "Perhaps as soon as tomorrow," he thought, "I shall no
longer ask anyone for food."

Suddenly pride flared up in him. He was no longer a samana, it was
no longer fitting for him to beg. He gave the rice cake to a dog and
remained without food.

"The life that people lead in the world here is simple," Siddhartha
thought. "It has no difficulties. Everything was difficult, toilsome,
and, when you come down to it, hopeless while I was still a samana.
Now everything is easy, easy as the lessons in kissing that Kamala is
giving me. I need clothes and money, nothing else; those are minor,
nearby goals that do not disturb anyone's sleep."

Längst hatte er das Stadthaus Kamalas erkundet, dort fand er sich am andern Tage ein.

»Es geht gut«, rief sie ihm entgegen. »Du wirst bei Kamaswami erwartet, er ist der reichste Kaufmann dieser Stadt. Wenn du ihm gefällst, wird er dich in Dienst nehmen. Sei klug, brauner Samana. Ich habe ihm durch andere von dir erzählen lassen. Sei freundlich gegen ihn, er ist sehr mächtig. Aber sei nicht zu bescheiden! Ich will nicht, daß du sein Diener wirst, du sollst seinesgleichen werden, sonst bin ich nicht mit dir zufrieden. Kamaswami fängt an, alt und bequem zu werden. Gefällst du ihm, so wird er dir viel anvertrauen.«

Siddhartha dankte ihr und lachte, und da sie erfuhr, er habe gestern und heute nichts gegessen, ließ sie Brot und Früchte bringen und bewirtete ihn.

»Du hast Glück gehabt«, sagte sie beim Abschied, »eine Tür um die andre tut sich dir auf. Wie kommt das wohl? Hast du einen Zauber?«

Siddhartha sagte: »Gestern erzählte ich dir, ich verstünde zu denken, zu warten und zu fasten, du aber fandest, das sei zu nichts nütze. Es ist aber zu vielem nütze, Kamala, du wirst es sehen. Du wirst sehen, daß die dummen Samanas im Walde viel Hübsches lernen und können, das ihr nicht könnt. Vorgestern war ich noch ein struppiger Bettler, gestern habe ich schon Kamala geküßt, und bald werde ich ein Kaufmann sein und Geld haben und all diese Dinge, auf die du Wert legst.«

»Nun ja«, gab sie zu. »Aber wie stünde es mit dir ohne mich? Was wärest du, wenn Kamala dir nicht hülfe?«

»Liebe Kamala«, sagte Siddhartha und richtete sich hoch auf, »als ich zu dir in deinen Hain kam, tat ich den ersten Schritt. Es war mein Vorsatz, bei dieser schönsten Frau die Liebe zu lernen. Von jenem Augenblick an, da ich den Vorsatz faßte, wußte ich auch, daß ich ihn ausführen werde. Ich wußte, daß du mir helfen würdest, bei deinem ersten Blick am Eingang des Haines wußte ich es schon.«

»Wenn ich aber nicht gewollt hätte?«

»Du hast gewollt. Sieh, Kamala: wenn du einen Stein ins Wasser wirfst, so eilt er auf dem schnellsten Wege zum Grunde des Wassers. So ist es, wenn Siddhartha ein Ziel, einen Vorsatz hat. Siddhartha tut nichts, er wartet, er denkt, er fastet, aber er geht durch die Dinge der Welt hindurch wie der Stein durchs Wasser, ohne etwas zu tun, ohne sich zu rühren; er wird gezogen, er läßt sich fallen. Sein Ziel zieht ihn an sich, denn er läßt nichts in seine Seele ein, was dem Ziel widerstreben könnte. Das ist es, was Siddhartha bei den Samanas gelernt hat. Es ist das, was die Toren Zauber nennen und wovon sie meinen, es werde durch

He had found out long before where Kamala's town house was, and he showed up there on the following day.

"Things are going well!" she called to him. "You are expected at Kamaswami's; he is the wealthiest merchant in town. If he likes you, he will take you into his service. Be clever, tan samana. I have arranged it for other people to tell him about you. Be friendly to him, he is very powerful. But do not be too modest! I do not want you to become his servant; you are to become his equal, or else I shall not be satisfied with you. Kamaswami is beginning to grow old and comfort-loving. If he likes you, he will entrust many things to you."

Siddhartha thanked her and laughed, and when she heard that he had eaten nothing that day or the day before, she had bread and fruit brought in, and invited him to eat.

"You have been lucky," she said while saying good-bye; "one door after the other is opening up for you. Now, how is that? Do you possess some magic?"

Siddhartha said: "Yesterday I told you that I knew how to think, to wait, and to fast; but you thought that it was all useless. But it is useful in many ways, Kamala, you will see. You will see that the stupid samanas in the forest learn many fine things and can do a lot that you cannot. The day before yesterday I was still a disheveled beggar; yesterday I already kissed Kamala; and soon I shall be a merchant and have money and all those things that you value."

"Well, yes," she admitted. "But what would your situation be if not for me? What would you be if Kamala were not helping you?"

"Dear Kamala," Siddhartha said, rising to his full height, "when I visited you in your grove, I took the first step. It was my intention to learn love from that most beautiful woman. From the moment that I formulated that intention, I also knew that I would carry it out. I knew that you would help me, I already knew it when you gave me that first look at the entrance to the grove."

"But if I had not been willing?"

"You *were* willing. Look, Kamala: if you throw a stone into the water, it hastens to the bottom by the quickest route. Thus it is when Siddhartha has a goal or an intention. Siddhartha does not act; he waits, he thinks, he fasts, but he pierces through the things of this world as the stone goes through the water, without performing any action, without bestirring himself; he is drawn, he lets himself fall. His goal draws him toward itself, because he admits nothing into his soul that could oppose that goal. That is what Siddhartha learned from the samanas. That is what fools call magic, in the belief that it is brought

die Dämonen bewirkt. Nichts wird von Dämonen bewirkt, es gibt keine Dämonen. Jeder kann zaubern, jeder kann seine Ziele erreichen, wenn er denken kann, wenn er warten kann, wenn er fasten kann.«

Kamala hörte ihm zu. Sie liebte seine Stimme, sie liebte den Blick seiner Augen.

»Vielleicht ist es so«, sagte sie leise, »wie du sprichst, Freund. Vielleicht ist es aber auch so, daß Siddhartha ein hübscher Mann ist, daß sein Blick den Frauen gefällt, daß darum das Glück ihm entgegenkommt.«

Mit einem Kuß nahm Siddhartha Abschied. »Möge es so sein, meine Lehrerin. Möge immer mein Blick dir gefallen, möge immer von dir mir Glück entgegenkommen!«

BEI DEN KINDERMENSCHEN

Siddhartha ging zum Kaufmann Kamaswami, in ein reiches Haus ward er gewiesen, Diener führten ihn zwischen kostbaren Teppichen in ein Gemach, wo er den Hausherrn erwartete.

Kamaswami trat ein, ein rascher, geschmeidiger Mann mit stark ergrauendem Haar, mit sehr klugen, vorsichtigen Augen, mit einem begehrlichen Mund. Freundlich begrüßten sich Herr und Gast.

»Man hat mir gesagt«, begann der Kaufmann, »daß du ein Brahmane bist, ein Gelehrter, daß du aber Dienste bei einem Kaufmann suchst. Bist du denn in Not geraten, Brahmane, daß du Dienste suchst?«

»Nein«, sagte Siddhartha, »ich bin nicht in Not geraten und bin nie in Not gewesen. Wisse, das ich von den Samanas komme, bei welchen ich lange Zeit gelebt habe.«

»Wenn du von den Samanas kommst, wie solltest du da nicht in Not sein? Sind nicht die Samanas völlig besitzlos?«

»Besitzlos bin´ich«, sagte Siddhartha, »wenn es das ist, was du meinst. Gewiß bin ich besitzlos. Doch bin ich es freiwillig, bin also nicht in Not.«

»Wovon aber willst du leben, wenn du besitzlos bist?«

»Ich habe daran noch nie gedacht, Herr. Ich bin mehr als drei Jahre besitzlos gewesen, und habe niemals daran gedacht, wovon ich leben solle.«

»So hast du vom Besitz anderer gelebt.«

»Vermutlich ist es so. Auch der Kaufmann lebt ja von der Habe anderer.«

about by demons. Nothing is brought about by demons, there are no demons. Anyone can work magic, anyone can attain his goals, if he can think, if he can wait, if he can fast."

Kamala listened to him. She loved his voice, she loved the look in his eyes.

"It may be as you say, my friend," she said softly. "But it may also be that good fortune comes Siddhartha's way because he is a handsome man, because women like his eyes."

Siddhartha said good-bye with a kiss. "Let it be so, my instructress. May you always like my eyes, may good fortune always come to me from you!"

WITH THE CHILD-PEOPLE

Siddhartha went to the merchant Kamaswami; he was shown into a wealthy home; servants led him past expensive tapestries into a room where he was to wait for the master of the house.

In came Kamaswami, a lively, limber man with heavily graying hair, with very clever, prudent eyes, with lips that betokened desire. Host and guest greeted each other in friendly fashion.

"I have been told," the merchant began, "that you are a Brahman, a learned man, but that you are seeking service with a merchant. Is it because you have fallen on hard times, Brahman, that you are seeking service?"

"No," said Siddhartha, "I have not fallen on hard times and I have never known hard times. Let me inform you that I have come from among the samanas, with whom I lived for a long period."

"If you are coming from the samanas, how can you not be in need? Are not the samanas completely without possessions?"

"I am without possessions," Siddhartha said, "if that is what you mean. Certainly, I am without possessions. But I am so voluntarily, and so I am not in need."

"But what do you expect to live on if you have no possessions?"

"I have never yet thought about it, sir. I have been without possessions for over three years and I have never thought about what I would live on."

"So you lived on the possessions of other people."

"Presumably so. Surely, a merchant, too, lives on other people's wealth."

»Wohl gesprochen. Doch nimmt er von den andern das Ihre nicht umsonst; er gibt ihnen seine Waren dafür.«

»So scheint es sich in der Tat zu verhalten. Jeder nimmt, jeder gibt, so ist das Leben.«

»Aber erlaube: wenn du besitzlos bist, was willst du geben?«

»Jeder gibt, was er hat. Der Krieger gibt Kraft, der Kaufmann gibt Ware, der Lehrer Lehre, der Bauer Reis, der Fischer Fische.«

»Sehr wohl. Und was ist es nun, was du zu geben hast? Was ist es, das du gelernt hast, das du kannst?«

»Ich kann denken. Ich kann warten. Ich kann fasten.«

»Das ist alles?«

»Ich glaube, es ist alles!«

»Und wozu nützt es? Zum Beispiel das Fasten – wozu ist es gut?«

»Es ist sehr gut, Herr. Wenn ein Mensch nichts zu essen hat, so ist Fasten das Allerklügste, was er tun kann. Wenn, zum Beispiel, Siddhartha nicht fasten gelernt hätte, so müßte er heute noch irgendeinen Dienst annehmen, sei es bei dir oder wo immer, denn der Hunger würde ihn dazu zwingen. So aber kann Siddhartha ruhig warten, er kennt keine Ungeduld, er kennt keine Notlage, lange kann er sich vom Hunger belagern lassen und kann dazu lachen. Dazu, Herr, ist Fasten gut.«

»Du hast recht, Samana. Warte einen Augenblick.«

Kamaswami ging hinaus und kehrte mit einer Rolle wieder, die er seinem Gaste hinreichte, indem er fragte: »Kannst du dies lesen?«

Siddhartha betrachtete die Rolle, in welcher ein Kaufvertrag niedergeschrieben war, und begann ihren Inhalt vorzulesen.

»Vortrefflich«, sagte Kamaswami. »Und willst du mir etwas auf dieses Blatt schreiben?«

Er gab ihm ein Blatt und einen Griffel, und Siddhartha schrieb und gab das Blatt zurück.

Kamaswami las: »Schreiben ist gut, Denken ist besser. Klugheit ist gut, Geduld ist besser.«

»Vorzüglich verstehst du zu schreiben«, lobte der Kaufmann. »Manches werden wir noch miteinander zu sprechen haben. Für heute bitte ich dich, sei mein Gast und nimm in diesem Hause Wohnung.«

Siddhartha dankte und nahm an, und wohnte nun im Hause des Händlers. Kleider wurden ihm gebracht, und Schuhe, und ein Diener bereitete ihm täglich das Bad. Zweimal am Tage wurde eine reichliche

"Well said. But he does not take people's money from them for nothing; he gives them his merchandise for it."

"Apparently that is actually the case. Everyone takes, everyone gives, such is life."

"But permit me: if you have no possessions, what do you expect to give?"

"Everyone gives what he has. The warrior gives his strength, the merchant gives his wares, the teacher his teachings, the farmer his rice, the fisherman his fish."

"Very good. And now, what is it that you have to give? What is it that you have learned, that you are able to do?"

"I can think. I can wait. I can fast."

"And that is all?"

"I believe that that is all!"

"And what good is that? For example, fasting—what is it good for?"

"It is very good, sir. If a person has nothing to eat, then to fast is the cleverest thing he can do. For example, if Siddhartha had not learned how to fast, this very day he would have to accept any position whatsoever, either with you or anywhere else, because hunger would compel him to. But, this way, Siddhartha can wait calmly, he knows no impatience, he knows no distress, he can let himself be besieged by hunger for a long time and can laugh at the situation. That, sir, is what fasting is good for."

"You are right, samana. Wait a moment."

Kamaswami went out and returned with a scroll, which he handed to his guest, asking: "Can you read this?"

Siddhartha looked at the scroll, on which a sales contract was written, and began to read its contents aloud.

"Excellent," said Kamaswami. "And do you mind writing something for me on this sheet?"

He gave him a sheet and a stylus; Siddhartha wrote and gave back the sheet.

Kamaswami read: "Writing is good, thinking is better. Cleverness is good, patience is better."

"You know how to write extremely well," the merchant said approvingly. "We will have much more to say to each other. For today I ask you to be my guest and take up residence in this house."

Siddhartha thanked him and accepted the position, and thereafter lived in the merchant's house. He was brought clothes and shoes, and every day a servant prepared his bath. Twice a day a copious meal was

Mahlzeit aufgetragen, Siddhartha aber aß nur einmal am Tage, und aß weder Fleisch noch trank er Wein. Kamaswami erzählte ihm von seinem Handel, zeigte ihm Waren und Magazine, zeigte ihm Berechnungen. Vieles Neue lernte Siddhartha kennen, er hörte viel und sprach wenig. Und der Worte Kamalas eingedenk, ordnete er sich niemals dem Kaufmann unter, zwang ihn, daß er ihn als seinesgleichen, ja als mehr denn seinesgleichen behandle. Kamaswami betrieb seine Geschäfte mit Sorglichkeit und oft mit Leidenschaft, Siddhartha aber betrachtete dies alles wie ein Spiel, dessen Regeln genau zu lernen er bemüht war, dessen Inhalt aber sein Herz nicht berührte.

Nicht lange war er in Kamaswamis Hause, da nahm er schon an seines Hausherrn Handel teil. Täglich aber zu der Stunde, die sie ihm nannte, besuchte er die schöne Kamala, in hübschen Kleidern, in feinen Schuhen, und bald brachte er ihr auch Geschenke mit. Vieles lehrte ihn ihr roter, kluger Mund. Vieles lehrte ihn ihre zarte, geschmeidige Hand. Ihn, der in der Liebe noch ein Knabe war und dazu neigte, sich blindlings und unersättlich in die Lust zu stürzen wie ins Bodenlose, lehrte sie von Grund auf die Lehre, daß man Lust nicht nehmen kann, ohne Lust zu geben, und daß jede Gebärde, jedes Streicheln, jede Berührung, jeder Anblick, jede kleinste Stelle des Körpers ihr Geheimnis hat, das zu wecken dem Wissenden Glück bereitet. Sie lehrte ihn, daß liebende nach einer Liebesfeier nicht voneinander gehen dürfen, ohne eins das andere zu bewundern, ohne ebenso besiegt zu sein, wie gesiegt zu haben, so daß bei keinem von beiden Übersättigung und Öde entstehe und das böse Gefühl, mißbraucht zu haben oder mißbraucht worden zu sein. Wunderbare Stunden brachte er bei der schönen und klugen Künstlerin zu, wurde ihr Schüler, ihr Liebhaber, ihr Freund. Hier bei Kamala lag der Wert und Sinn seines jetzigen Lebens, nicht im Handel des Kamaswami.

Der Kaufmann übertrug ihm das Schreiben wichtiger Briefe und Verträge und gewöhnte sich daran, alle wichtigen Angelegenheiten mit ihm zu beraten. Er sah bald, daß Siddhartha von Reis und Wolle, von Schiffahrt und Handel wenig verstand, daß aber seine Hand eine glückliche war, und daß Siddhartha ihn, den Kaufmann, übertraf an Ruhe und Gleichmut, und in der Kunst des Zuhörenkönnens und Eindringens in fremde Menschen. »Dieser Brahmane«, sagte er zu einem Freunde, »ist kein richtiger Kaufmann und wird nie einer werden, nie ist seine Seele mit Leidenschaft bei den Geschäften. Aber er hat das Geheimnis jener Menschen, zu welchen der Erfolg von selber kommt, sei das nun ein angeborener guter Stern, sei es Zauber, sei es etwas, das er bei den Samanas gelernt hat. Immer scheint er mit den

served, but Siddhartha ate only once a day; moreover, he ate no meat and he drank no wine. Kamaswami told him about his business, showed him merchandise and storehouses, showed him ledgers. Siddhartha became acquainted with many new things, listening carefully but saying little. And, mindful of what Kamala had said, he never subordinated himself to the merchant, but compelled him to treat him as an equal, indeed as more than an equal. Kamaswami ran his business conscientiously and often passionately, but Siddhartha regarded it all as a game, the rules of which he strove to learn accurately, but the substance of which did not touch his heart.

Before he had been in Kamaswami's house very long, he was already taking part in his host's dealings. But every day, at the time she designated, he visited the beautiful Kamala, wearing handsome clothes and elegant shoes, and soon he even brought along gifts for her. Her clever red lips taught him much. Her delicate, supple hands taught him much. Still a boy when it came to love and, moreover, inclined to plunge into his pleasure blindly and insatiably as into a bottomless pit, he learned thoroughly from her that pleasure cannot be taken without giving pleasure in return, and that every gesture, every caress, every touch, every look, every inch of the body, has its secret, the awakening of which affords happiness to the knowing person. She taught him that lovers should not part after a love fest without admiring each other, without feeling they have been conquered as much as they themselves have conquered, so that neither one of them suffers from satiety, boredom, or the unpleasant sensation of having abused the other or having been abused. He spent marvelous hours with the beautiful, clever artiste; he became her pupil, her lover, her friend. Here, with Kamala, lay the value and meaning of his present life, not in Kamaswami's commerce.

The merchant entrusted to him the writing of important letters and contracts, and became accustomed to discussing every important matter with him. He soon saw that Siddhartha understood little about rice or wool, ship transport or business, but that he had a knack for what he was doing, and that Siddhartha surpassed him, the merchant, in calmness and equanimity and in the art of listening and the accurate evaluation of strangers. "This Brahman," he said to a friend, "is no real merchant and will never become one, he is never passionately involved in the business. But he possesses the secret of those people to whom success comes all on its own, whether because a lucky star was shining when they were born, or through magic, or through something he learned from the samanas. He always appears

Geschäften nur zu spielen, nie gehen sie ganz in ihn ein, nie beherrschen sie ihn, nie fürchtet er Mißerfolg, nie bekümmert ihn ein Verlust.«

Der Freund riet dem Händler: »Gib ihm von den Geschäften, die er für dich treibt, ein Drittel vom Gewinn, laß ihn aber auch denselben Anteil des Verlustes treffen, wenn Verlust entsteht. So wird er eifriger werden.«

Kamaswami folgte dem Rat. Siddhartha aber kümmerte sich wenig darum. Traf ihn Gewinn, so nahm er ihn gleichgültig hin; traf ihn Verlust, so lachte er und sagte: »Ei sieh, dies ist also schlecht gegangen!«

Es schien in der Tat, als seien die Geschäfte ihm gleichgültig. Einmal reiste er in ein Dorf, um dort eine große Reisernte aufzukaufen. Als er ankam, war aber der Reis schon an einen andern Händler verkauft. Dennoch blieb Siddhartha manche Tage in jenem Dorf, bewirtete die Bauern, schenkte ihren Kindern Kupfermünzen, feierte eine Hochzeit mit und kam überaus zufrieden von der Reise zurück. Kamaswami machte ihm Vorwürfe, daß er nicht sogleich umgekehrt sei, daß er Zeit und Geld vergeudet habe. Siddhartha antwortete: »Laß das Schelten, lieber Freund! Noch nie ist mit Schelten etwas erreicht worden. Ist Verlust entstanden, so laß mich den Verlust tragen. Ich bin sehr zufrieden mit dieser Reise. Ich habe vielerlei Menschen kennengelernt, ein Brahmane ist mein Freund geworden, Kinder sind auf meinen Knien geritten, Bauern haben mir ihre Felder gezeigt, niemand hat mich für einen Händler gehalten.«

»Sehr hübsch ist dies alles«, rief Kamaswami unwillig, »aber tatsächlich bist du doch ein Händler, sollte ich meinen! Oder bist du denn nur zu deinem Vergnügen gereist?«

»Gewiß«, lachte Siddhartha, »gewiß bin ich zu meinem Vergnügen gereist. Wozu denn sonst? Ich habe Menschen und Gegenden kennengelernt, ich habe Freundlichkeit und Vertrauen genossen, ich habe Freundschaft gefunden. Sieh, Lieber, wenn ich Kamaswami gewesen wäre, so wäre ich sofort, als ich meinen Kauf vereitelt sah, voll Ärger und in Eile wieder zurückgereist, und Zeit und Geld wäre in der Tat verloren gewesen. So aber habe ich gute Tage gehabt, habe gelernt, habe Freude genossen, habe weder mich noch andere durch Ärger und durch Eilfertigkeit geschädigt. Und wenn ich jemals wieder dorthin komme, vielleicht um eine spätere Ernte zu kaufen, oder zu welchem Zwecke es sei, so werden freundliche Menschen mich freundlich und heiter empfangen, und ich werde mich dafür

to be merely playing with business, it never completely occupies his mind, it never dominates him, he is never afraid of failure, he never frets over a loss."

The friend advised the merchant: "Give him a third of the profits from the deals he makes for you, but let him also lose the same percentage when the business suffers a loss. That way he will become more enthusiastic."

Kamaswami followed the advice. But Siddhartha was not much concerned about it. If he made a profit, he accepted it with indifference; if he suffered a loss, he laughed, saying: "Just look, this turned out badly!"

It really seemed as if business did not matter to him. On one occasion, he traveled to a village to purchase a sizable rice crop there. When he arrived, however, the rice had already been sold to another dealer. Nevertheless, Siddhartha remained in that village for many days; he treated the farmers to meals, he gave their children copper coins, he was a guest at a wedding, and returned from his trip highly satisfied. Kamaswami reproached him for not having come back at once, for wasting time and money. Siddhartha replied: "Stop scolding, my dear friend! Nothing has ever yet been achieved by scolding. If there has been a loss, then let me bear the loss. I am very satisfied with this trip. I met all sorts of people, I made friends with a Brahman, I dandled children on my knee, farmers showed me their fields, no one took me for a businessman."

"That is all very fine!" Kamaswami cried indignantly. "But in reality you *are* a businessman, I should think! Or were you just taking a pleasure trip?"

"Of course," Siddhartha laughed. "Of course, I was taking a pleasure trip. Why else should I travel? I got to know people and places, I enjoyed friendliness and trust, I found friendship. Look, dear friend, if I had been Kamaswami, as soon as I saw that my deal was nullified, I would have come back again in haste, filled with vexation, and my time and money would really have been lost. But, this way, I had a good time, I learned things, I tasted joy, and I harmed neither myself nor others through vexation or through hastiness. And if I ever go back there again, perhaps to buy a future crop, or for any other reason, friendly people will receive me in a friendly and cheerful way, and I shall applaud myself for not having exhibited haste or displeasure on the former occasion. So let it go, my friend, and do not do yourself

loben, daß ich damals nicht Eile und Unmut gezeigt habe. Also laß gut
sein, Freund, und schade dir nicht durch Schelten! Wenn der Tag
kommt, an dem du sehen wirst: Schaden bringt mir dieser Siddhartha,
dann sprich ein Wort, und Siddhartha wird seiner Wege gehen. Bis
dahin aber laß uns einer mit dem andern zufrieden sein.«

Vergeblich waren auch die Versuche des Kaufmanns, Siddhartha zu
überzeugen, daß er sein, Kamaswamis, Brot esse. Siddhartha aß sein
eignes Brot, vielmehr sie beide aßen das Brot anderer, das Brot aller.
Niemals hatte Siddhartha ein Ohr für Kamaswamis Sorgen, und
Kamaswami machte sich viele Sorgen. War ein Geschäft im Gange,
welchem Mißerfolg drohte, schien eine Warensendung verloren, schien
ein Schuldner nicht zahlen zu können, nie konnte Kamaswami seinen
Mitarbeiter überzeugen, daß es nützlich sei, Worte des Kummers oder
des Zornes zu verlieren, Falten auf der Stirn zu haben, schlecht zu
schlafen. Als ihm Kamaswami einstmals vorhielt, er habe alles, was er verstehe, von ihm gelernt, gab er zu Antwort: »Wolle mich doch nicht mit
solchen Späßen zum besten haben! Von dir habe ich gelernt, wieviel ein
Korb voll Fische kostet, und wieviel Zins man für geliehenes Geld
fordern kann. Das sind deine Wissenschaften. Denken habe ich nicht bei
dir gelernt, teurer Kamaswami, suche lieber du, es von mir zu lernen.«

In der Tat war seine Seele nicht beim Handel. Die Geschäfte waren
gut, um ihm Geld für Kamala einzubringen, und sie brachten weit
mehr ein, als er brauchte. Im übrigen war Siddharthas Teilnahme und
Neugierde nur bei den Menschen, deren Geschäfte, Handwerke,
Sorgen, Lustbarkeiten und Torheiten ihm früher fremd und fern
gewesen waren wie der Mond. So leicht es ihm gelang, mit allen zu
sprechen, mit allen zu leben, von allen zu lernen, so sehr ward ihm
dennoch bewußt, daß etwas sei, was ihn von ihnen trennte, und dies
Trennende war sein Samanatum. Er sah die Menschen auf eine
kindliche oder tierhafte Art dahinleben, welche er zugleich liebte und
auch verachtete. Er sah sie sich mühen, sah sie leiden und grau werden um Dinge, die ihm dieses Preises ganz unwert schienen, um
Geld, um kleine Lust, um kleine Ehren, er sah sie einander schelten
und beleidigen, er sah sie um Schmerzen wehklagen, über die der
Samana lächelt, und unter Entbehrungen leiden, die ein Samana
nicht fühlt.

Allem stand er offen, was diese Menschen ihm zubrachten.
Willkommen war ihm der Händler, der ihm Leinwand zum Kauf
anbot, willkommen der Verschuldete, der ein Darlehen suchte,
willkommen der Bettler, der ihm eine Stunde lang die Geschichte

harm by scolding! When the day comes on which you see, 'This Siddhartha is doing me damage,' then just say the word and Siddhartha will go his way. But till then let us be satisfied with each other."

Just as futile were the merchant's attempts to convince Siddhartha that he was eating his, Kamaswami's, bread. Siddhartha was eating his own bread; or, rather, both of them were eating other people's bread, everybody's bread. Siddhartha never lent an ear to Kamaswami's worries, and Kamaswami worried a lot. If a business deal in progress threatened to be unsuccessful, if a shipment seemed to be lost, if a debtor seemed unable to pay, Kamaswami was never able to convince his associate that it was a useful thing to utter words of concern or anger, to knit one's brows, or to lose sleep. When Kamaswami, on one occasion, rebuked him, saying he had learned everything he knew from him, he replied: "Please do not pull my leg with that sort of joke! I have learned from you how much a basket of fish costs, and how much interest can be demanded for a loan of money. That is your corpus of knowledge. But I did not learn how to think from you, my dear Kamaswami; it would be better if you tried to learn that from me."

In truth, his heart was not in commerce. Business was good for making money that he could spend on Kamala, and he made much more at it than he needed. Otherwise, Siddhartha's interests and curiosity were only about people, whose business dealings, artisanry, worries, entertainments, and follies had previously been as foreign to him and remote from him as the moon. No matter how easy it was for him to talk to everyone, to live with everyone, to learn from everyone, he was nevertheless fully aware that there was something that set him apart from them, and that this alienating factor was his experience as a samana. He saw people going through life like children or animals, and he both loved and looked down on that way of life. He saw them laboring, suffering, and growing gray for the sake of things that seemed to him not at all worth that price: for money, for petty pleasures, for petty honors. He saw them scold and insult one another, he saw them complain about pains that a samana smiles at, and suffer from privations that a samana fails to notice.

He was open to everything these people could give him. He welcomed the merchant who offered to sell him linen, he welcomed the debtor who asked him for a loan, he welcomed the beggar who told him the history of his poverty for a full hour, although he was not half

seiner Armut erzählte, und welcher nicht halb so arm war als ein jeder
Samana. Den reichen ausländischen Händler behandelte er nicht anders als den Diener, der ihn rasierte, und den Straßenverkäufer, von
dem er sich beim Bananenkauf um kleine Münze betrügen ließ.
Wenn Kamaswami zu ihm kam, um über seine Sorgen zu klagen oder
ihm wegen eines Geschäftes Vorwürfe zu machen, so hörte er
neugierig und heiter zu, wunderte sich über ihn, suchte ihn zu verstehen, ließ ihn ein wenig recht haben, ebensoviel als ihm unent-
behrlich schien, und wandte sich von ihm ab, dem Nächsten zu, der
ihn begehrte. Und es kamen viele zu ihm, viele, um mit ihm zu handeln, viele, um ihn zu betrügen, viele, um ihn auszuhorchen, viele, um
sein Mitleid anzurufen, viele, um seinen Rat zu hören. Er gab Rat, er
bemitleidete, er schenkte, er ließ sich ein wenig betrügen, und dieses
ganze Spiel und die Leidenschaft mit welcher alle Menschen dies
Spiel betrieben, beschäftigte seine Gedanken ebensosehr, wie einst
die Götter und das Brahman sie beschäftigt hatten.

Zuzeiten spürte er, tief in der Brust, eine sterbende, leise Stimme,
die mahnte leise, klagte leise, kaum daß er sie vernahm. Alsdann kam
ihm für eine Stunde zum Bewußtsein, daß er ein seltsames Leben
führe, daß er da lauter Dinge tue, die bloß ein Spiel waren, daß er
wohl heiter sei und zuweilen Freude fühle, daß aber das eigentliche
Leben dennoch an ihm vorbeifließe und ihn nicht berühre. Wie ein
Ballspieler mit seinen Bällen spielt, so spielte er mit seinen
Geschäften, mit den Menschen seiner Umgebung, sah ihnen zu, fand
seinen Spaß an ihnen; mit dem Herzen, mit der Quelle seines Wesens
war er nicht dabei. Die Quelle lief irgendwo, wie fern von ihm, lief
und lief unsichtbar, hatte nichts mehr mit seinem Leben zu tun. Und
einigemal erschrak er ob solchen Gedanken und wünschte sich, es
möge doch auch ihm gegeben sein, bei all dem kindlichen Tun des
Tages mit Leidenschaft und mit dem Herzen beteiligt zu sein, wirklich zu leben, wirklich zu tun, wirklich zu genießen und zu leben, statt
nur so als ein Zuschauer daneben zu stehen.

Immer aber kam er wieder zur schönen Kamala, lernte
Liebeskunst, übte den Kult der Lust, bei welchem mehr als irgendwo
Geben und Nehmen zu einem wird, plauderte mit ihr, lernte von ihr,
gab ihr Rat, empfing Rat. Sie verstand ihn besser, als Govinda ihn
einst verstanden hatte, sie war ihm ähnlicher.

Einmal sagte er zu ihr: »Du bist wie ich, du bist anders als die meisten Menschen. Du bist Kamala, nichts andres, und in dir innen ist
eine Stille und Zuflucht, in welche du zu jeder Stunde eingehen und

as poor as any samana. He treated wealthy foreign merchants just as he treated the servant who shaved him, or the street vendor, whom he allowed to cheat him out of small change when he bought plantains. When Kamaswami came to him to complain about his worries or to reproach him over some business deal, he listened inquisitively and serenely, was amazed at him, tried to understand him, let him have his own way to some extent, just as much as he considered indispensable, and then turned away from him and on to the next person who wanted him. And many people came to him, many to do business with him, many to cheat him, many to sound him out, many to call upon his sympathy, many to hear his advice. He gave advice, he offered sympathy, he made gifts, he allowed himself to be cheated a little; and this entire game, and the passion with which all people played this game, occupied his thoughts just as much as the gods and the *Brahman* had occupied them in the past.

At times he heard, deep in his heart, a very faint, still voice that quietly admonished him, quietly lamented, so it could barely be perceived. At such times he became aware for an hour or so that he was leading a strange life, that he was doing nothing but playing a mere game, that although he might be serene and might sometimes feel joy, true life was nevertheless passing him by without touching him. The way a ball player plays with the ball, so did he play with his business, with the people around him, watching them, finding amusement in them; his heart, the wellspring of his being, was not in it. The wellspring flowed elsewhere, as if far from him; it flowed on and on invisibly, and had nothing more to do with his life. And a few times he was alarmed at these thoughts and wished that it might be vouchsafed to him, as well, to take part in all the childlike activity of each day passionately and wholeheartedly, really to live, really to act, really to enjoy and to live instead of merely standing by in that way like a spectator.

But he went on visiting the beautiful Kamala; he learned the art of love; he practiced the cult of pleasure, in which more than anywhere else giving and taking become one and the same; he chatted with her, learned from her, gave her advice, received advice. She understood him better than Govinda had formerly understood him; she was more like him.

On one occasion, he said to her: "You are like me, you are different from most people. You are Kamala, nothing else, and within you there is a tranquillity and refuge, in which you can take shelter at any time

bei dir daheim sein kannst, so wie auch ich es kann. Wenige Menschen haben das, und doch könnten alle es haben.«

»Nicht alle Menschen sind klug«, sagte Kamala.

»Nein«, sagte Siddhartha, »nicht daran liegt es. Kamaswami ist ebenso klug wie ich, und hat doch keine Zuflucht in sich. Andre haben sie, die an Verstand kleine Kinder sind. Die meisten Menschen, Kamala, sind wie ein fallendes Blatt, das weht und dreht sich durch die Luft, und schwankt, und taumelt zu Boden. Andre aber, wenige, sind wie Sterne, die gehen eine feste Bahn, kein Wind erreicht sie, in sich selber haben sie ihr Gesetz und ihre Bahn. Unter allen Gelehrten und Samanas, deren ich viele kannte, war einer von dieser Art ein Vollkommener, nie kann ich ihn vergessen. Es ist jener Gotama, der Erhabene, der Verkünder jener Lehre. Tausend Jünger hören jeden Tag seine Lehre, folgen jede Stunde seiner Vorschrift, aber sie alle sind fallendes Laub, nicht in sich selbst haben sie Lehre und Gesetz.«

Kamala betrachtete ihn mit Lächeln. »Wieder redest du von ihm«, sagte sie, »wieder hast du Samanagedanken.«

Siddhartha schwieg, und sie spielten das Spiel der Liebe, eines von den dreißig oder vierzig verschiedenen Spielen, welche Kamala wußte. Ihr Leib war biegsam wie der eines Jaguars und wie der Bogen eines Jägers; wer von ihr die Liebe gelernt hatte, war vieler Lüste, vieler Geheimnisse kundig. Lange spielte sie mit Siddhartha, lockte ihn, wies ihn zurück, zwang ihn, umspannte ihn, freute sich seiner Meisterschaft, bis er besiegt war und erschöpft an ihrer Seite ruhte.

Die Hetäre beugte sich über ihn, sah lang in sein Gesicht, in seine müdgewordenen Augen.

»Du bist der beste Liebende«, sagte sie nachdenklich, »den ich gesehen habe. Du bist stärker als andre, biegsamer, williger. Gut hast du meine Kunst gelernt, Siddhartha. Einst, wenn ich älter bin, will ich von dir ein Kind haben. Und dennoch, Lieber, bist du ein Samana geblieben, dennoch liebst du mich nicht, du liebst keinen Menschen. Ist es nicht so?«

»Es mag wohl so sein«, sagte Siddhartha müde. »Ich bin wie du. Auch du liebst nicht – wie könntest du sonst die Liebe als eine Kunst betreiben? Die Menschen von unserer Art können vielleicht nicht lieben. Die Kindermenschen können es; das ist ihr Geheimnis.«

and be at home with yourself, just as I can, too. Not many people have that, and yet everybody could have it."

"Not all people are clever," Kamala said.

"No," Siddhartha said, "that is not the reason. Kamaswami is just as clever as I am, and yet has no refuge within himself. Others have it, although they have the minds of little children. Most people, Kamala, are like a falling leaf, which drifts and turns in the air, and sways, and zigzags to the ground. But others, just a few, are like stars; they travel a fixed route, no wind reaches them; their law and their route lie within themselves. Among all the many learned men and samanas I have known, one man of this type had attained perfection; I can never forget him. I mean Gotama, the Sublime One, who proclaims that doctrine. A thousand disciples hear his teachings every day, and follow his regulations every hour, but they are all falling leaves; they do not possess the doctrine and the Law within themselves."

Kamala studied him, smiling. "You are talking about him again," she said; "again you are thinking like a samana."

Siddhartha was silent, and they played the game of love, one of the thirty or forty different varieties of the game that Kamala knew. Her body was as lithe as a jaguar's[9] or as a hunter's bow; a man who had learned love from her was acquainted with many pleasures, many secrets. For a long while she sported with Siddhartha, luring him on, repulsing him, forcing his will, encircling him, enjoying his mastery, until he was vanquished and lay exhausted at her side.

The hetaera leaned over him, taking a long look at his face, at his eyes that had grown weary.

She said reflectively, "You are the best lover I have seen. You are stronger than others, more supple, more willing. You have learned my art well, Siddhartha. Sometime when I am older, I want to bear your child. And yet, dear, you have remained a samana; and yet, you do not love me, you do not love anyone. Am I not right?"

"It may be so," said Siddhartha wearily. "I am like you. You do not love anyone, either—otherwise, how could you practice love as an art? Perhaps people of our kind are unable to love. The child-people can; that is their secret."

---

[9] An odd comparison in the context of the novel; the jaguar is a New World animal.

SANSARA

Lange Zeit hatte Siddhartha das Leben der Welt und der Lüste gelebt, ohne ihm doch anzugehören. Seine Sinne, die er in heißen Samana-Jahren ertötet hatte, waren wieder erwacht, er hatte Reichtum gekostet, hatte Wollust gekostet, hatte Macht gekostet; dennoch war er lange Zeit im Herzen noch ein Samana geblieben, dies hatte Kamala, die Kluge, richtig erkannt. Immer war es die Kunst des Denkens, des Wartens, des Fastens, von welcher sein Leben gelenkt wurde, immer noch waren die Menschen der Welt, die Kindermenschen, ihm fremd geblieben, wie er ihnen fremd war.

Die Jahre liefen dahin, in Wohlergehen eingehüllt fühlte Siddhartha ihr Schwinden kaum. Er war reich geworden, er besaß längst ein eigenes Haus und eigene Dienerschaft, und einen Garten vor der Stadt am Flusse. Die Menschen hatten ihn gerne, sie kamen zu ihm, wenn sie Geld oder Rat brauchten, niemand aber stand ihm nahe, außer Kamala.

Jenes hohe, helle Wachsein, welches er einst, auf der Höhe seiner Jugend, erlebt hatte, in den Tagen nach Gotamas Predigt, nach der Trennung von Govinda, jene gespannte Erwartung, jenes stolze Alleinstehen ohne Lehren und ohne Lehrer, jene geschmeidige Bereitschaft, die göttliche Stimme im eigenen Herzen zu hören, war allmählich Erinnerung geworden, war vergänglich gewesen; fern und leise rauschte die heilige Quelle, die einst nahe gewesen war, die einst in ihm selber gerauscht hatte. Vieles zwar, das er von den Samanas gelernt, das er von Gotama gelernt, das er von seinem Vater, dem Brahmanen, gelernt hatte, war noch lange Zeit in ihm geblieben: mäßiges Leben, Freude am Denken, Stunden der Versenkung, heimliches Wissen vom Selbst, vom ewigen Ich, das nicht Körper noch Bewußtsein ist. Manches davon war in ihm geblieben, eines ums andere aber war untergesunken und hatte sich mit Staub bedeckt. Wie die Scheibe des Töpfers, einmal angetrieben, sich noch lange dreht und nur langsam ermüdet und ausschwingt, so hatte in Siddharthas Seele das Rad der Askese, das Rad des Denkens, das Rad der Unterscheidung lange weiter geschwungen, schwang immer noch, aber es schwang langsam und zögernd und war dem Stillstand nahe. Langsam, wie Feuchtigkeit in den absterbenden Baumstrunk dringt, ihn langsam füllt und faulen macht, war Welt und Trägheit in Siddharthas Seele gedrungen, langsam füllte sie seine Seele, machte sie schwer, machte sie müde, schläferte sie ein. Dafür waren seine Sinne lebendig geworden, viel hatten sie gelernt, viel erfahren.

SAMSARA

For a long time Siddhartha had lived the life of the world and its pleasures without really belonging to it. His senses, which he had mortified in his ardent samana years, had reawakened; he had tasted
wealth, had tasted sensual delights, had tasted power; and yet, for a
long time he had still remained a samana in his heart; clever Kamala
had realized that correctly. It was always the art of thinking, waiting,
and fasting that directed his life; the people of the world, the child-
people, had always still remained foreign to him, just as he was foreign
to them.

The years sped by; cushioned by prosperity, Siddhartha barely felt
their passing. He had become wealthy; for some time he had had a
house of his own, his own servants, and a garden in the suburbs by the
river. People liked him; they came to him when they needed money
or advice; but no one was close to him except Kamala.

That lofty, clear sensation of wakefulness he had once experienced in the prime of his youth, in the days after Gotama's preaching, after his separation from Govinda, that tense feeling of ex-
pectancy, that proud independence from teachings and teachers,
that pliant readiness to hear the divine voice in his own heart, had
gradually become just a memory, it had been transitory. Distantly
and quietly murmured the sacred wellspring that had once been
nearby, that had once resounded within himself. To be sure, for a
long time he had retained much of what he had learned from the
samanas, from Gotama, from his father the Brahman: a moderate
way of life, pleasure in thinking, hours of concentration, secret
knowledge of the self, of the eternal "I" that is neither body nor
consciousness. He had retained much of that, but one thing after
another had been submerged and had become covered with dust.
Just as a potter's wheel, once set in motion, still turns for a long
time and only slowly slackens and comes to rest, thus in
Siddhartha's soul the wheel of asceticism, the wheel of thought, the
wheel of discernment, had kept on turning for some time, and was
still turning, but turning slowly and hesitantly, and it was close to
stopping. Slowly, the way that moisture penetrates a dying tree
stump, slowly filling it and making it rot, the world and indolence
had penetrated Siddhartha's soul; slowly it filled his soul, making it
heavy, making it weary, lulling it to sleep. In compensation for that,
his senses had become alert; they had learned a great deal, experienced a great deal.

Siddhartha hatte gelernt, Handel zu treiben, Macht über Menschen auszuüben, sich mit dem Weibe zu vergnügen, er hatte gelernt, schöne Kleider zu tragen, Dienern zu befehlen, sich in wohlriechenden Wassern zu baden. Er hatte gelernt, zart und sorgfältig bereitete Speisen zu essen, auch den Fisch, auch Fleisch und Vogel, Gewürze und Süßigkeiten, und den Wein zu trinken, der träge und vergessen macht. Er hatte gelernt, mit Würfeln und auf dem Schachbrette zu spielen, Tänzerinnen zuzusehen, sich in der Sänfte tragen zu lassen, auf einem weichen Bett zu schlafen. Aber immer noch hatte er sich von den andern verschieden und ihnen überlegen gefühlt, immer hatte er ihnen mit ein wenig Spott zugesehen, mit ein wenig spöttischer Verachtung, mit eben jener Verachtung, wie sie ein Samana stets für Weltleute fühlt. Wenn Kamaswami kränklich war, wenn er ärgerlich war, wenn er sich beleidigt fühlte, wenn er von seinen Kaufmannssorgen geplagt wurde, immer hatte Siddhartha es mit Spott angesehen. Langsam und unmerklich nur, mit den dahingehenden Erntezeiten und Regenzeiten, war sein Spott müder geworden, war seine Überlegenheit stiller geworden. Langsam nur, zwischen seinen wachsenden Reichtümern, hatte Siddhartha selbst etwas von der Art der Kindermenschen angenommen, etwas von ihrer Kindlichkeit und von ihrer Ängstlichkeit. Und doch beneidete er sie, beneidete sie desto mehr, je ähnlicher er ihnen wurde. Er beneidete sie um das Eine, was ihm fehlte und was sie hatten, um die Wichtigkeit, welche sie ihrem leben beizulegen vermochten, um die Leidenschaftlichkeit ihrer Freuden und Ängste, um das bange, aber süße Glück ihrer ewigen Verliebtheit. In sich selbst, in Frauen, in ihre Kinder, in Ehre oder Geld, in Pläne oder Hoffnungen verliebt waren diese Menschen immerzu. Er aber lernte dies nicht von ihnen, gerade dies nicht, diese Kinderfreude und Kindertorheit; er lernte von ihnen gerade das Unangenehme, was er selbst verachtete. Es geschah immer öfter, daß er am Morgen nach einem geselligen Abend lange liegenblieb und sich dumm und müde fühlte. Es geschah, daß er ärgerlich und ungeduldig wurde, wenn Kamaswami ihn mit seinen Sorgen langweilte. Es geschah, daß er allzu laut lachte, wenn er im Würfelspiel verlor. Sein Gesicht war noch immer klüger und geistiger als andre, aber es lachte selten und nahm einen um den andern jene Züge an, die man im Gesicht reicher Leute so häufig findet, jene Züge der Unzufriedenheit, der Kränklichkeit, des Mißmutes, der Trägheit, der Lieblosigkeit. Langsam ergriff ihn die Seelenkrankheit der Reichen.

Wie ein Schleier, wie ein dünner Nebel senkte sich Müdigkeit über Siddhartha, langsam, jeden Tag ein wenig dichter, jeden Monat ein

Siddhartha had learned how to conduct business, how to exercise power over people, how to enjoy women; he had learned to wear beautiful clothes, to give orders to servants, to bathe in scented water. He had learned to eat delicately and carefully prepared dishes, even fish, even meat and poultry, spices and sweets, and to drink wine, which makes you indolent and forgetful. He had learned to play dice and chess, to watch dancing girls, to be carried in a sedan chair, to sleep on a soft bed. But still he had always set himself apart from the rest, feeling superior to them; he had always watched them with a little mockery, with a little mocking contempt, with precisely that contempt which a samana always feels for worldlings. Whenever Kamaswami felt unwell, whenever he was peevish, whenever he felt insulted, whenever he was plagued by his business worries, Siddhartha had always looked on mockingly. Only slowly and imperceptibly, with the passing harvest seasons and rainy seasons, had his mockery grown wearier, had his superiority become quieter. Only slowly, amid his growing riches, had Siddhartha himself taken on something of the nature of the child-people, something of their childlikeness and of their anxiety. And yet he envied them; he envied them more, the more he became like them. He envied them for the one thing that he lacked and they had, for the importance they were able to attach to their life, for the passionate quality of their joys and fears, for the anxious but sweet happiness of their perpetual loving. These people were always in love: with themselves or with women; they loved their children, they loved honor or money, plans or hopes. But it was this, precisely this, that he did not learn from them, this childlike joy and childlike folly; what he did learn from them was precisely what he found unpleasant and had contempt for. It occurred more and more frequently that on the morning after an evening of partying he lay in bed for a long time, feeling stupid and tired. He would become peevish and impatient when Kamaswami bored him with his worries. He would laugh too loud when he lost at dice. His face was still cleverer and more intellectual than other people's, but it seldom laughed, and, one by one, it acquired those lines so frequently found in rich people's faces, those lines of dissatisfaction, sickliness, bad temper, indolence, lovelessness. Slowly the mental malady of the rich was taking hold of him.

Like a veil, like a thin mist, weariness descended upon Siddhartha, slowly, every day a little denser, every month a little more opaque,

wenig trüber, jedes Jahr ein wenig schwerer. Wie ein neues Kleid mit der Zeit alt wird, mit der Zeit seine schöne Farbe verliert, Flecken bekommt, Falten bekommt, an den Säumen abgestoßen wird und hier und dort blöde, fädige Stellen zu zeigen beginnt, so war Siddharthas neues Leben, das er nach seiner Trennung von Govinda begonnen hatte, alt geworden, so verlor es mit den hinrinnenden Jahren Farbe und Glanz, so sammelten sich Falten und Flecken auf ihm, und im Grunde verborgen, hier und dort schon häßlich hervorblickend, wartete Enttäuschung und Ekel. Siddhartha merkte es nicht. Er merkte nur, daß jene helle und sichere Stimme seines Innern, die einst in ihm erwacht war und ihn in seinen glänzenden Zeiten je und je geleitet hatte, schweigsam geworden war.

Die Welt hatte ihn eingefangen, die Lust, die Begehrlichkeit, die Trägheit, und zuletzt auch noch jenes Laster, das er als das törichteste stets am meisten verachtet und gehöhnt hatte: die Habgier. Auch das Eigentum, der Besitz und Reichtum hatte ihn schließlich eingefangen, war ihm kein Spiel und Tand mehr, war Kette und Last geworden. Auf einem seltsamen und listigen Wege war Siddhartha in diese letzte und schnödeste Abhängigkeit geraten, durch das Würfelspiel. Seit der Zeit nämlich, da er im Herzen aufgehört hatte, ein Samana zu sein, begann Siddhartha das Spiel um Geld und Kostbarkeiten, das er sonst lächelnd und lässig als eine Sitte der Kindermenschen mitgemacht hatte, mit einer zunehmenden Wut und Leidenschaft zu treiben. Er war ein gefürchteter Spieler, wenige wagten es mit ihm, so hoch und frech waren seine Einsätze. Er trieb das Spiel aus der Not seines Herzens, das Verspielen und Verschleudern des elenden Geldes schuf ihm eine zornige Freude, auf keine andere Weise konnte er seine Verachtung des Reichtums, des Götzen der Kaufleute, deutlicher und höhnischer zeigen. So spielte er hoch und schonungslos, sich selbst hassend, sich selbst verhöhnend, strich Tausende ein, warf Tausende weg, verspielte Geld, verspielte Schmuck, verspielte ein Landhaus, gewann wieder, verspielte wieder. Jene Angst, jene furchtbare und beklemmende Angst, welche er während des Würfelns, während des Bangens um hohe Einsätze empfand, jene Angst liebte er und suchte sie immer zu erneuern, immer zu steigern, immer höher zu kitzeln, denn in diesem Gefühl allein noch fühlte er etwas wie Glück, etwas wie Rausch, etwas wie erhöhtes Leben inmitten seines gesättigten, lauen, faden Lebens. Und nach jedem großen Verluste sann er auf neuen Reichtum, ging eifriger dem Handel nach, zwang strenger seine Schuldner zum Zahlen, denn er wollte weiter spielen, er wollte weiter vergeuden, weiter dem Reichtum seine

every year a little heavier. Just as a new garment becomes old with time, loses its beautiful color with time, gets stained, gets creased, gets frayed at the seams, and begins to show worn-out, threadbare places here and there, thus had Siddhartha's new life, which he had begun after his separation from Govinda, become old; thus, with the fleeting years, it was losing its color and brightness; thus creases and stains gathered on it; and, concealed below, but already showing through in their ugliness here and there, disappointment and disgust lay in wait. Siddhartha did not notice this. He only noticed that that bright, confident voice within him, that had once awakened in him and had constantly directed him in his most brilliant days, had become taciturn.

The world had entrapped him, pleasure, covetousness, indolence, and finally even the vice he had always despised and scorned most, as being the most foolish: avarice. Property, too, possessions and wealth had finally entrapped him; they were no longer a game or toy to him, but had become a chain and a burden. Siddhartha had fallen into this ultimate, vilest dependency by way of an unusual, deceitful path: through dice playing. For, from the time he had ceased in his heart to be a samana, Siddhartha had begun to gamble for money and expensive things with increasing fury and passion, whereas earlier he had only been participating, smiling and unconcerned, in a custom of the child-people. He was a dreaded player; not many people dared to oppose him, his stakes were so high and reckless. He played out of his heart's distress; to lose and squander his wretched money gave him an angry joy; in no other way could he show more clearly and scornfully his contempt for wealth, the false idol of the merchant class. And so he played for high stakes, ruthlessly, hating himself, scorning himself; he raked in thousands, threw away thousands, lost money, lost jewelry, lost a country villa, won again, lost again. He loved the fear, that awful, oppressive fear that he felt during a dice game, while he was anxious over his high stakes; he strove to renew that fear again and again, to keep intensifying it, to keep titillating it, for only in this sensation did he still feel something like happiness, something like intoxication, something like a heightened form of life, in the midst of his surfeited, tepid, dull existence. And after every big loss he thought about new wealth, he pursued his business interests more enthusiastically, he was firmer in forcing his debtors to pay up, because he wanted to continue gambling, he wanted to continue squandering wealth and showing his contempt for it. Siddhartha lost his calmness when the dice went against him; he lost his patience

Verachtung zeigen. Siddhartha verlor die Gelassenheit bei Verlusten,
er verlor die Geduld gegen säumige Zahler, verlor die Gutmütigkeit
gegen Bettler, verlor die Lust am Verschenken und Wegleihen des
Geldes an Bittende. Er, der zehntausend auf einen Wurf verspielte
und dazu lachte, wurde im Handel strenger und kleinlicher, träumte
nachts zuweilen von Geld! Und so oft er aus dieser häßlichen Bezauberung erwachte, so oft er sein Gesicht im Spiegel an der Schlafzim-
merwand gealtert und häßlicher geworden sah, so oft Scham und Ekel
ihn überfiel, floh er weiter, floh in neues Glücksspiel, floh in
Betäubungen der Wollust, des Weines, und von da zurück in den
Trieb des Häufens und Erwerbens. In diesem sinnlosen Kreislauf lief
er sich müde, lief er sich alt, lief sich krank.

Da mahnte ihn einst ein Traum. Er war die Abendstunden bei Kamala
gewesen, in ihrem schönen Lustgarten. Sie waren unter den Bäumen
gesessen, im Gespräch, und Kamala hatte nachdenkliche Worte gesagt,
Worte, hinter welchen sich eine Trauer und Müdigkeit verbarg. Von
Gotama hatte sie ihn gebeten zu erzählen, und konnte nicht genug von
ihm hören, wie rein sein Auge, wie still und schön sein Mund, wie gütig
sein Lächeln, wie friedevoll sein Gang gewesen. Lange hatte er ihr vom
erhabenen Buddha erzählen müssen, und Kamala hatte geseufzt, und
hatte gesagt: »Einst, vielleicht bald, werde auch ich diesem Buddha folgen. Ich werde ihm meinen Lustgarten schenken, und werde meine
Zuflucht zu seiner Lehre nehmen.« Darauf aber hatte sie ihn gereizt und
ihn im Liebesspiel mit schmerzlicher Inbrunst an sich gefesselt, unter
Bissen und unter Tränen, als wolle sie noch einmal aus dieser eiteln,
vergänglichen Lust den letzten süßen Tropfen pressen. Nie war es
Siddhartha so seltsam klargeworden, wie nahe die Wollust dem Tode ver-
wandt ist. Dann war er an ihrer Seite gelegen, und Kamalas Antlitz war
ihm nahe gewesen, und unter ihren Augen und neben ihren
Mundwinkeln hatte er deutlich wie noch niemals eine bange Schrift gelesen, eine Schrift von feinen Linien, von leisen Furchen, eine Schrift, die
an den Herbst und an das Alter erinnerte, wie denn auch Siddhartha
selbst, der erst in den Vierzigen stand, schon hier und dort ergraute
Haare zwischen seinen schwarzen bemerkt hatte. Müdigkeit stand auf
Kamalas schönem Gesicht geschrieben, Müdigkeit vom Gehen eines langen Weges, der kein frohes Ziel hat, Müdigkeit und beginnende Welke,
und verheimlichte, noch nicht gesagte, vielleicht noch nicht einmal
gewußte Bangigkeit: Furcht vor dem Alter, Furcht vor dem Herbste,
Furcht vor dem Sterbenmüssen. Seufzend hatte er von ihr Abschied
genommen, die Seele voll Unlust und voll verheimlichter Bangigkeit.

Dann hatte Siddhartha die Nacht in seinem Hause mit Tänzerinnen

with those slow to pay him, lost his kindly feeling for beggars, lost his pleasure in giving away or lending money to those who asked for it. Although he would lose ten thousand on a single cast and laugh over it, he became stricter and pettier in his business dealings; he sometimes dreamed of money at night! And every time he awoke from that hateful enchantment, every time he saw in the mirror on his bedroom wall how much his face had aged and grown uglier, every time he was seized by shame and disgust, he ran farther away; he fled to new games of chance, he fled to mind-numbing sensual pleasures and wine, and from there back to the urge to accumulate and gain. In this meaningless cycle he ran himself weary, ran himself old, ran himself sick.

Then, one night, a dream warned him. He had spent the evening hours with Kamala, in her beautiful pleasure garden. They had sat beneath the trees, talking, and Kamala had spoken thoughtful words, words behind which sadness and weariness lay concealed. She had asked him to tell her about Gotama, and she could not hear enough about him, how pure his eyes had been, how calm and beautiful his lips, how kindly his smile, how peaceful his walk. He had had to give her a long account of the sublime Buddha, and Kamala had sighed, saying: "Sometime, maybe soon, I, too, shall follow this Buddha. I shall make him a gift of my pleasure garden, and shall take refuge in his Law." But, after that, she had incited him and had chained him to her in love play with painful ardor, with bites and with tears, as if she wanted just once more to squeeze the last drop of sweetness out of this vain, transitory pleasure. Never had it become so unusually clear to Siddhartha how closely sex is related to death. Afterward he had lain at her side, and Kamala's face had been near him, and below her eyes and at the corners of her mouth he had read more clearly than ever before an anxious message, written in fine lines, in light wrinkles, a message reminding him of autumn and old age—for Siddhartha himself, who was only in his forties, had already noticed gray hairs among his black hair here and there. Weariness was written on Kamala's beautiful face, weariness from traveling a long path that has no happy goal, weariness and the onset of fading, and an anxiety that was kept secret, not yet uttered, perhaps not yet even conscious: fear of old age, fear of the autumn, fear of the necessity of dying. He had taken leave of her with a sigh, his soul filled with aversion and filled with concealed anxiety.

Then Siddhartha had spent the night at home with dancing girls

beim Weine zugebracht, hatte gegen seine Standesgenossen den Über-
legenen gespielt, welcher er nicht mehr war, hatte viel Wein getrunken
und spät nach Mitternacht sein Lager aufgesucht, müde und dennoch
erregt, dem Weinen und der Verzweiflung nahe, und hatte lange vergeblich den Schlaf gesucht, das Herz voll eines Elendes, das er nicht mehr
ertragen zu können meinte, voll eines Ekels, von dem er sich durchdrungen fühlte wie vom lauen, widerlichen Geschmack des Weines, der
allzu süßen, öden Musik, dem allzu weichen Lächeln der Tänzerinnen,
dem allzu süßen Duft ihrer Haare und Brüste. Mehr aber als vor allem
anderen ekelte ihm vor sich selbst, vor seinen duftenden Haaren, vor
dem Weingeruch seines Mundes, vor der schlaffen Müdigkeit und
Unlust seiner Haut. Wie wenn einer, der allzuviel gegessen oder
getrunken hat, es unter Qualen wieder erbricht und doch der
Erleichterung froh ist, so wünschte sich der Schlaflose, in einem ungeheuren Schwall von Ekel sich dieser Genüsse, dieser Gewohnheiten,
dieses ganzen sinnlosen Lebens und seiner selbst zu entledigen. Erst
beim Schein des Morgens und dem Erwachen der ersten Geschäftigkeit
auf der Straße vor seinem Stadthause war er eingeschlummert, hatte für
wenige Augenblicke eine halbe Betäubung, eine Ahnung von Schlaf gefunden. In diesen Augenblicken hatte er einen Traum:
Kamala besaß in einem goldenen Käfig einen kleinen seltenen
Singvogel. Von diesem Vogel träumte er. Er träumte: dieser Vogel war
stumm geworden, der sonst stets in der Morgenstunde sang, und da
dies ihm auffiel, trat er vor den Käfig und blickte hinein, da war der
kleine Vogel tot und lag steif am Boden. Er nahm ihn heraus, wog ihn
einen Augenblick in der Hand und warf ihn dann weg, auf die Gasse
hinaus, und im gleichen Augenblick erschrak er furchtbar, und das
Herz tat ihm weh, so, als habe er mit diesem toten Vogel allen Wert
und alles Gute von sich geworfen.
Aus diesem Traum auffahrend, fühlte er sich von tiefer Traurigkeit
umfangen. Wertlos, so schien ihm, wertlos und sinnlos hatte er sein
Leben dahingeführt; nichts Lebendiges, nichts irgendwie Köstliches
oder Behaltenswertes war ihm in Händen geblieben. Allein stand er
und leer, wie ein Schiffbrüchiger am Ufer.
Finster begab sich Siddhartha in einen Lustgarten, der ihm
gehörte, verschloß die Pforte, setzte sich unter einem Mangobaum
nieder, fühlte den Tod im Herzen und das Grauen in der Brust, saß
und spürte, wie es in ihm starb, in ihm welkte, in ihm zu Ende ging.
Allmählich sammelte er seine Gedanken und ging im Geiste
nochmals den ganzen Weg seines Lebens, von den ersten Tagen an,
auf welche er sich besinnen konnte. Wann denn hatte er ein Glück er-

and wine; he had played the part of a superior man vis-à-vis his peers, although he no longer was one; he had drunk much wine and had gone to bed long after midnight, weary and yet agitated, close to tears and despair; for a long time he had tried in vain to fall asleep, his heart full of a misery that he thought he could no longer bear, full of a disgust that he felt permeating him like the tepid, repellent taste of the wine, like the oversweet, monotonous music, like the too simpering smiles of the dancing girls and the oversweet fragrance of their hair and breasts. But, more than with anything else, he was disgusted with himself, with his scented hair, with the smell of wine from his mouth, with the flabby tiredness and irritability of his skin. Just as someone who has eaten or drunk too much vomits it out again in great discomfort but nevertheless is glad of the relief, thus the insomniac wished he could rid himself of these pleasures, of these habits, of this whole pointless life, and of himself, in one enormous surge of nausea. He had not dropped off to sleep until the morning light and the first flurry of activity on the street in front of his town house; for a few moments he had achieved semiconsciousness, a foretaste of sleep. During these moments he had a dream:

Kamala owned a small, rare songbird that she kept in a golden cage. It was this bird he dreamt about. In his dream, this bird, which usually always sang at the morning hour, remained silent; and, since this attracted his attention, he stepped up to the cage and looked in; the little bird was dead, and lay rigid on the floor of the cage. He took it out, weighed it in his hand for a moment, and then threw it away, out into the lane; and, at the same moment, he received a terrible fright, and his heart ached as if he had cast away everything valuable and good from himself together with that dead bird.

Starting up out of that dream, he felt hemmed in by a profound sadness. It appeared to him that he had been living his life in a worthless way, worthless and pointless; nothing alive, nothing in the least way valuable or worth keeping, had remained in his hands. He stood there alone and empty like a shipwrecked man on the shore.

Gloomily Siddhartha went to a pleasure garden he owned, locked the gate, sat down beneath a mango tree, felt death in his heart and terror in his bosom; he sat there and physically felt a dying, fading, and ending within him. Gradually he collected his thoughts and mentally retraced the entire course of his life, from the very first days he was able to recall. When had he ever experienced happiness, felt true bliss? Oh, yes, he had experienced it several times. As a boy

lebt, eine wahre Wonne gefühlt? O ja, mehrere Male hatte er solches erlebt. In den Knabenjahren hatte er es gekostet, wenn er von den Brahmanen Lob errungen hatte, wenn er, den Altersgenossen weit voraus, sich mit dem Hersagen der heiligen Verse, im Disput mit den Gelehrten, als Gehilfe beim Opfer ausgezeichnet hatte. Da hatte er es in seinem Herzen gefühlt: »Ein Weg liegt vor dir, zu dem du berufen bist, auf dich warten die Götter.« Und wieder als Jüngling, da ihn das immer höher emporfliehende Ziel alles Nachdenkens aus der Schar Gleichstrebender heraus- und hinangerissen hatte, da er in Schmerzen um den Sinn des Brahman rang, da jedes erreichte Wissen nur neuen Durst in ihm entfachte, da wieder hatte er, mitten im Durst, mitten im Schmerze dieses selbe gefühlt: »Weiter! Weiter! Du bist berufen!« Diese Stimme hatte er vernommen, als er seine Heimat verlassen und das Leben des Samana gewählt hatte, und wieder, als er von den Samanas hinweg zu jenem Vollendeten, und auch von ihm hinweg ins Ungewisse gegangen war. Wie lange hatte er diese Stimme nicht gehört, wie lange keine Höhe mehr erreicht, wie eben und öde war sein Weg dahingegangen, viele lange Jahre, ohne hohes Ziel, ohne Durst, ohne Erhebung, mit kleinen Lüsten zufrieden und dennoch nie begnügt! Alle diese Jahre hatte er, ohne es selbst zu wissen, sich bemüht und danach gesehnt, ein Mensch wie diese vielen zu werden, wie diese Kinder, und dabei war sein Leben viel elender und ärmer gewesen als das ihre, denn ihre Ziele waren nicht die seinen, noch ihre Sorgen, diese ganze Welt der Kamaswami-Menschen war ihm ja nur ein Spiel gewesen, ein Tanz, dem man zusieht, eine Komödie. Einzig Kamala war ihm lieb, war ihm wertvoll gewesen – aber war sie es noch? Brauchte er sie noch, oder sie ihn? Spielten sie nicht ein Spiel ohne Ende? War es notwendig, dafür zu leben? Nein, es war nicht notwendig! Dieses Spiel hieß Sansara, ein Spiel für Kinder, ein Spiel, vielleicht hold zu spielen, einmal, zweimal, zehnmal – aber immer und immer wieder?

Da wußte Siddhartha, daß das Spiel zu Ende war, daß er es nicht mehr spielen könne. Ein Schauder lief ihm über den Leib, in seinem Innern, so fühlte er, war etwas gestorben.

Jenen ganzen Tag saß er unter dem Mangobaume, seines Vaters gedenkend, Govindas gedenkend, Gotamas gedenkend. Hatte er diese verlassen müssen, um ein Kamaswami zu werden? Er saß noch, als die Nacht angebrochen war. Als er aufschauend die Sterne erblickte, dachte er: »Hier sitze ich unter meinem Mangobaume, in meinem Lustgarten.« Er lächelte ein wenig – war es denn notwendig,

he had tasted it when he had elicited praise from the Brahmans, when, far surpassing the others of his age, he had distinguished himself in reciting the holy verses, in disputations with the learned men, as an assistant at the sacrifices. At such times he had felt in his heart: "A path lies before you to which you are called, the gods are waiting for you." And, then, as a young man, when the ever-elusive goal of all reflective thought had plucked him out of the mass of all the other contenders and had borne him upward; when he was painfully struggling for the meaning of *Brahman,* when every bit of knowledge he acquired merely kindled fresh thirst in him—there too, amid his thirst, amid his pain, he had had the same feeling: "Onward! Onward! You have a calling!" He had heard that voice when he had left home and chosen a samana's life, and again when he had departed from the samanas and gone to that Perfect One, and then when he had departed from him and gone into the unknown. How long it was now since he had heard that voice, how long since he had scaled any heights; how evenly and monotonously his journey had gone on, many long years without a lofty goal, knowing no thirst or elevation of spirit, contented with petty pleasures and yet never satisfied! For all these years, without knowing it, he had labored and longed to become a human being like all these others, like these children, and all that time his life had been much more wretched and poor than theirs, because their goals were not his, nor their worries; in fact, this whole world of Kamaswami-people had been just a game to him, a dance that you watch, a comedy. Only Kamala had been dear to him, had had value for him—but did she still? Did he still need her, or she him? Were they not playing a game that had no end? Was it necessary to go on living for that? No, it was not necessary! This game was called *samsara,* a game for children, a game it might be pleasant to play once, twice, ten times— but over and over again?

Then Siddhartha knew that the game was over, that he could not play it anymore. He shuddered all over his body, and inside him, and he felt that something had died.

That whole day he sat beneath the mango tree, recalling his father, recalling Govinda, recalling Gotama. Had it been necessary to abandon them in order to become a Kamaswami? He was still sitting there when night fell. When he looked up and caught sight of the stars, he thought: "Here I am sitting beneath my mango tree in my pleasure garden." He smiled slightly—was it necessary, then, was it

war es richtig, war es nicht ein törichtes Spiel, daß er einen Mangobaum, daß er einen Garten besaß?

Auch damit schloß er ab, auch das starb in ihm. Er erhob sich,
nahm Abschied vom Mangobaum, Abschied vom Lustgarten. Da er
den Tag ohne Speise geblieben war, fühlte er heftigen Hunger, und
gedachte an sein Haus in der Stadt, an sein Gemach und Bett, an den
Tisch mit den Speisen. Er lächelte müde, schüttelte sich und nahm
Abschied von diesen Dingen.

In derselben Nachtstunde verließ Siddhartha seinen Garten,
verließ die Stadt und kam niemals wieder. Lange ließ Kamaswami
nach ihm suchen, der ihn in Räuberhand gefallen glaubte. Kamala
ließ nicht nach ihm suchen. Als sie erfuhr, daß Siddhartha verschwunden sei, wunderte sie sich nicht. Hatte sie es nicht immer erwartet? War er nicht ein Samana, ein Heimloser, ein Pilger? Und am
meisten hatte sie dies beim letzten Zusammensein gefühlt, und sie
freute sich mitten im Schmerz des Verlustes, daß sie ihn dieses letzte
Mal noch so innig an ihr Herz gezogen, sich noch einmal so ganz von
ihm besessen und durchdrungen gefühlt hatte.

Als sie die erste Nachricht von Siddharthas Verschwinden bekam,
trat sie ans Fenster, wo sie in einem goldenen Käfig einen seltenen
Singvogel gefangen hielt. Sie öffnete die Tür des Käfigs, nahm den
Vogel heraus und ließ ihn fliegen. Lange sah sie ihm nach, dem fliegen-
den Vogel. Sie empfing von diesem Tage an keine Besucher mehr und
hielt ihr Haus verschlossen. Nach einiger Zeit aber ward sie inne, daß
sie von dem letzten Zusammensein mit Siddhartha schwanger sei.

AM FLUSSE

Siddhartha wanderte im Walde, schon fern von der Stadt, und wußte
nichts als das eine, daß er nicht mehr zurück konnte, daß dies Leben,
wie er es nun viele Jahre lang geführt, vorüber und dahin und bis zum
Ekel ausgekostet und ausgesogen war. Tot war der Singvogel, von
dem er geträumt. Tot war der Vogel in seinem Herzen. Tief war er in
Sansara verstrickt, Ekel und Tod hatte er von allen Seiten in sich
eingesogen, wie ein Schwamm Wasser einsaugt, bis er voll ist. Voll war
er von Überdruß, voll von Elend, voll von Tod, nichts mehr gab es in
der Welt, das ihn locken, das ihn freuen, das ihn trösten konnte.

Sehnlich wünschte er, nichts mehr von sich zu wissen, Ruhe zu
haben, tot zu sein. Käme doch ein Blitz und erschlüge ihn! Käme
doch ein Tiger und fräße ihn! Gäbe es doch einen Wein, ein Gift, das

proper, was it not just a foolish game, for him to own a mango tree and a garden?

He called it quits with that, as well; that, too, died within him. He got up, said good-bye to the mango tree, good-bye to the pleasure garden. Since he had spent the whole day without eating, he felt a ravenous hunger, and recalled his house in town, his room and bed, the table laden with food. He smiled wearily, shook himself, and said good-bye to those things.

In the same hour of the night, Siddhartha abandoned his garden, abandoned the town, and never returned. For a long time Kamaswami had him searched for, believing he had fallen into the hands of highwaymen. Kamala did not have him searched for. When she learned that Siddhartha had disappeared, she was not surprised. Had she not always expected it? Was he not a samana, a homeless man, a wanderer? And she had felt this most strongly the last time they were together; and, amid the pain of her loss, she was glad that, on that last occasion, she had still drawn him so lovingly to her heart, that she had once again felt so fully possessed and permeated by him.

When she received the first news of Siddhartha's disappearance, she went to the window where she kept a rare songbird in a golden cage. She opened the cage door, took the bird out, and let it fly away. For a long time she watched it go, that flying bird. From that day on, she accepted no more visits and kept her house locked up. But after a while she became aware that her last meeting with Siddhartha had left her pregnant.

BY THE RIVER

Siddhartha wandered through the forest, already far from the town; he knew only this: that he could not return, that the life he had now been leading for many years was over and done with, that he had tasted and drained it to the surfeiting point. Dead was the songbird of which he had dreamed. Dead was the bird in his heart. He was tightly entangled in *samsara*; he had imbibed disgust and death from all sides, as a sponge soaks up water until it is full. He was full of distaste, full of misery, full of death; there was nothing more in the world that could entice him, gladden him, console him.

He ardently wished to know nothing more about himself, to enjoy repose, to be dead. If only a lightning bolt would come and kill him! If only a tiger would come and devour him! If only there were a wine,

ihm Betäubung brächte, Vergessen und Schlaf, und kein Erwachen mehr! Gab es denn noch irgendeinen Schmutz, mit dem er sich nicht beschmutzt hatte, eine Sünde und Torheit, die er nicht begangen, eine Seelenöde, die er nicht auf sich geladen hatte? War es denn noch möglich zu leben? War es möglich, nochmals und nochmals wieder Atem zu ziehen, Atem auszustoßen, Hunger zu fühlen, wieder zu essen, wieder zu schlafen, wieder beim Weibe zu liegen? War dieser Kreislauf nicht für ihn erschöpft und abgeschlossen?

Siddhartha gelangte an den großen Fluß im Walde, an denselben Fluß, über welchen ihn einst, als er noch ein junger Mann war und von der Stadt des Gotama kam, ein Fährmann geführt hatte. An diesem Flusse machte er halt, blieb zögernd beim Ufer stehen. Müdigkeit und Hunger hatten ihn geschwächt, und wozu auch sollte er weitergehen, wohin denn, zu welchem Ziel? Nein, es gab keine Ziele mehr, es gab nichts mehr als die tiefe, leidvolle Sehnsucht, diesen ganzen wüsten Traum von sich zu schütteln, diesen schalen Wein von sich zu speien, diesem jämmerlichen und schmachvollen Leben ein Ende zu machen.

Über das Flußufer hing ein Baum gebeugt, ein Kokosbaum, an dessen Stamm lehnte sich Siddhartha mit der Schulter, legte den Arm um den Stamm und blickte in das grüne Wasser hinab, das unter ihm zog und zog, blickte hinab und fand sich ganz und gar von dem Wunsche erfüllt, sich loszulassen und in diesem Wasser unterzugehen. Eine schauerliche Leere spiegelte ihm aus dem Wasser entgegen, welcher die furchtbare Leere in seiner Seele Antwort gab. Ja, er war am Ende. Nichts mehr gab es für ihn, als sich auszulöschen, als das mißlungene Gebilde seines Lebens zu zerschlagen, es wegzuwerfen, hohnlachenden Göttern vor die Füße. Dies war das große Erbrechen, nach dem er sich gesehnt hatte: der Tod, das Zerschlagen der Form, die er haßte! Mochten ihn die Fische fressen, diesen Hund von Siddhartha, diesen Irrsinnigen, diesen verdorbenen und verfaulten Leib, diese erschlaffte und mißbrauchte Seele! Mochten die Fische und Krokodile ihn fressen, mochten die Dämonen ihn zerstücken!

Mit verzerrtem Gesichte starrte er ins Wasser, sah sein Gesicht gespiegelt und spie danach. In tiefer Müdigkeit löste er den Arm vom Baumstamme und drehte sich ein wenig, um sich senkrecht hinabfallen zu lassen, um endlich unterzugehen. Er sank, mit geschlossenen Augen, dem Tod entgegen.

a poison, that could bring him unconsciousness, oblivion, and sleep without any more awakening! For was there any kind of filth he had not filthied himself with, any sin and folly he had not committed, any barrenness of the soul he had not burdened himself with? Was it possible to go on living? Was it possible to keep on constantly breathing in, breathing out, feeling hunger, eating again, sleeping again, lying with a woman again? Was not this cycle exhausted and terminated for him?

Siddhartha reached the wide river in the forest, the same river over which a ferryman had once taken him when he was still a young man coming from Gotama's town. By that river he halted, lingering hesitantly on its bank. Fatigue and hunger had weakened him—and, then, what reason had he to continue on, and where to, toward what goal? No, there were no longer any goals, nothing was left but the deep-seated, sorrowful longing to shake off that entire chaotic dream, to spit out that flat wine, to make an end of that pathetic, shameful life.

A tree leaned forward over the riverbank, a coconut palm. Siddhartha rested his shoulder against its trunk, placed his arm around the trunk, and looked down into the green water that continued to flow by below him. He looked down and discovered that he was totally imbued with the desire to let himself go and sink in that water. He saw a frightful void reflected in that water, corresponding to the terrible void in his soul. Yes, he had reached the end. There was nothing left for him but to obliterate himself, to shatter the abortive structure of his life, to throw it away at the feet of gods who would laugh in scorn. This was the great fit of vomiting he had longed for: death, the shattering of the mold that he hated! Let the fish devour him, that dog Siddhartha, that lunatic, that corrupt, decayed body, that flaccid, misused soul! Let the fish and crocodiles devour him, let the demons[10] tear him apart!

His features distorted, he stared into the water; seeing the reflection of his face, he spat at it. In profound weariness he detached his arm from the tree trunk and turned his body slightly so that he would fall vertically, and finally perish. His eyes closed, he was dropping to his death.

---

[10] Siddhartha has claimed earlier that there are no demons. Perhaps here the term is merely a poetical equivalent of the crocodiles and other deadly creatures.

Da zuckte aus entlegenen Bezirken seiner Seele, aus Vergangenheiten seines ermüdeten Lebens her ein Klang. Es war ein Wort, eine Silbe, die er ohne Gedanken mit lallender Stimme vor sich hinsprach, das alte Anfangswort und Schlußwort aller brahmanischen Gebete, das heilige »Om«, das so viel bedeutet wie »das Vollkommene« oder »die Vollendung.«. Und im Augenblick, da der Klang »Om« Siddharthas Ohr berührte, erwachte sein entschlummerter Geist plötzlich, und erkannte die Torheit seines Tuns.

Siddhartha erschrak tief. So also stand es um ihn, so verloren war er, so verirrt und von allem Wissen verlassen, daß er den Tod hatte suchen können, daß dieser Wunsch, dieser Kinderwunsch in ihm hatte groß werden können: Ruhe zu finden, indem er seinen Leib auslöschte! Was alle Qual dieser letzten Zeiten, alle Ernüchterung, alle Verzweiflung nicht bewirkt hatte, das bewirkte dieser Augenblick, da das Om in sein Bewußtsein drang: daß er sich in seinem Elend und in seinem Irrsal erkannte.

»Om!« sprach er vor sich hin: »Om!« Und wußte um Brahman, wußte um die Unzerstörbarkeit des Lebens, wußte um alles Göttliche wieder, das er vergessen hatte.

Doch war dies nur ein Augenblick, ein Blitz. Am Fuß des Kokosbaumes sank Siddhartha nieder, legte sein Haupt auf die Wurzel des Baumes und sank in tiefen Schlaf.

Tief war sein Schlaf und frei von Träumen, seit langer Zeit hatte er einen solchen Schlaf nicht mehr gekannt. Als er nach manchen Stunden erwachte, war ihm, als seien zehn Jahre vergangen, er hörte das leise Strömen des Wassers, wußte nicht, wo er sei und wer ihn hierher gebracht habe, schlug die Augen auf, sah mit Verwunderung Bäume und Himmel über sich, und erinnerte sich, wo er wäre und wie er hierher gekommen sei. Doch bedurfte er hierzu einer langen Weile, und das Vergangene erschien ihm wie von einem Schleier überzogen, unendlich fern, unendlich weit weg gelegen, unendlich gleichgültig. Er wußte nur, daß er sein früheres Leben (im ersten Augenblick der Besinnung erschien ihm dies frühere Leben wie eine weit zurückliegende, einstige Verkörperung, wie eine frühe Vorgeburt seines jetzigen Ich) – , daß er sein früheres Leben verlassen habe, daß er voll Ekel und Elend sogar sein Leben habe wegwerfen wollen, daß er aber an einem Flusse, unter einem Kokosbaume, zu sich gekommen sei, das heilige Wort Om auf den Lippen, dann entschlummert sei, und nun erwacht als ein neuer Mensch in die Welt blicke. Leise sprach er das Wort Om vor sich hin, über welchem er eingeschlafen war, und ihm schien, sein ganzer langer Schlaf sei nichts als ein langes, versunkenes

Just then, from remote regions of his soul, from past periods of his tired life, a sound ran through his mind like a flash. It was a word, a syllable, that he spoke to himself involuntarily in a slurred voice, that old word which begins and ends every Brahmanist prayer, the sacred *om*, which is equivalent in meaning to "perfection" or "the absolute." And at the moment that the sound *om* touched Siddhartha's ears, his intellect, which had fallen asleep, suddenly awakened and realized the folly of what he was doing.

Siddhartha was thoroughly frightened. So, then, things were so bad for him, he was so lost, so far astray and abandoned by all knowledge, that he had been able to seek death; that that wish, that childish wish, had been able to grow strong within him: to find peace by obliterating his body! What all the torment of those recent days, all his sober reflections, all his despair, had not accomplished, was accomplished by the moment when *om* penetrated his consciousness: he understood himself in his misery and his maze of error.

"*Om!*" he said to himself: "*Om!*" And once more he knew about *Brahman,* he knew about the indestructibility of life, he knew about all the divine things he had forgotten.

But this was only a moment, a lightning flash. Siddhartha sank down at the foot of the coconut palm, laid his head on the tree's roots, and sank into deep sleep.

His sleep was deep and dreamless; for a long time he had not known such sleep. When he awakened many hours later, he felt as if ten years had gone by; he heard the quiet flowing of the water; he did not know where he was or who had brought him there; he opened his eyes, and in surprise saw trees and sky above him, and remembered where he was and how he had gotten there. But this took him a long time, and the past seemed to him to lie under a veil, to be infinitely distant, infinitely far away, infinitely unimportant. All he knew was that he had left his earlier life behind (in the first moments of his return to his senses, that earlier life resembled a previous incarnation in the remote past, an early prenatal state of his present self); he knew that, filled with disgust and misery, he had even wanted to throw away his life, but that he had regained consciousness by a river, under a coconut palm, the sacred word *om* on his lips; he had then fallen asleep, and now, awake again, he was looking at the world like a new person. Softly he spoke the word *om* to himself, the word that had been in his thoughts when he fell asleep, and he felt as if all of his long sleep had been nothing but a long utterance of *om* in a state of concen-

Om-Sprechen gewesen, ein Om-Denken, ein Untertauchen und völliges Eingehen in Om, in das Namenlose, Vollendete.

Was für ein wunderbarer Schlaf war dies doch gewesen! Niemals hatte ein Schlaf ihn so erfrischt, so erneut, so verjüngt! Vielleicht war er wirklich gestorben, war untergegangen und in einer neuen Gestalt wiedergeboren? Aber nein, er kannte sich, er kannte seine Hand und seine Füße, kannte den Ort, an dem er lag, kannte dies Ich in seiner Brust, diesen Siddhartha, den Eigenwilligen, den Seltsamen, aber dieser Siddhartha war dennoch verwandelt, war erneut, war merkwürdig ausgeschlafen, merkwürdig wach, freudig und neugierig.

Siddhartha richtete sich empor, da sah er sich gegenüber einen Menschen sitzen, einen fremden Mann, einen Mönch in gelbem Gewande mit rasiertem Kopfe, in der Stellung des Nachdenkens. Er betrachtete den Mann, der weder Haupthaar noch Bart an sich hatte, und nicht lange hatte er ihn betrachtet, da erkannte er in diesem Mönche Govinda, den Freund seiner Jugend, Govinda, der seine Zuflucht zum erhabenen Buddha genommen hatte. Govinda war gealtert, auch er, aber noch immer trug sein Gesicht die alten Züge, sprach von Eifer, von Treue, von Suchen, von Ängstlichkeit. Als nun aber Govinda, seinen Blick fühlend, das Auge aufschlug und ihn anschaute, sah Siddhartha, daß Govinda ihn nicht erkenne. Govinda freute sich, ihn wach zu finden, offenbar hatte er lange hier gesessen und auf sein Erwachen gewartet, obwohl er ihn nicht kannte.

»Ich habe geschlafen«, sagte Siddhartha. »Wie bist denn du hierher gekommen?«

»Du hast geschlafen«, antwortete Govinda. »Es ist nicht gut, an solchen Orten zu schlafen, wo häufig Schlangen sind und die Tiere des Waldes ihre Wege haben. Ich, o Herr, bin ein Jünger des erhabenen Gotama, des Buddha, des Sakyamuni, und bin mit einer Zahl der Unsrigen diesen Weg gepilgert, da sah ich dich liegen und schlafen an einem Orte, wo es gefährlich ist zu schlafen. Darum suchte ich dich zu wecken, o Herr, und da ich sah, daß dein Schlaf sehr tief war, blieb ich hinter den Meinigen zurück und saß bei dir. Und dann, so scheint es, bin ich selbst eingeschlafen, der ich deinen Schlaf bewachen wollte. Schlecht habe ich meinen Dienst versehen, Müdigkeit hat mich übermannt. Aber nun, da du ja wach bist, laß mich gehen, damit ich meine Brüder einhole.«

»Ich danke dir, Samana, daß du meinen Schlaf behütet hast«, sprach Siddhartha. »Freundlich seid ihr Jünger des Erhabenen. Nun magst du denn gehen.«

»Ich gehe, Herr. Möge der Herr sich immer wohl befinden.«

»Ich danke dir, Samana.«

tration, a meditation on *om,* an immersion and total absorption into *om,* into the nameless, the absolute.

Really, what a marvelous sleep that had been! Never had sleep so refreshed him, so renewed him, so rejuvenated him! Perhaps he had really died, had perished, and was now reborn in a new shape? But no, he recognized himself, he recognized his hands and feet, he recognized the place where he was lying, he recognized that "I" in his bosom, that Siddhartha, that willful, strange man; and yet this Siddhartha was transformed, he was renewed, he was remarkably rested, remarkably awake, joyful and inquisitive.

Siddhartha sat up, whereupon he saw someone sitting opposite him, a stranger, a monk in a yellow robe, with a shaved head, in the pose of contemplation. He observed the man, who had neither hair on his head nor a beard; but he had not been observing him very long when he recognized in that monk Govinda, the friend of his youth, Govinda, who had taken refuge in the sublime Buddha. Govinda had aged, too, but his face still bore the same old features, betokening enthusiasm, loyalty, questing, anxiety. But now, when Govinda, feeling his eyes upon him, opened his own eyes and looked at him, Siddhartha saw that Govinda did not recognize him. Govinda was glad to find him awake; obviously he had been sitting there for some time waiting for him to awaken, even though he did not know him.

"I have been sleeping," Siddhartha said. "How did you get here?"

"You have been sleeping," Govinda replied. "It is not good to sleep in places like this, where there are often snakes and where the forest animals have their trails. I, sir, am a disciple of the sublime Gotama, the Buddha, the Sakyamuni, and I was wandering this way with a group of my fellows when I saw you lying asleep in a place where it is dangerous to sleep. Therefore I tried to awaken you, sir, and when I saw that your sleep was very deep, I remained behind while my friends went on, and I sat with you. And then, it seems, I fell asleep myself, I who wanted to guard you while you slept. I have done my duty badly, fatigue overpowered me. But now that you are awake, let me go so that I can overtake my brothers."

"Thank you, samana, for watching over me while I slept," Siddhartha said. "You disciples of the Sublime One are friendly. Now you may go."

"I am going, sir. May you always enjoy good health, sir."

"Thank you, samana."

Govinda machte das Zeichen des Grußes und sagte: »Lebe wohl.«
»Lebe wohl, Govinda«, sagte Siddhartha.

Der Mönch blieb stehen.

»Erlaube, Herr, woher kennst du meinen Namen?«

Da lächelte Siddhartha.

»Ich kenne dich, o Govinda, aus der Hütte deines Vaters, und aus der Brahmanenschule, und von den Opfern, und von unsrem Gang zu den Samanas, und von jener Stunde, da du im Hain Jetavana deine Zuflucht zum Erhabenen nahmest.«

»Du bist Siddhartha!« rief Govinda laut. »Jetzt erkenne ich dich, und begreife nicht mehr, wie ich dich nicht sogleich erkennen konnte. Sei willkommen, Siddhartha, groß ist meine Freude, dich wiederzusehen.«

»Auch mich erfreut es, dich wiederzusehen. Du bist der Wächter meines Schlafes gewesen, nochmals danke ich dir dafür, obwohl ich keines Wächters bedurft hätte. Wohin gehst du, o Freund?«

»Nirgendhin gehe ich. Immer sind wir Mönche unterwegs, solange nicht Regenzeit ist, immer ziehen wir von Ort zu Ort, leben nach der Regel, verkündigen die Lehre, nehmen Almosen, ziehen weiter. Immer ist es so. Du aber, Siddhartha, wo gehst du hin?«

Sprach Siddhartha: »Auch mit mir steht es so, Freund, wie mit dir. Ich gehe nirgendhin. Ich bin nur unterwegs. Ich pilgere.«

Govinda sprach: »Du sagst, du pilgerst, und ich glaube dir. Doch verzeih, o Siddhartha, nicht wie ein Pilger siehst du aus. Du trägst das Kleid eines Reichen, du trägst die Schuhe eines Vornehmen, und dein Haar, das nach wohlriechendem Wasser duftet, ist nicht das Haar eines Pilgers, nicht das Haar eines Samanas.«

»Wohl, Lieber, gut hast du beobachtet, alles sieht dein scharfes Auge. Doch habe ich nicht zu dir gesagt, daß ich ein Samana sei. Ich sagte: ich pilgere. Und so ist es: ich pilgere.«

»Du pilgerst«, sagte Govinda. »Aber wenige pilgern in solchem Kleide, wenige in solchen Schuhen, wenige mit solchen Haaren. Nie habe ich, der ich schon viele Jahre pilgere, solch einen Pilger angetroffen.«

»Ich glaube es dir, mein Govinda. Aber nun, heute, hast du eben einen solchen Pilger angetroffen, in solchen Schuhen, mit solchem Gewande. Erinnere dich, Lieber: vergänglich ist die Welt der Gestaltungen, vergänglich, höchst vergänglich sind unsere Gewänder, und die Tracht unserer Haare, und unsere Haare und Körper selbst. Ich trage die Kleider eines Reichen, da hast du recht gesehen. Ich trage

Govinda made the sign of leavetaking and said: "Farewell."

"Farewell, Govinda," Siddhartha said.

The monk stopped short.

"Pardon me, sir, how do you know my name?"

Thereupon Siddhartha smiled.

"I know you, O Govinda, from your father's cottage, and from the Brahmanic school, and from the sacrifices, and from our journey to the samanas, and from the hour when you took refuge in the Sublime One in the grove of Jetavana."

"You are Siddhartha!" Govinda shouted out loud. "Now I recognize you, and I fail to understand how I did not recognize you at once. Welcome, Siddhartha, great is my joy at seeing you again."

"I, too, am pleased to see you again. You have been the guardian of my slumbers, for which I thank you again, even though I needed no guardian. Where are you headed for, my friend?"

"Nowhere in particular. We monks are always journeying, except in the rainy season; we are always proceeding from one place to another, living by our rules, proclaiming the doctrine, accepting alms, journeying further. It is always like that. But you, Siddhartha, where are you headed for?"

Siddhartha said: "It is the same with me, too, friend, as with you. I am going nowhere in particular. I am merely journeying. I am wandering."

Govinda said: "You say you are wandering and I believe you. But forgive me, O Siddhartha, you do not look like a wanderer. You are wearing a rich man's garment, you are wearing an aristocrat's shoes, and your hair, with its fragrance of scented water, is not the hair of a wanderer, not the hair of a samana."

"Yes, my dear friend, you have observed well; your sharp eyes see everything. But I did not say I was a samana. I said I was wandering. And it is true: I am wandering."

"You are wandering," Govinda said. "But not many people go wandering in such a garment, in such shoes, with such well-groomed hair. I, who have been wandering for many years now, have never run across a wanderer of that sort."

"I believe you, my Govinda. But now, today, you have run across just such a wanderer, in such shoes, in such a garment. Remember, my dear friend: the world of created forms is transitory; transitory, extremely transitory, are our garments, and the way we do our hair, and our hair and body themselves. I am wearing a rich man's clothes, you have seen that rightly. I am wearing them because I have been a rich

sie, denn ich bin ein Reicher gewesen, und trage das Haar wie die
Weltleute und Lüstlinge, denn einer von ihnen bin ich gewesen.«

»Und jetzt, Siddhartha, was bist du jetzt?«

»Ich weiß es nicht, ich weiß es so wenig wie du. Ich bin unterwegs.
Ich war ein Reicher, und bin es nicht mehr; und was ich morgen sein
werde, weiß ich nicht.«

»Du hast deinen Reichtum verloren?«

»Ich habe ihn verloren, oder er mich. Er ist mir abhanden gekommen.
Schnell dreht sich das Rad der Gestaltungen, Govinda. Wo ist der
Brahmane Siddhartha? Wo ist der Samana Siddhartha? Wo ist der Reiche
Siddhartha? Schnell wechselt das Vergängliche, Govinda, du weißt es.«

Govinda blickte den Freund seiner Jugend lange an, Zweifel im
Auge. Darauf grüßte er ihn, wie man Vornehme grüßt, und ging
seines Weges.

Mit lächelndem Gesicht schaute Siddhartha ihm nach, er liebte ihn
noch immer, diesen Treuen, diesen Ängstlichen. Und wie hätte er, in
diesem Augenblick, in dieser herrlichen Stunde nach seinem wun-
derbaren Schlafe, durchdrungen von Om, irgend jemand und irgend
etwas nicht lieben sollen! Eben darin bestand die Verzauberung,
welche im Schlafe und durch das Om in ihm geschehen war, daß er
alles liebte, daß er voll froher Liebe war zu allem, was er sah. Und
eben daran, so schien es ihm jetzt, war er vorher so sehr krank gewesen, daß er nichts und niemand hatte lieben können.

Mit lächelndem Gesichte schaute Siddhartha dem hinweggehenden
Mönche nach. Der Schlaf hatte ihn sehr gestärkt, sehr aber quälte ihn
der Hunger, denn er hatte nun zwei Tage nichts gegessen, und lange
war die Zeit vorüber, da er hart gegen den Hunger gewesen war. Mit
Kummer, und doch auch mit Lachen, gedachte er jener Zeit. Damals,
so erinnerte er sich, hatte er sich vor Kamala dreier Dinge gerühmt,
hatte drei edle und unüberwindliche Künste gekonnt: Fasten – Warten
– Denken. Dies war sein Besitz gewesen, seine Macht und Kraft, sein
fester Stab, in den fleißigen, mühseligen Jahren seiner Jugend hatte er
diese drei Künste gelernt, nichts anderes. Und nun hatten sie ihn verlassen, keine von ihnen war mehr sein, nicht Fasten, nicht Warten,
nicht Denken. Um das Elendeste hatte er sie hingegeben, um das
Vergänglichste, um Sinnenlust, um Wohlleben, um Reichtum! Seltsam
war es ihm in der Tat ergangen. Und jetzt, so schien es, jetzt war er
wirklich ein Kindermensch geworden.

Siddhartha dachte über seine Lage nach. Schwer fiel ihm das
Denken, er hatte im Grunde keine Lust dazu, doch zwang er sich.

Nun, dachte er, da alle diese vergänglichsten Dinge mir wieder ent-

man, and my hair is dressed like that of worldlings and voluptuaries because I have been one."

"And now, Siddhartha, what are you now?"

"I do not know, I know no more about it than you do. I am journeying. I was a rich man and I no longer am; and what I shall be tomorrow I do not know."

"You have lost your wealth?"

"I have lost it, or it has lost me. It got away from me. The wheel of created forms turns swiftly, Govinda. Where is Siddhartha the Brahman? Where is Siddhartha the samana? Where is Siddhartha the rich man? Transitory things change swiftly, Govinda, as you know."

Govinda took a long look at the friend of his youth, with doubt in his eyes. Then he took leave of him as one takes leave of aristocrats, and went his way.

With a smile on his face Siddhartha watched him go; he still loved that loyal, anxious man. And how could he fail to love any person or any thing at this moment, at this splendid hour following his miraculous sleep, when he was permeated with *om*! This was the very nature of the enchantment that had befallen him through the *om* while sleeping: that he loved everything, that he was filled with happy love for everything he saw. And it now appeared to him that it had been his inability to love anything or anyone that had previously made him so ill.

With a smile on his face, Siddhartha watched the departing monk. His sleep had greatly strengthened him, but he had severe hunger pangs because he had not eaten for two days now, and that time was long past when he had been fortified against hunger. He remembered that time with sorrow, yet with a laugh, too. Back then, he recalled, he had boasted to Kamala of three things; he had mastered three noble, invincible arts: fasting, waiting, thinking. Those had been his possessions, his power and strength, his firm rod; in the diligent, laborious years of his youth he had learned those three arts and nothing else. And now they had deserted him; not one of them was his any longer, neither fasting, nor waiting, nor thinking. He had given them up for the sake of the most wretched things, the most transitory things, for sensual pleasure, for luxury, for wealth! His experience had really been a strange one. And now, it seemed, now he had truly become a child-person.

Siddhartha reflected on his situation. It was hard for him to think; he really had no inclination to do so, but he forced himself.

"Now," he thought, "now that all these most transitory things have

glitten sind, nun stehe ich wieder unter der Sonne, wie ich einst als
kleines Kind gestanden bin, nichts ist mein, nichts kann ich, nichts
vermag ich, nichts habe ich gelernt. Wie ist dies wunderlich! Jetzt, wo
ich nicht mehr jung bin, wo meine Haare schon halb grau sind, wo die
Kräfte nachlassen, jetzt fange ich wieder von vorn und beim Kinde an!
Wieder mußte er lächeln. Ja, seltsam war sein Geschick! Es ging abwärts mit ihm, und nun stand er wieder leer und nackt und dumm in
der Welt. Aber Kummer darüber konnte er nicht empfinden, nein, er
fühlte sogar großen Anreiz zum Lachen, zum Lachen über sich, zum
Lachen über diese seltsame törichte Welt.

»Abwärts geht es mit dir!« sagte er zu sich selber und lachte dazu,
und wie er es sagte, fiel sein Blick auf den Fluß, und auch den Fluß
sah er abwärts gehen, immer abwärts wandern, und dabei singen und
fröhlich sein. Das gefiel ihm wohl, freundlich lächelte er dem Flusse
zu. War dies nicht der Fluß, in welchem er sich hatte ertränken
wollen, einst, vor hundert Jahren, oder hatte er das geträumt?

Wunderlich in der Tat war mein Leben, so dachte er, wunderliche
Umwege hat es genommen. Als Knabe habe ich nur mit Göttern und
Opfern zu tun gehabt. Als Jüngling habe ich nur mit Askese, mit Denken
und Versenkung zu tun gehabt, war auf der Suche nach Brahman,
verehrte das Ewige im Atman. Als junger Mann aber zog ich den Büßern
nach, lebte im Walde, litt Hitze und Frost, lernte hungern, lehrte meinen
Leib absterben. Wunderbar kam mir alsdann in der Lehre des großen
Buddha Erkenntnis entgegen, ich fühlte Wissen um die Einheit der Welt
in mir kreisen wie mein eigenes Blut. Aber auch von Buddha und von
dem großen Wissen mußte ich wieder fort. Ich ging und lernte bei
Kamala die Liebeslust, lernte bei Kamaswami den Handel, häufte Geld,
vertat Geld, lernte meinen Magen lieben, lernte meinen Sinnen schmei-
cheln. Viele Jahre mußte ich damit hinbringen, den Geist zu verlieren,
das Denken wieder zu verlernen, die Einheit zu vergessen. Ist es nicht so,
als sei ich langsam und auf großen Umwegen aus einem Mann ein Kind
geworden, aus einem Denker ein Kindermensch? Und doch ist dieser
Weg sehr gut gewesen, und doch ist der Vogel in meiner Brust nicht
gestorben. Aber welch ein Weg war das! Ich habe durch so viel
Dummheit, durch so viel Laster, durch so viel Irrtum, durch so viel Ekel
und Enttäuschung und Jammer hindurchgehen müssen, bloß um wieder
ein Kind zu werden und neu anfangen zu können. Aber es war richtig so,
mein Herz sagt ja dazu, meine Augen lachen dazu. Ich habe Verzweiflung
erleben müssen, ich habe hinabsinken müssen bis zum törichtesten aller
Gedanken, zum Gedanken des Selbstmordes, um Gnade erleben zu können, um wieder Om zu vernehmen, um wieder richtig schlafen und

slipped away from me again, I am standing once more in the sunshine, as I once stood as a little child; nothing belongs to me; there is nothing I know how to do, nothing I am able to do, nothing that I have learned. How peculiar it is! Now, when I am no longer young, when my hair is already half gray, when my strength is giving out, now I am starting from the beginning again, from childhood!" Again he had to smile. Yes, his destiny was strange! Things were going downhill for him, and now once again he stood in the world empty, naked, and stupid. But he was unable to feel sorrow over it; no, he even felt a great urge to laugh, to laugh at himself, to laugh at this strange, foolish world.

"Things are going downhill for me!" he said to himself, laughing the while; and, as he said this, his glance fell on the river, and he saw the river going downward, too, moving constantly downstream, but singing merrily as it went. He was greatly pleased with that, and smiled at the river in a friendly way. Was this not the river in which he had wanted to drown, long ago, a hundred years ago, or had he just dreamed that?

"My life was truly peculiar," he thought; "it followed strange, roundabout paths. As a boy I was only occupied with gods and sacrifices. As a youth I was only occupied with ascetic practices, with thinking and concentrating; I was questing after *Brahman*, revering the eternal in the *Atman*. But as a young man I followed the penitents, lived in the forest, suffered from heat and cold, learned to fast, taught my body to go dead. Then, in the teachings of the great Buddha, realization came to me miraculously, I felt knowledge of the unity of the world circulating inside me like my own blood. But I had to depart even from the Buddha and the great knowledge. I went and learned the pleasures of love from Kamala, I learned business from Kamaswami, I accumulated money, I squandered money, I learned to love my belly, I learned to flatter my senses. I had to spend many years losing my intellectual powers, unlearning my ability to think, forgetting the principle of oneness. Is it not as if, slowly and wandering far from the direct path, I have changed from a man to a child, from a thinker to a child-person? And yet this journey has been very good, and yet the bird in my heart has not died. But what a journey it was! I have had to pass through so much stupidity, through so much vice, through so much error, through so much disgust and disappointment and misery, merely to become a child again and to be able to make a new start. But it all happened for the best; my heart tells me so, my eyes agree laughingly. I had to experience despair, I had to descend to the most foolish thought of all, the thought of suicide, in order to experience grace, in order to hear *om* again, to be able to

richtig erwachen zu können. Ich habe ein Tor werden müssen, um Atman
wieder in mir zu finden. Ich habe sündigen müssen, um wieder leben zu
können. Wohin noch mag mein Weg mich führen? Närrisch ist er, dieser
Weg, er geht in Schleifen, er geht vielleicht im Kreise. Mag er gehen, wie
er will, ich will ihn gehen.

Wunderbar fühlte er in seiner Brust die Freude wallen.

Woher denn, fragte er sein Herz, woher hast du diese Fröhlichkeit?
Kommt sie wohl aus diesem langen, guten Schlafe her, der mir so sehr
wohlgetan hat? Oder von dem Worte Om, das ich aussprach? Oder
davon, daß ich entronnen bin, daß meine Flucht vollzogen ist, daß ich
endlich wieder frei bin und wie ein Kind unter dem Himmel stehe?
O wie gut ist dies Geflohensein, dies Freigewordensein! Wie rein und
schön ist hier die Luft, wie gut zu atmen! Dort, von wo ich entlief,
dort roch alles nach Salbe, nach Gewürzen, nach Wein, nach
Überfluß, nach Trägheit. Wie haßte ich diese Welt der Reichen, der
Schlemmer, der Spieler! Wie habe ich mich selbst gehaßt, daß ich so
lang in dieser schrecklichen Welt geblieben bin! Wie habe ich mich
gehaßt, habe mich beraubt, vergiftet, gepeinigt, habe mich alt und
böse gemacht! Nein, nie mehr werde ich, wie ich es einst so gerne tat,
mir einbilden, daß Siddhartha weise sei! Dies aber habe ich gut
gemacht, dies gefällt mir, dies muß ich loben, daß es nun ein Ende hat
mit jenem Haß gegen mich selber, mit jenem törichten und öden
Leben! Ich lobe dich, Siddhartha, nach so viel Jahren der Torheit hast
du wieder einmal einen Einfall gehabt, hast etwas getan, hast den
Vogel in deiner Brust singen hören und bist ihm gefolgt!

So lobte er sich, hatte Freude an sich, hörte neugierig seinem
Magen zu, der vor Hunger knurrte. Ein Stück Leid, ein Stück Elend
hatte er nun, so fühlte er, in diesen letzten Zeiten und Tagen ganz und
gar durchgekostet und ausgespien, bis zur Verzweiflung und bis zum
Tode ausgefressen. So war es gut. Lange noch hätte er bei
Kamaswami bleiben können, Geld erwerben, Geld vergeuden, seinen
Bauch mästen und seine Seele verdursten lassen, lange noch hätte er
in dieser sanften, wohlgepolsterten Hölle wohnen können, wäre dies
nicht gekommen: der Augenblick der vollkommenen Trostlosigkeit
und Verzweiflung, jener äußerste Augenblick, da er über dem strömenden Wasser hing und bereit war, sich zu vernichten. Daß er diese
Verzweiflung, diesen tiefsten Ekel gefühlt hatte, und daß er ihm nicht
erlegen war, daß der Vogel, die frohe Quelle und Stimme in ihm doch
noch lebendig war, darüber fühlte er diese Freude, darüber lachte er,
darüber strahlte sein Gesicht unter den ergrauten Haaren.

»Es ist gut«, dachte er, »alles selber zu kosten, was man zu wissen

sleep and awaken properly again. I had to become a fool in order to find *Atman* within myself again. I had to sin so that I could live again. Where else may my path lead me? This path is foolish, it makes wide loops, maybe it is going in a circle. Let it go wherever it wishes, I shall follow it."

He felt joy surging miraculously in his heart.

"Where," he asked his heart, "where is your jollity coming from? Is it coming from that long, good sleep that did me so much good? Or from the word *om* that I uttered? Or because I have escaped, because my getaway is accomplished, because I am finally free again and standing beneath the sky like a child? Oh, how good this escape and this liberation are! How fresh and beautiful the air is here, so good to breathe! In the place I escaped from, everything smelled of ointments, spices, wine, overabundance, indolence. How I hated that world of rich people, gourmands, gamblers! How I hated myself for remaining so long in that frightful world! How I hated myself, robbed myself, poisoned myself, tortured myself, made myself old and malevolent! No, never again will I take it into my head, as it once pleased me to do, that Siddhartha is wise! But in this I have acted well; I am glad, and I give praise for it, that that hatred for myself, that foolish, dismal life, is over and done with! I applaud you, Siddhartha; after so many years of folly, you have once again had an inspiration, you have done something, you have heard the bird in your heart singing, and you have followed it!"

Thus he applauded himself, took pleasure in himself, listened inquisitively to his stomach, which was growling with hunger. He felt that, in those last times and days, he had now thoroughly tasted and spat out a piece of sorrow, a piece of misery; he had gobbled it up to the point of despair and death. And it was good so. He might still have remained with Kamaswami for a long time, earning money, wasting money, fattening his belly and letting his soul die of thirst; he might have dwelt for a long time in that soft, well-upholstered hell, had *that* not arrived: the moment of absolute disconsolateness and despair, that extreme moment when he was suspended above the rushing waters, ready to annihilate himself. Because he had felt that despair, that most profound loathing, and had not succumbed to it; because the bird, the happy wellspring, and the voice within him were still alive after all: that is why he felt this joy, why he was laughing, why his face was beaming beneath his grayed hair.

"It is good," he thought, "to taste for yourself everything you need

nötig hat. Daß Weltlust und Reichtum nicht vom Guten sind, habe ich schon als Kind gelernt. Gewußt habe ich es lange, erlebt habe ich es erst jetzt. Und nun weiß ich es, weiß es nicht nur mit dem Gedächtnis, sondern mit meinen Augen, mit meinem Herzen, mit meinem Magen. Wohl mir, daß ich es weiß!«

Lange sann er nach über seine Verwandlung, lauschte dem Vogel, wie er vor Freude sang. War nicht dieser Vogel in ihm gestorben, hatte er nicht seinen Tod gefühlt? Nein, etwas anderes in ihm war gestorben, etwas, das schon lange sich nach Sterben gesehnt hatte. War es nicht das, was er einst in seinen glühenden Büßerjahren hatte abtöten wollen? War es nicht sein Ich, sein kleines, banges und stolzes Ich, mit dem er so viele Jahre gekämpft hatte, das ihn immer wieder besiegt hatte, das nach jeder Abtötung wieder da war, Freude verbot, Furcht empfand? War es nicht dies, was heute endlich seinen Tod gefunden hatte, hier im Walde an diesem lieblichen Flusse? War es nicht dieses Todes wegen, daß er jetzt wie ein Kind war, so voll Vertrauen, so ohne Furcht, so voll Freude?

Nun auch ahnte Siddhartha, warum er als Brahmane, als Büßer vergeblich mit diesem Ich gekämpft hatte. Zu viel Wissen hatte ihn gehindert, zu viel heilige Verse, zu viel Opferregeln, zu viel Kasteiung, zu viel Tun und Streben! Voll Hochmut war er gewesen, immer der Klügste, immer der Eifrigste, immer allen um einen Schritt voran, immer der Wissende und Geistige, immer der Priester oder Weise. In dies Priestertum, in diesen Hochmut, in diese Geistigkeit hinein hatte sein Ich sich verkrochen, dort saß es fest und wuchs, während er es mit Fasten und Buße zu töten meinte. Nun sah er es, und sah, daß die heimliche Stimme recht gehabt hatte, daß kein Lehrer ihn je hätte erlösen können. Darum hatte er in die Welt gehen müssen, sich an Lust und Macht, an Weib und Geld verlieren müssen, hatte ein Händler, ein Würfelspieler, Trinker und Habgieriger werden müssen, bis der Priester und Samana in ihm tot war. Darum hatte er weiter diese häßlichen Jahre ertragen müssen, den Ekel ertragen, die Leere, die Sinnlosigkeit eines öden und verlorenen Lebens, bis zum Ende, bis zur bittern Verzweiflung, bis auch der Lüstling Siddhartha, der Habgierige Siddhartha sterben konnte. Er war gestorben, ein neuer Siddhartha war aus dem Schlaf erwacht. Auch er würde alt werden, auch er würde einst sterben müssen, vergänglich war Siddhartha, vergänglich war jede Gestaltung. Heute aber war er jung, war ein Kind, der neue Siddhartha, und war voll Freude.

Diese Gedanken dachte er, lauschte lächelnd auf seinen Magen, hörte dankbar einer summenden Biene zu. Heiter blickte er in den

to know. That worldly pleasures and wealth are not good things, I learned even as a child. I knew it for a long time, but only now have I experienced it. And now I know it, I know it not only because I remember hearing it, but with my eyes, with my heart, with my stomach. And it is good for me to know it!"

He reflected for some time upon his transformation; he listened to the bird that was singing for joy. Had not that bird within him died, had he not felt its death? No, something else inside him had died, something that had long been yearning to die. Was it not the thing that he had once wanted to mortify during his ardent years as a penitent? Was it not his self, his petty, timid, proud self, with which he had battled for so many years, which had conquered him time and again, which had reemerged after every mortification, forbidding him to be happy, experiencing fear? Was it not this that had finally met its death that day, there in the forest beside that lovely river? Was it not because of that death that he was now like a child, so full of trust, so free from fear, so full of joy?

Now Siddhartha also suspected why, as a Brahman, as a penitent, he had battled in vain with that self. He had been hindered by too much knowledge, too many sacred verses, too many sacrificial rules, too much castigation, too much activity and ambition! He had been full of pride, always the cleverest, always the most eager, always one step ahead of the others, always the scholar and intellectual, always the priest or the sage. His self had wormed its way into that priesthood, into that pridefulness, into that intellectuality; there it took a firm hold and grew, while he thought he was killing it by fasting and doing penance. Now he saw it, and saw that the secret voice had been right, that no teacher would ever have been able to liberate him. For that, he had had to go into the world, he had had to lose himself to pleasure and power, to women and money; he had had to become a merchant, a dice player, a drinker, and an avaricious man, until the priest and samana within him were dead. For that, he had had to go on enduring those hateful years, enduring the disgust, the emptiness, the meaninglessness of a barren, lost life, to the very end, to the point of bitter despair, until Siddhartha the voluptuary and Siddhartha the avaricious man could also die. He *had* died; a new Siddhartha had awakened from sleep. He, too, would grow old; he, too, would have to die sometime; Siddhartha was mortal, every created thing was mortal. But today he was young, he was a child, this new Siddhartha, and he was full of joy.

These were the thoughts he was thinking as he listened smilingly to his stomach, and gratefully paid attention to the buzzing of a bee.

strömenden Fluß, nie hatte ihm ein Wasser so wohl gefallen wie
dieses, nie hatte er Stimme und Gleichnis des ziehenden Wassers so
stark und schön vernommen. Ihm schien, es habe der Fluß ihm etwas
Besonderes zu sagen, etwas, das er noch nicht wisse, das noch auf ihn
warte. In diesem Fluß hatte sich Siddhartha ertränken wollen, in ihm
war der alte, müde, verzweifelte Siddhartha heute ertrunken. Der
neue Siddhartha aber fühlte eine tiefe Liebe zu diesem strömenden
Wasser und beschloß bei sich, es nicht so bald wieder zu verlassen.

DER FÄHRMANN

An diesem Fluß will ich bleiben, dachte Siddhartha, es ist derselbe,
über den ich einstmals auf dem Wege zu den Kindermenschen gekommen bin, ein freundlicher Fährmann hat mich damals geführt, zu ihm
will ich gehen, von seiner Hütte aus führte mich einst mein Weg in ein
neues Leben, das nun alt geworden und tot ist – möge auch mein jet-
ziger Weg, mein jetziges neues Leben dort seinen Ausgang nehmen!
    Zärtlich blickte er in das strömende Wasser, in das durchsichtige
Grün, in die kristallenen Linien seiner geheimnisreichen Zeichnung.
Lichte Perlen sah er aus der Tiefe steigen, stille Luftblasen auf dem
Spiegel schwimmen, Himmelsbläue darin abgebildet. Mit tausend
Augen blickte der Fluß ihn an, mit grünen, mit weißen, mit kristall-
nen, mit himmelblauen. Wie liebte er dies Wasser, wie entzückte es
ihn, wie war er ihm dankbar! Im Herzen hörte er die Stimme
sprechen, die neu erwachte, und sie sagte ihm: Liebe dies Wasser!
Bleibe bei ihm! Lerne von ihm! O ja, er wollte von ihm lernen, er
wollte ihm zuhören. Wer dies Wasser und seine Geheimnisse verstünde, so schien ihm, der würde auch viel anderes verstehen, viele
Geheimnisse, alle Geheimnisse.
    Von den Geheimnissen des Flusses aber sah er heute nur eines, das
ergriff seine Seele. Er sah: dies Wasser lief und lief, immerzu lief es,
und war doch immer da, war immer und allezeit dasselbe und doch
jeden Augenblick neu! Oh, wer dies faßte, dies verstünde! Er verstand
und faßte es nicht, fühlte nur Ahnung sich regen, ferne Erinnerung,
göttliche Stimmen.
    Siddhartha erhob sich, unerträglich wurde das Treiben des
Hungers in seinem Leibe. Hingenommen wanderte er weiter, den
Uferpfad hinan, dem Strom entgegen, lauschte auf die Strömung,
lauschte auf den knurrenden Hunger in seinem Leibe.
    Als er die Fähre erreichte, lag eben das Boot bereit, und derselbe

Serenely he gazed into the flowing river; never had any water pleased him as much as this did, never had he perceived the voice and the allegory of the moving current so strongly and beautifully. He felt as if the river had something special to tell him, something he did not yet know but was still awaiting him. In this river Siddhartha had wanted to drown; in it the old, tired, despairing Siddhartha *had* drowned that day. But the new Siddhartha felt a profound love for that flowing water, and resolved in his mind not to leave it behind for quite some time.

THE FERRYMAN

"I shall remain by this river," thought Siddhartha. "It is the same one that I once crossed on my way to the child-people; at that time a friendly ferryman took me across. I shall go to him; from his hut my path once led me to a new life, which has now grown old and has died—let my present path, too, my present new life, take its start there!"

He looked tenderly into the flowing water, into the transparent green, into the crystalline lines of its mysterious design. He saw bright pearls rising from the depths, quiet air bubbles floating on the surface, with the blue of the sky depicted in them. With a thousand eyes the river looked at him, with green ones, with white ones, with crystal ones, with sky-blue ones. How he loved that water, how it delighted him, how grateful he was to it! In his heart he heard the voice speak, the newly awakened one, and it said to him: "Love this water! Remain by it! Learn from it!" Oh, yes, he wanted to learn from it, he wanted to listen to it. Whoever understood that water and its secrets, he felt, would also understand much more, many secrets, all secrets.

But today, of all the secrets of the river, he saw just one, which gripped his soul. He saw: this water flowed and flowed, it kept on flowing, and yet it was always there; it was always and at all times the same and yet new every moment! Oh, if he could only grasp that, understand that! He did not understand or grasp it; he merely felt the stirrings of a premonition, a distant recollection, divine voices.

Siddhartha rose; the pangs of hunger in his body became unbearable. In its toils, he walked onward, up the path along the riverbank, upstream, listening to the current, listening to the growling hunger in his body.

When he reached the ferry, the boat was just in readiness, and the

Fährmann, welcher einst den jungen Samana über den Fluß gesetzt
hatte, stand im Boot, Siddhartha erkannte ihn wieder, auch er war
stark gealtert.

»Willst du mich übersetzen?« fragte er.

Der Fährmann, erstaunt, einen so vornehmen Mann allein und zu
Fuße wandern zu sehen, nahm ihn ins Boot und stieß ab.

»Ein schönes Leben hast du dir erwählt«, sprach der Gast. »Schön muß
es sein, jeden Tag an diesem Wasser zu leben und auf ihm zu fahren.«

Lächelnd wiegte sich der Ruderer: »Es ist schön, Herr, es ist, wie
du sagst. Aber ist nicht jedes Leben, ist nicht jede Arbeit schön?«

»Es mag wohl sein. Dich aber beneide ich um die deine.«

»Ach, du möchtest bald die Lust an ihr verlieren. Das ist nichts für
Leute in feinen Kleidern.«

Siddhartha lachte. »Schon einmal bin ich heute um meiner Kleider
willen betrachtet worden, mit Mißtrauen betrachtet. Willst du nicht,
Fährmann, diese Kleider, die mir lästig sind, von mir annehmen? Denn
du mußt wissen, ich habe kein Geld, dir einen Fährlohn zu zahlen.«

»Der Herr scherzt«, lachte der Fährmann.

»Ich scherze nicht, Freund. Sieh, schon einmal hast du mich in
deinem Boot über dies Wasser gefahren, um Gotteslohn. So tue es
auch heute, und nimm meine Kleider dafür an.«

»Und will der Herr ohne Kleider weiterreisen?«

»Ach, am liebsten wollte ich gar nicht weiterreisen. Am liebsten
wäre es mir, Fährmann, wenn du mir eine alte Schürze gäbest und be-
hieltest mich als deinen Gehilfen bei dir, vielmehr als deinen
Lehrling, denn erst muß ich lernen, mit dem Boot umzugehen.«

Lange blickte der Fährmann den Fremden an, suchend.

»Jetzt erkenne ich dich«, sagte er endlich. »Einst hast du in meiner
Hütte geschlafen, lange ist es her, wohl mehr als zwanzig Jahre mag
das her sein, und bist von mir über den Fluß gebracht worden, und
wir nahmen Abschied voneinander wie gute Freunde. Warst du nicht
ein Samana? Deines Namens kann ich mich nicht mehr entsinnen.«

»Ich heiße Siddhartha, und ich war ein Samana, als du mich zuletzt
gesehen hast.«

»So sei willkommen, Siddhartha. Ich heiße Vasudeva. Du wirst, so
hoffe ich, auch heute mein Gast sein und in meiner Hütte schlafen,
und mir erzählen, woher du kommst, und warum deine schönen
Kleider dir so lästig sind.«

Sie waren in die Mitte des Flusses gelangt, und Vasudeva legte sich
stärker ins Ruder, um gegen die Strömung anzukommen. Ruhig arbeitete er, den Blick auf der Bootspitze, mit kräftigen Armen. Siddhartha

same ferryman who had once taken the young samana across the river was standing in the boat. Siddhartha recognized him; he, too, had greatly aged.

"Will you take me across?" he asked.

The ferryman, astonished to see such an elegant man alone and on foot, took him into the boat and shoved off.

"You have chosen a fine life," the passenger said. "It must be beautiful to live by this water every day and to travel on it."

The oarsman rocked to and fro, smiling: "It is beautiful, sir; it is just as you say. But is not every life, is not every occupation, beautiful?"

"That may be. But I envy you for yours."

"Oh, you would soon lose your pleasure in it. It is not for people in fine clothes."

Siddhartha laughed. "Earlier today I was also judged by my clothes, and was looked on with distrust. Ferryman, will you accept as a gift from me these clothes, which are a burden to me? For you ought to know, I have no money to pay you for my passage."

"You are joking, sir," the ferryman laughed.

"I am not joking, my friend. Look, once before you took me across this river in your boat, with only God repaying you. Then, do it again today, and accept my clothes in exchange."

"And do you intend to travel on without clothes, sir?"

"Oh, I would like best of all not to travel on. I would like it best of all, ferryman, if you were to give me an old apron and keep me on as your assistant—as your apprentice, rather, for I must first learn how to handle the boat."

For some time the ferryman looked at the stranger, examining him.

"Now I recognize you," he finally said. "You once slept in my hut, long ago, it must be over twenty years ago, and I took you across the river, and we said good-bye like good friends. Were you not a samana? I can no longer remember your name."

"My name is Siddhartha, and I *was* a samana when you last saw me."

"Then, welcome, Siddhartha. My name is Vasudeva. I hope you will be my guest today, too, and sleep in my hut, and tell me where you are coming from, and why your beautiful clothes are such a burden to you."

They had reached the middle of the river, and Vasudeva began to row more vigorously, to cope with the current. He worked calmly, his eyes on the bow, with powerful arms. Siddhartha sat and watched

saß und sah ihm zu, und erinnerte sich, wie schon einstmals, an jenem letzten Tage seiner Samana-Zeit, Liebe zu diesem Manne sich in seinem Herzen geregt hatte. Dankbar nahm er Vasudevas Einladung an. Als sie am Ufer anlegten, half er ihm das Boot an den Pflöcken festbinden, darauf bat ihn der Fährmann, in die Hütte zu treten, bot ihm Brot und Wasser, und Siddhartha aß mit Lust, und aß mit Lust auch von den Mangofrüchten, die ihm Vasudeva anbot.

Danach setzten sie sich, es ging gegen Sonnenuntergang, auf einen Baumstamm am Ufer, und Siddhartha erzählte dem Fährmann seine Herkunft und sein Leben, wie er es heute, in jener Stunde der Verzweiflung, vor seinen Augen gesehen hatte. Bis tief in die Nacht währte sein Erzählen.

Vasudeva hörte mit großer Aufmerksamkeit zu. Alles nahm er lauschend in sich auf, Herkunft und Kindheit, all das Lernen, all das Suchen, alle Freude, alle Not. Dies war unter des Fährmanns Tugenden eine der größten: er verstand wie wenige das Zuhören. Ohne daß er ein Wort gesprochen hätte, empfand der Sprechende, wie Vasudeva seine Worte in sich einließ, still, offen, wartend, wie er keines verlor, keines mit Ungeduld erwartete, nicht Lob noch Tadel daneben stellte, nur zuhörte. Siddhartha empfand, welches Glück es ist, einem solchen Zuhörer sich zu bekennen, in sein Herz das eigene Leben zu versenken, das eigene Suchen, das eigene Leiden.

Gegen das Ende von Siddharthas Erzählung aber, als er von dem Baum am Flusse sprach und von seinem tiefen Fall, vom heiligen Om, und wie er nach seinem Schlummer eine solche Liebe zu dem Flusse gefühlt hatte, da lauschte der Fährmann mit verdoppelter Aufmerksamkeit, ganz und völlig hingegeben, mit geschlossnem Auge.

Als aber Siddhartha schwieg und eine lange Stille gewesen war, da sagte Vasudeva: »Es ist so, wie ich dachte. Der Fluß hat zu dir gesprochen. Auch dir ist er Freund, auch zu dir spricht er. Das ist gut, das ist sehr gut. Bleibe bei mir, Siddhartha, mein Freund. Ich hatte einst eine Frau, ihr Lager war neben dem meinen, doch ist sie schon lange gestorben, lange habe ich allein gelebt. Lebe nun du mit mir, es ist Raum und Essen für beide vorhanden.«

»Ich danke dir«, sagte Siddhartha, »ich danke dir und nehme an. Und auch dafür danke ich dir, Vasudeva, daß du mir so gut zugehört hast! Selten sind die Menschen, welche das Zuhören verstehen, und keinen traf ich, der es verstand wie du. Auch hierin werde ich von dir lernen.«

»Du wirst es lernen«, sprach Vasudeva, »aber nicht von mir. Das Zuhören hat mich der Fluß gelehrt, von ihm wirst auch du es lernen. Er weiß alles, der Fluß, alles kann man von ihm lernen. Sieh, auch das

him, recalling that, even in the past, on that last day of his life as a samana, love for that man had stirred in his heart. He gratefully accepted Vasudeva's invitation. When they reached the bank, he helped him tie the boat fast to its posts; then the ferryman asked him to enter the hut, and offered him bread and water; Siddhartha ate with pleasure, and also ate with pleasure the mangos that Vasudeva offered him.

Afterward, they sat down on a tree trunk by the riverbank—it was getting on toward sunset—and Siddhartha told the ferryman about his family and his life, as he had seen it before his eyes that very day, in that hour of despair. His story lasted deep into the night.

Vasudeva listened most attentively. As he listened, he absorbed it all, family and childhood, all the learning, all the seeking, all the joy, all the distress. Among the ferryman's virtues this was one of the greatest: he knew how to listen as only few people do. Although Vasudeva said not a word, the speaker felt that he was taking in his words, quietly, openly, expectantly; that he was not losing one of them, was not awaiting them impatiently, was not assigning praise or blame to them, but was merely listening. Siddhartha realized what a great good fortune it is to confess oneself to a listener like that, to confide one's own life to his heart, one's own questing, one's own suffering.

But toward the end of Siddhartha's narrative, when he spoke about the tree by the river and his deep plunge, about the sacred *om*, and how, after his slumber, he had felt such a great love for the river, the ferryman listened with redoubled attentiveness, with total and complete devotion, his eyes closed.

But when Siddhartha ended, and a long silence had ensued, Vasudeva said: "It is just as I thought. The river spoke to you. It is a friend to you, too; it speaks to you, too. That is good, that is very good. Stay with me, Siddhartha, my friend. I once had a wife; her bed was next to mine, but she died long ago, and I have long lived alone. Now live with me, there is room and food for both."

"Thank you," said Siddhartha, "I thank you and I accept. And I also thank you, Vasudeva, for listening to me so well! It is a rare person who knows how to listen, and I have never met anyone who could do it as well as you. That is another area in which I shall learn from you."

"You will learn it," said Vasudeva, "but not from me. The river taught me how to listen, and you will learn that from it, too. It knows everything, the river, a person can learn anything from it. Look, you

hast du schon vom Wasser gelernt, daß es gut ist, nach unten zu streben, zu sinken, die Tiefe zu suchen. Der reiche und vornehme Siddhartha wird ein Ruderknecht, der gelehrte Brahmane Siddhartha wird ein Fährmann: auch dies ist dir vom Fluß gesagt worden. Du wirst auch das andere von ihm lernen.«

Sprach Siddhartha, nach einer langen Pause: »Welches andere, Vasudeva?«

Vasudeva erhob sich. »Spät ist es geworden«, sagte er, »laß uns schlafen gehen. Ich kann dir das ›andere‹ nicht sagen, o Freund. Du wirst es lernen, vielleicht auch weißt du es schon. Sieh, ich bin kein Gelehrter, ich verstehe nicht zu sprechen, ich verstehe auch nicht zu denken. Ich verstehe nur zuzuhören und fromm zu sein, sonst habe ich nichts gelernt. Könnte ich es sagen und lehren, so wäre ich vielleicht ein Weiser, so aber bin ich nur ein Fährmann, und meine Aufgabe ist es, Menschen über diesen Fluß zu setzen. Viele habe ich übergesetzt, Tausende, und ihnen allen ist mein Fluß nichts anderes gewesen als ein Hindernis auf ihren Reisen. Sie reisten nach Geld und Geschäften, und zu Hochzeiten, und zu Wallfahrten, und der Fluß war ihnen im Wege, und der Fährmann war dazu da, sie schnell über das Hindernis hinwegzubringen. Einige unter den Tausenden aber, einige wenige, vier oder fünf, denen hat der Fluß aufgehört, ein Hindernis zu sein, sie haben seine Stimme gehört, sie haben ihm zugehört, und der Fluß ist ihnen heilig geworden, wie er es mir geworden ist. Laß uns nun zur Ruhe gehen, Siddhartha.«

Siddhartha blieb bei dem Fährmann und lernte das Boot bedienen, und wenn nichts an der Fähre zu tun war, arbeitete er mit Vasudeva im Reisfelde, sammelte Holz, pflückte die Früchte der Pisangbäume. Er lernte ein Ruder zimmern, und lernte das Boot ausbessern, und Körbe flechten, und war fröhlich über alles, was er lernte, und die Tage und Monate liefen schnell hinweg. Mehr aber, als Vasudeva ihn lehren konnte, lehrte ihn der Fluß. Von ihm lernte er unaufhörlich. Vor allem lernte er von ihm das Zuhören, das Lauschen mit stillem Herzen, mit wartender, geöffneter Seele, ohne Leidenschaft, ohne Wunsch, ohne Urteil, ohne Meinung.

Freundlich lebte er neben Vasudeva, und zuweilen tauschten sie Worte miteinander, wenige und lang bedachte Worte. Vasudeva war kein Freund der Worte, selten gelang es Siddhartha, ihn zum Sprechen zu bewegen.

have already learned this, too, from the water: that it is good to make your way downward, to move lower, to seek the depths. The wealthy aristocrat Siddhartha is becoming a hired oarsman; the learned Brahman Siddhartha is becoming a ferryman: that, too, was told you by the river. You will learn the rest from it, as well."

Siddhartha said, after a long pause: "What is the rest, Vasudeva?"

Vasudeva arose. "It has grown late," he said, "let us go to bed. I cannot tell you the 'rest,' O friend. You will learn it; perhaps you already know it. Look, I am no scholar, I do not understand how to speak, nor do I understand how to think. All I know how to do is to listen, and to be pious; more than that I have never learned. If I could say it and teach it, perhaps I would be a sage, but as it is I am only a ferryman, and my task is to take people across this river. I have taken many across, thousands, and for all of them my river has meant nothing but an obstacle on their travels. They were traveling for money and on business, or to a wedding, or on a pilgrimage, and the river was in their way, and the ferryman existed only to take them past that obstacle quickly. For some among those thousands, however—just a few, four or five—the river ceased to be an obstacle; they heard its voice, they listened to it; and the river became holy for them, as it has become for me. Let us now seek repose, Siddhartha."

Siddhartha remained with the ferryman and learned how to manipulate the boat; and when there was no business at the ferry, he worked with Vasudeva in the rice paddy, gathered wood, and picked the fruit of the *pisang* trees.[11] He learned how to fashion an oar, and learned how to repair the boat, and weave baskets; and he was happy over everything he learned, and the days and months sped rapidly by. But more than Vasudeva could teach him, the river taught him. He never stopped learning from it. Above all it taught him how to listen, to listen with a quiet heart, with an open, expectant soul, without passion, without a desire, without judging, without forming an opinion.

He lived alongside Vasudeva like a friend; and at times they exchanged words with each other, words few in number but maturely considered. Vasudeva was no friend of words; Siddhartha rarely succeeded in inducing him to speak.

---

[11] Plantain (*Musa paradisiaca*), Hesse's use of *pisang*, a Malayan word (not related to any language of India), reminds the alert reader of the true site of his so-called "Indian" sojourn.

»Hast du«, so fragte er ihn einst, »hast auch du vom Flusse jenes Geheime gelernt: daß es keine Zeit gibt?«

Vasudevas Gesicht überzog sich mit hellem Lächeln.

»Ja, Siddhartha«, sprach er. »Es ist doch dieses, was du meinst: daß der Fluß überall zugleich ist, am Ursprung und an der Mündung, am Wasserfall, an der Fähre, an der Stromschnelle, im Meer, im Gebirge, überall, zugleich, und daß es für ihn nur Gegenwart gibt, nicht den Schatten Zukunft?«

»Dies ist es«, sagte Siddhartha. »Und als ich es gelernt hatte, da sah ich mein Leben an, und es war auch ein Fluß und es war der Knabe Siddhartha vom Manne Siddhartha und vom Greis Siddhartha nur durch Schatten getrennt, nicht durch Wirkliches. Es waren auch Siddharthas frühere Geburten keine Vergangenheit, und sein Tod und seine Rückkehr zu Brahma keine Zukunft. Nichts war, nichts wird sein; alles ist, alles hat Wesen und Gegenwart.«

Siddhartha sprach mit Entzücken, tief hatte diese Erleuchtung ihn beglückt. Oh, war denn nicht alles Leiden Zeit, war nicht alles Sichquälen und Sichfürchten Zeit, war nicht alles Schwere, alles Feindliche in der Welt weg und überwunden, sobald man die Zeit überwunden hatte, sobald man die Zeit wegdenken konnte? Entzückt hatte er gesprochen. Vasudeva aber lächelte ihn strahlend an und nickte Bestätigung, schweigend nickte er, strich mit der Hand über Siddharthas Schulter, wandte sich zu seiner Arbeit zurück.

Und wieder einmal, als eben der Fluß in der Regenzeit geschwollen war und mächtig rauschte, da sagte Siddhartha: »Nicht wahr, o Freund, der Fluß hat viele Stimmen, sehr viele Stimmen? Hat er nicht die Stimme eines Königs, und eines Kriegers, und eines Stieres, und eines Nachtvogels, und einer Gebärenden, und eines Seufzenden, und noch tausend andere Stimmen?«

»Es ist so«, nickte Vasudeva, »alle Stimmen der Geschöpfe sind in seiner Stimme.«

»Und weißt du«, fuhr Siddhartha fort, »welches Wort er spricht, wenn es dir gelingt, alle seine zehntausend Stimmen zugleich zu hören?«

Glücklich lachte Vasudevas Gesicht, er neigte sich gegen Siddhartha und sprach ihm das heilige Om ins Ohr. Und eben dies war es, was auch Siddhartha gehört hatte.

Und von Mal zu Mal ward sein Lächeln dem des Fährmanns ähnlicher, ward beinahe ebenso strahlend, beinahe ebenso von Glück durchglänzt, ebenso aus tausend kleinen Falten leuchtend, ebenso kindlich, ebenso greisenhaft. Viele Reisende, wenn sie die beiden Fährmänner sahen, hielten sie für Brüder. Oft saßen sie am Abend

On one occasion, he asked him: "Have you, too, learned that secret from the river: that there is no such thing as time?"

A bright smile spread over Vasudeva's face.

"Yes, Siddhartha," he said. "Surely this is what you really mean: that the river is everywhere at once, at its source and at its mouth, at the waterfall, at the ferry, at the rapids, at the sea, in the mountains, everywhere, at the same time, and that it possesses only a present, without any shadow of a future?"

"That is it," said Siddhartha. "And when I had learned that, I looked at my life, and it, too, was a river, and Siddhartha the boy was separated from Siddhartha the man and from Siddhartha the old man merely by shadows, not by anything real. Moreover, Siddhartha's prior births did not constitute a past, and his death and his return to Brahma were not a future. There was nothing, there will be nothing; everything *is,* everything has substantiality and presence."

Siddhartha spoke with rapture; this enlightenment had given him profound happiness. Oh, was not all suffering time, then? Were not all self-torture and self-fearing time? Was not everything difficult, everything hostile in the world done away with and conquered as soon as you had conquered time, as soon as you could think away time? He had spoken in rapture. But Vasudeva beamed and smiled at him, nodding in confirmation; he nodded silently, stroked Siddhartha's shoulder, and turned back to his work.

And on another occasion, when the river ran high in the rainy season and roared mightily, Siddhartha said: "Is it not true, O friend, the river has many voices, very many voices? Does it not have the voice of a king, and of a warrior, and of a bull, and of a night bird, and of a woman in labor, and of a man sighing, and a thousand other voices, as well?"

"It is so," Vasudeva nodded; "the voices of all creatures are in its voice."

"And do you know," Siddhartha continued, "what word it speaks, when you succeed in hearing all its ten thousand voices at once?"

Vasudeva's face laughed happily; he leaned over to Siddhartha and pronounced the sacred *om* in his ear. And it was precisely that which Siddhartha had heard, also.

And from one occasion to another, his smile became more like the ferryman's; it became nearly as radiant, nearly as glowing with happiness, just as beaming from a thousand little wrinkles, just as childlike, just as similar to an old man's. Many travelers, seeing the two ferrymen, took them for brothers. Often, in the evening, they sat together

gemeinsam beim Ufer auf dem Baumstamm, schwiegen und hörten beide dem Wasser zu, welches für sie kein Wasser war, sondern die Stimme des Lebens, die Stimme des Seienden, des ewig Werdenden. Und es geschah zuweilen, daß beide beim Anhören des Flusses an dieselben Dinge dachten, an ein Gespräch von vorgestern, an einen ihrer Reisenden, dessen Gesicht und Schicksal sie beschäftigte, an den Tod, an ihre Kindheit, und daß sie beide im selben Augenblick, wenn der Fluß ihnen etwas Gutes gesagt hatte, einander anblickten, beide genau dasselbe denkend, beide beglückt über dieselbe Antwort auf dieselbe Frage.

Es ging von der Fähre und von den beiden Fährleuten etwas aus, das manche von den Reisenden spürten. Es geschah zuweilen, daß ein Reisender, nachdem er in das Gesicht eines der Fährmänner geblickt hatte, sein Leben zu erzählen begann, Leid erzählte, Böses bekannte, Trost und Rat erbat. Es geschah zuweilen, daß einer um Erlaubnis bat, einen Abend bei ihnen zu verweilen, um dem Flusse zuzuhören. Es geschah auch, daß Neugierige kamen, welchen erzählt worden war, an dieser Fähre lebten zwei Weise oder Zauberer oder Heilige. Die Neugierigen stellten viele Fragen, aber sie bekamen keine Antworten, und sie fanden weder Zauberer noch Weise, sie fanden nur zwei alte freundliche Männlein, welche stumm zu sein und etwas sonderbar und verblödet schienen. Und die Neugierigen lachten und unterhielten sich darüber, wie töricht und leichtgläubig doch das Volk solche leere Gerüchte verbreite.

Die Jahre gingen hin, und keiner zählte sie. Da kamen einst Mönche gepilgert, Anhänger des Gotama, des Buddha, welche baten, sie über den Fluß zu setzen, und von ihnen erfuhren die Fährmänner, daß sie eiligst zu ihrem großen Lehrer zurückwanderten, denn es habe sich die Nachricht verbreitet, der Erhabene sei todkrank und werde bald seinen letzten Menschentod sterben, um zur Erlösung einzugehen. Nicht lange, so kam eine neue Schar Mönche gepilgert, und wieder eine, und sowohl die Mönche wie die meisten der übrigen Reisenden und Wanderer sprachen von nichts anderem als von Gotama und seinem nahen Tode. Und wie zu einem Kriegszug oder zur Krönung eines Königs von überall und allen Seiten her die Menschen strömen und sich gleich Ameisen in Scharen sammeln, so strömten sie, wie von einem Zauber gezogen, dahin, wo der große

by the riverbank on the tree trunk, in silence, both listening to the water, which was not water to them, but the voice of life, the voice of Being, of eternal Becoming. And it occurred at times that, when hearing the river, both of them thought of the same things, of a conversation they had had two days earlier, of one of their passengers whose face and destiny occupied their minds, of death, of their childhood; and, at such times, when the river had told them something good, they would look at each other simultaneously, both thinking exactly the same thing, both made happy by the identical answer to the identical question.

Something emanated from the ferry and the two ferrymen that many of their passengers perceived. It occurred at times that, after a passenger had looked into the face of one of the ferrymen, he began to recount his life; he recounted his sorrow, confessed ill deeds, sought consolation and advice. It occurred at times that one of them asked permission to spend an evening with them, in order to listen to the river. It also occurred that curiosity seekers showed up who had been told that two sages or sorcerers or saints lived at that ferry. These inquisitive people posed many questions but received no answers, and they found neither sorcerers nor sages; they found merely two friendly little old men who seemed to be mute and somewhat peculiar and simple-minded. And the inquisitive people laughed and amused themselves over the foolish and gullible way in which the common people spread such empty rumors.

The years went by, and no one counted them. Then, one day, monks came wandering by, adherents of Gotama the Buddha; they asked to be taken across the river, and from them the ferrymen learned that they were making an urgent journey back to their great teacher, because the news had spread that the Sublime One was mortally ill and would soon die his final human death,[12] in order to enter the state of salvation. Not long after that, another group of monks came by, and then another, and the monks, as well as most of the other travelers and wanderers, spoke of nothing but Gotama and his impending death. And just as, on the occasion of a military expedition or a king's coronation, people pour in from every direction and every side, and swarm like ants: in like fashion, as if drawn by a magic spell, they thronged to the place where the great Buddha awaited his death, where the

---

[12] This circumlocution corresponds to what is called in Buddhist writings the *parinirvana* of the Buddha, the "ultimate extinction" after which he would not be reborn—historically speaking, the death of Siddhartha Gautama of the Sakya clan.

Buddha seinen Tod erwartete, wo das Ungeheure geschehen und der große Vollendete eines Weltalters zur Herrlichkeit eingehen sollte. Viel gedachte Siddhartha in dieser Zeit des sterbenden Weisen, des großen Lehrers, dessen Stimme Völker ermahnt und Hunderttausende erweckt hatte, dessen Stimme auch er einst vernommen, dessen heiliges Antlitz auch er einst mit Ehrfurcht geschaut hatte. Freundlich gedachte er seiner, sah seinen Weg der Vollendung vor Augen und erinnerte sich mit Lächeln der Worte, welche er einst als junger Mann an ihn, den Erhabenen, gerichtet hatte. Es waren, so schien ihm, stolze und altkluge Worte gewesen, lächelnd erinnerte er sich ihrer. Längst wußte er sich nicht mehr von Gotama getrennt, dessen Lehre er doch nicht hatte annehmen können. Nein, keine Lehre konnte ein wahrhaft Suchender annehmen, einer, der wahrhaft finden wollte. Der aber, der gefunden hat, der konnte jede, jede Lehre gutheißen, jeden Weg, jedes Ziel, ihn trennte nichts mehr von all den tausend anderen, welche im Ewigen lebten, welche das Göttliche atmeten.

An einem dieser Tage, da so viele zum sterbenden Buddha pilgerten, pilgerte zu ihm auch Kamala, einst die schönste der Kurtisanen. Längst hatte sie sich aus ihrem vorigen Leben zurückgezogen, hatte ihren Garten den Mönchen Gotamas geschenkt, hatte ihre Zuflucht zur Lehre genommen, gehörte zu den Freundinnen und Wohltäterinnen der Pilgernden. Zusammen mit dem Knaben Siddhartha, ihrem Sohne, hatte sie auf die Nachricht vom nahen Tode Gotamas hin sich auf den Weg gemacht, in einfachem Kleide, zu Fuß. Mit ihrem Söhnlein war sie am Flusse unterwegs; der Knabe aber war bald ermüdet, begehrte nach Hause zurück, begehrte zu rasten, begehrte zu essen, wurde trotzig und weinerlich. Kamala mußte häufig mit ihm rasten, er war gewohnt, seinen Willen gegen sie zu behaupten, sie mußte ihn füttern, mußte ihn trösten, mußte ihn schelten. Er begriff nicht, warum er mit seiner Mutter diese mühsame und traurige Pilgerschaft habe antreten müssen, an einen unbekannten Ort, zu einem fremden Manne, welcher heilig war und welcher im Sterben lag. Mochte er sterben, was ging dies den Knaben an?

Die Pilgernden waren nicht mehr ferne von Vasudevas Fähre, als der kleine Siddhartha abermals seine Mutter zu einer Rast nötigte. Auch sie selbst, Kamala, war ermüdet, und während der Knabe an einer Banane kaute, kauerte sie sich am Boden nieder, schloß ein wenig die Augen und ruhte. Plötzlich aber stieß sie einen klagenden Schrei aus, der Knabe sah sie erschrocken an und sah ihr Gesicht von

tremendous event was to take place and the great Perfect One of the age was to enter into glory.

At that time Siddhartha frequently recalled the dying sage, the great teacher, whose voice had admonished nations and had awakened hundreds of thousands, whose voice he, too, had once heard, whose holy countenance he, too, had once looked upon with respect. He recalled him in a friendly way, saw his path of perfection before his eyes, and smilingly recollected the words that, as a young man, he had once addressed to him, the Sublime One. It now seemed to him that they had been prideful and precocious words; he recollected them with a smile. For some time he had known that he was no longer separated from Gotama, even though he had been unable to accept his doctrine. No, a true seeker, one who truly wished to find, could accept no doctrine. But the man who has found what he sought, such a man could approve of every doctrine, each and every one, every path, every goal; nothing separated him any longer from all those thousands of others who lived in the Eternal, who breathed the Divine.

On one of those days when so many were journeying to the dying Buddha, Kamala, too, journeyed his way, she who was formerly the most beautiful of courtesans. For some time she had retired from her previous life; she had given her garden to Gotama's monks, she had taken refuge in the Law, and was one of the friends and benefactresses of the journeying monks. Together with the boy Siddhartha, her son, upon hearing the news of Gotama's impending death, she had set out, in a simple dress, on foot. She and her young son were journeying along the river; but the boy had soon grown tired; he wanted to go back home, he wanted to rest, he wanted to eat, he became defiant and querulous. Kamala had to stop and rest with him frequently; he was accustomed to get his way where she was concerned; she had to feed him, had to console him, had to scold him. He failed to understand why he and his mother had had to undertake that laborious and sad journey to an unfamiliar place, to a man he did not know, a man who was holy and who lay dying. Let him die; what was that to the boy?

The travelers were no longer far from Vasudeva's ferry when little Siddhartha once more pleaded with his mother to take a rest. She, too, Kamala, was tired out and, while the boy chewed on a plantain, she crouched down on the ground, closed her eyes a little, and rested. But suddenly she uttered a lamenting cry; the boy looked at her in alarm and saw her face pale with horror; out from

Entsetzen gebleicht, und unter ihrem Kleide hervor entwich eine kleine schwarze Schlange, von welcher Kamala gebissen war.

Eilig liefen sie nun beide des Weges, um zu Menschen zu kommen, und kamen bis in die Nähe der Fähre, dort sank Kamala zusammen und vermochte nicht weiterzugehen. Der Knabe aber erhob ein klägliches Geschrei, dazwischen küßte und umhalste er seine Mutter, und auch sie stimmte in seine lauten Hilferufe ein, bis die Töne Vasudevas Ohr erreichten, der bei der Fähre stand. Schnell kam er gegangen, nahm die Frau auf die Arme, trug sie ins Boot, der Knabe lief mit, und bald kamen sie alle in der Hütte an, wo Siddhartha am Herde stand und eben Feuer machte. Er blickte auf und sah zuerst das Gesicht des Knaben, das ihn wunderlich erinnerte, an Vergessenes mahnte. Dann sah er Kamala, die er alsbald erkannte, obwohl sie besinnungslos im Arm des Fährmanns lag, und nun wußte er, daß es sein eigner Sohn sei, dessen Gesicht ihn so sehr gemahnt hatte, und das Herz bewegte sich in seiner Brust.

Kamalas Wunde wurde gewaschen, war aber schon schwarz und ihr Leib angeschwollen, ein Heiltrank wurde ihr eingeflößt. Ihr Bewußtsein kehrte zurück, sie lag auf Siddharthas Lager in der Hütte, und über sie gebeugt stand Siddhartha, der sie einst so sehr geliebt hatte. Es schien ihr ein Traum zu sein, lächelnd blickte sie in ihres Freundes Gesicht, nur langsam erkannte sie ihre Lage, erinnerte sich des Bisses, rief ängstlich nach dem Knaben.

»Er ist bei dir, sei ohne Sorge«, sagte Siddhartha.

Kamala blickte in seine Augen. Sie sprach mit schwerer Zunge, vom Gift gelähmt. »Du bist alt geworden, Lieber«, sagte sie, »grau bist du geworden. Aber du gleichst dem jungen Samana, der einst ohne Kleider mit staubigen Füßen zu mir in den Garten kam. Du gleichst ihm viel mehr, als du ihm damals glichest, da du mich und Kamaswami verlassen hast. In den Augen gleichst du ihm, Siddhartha. Ach, auch ich bin alt geworden, alt – kanntest du mich denn noch?«

Siddhartha lächelte: »Sogleich kannte ich dich, Kamala, Liebe.«

Kamala deutete auf ihren Knaben und sagte: »Kanntest du auch ihn? Er ist dein Sohn.«

Ihre Augen wurden irr und fielen zu. Der Knabe weinte, Siddhartha nahm ihn auf seine Knie, ließ ihn weinen, streichelte sein Haar, und beim Anblick des Kindergesichtes fiel ein brahmanisches Gebet ihm ein, das er einst gelernt hatte, als er selbst ein kleiner Knabe war. Langsam, mit singender Stimme, begann er es zu sprechen, aus der Vergangenheit und Kindheit her kamen ihm die Worte geflossen. Und unter seinem Singsang wurde der Knabe ruhig,

under her dress escaped a little black snake, by which Kamala had been bitten.

Now they both ran hurriedly along the path, in order to reach other people, and arrived very close to the ferry, when Kamala collapsed and was unable to continue on. But the boy raised a piteous cry, from time to time kissing and hugging his mother, and she, too, added her loud calls for help to his, until the sounds reached the ears of Vasudeva, who was standing near the ferry. He ran over quickly, took the woman in his arms, and carried her into the boat; the boy ran along with them, and soon they all reached the hut, where Siddhartha was standing by the hearth engaged in lighting a fire. He looked up, and the first thing he saw was the boy's face, which strangely jogged his memory, reminding him of things forgotten. Then he saw Kamala, whom he recognized at once, although she was lying unconscious in the ferryman's arms; and then he knew that it was his own son whose face had been such a reminder to him, and his heart jumped in his bosom.

Kamala's wound was washed, but it was already black and her body had swelled; a medicinal potion was administered to her. She regained consciousness, and lay on Siddhartha's bed in the hut; and leaning over her stood Siddhartha, who had once loved her so much. It seemed like a dream to her; with a smile she looked into her friend's face; only gradually did she take in her situation, remembering the bite, and she called anxiously for the boy.

"He is here with you, do not worry," said Siddhartha.

Kamala looked into his eyes. She spoke with a heavy tongue, paralyzed by the poison. "You have grown old, dear," she said; "you have grown gray. But you look like the young samana who once came into my garden without clothes and with dusty feet. You look much more like him now than you did when you left me and Kamaswami. It is your eyes that resemble his, Siddhartha. Oh, I have grown old, too, old—did you still recognize me?"

Siddhartha smiled: "I recognized you at once, Kamala, dear."

Kamala pointed to her boy, saying: "Did you recognize him, too? He is your son."

Her eyes started to wander, and closed. The boy wept, Siddhartha took him on his knee, let him weep, stroked his hair, and, at the sight of that child's face, he recalled a Brahmanic prayer he had once learned when he himself was a little boy. Slowly, in a chanting voice, he began to say it; the words came rushing back to him from the past and his childhood. And, as he chanted, the boy grew calm, gave just a few more sobs at moments, and fell asleep. Siddhartha placed him on

schluchzte noch hin und wieder auf und schlief ein. Siddhartha legte ihn auf Vasudevas Lager. Vasudeva stand am Herd und kochte Reis. Siddhartha warf ihm einen Blick zu, den er lächelnd erwiderte.

»Sie wird sterben«, sagte Siddhartha leise.

Vasudeva nickte, über sein freundliches Gesicht lief der Feuerschein vom Herde.

Nochmals erwachte Kamala zum Bewußtsein. Schmerz verzog ihr Gesicht, Siddharthas Auge las das Leiden auf ihrem Munde, auf ihren erblaßten Wangen. Stille las er es, aufmerksam, wartend, in ihr Leiden versenkt. Kamala fühlte es, ihr Blick suchte sein Auge.

Ihn anblickend, sagte sie:»Nun sehe ich, daß auch deine Augen sich verändert haben. Ganz anders sind sie geworden. Woran doch erkenne ich noch, daß du Siddhartha bist? Du bist es, und bist es nicht.«

Siddhartha sprach nicht, still blickten seine Augen in die ihren.

»Du hast es erreicht?« fragte sie. »Du hast Friede gefunden?«

Er lächelte und legte seine Hand auf ihre.

»Ich sehe es«, sagte sie, »ich sehe es. Auch ich werde Friede finden.«

»Du hast ihn gefunden«, sprach Siddhartha flüsternd.

Kamala blickte ihm unverwandt in die Augen. Sie dachte daran, daß sie zu Gotama hatte pilgern wollen, um das Gesicht eines Vollendeten zu sehen, um seinen Frieden zu atmen, und daß sie statt seiner nun ihn gefunden, und daß es gut war, ebenso gut, als wenn sie jenen gesehen hätte. Sie wollte es ihm sagen, aber die Zunge gehorchte ihrem Willen nicht mehr. Schweigend sah sie ihn an, und er sah in ihren Augen das Leben erlöschen. Als der letzte Schmerz ihr Auge erfüllte und brach, als der letzte Schauder über ihre Glieder lief, schloß sein Finger ihre Lider.

Lange saß er und blickte auf ihr entschlafenes Gesicht. Lange betrachtete er ihren Mund, ihren alten, müden Mund mit den schmal gewordenen Lippen, und erinnerte sich, daß er einst, im Frühling seiner Jahre, diesen Mund einer frisch aufgebrochenen Feige verglichen hatte. Lange saß er, las in dem bleichen Gesicht, in den müden Falten, füllte sich mit dem Anblick, sah sein eigenes Gesicht ebenso liegen, ebenso weiß, ebenso erloschen, und sah zugleich sein Gesicht und das ihre jung, mit den roten Lippen, mit dem brennenden Auge, und das Gefühl der Gegenwart und Gleichzeitigkeit durchdrang ihn völlig, das Gefühl der Ewigkeit. Tief empfand er, tiefer als jemals, in dieser Stunde die Unzerstörbarkeit jedes Lebens, die Ewigkeit jedes Augenblicks.

Da er sich erhob, hatte Vasudeva Reis für ihn bereitet. Doch aß Siddhartha nicht. Im Stall, wo ihre Ziege stand, machten sich die beiden Alten eine Streu zurecht, und Vasudeva legte sich schlafen.

Vasudeva's bed. Vasudeva stood at the hearth cooking rice. Siddhartha threw him a glance that he returned with a smile.

"She is going to die," Siddhartha said softly.

Vasudeva nodded; the firelight from the hearth flickered over his friendly face.

Again Kamala regained consciousness. Her face was distorted by pain; Siddhartha's eyes read the suffering on her lips, on her pallid cheeks. He read it quietly, attentively, expectantly, absorbed in her suffering. Kamala felt it; her eyes sought his.

Looking at him, she said: "Now I see that your eyes have changed, too. They have become entirely different. What is it, then, that makes me still recognize you as being Siddhartha? You are, and you are not."

Siddhartha did not speak; silently his eyes looked into hers.

"Have you attained it?" she asked. "Have you found peace?"

He smiled and laid his hand on hers.

"I see it," she said, "I see it. I, too, shall find peace."

"You have found it," said Siddhartha in a whisper.

Kamala looked into his eyes unflinchingly. She thought about her intention to journey to Gotama to see the face of a perfected man, to absorb his peace; and she reflected that she had now found Siddhartha instead, and that it was good, just as good as if she had seen Gotama. She wanted to tell him that, but her tongue no longer obeyed her will. She looked at him in silence, and he saw life fading away in her eyes. When the final stab of pain filled her eyes and ended, when the final shudder ran through her limbs, his fingers closed her eyelids.

For a long while he sat there looking at her dead face. For a long while he contemplated her mouth, her old, tired mouth with the lips that had grown narrow, and he remembered that, once, in the spring-time of his years, he had likened that mouth to a newly opened fig. For a long while he sat there, reading the pale face, the weary wrinkles; he filled himself with the sight, he saw his own face lying in the same way, just as white, just as burnt-out; and, at the same time, he saw his face and hers young, with red lips, with glowing eyes; and he was completely permeated by the feeling of present time and simultaneity, the feeling of eternity. At that moment, he felt deeply, more deeply than ever before, the indestructibility of all life, the eternity of every moment.

When he arose, Vasudeva had prepared rice for him. But Siddhartha did not eat. In the shed where they kept their goat, the two old men arranged a pallet of straw, and Vasudeva lay down to sleep.

Siddhartha aber ging hinaus und saß die Nacht vor der Hütte, dem
Flusse lauschend, von Vergangenheit umspült, von allen Zeiten seines
Lebens zugleich berührt und umfangen. Zuweilen aber erhob er sich,
trat an die Hüttentür und lauschte, ob der Knabe schlafe.

Früh am Morgen, noch ehe die Sonne sichtbar ward, kam Vasudeva
aus dem Stalle und trat zu seinem Freunde.

»Du hast nicht geschlafen«, sagte er.

»Nein, Vasudeva. Ich saß hier, ich hörte dem Flusse zu. Viel hat er
mir gesagt, tief hat er mich mit dem heilsamen Gedanken erfüllt, mit
dem Gedanken der Einheit.«

»Du hast Leid erfahren, Siddhartha, doch ich sehe, es ist keine
Traurigkeit in dein Herz gekommen.«

»Nein, Lieber, wie sollte ich denn traurig sein? Ich, der ich reich
und glücklich war, bin jetzt noch reicher und glücklicher geworden.
Mein Sohn ist mir geschenkt worden.«

»Willkommen sei dein Sohn auch mir. Nun aber, Siddhartha, laß
uns an die Arbeit gehen, viel ist zu tun. Auf demselben Lager ist
Kamala gestorben, auf welchem einst mein Weib gestorben ist. Auf
demselben Hügel auch wollen wir Kamalas Scheiterhaufen bauen,
auf welchem ich einst meines Weibes Scheiterhaufen gebaut habe.«

Während der Knabe noch schlief, bauten sie den Scheiterhaufen.

DER SOHN

Scheu und weinend hatte der Knabe der Bestattung seiner Mutter
beigewohnt, finster und scheu hatte er Siddhartha angehört, der ihn
als seinen Sohn begrüßte und ihn bei sich in Vasudevas Hütte
willkommen hieß. Bleich saß er tagelang am Hügel der Toten, mochte
nicht essen, verschloß seinen Blick, verschloß sein Herz, wehrte und
sträubte sich gegen das Schicksal.

Siddhartha schonte ihn und ließ ihn gewähren, er ehrte seine
Trauer. Siddhartha verstand, daß sein Sohn ihn nicht kenne, daß er
ihn nicht lieben könne wie einen Vater. Langsam sah und verstand er
auch, daß der Elfjährige ein verwöhnter Knabe war, ein Mutterkind,
und in Gewohnheiten des Reichtums aufgewachsen, gewöhnt an
feinere Speisen, an ein weiches Bett, gewohnt, Dienern zu befehlen.
Siddhartha verstand, daß der Trauernde und Verwöhnte nicht plötzlich und gutwillig in der Fremde und Armut sich zufrieden geben
könne. Er zwang ihn nicht, er tat manche Arbeit für ihn, suchte stets

But Siddhartha went outside and sat in front of the hut all night long, listening to the river, with the past washing all around him, touched and surrounded by all the phases of his life simultaneously. But every once in a while he got up, stepped over to the door of the hut, and listened to hear whether the boy was sleeping.

Early in the morning, even before the sun became visible, Vasudeva stepped out of the shed and came over to his friend.

"You have not slept," he said.

"No, Vasudeva. I was sitting here listening to the river. It told me many things, it filled me full of healing thoughts, with the concept of oneness."

"You have experienced sorrow, Siddhartha, but I see that no sadness has entered your heart."

"No, my dear friend, why should I be sad? I, who used to be rich and happy, have now become even richer and happier. My son has been given to me."

"Let your son be welcome to me, also. But now, Siddhartha, let us go to work, there is much to be done. Kamala died on the same bed on which my wife once died. We shall also build Kamala's pyre on the same hill on which I once built my wife's pyre."

While the boy was still asleep, they built the pyre.

THE SON

Timidly weeping, the boy had attended his mother's funeral; gloomy and timid, he had heard Siddhartha greet him as his son and welcome him into Vasudeva's hut. He sat pale for days on end on the dead woman's hill; he refused to eat, he averted his gaze, he locked up his heart, he resisted and fought against his destiny.

Siddhartha treated him considerately and let him have his way, out of respect for his loss. Siddhartha understood that his son did not know him, that he could not love him like a father. Gradually he also saw and understood that the eleven-year-old was a spoiled child, a mother's boy, who had grown up accustomed to riches, used to more delicate food and to a soft bed, with the habit of ordering around servants. Siddhartha understood that a spoiled child who was mourning a loss could not suddenly and voluntarily be contented with strange surroundings and poverty. He put no pressure on him, he performed many tasks for him, he always picked out the choicest pieces of food

den besten Bissen für ihn aus. Langsam hoffte er, ihn zu gewinnen, durch freundliche Geduld.

Reich und glücklich hatte er sich genannt, als der Knabe zu ihm gekommen war. Da indessen die Zeit hinfloß, und der Knabe fremd und finster blieb, da er ein stolzes und trotziges Herz zeigte, keine Arbeit tun wollte, den Alten keine Ehrfurcht erwies, Vasudevas Fruchtbäume beraubte, da begann Siddhartha zu verstehen, daß mit seinem Sohne nicht Glück und Friede zu ihm gekommen war, sondern Leid und Sorge. Aber er liebte ihn, und lieber war ihm Leid und Sorge der Liebe, als ihm Glück und Freude ohne den Knaben gewesen war.

Seit der junge Siddhartha in der Hütte war, hatten die Alten sich in die Arbeit geteilt. Vasudeva hatte das Amt des Fährmanns wieder allein übernommen, und Siddhartha, um bei seinem Sohne zu sein, die Arbeit in Hütte und Feld.

Lange Zeit, lange Monate wartete Siddhartha darauf, daß sein Sohn ihn verstehe, daß er seine Liebe annehme, daß er sie vielleicht erwidere. Lange Monate wartete Vasudeva, zusehend, wartete und schwieg. Eines Tages, als Siddhartha der Junge seinen Vater wieder sehr mit Trotz und Launen gequält und ihm beide Reisschüsseln zerbrochen hatte, nahm Vasudeva seinen Freund am Abend beiseite und sprach mit ihm.

»Entschuldige mich«, sagte er, »aus freundlichem Herzen rede ich zu dir. Ich sehe, daß du dich quälst, ich sehe, daß du Kummer hast. Dein Sohn, Lieber, macht dir Sorge, und auch mir macht er Sorge. An ein anderes Leben, an ein anderes Nest ist der junge Vogel gewöhnt. Nicht wie du ist er dem Reichtum und der Stadt entlaufen aus Ekel und Überdruß, er hat wider seinen Willen dies alles dahinten lassen müssen. Ich fragte den Fluß, o Freund, viele Male habe ich ihn gefragt. Der Fluß aber lacht, er lacht mich aus, mich und dich lacht er aus, und schüttelt sich über unsre Torheit. Wasser will zu Wasser, Jugend will zu Jugend, dein Sohn ist nicht an dem Orte, wo er gedeihen kann. Frage auch du den Fluß, höre auch du auf ihn!«

Bekümmert blickte Siddhartha ihm in das freundliche Gesicht, in dessen vielen Runzeln beständige Heiterkeit wohnte.

»Kann ich mich denn von ihm trennen?« fragte er leise, beschämt. »Laß mir noch Zeit, Lieber! Sieh, ich kämpfe um ihn, ich werbe um sein Herz, mit Liebe und mit freundlicher Geduld will ich es fangen. Auch zu ihm soll einst der Fluß reden, auch er ist berufen.«

Vasudevas Lächeln blühte wärmer. »O ja, auch er ist berufen, auch er ist vom ewigen Leben. Aber wissen wir denn, du und ich, wozu er

for him. He hoped he could gradually win him over through friendliness and patience.

He had considered himself rich and fortunate when the boy had come to him. But since time had gone by since then, and the boy remained a gloomy stranger, since he gave signs of having a prideful, defiant heart, refusing to do any work, showing no respect for the old men, and stealing fruit from Vasudeva's trees, Siddhartha began to understand that his son had brought him not happiness and peace but sorrow and care. But he loved him, and the sorrow and care that came with love were dearer to him than happiness and joy had been without the boy.

Ever since young Siddhartha had been in the hut, the old men had decided on a division of labor. Vasudeva had once again taken over the duties of a ferryman on his own, and Siddhartha, to be near his son, had taken over the work in the hut and the paddy.

For a long time, for long months, Siddhartha waited for his son to understand him, to accept his love, and perhaps reciprocate it. For long months Vasudeva waited, looking on, waited and kept silent. One day, when young Siddhartha had once again severely tormented his father with rebelliousness and moodiness, breaking both of his rice bowls, Vasudeva took his friend aside in the evening and spoke to him.

"Excuse me," he said, "I am talking to you like a friend. I see that you are tormenting yourself, I see that you are grieved. My dear friend, your son is giving you worries, and he is giving me worries, too. This young bird is used to a different life, a different nest. He did not, like you, run away from riches and the town out of disgust and surfeit; he had to leave all that behind against his will. I questioned the river, O friend, many times have I questioned it. But the river laughs, it laughs at me, it laughs at me and you, shaking its sides over our foolishness. Water seeks out water, the young seek out the young; your son is not in a place where he can thrive. Question the river yourself, listen to it yourself!"

Sadly Siddhartha looked into his friendly face, in the many wrinkles of which unchanging serenity dwelt.

"But can I part with him?" he asked softly, feeling ashamed. "Give me more time, dear friend! Look, I am fighting for him, I am courting his heart; I shall capture it with love and with friendly patience. Some day the river will speak to him, too; he, too, has a vocation."

Vasudeva's smile grew warmer, blossoming out. "Oh, yes, he, too, has a vocation; he, too, partakes of eternal life. But do we know, you

berufen ist, zu welchem Wege, zu welchen Taten, zu welchen Leiden? Nicht klein wird sein Leiden sein, stolz und hart ist ja sein Herz, viel müssen solche leiden, viel irren, viel Unrecht tun, sich viel Sünde aufladen. Sage mir, mein Lieber: du erziehst deinen Sohn nicht? Du zwingst ihn nicht? Schlägst ihn nicht? Strafst ihn nicht?«

»Nein, Vasudeva, das tue ich alles nicht.«

»Ich wußte es. Du zwingst ihn nicht, schlägst ihn nicht, befiehlst ihm nicht, weil du weißt, daß Weich stärker ist als Hart, Wasser stärker als Fels, Liebe stärker als Gewalt. Sehr gut, ich lobe dich. Aber ist es nicht ein Irrtum von dir, zu meinen, daß du ihn nicht zwingst, nicht strafest? Bindest du ihn nicht in Bande mit deiner Liebe? Beschämst du ihn nicht täglich, und machst es ihm noch schwerer, mit deiner Güte und Geduld? Zwingst du ihn nicht, den hochmütigen und verwöhnten Knaben, in einer Hütte bei zwei alten Bananenessern zu leben, welchen schon Reis ein Leckerbissen ist, deren Gedanken nicht seine sein können, deren Herz alt und still ist und anderen Gang hat als das seine? Ist er mit alledem nicht gezwungen, nicht gestraft?«

Betroffen blickte Siddhartha zur Erde. Leise fragte er: »Was meinst du, soll ich tun?«

Sprach Vasudeva: »Bring ihn zur Stadt, bringe ihn in seiner Mutter Haus, es werden noch Diener dort sein, denen gib ihn. Und wenn keine mehr da sind, so bringe ihn einem Lehrer, nicht der Lehre wegen, aber daß er zu anderen Knaben komme, und zu Mädchen, und in die Welt, welche die seine ist. Hast du daran nie gedacht?«

»Du siehst in mein Herz«, sprach Siddhartha traurig. »Oft habe ich daran gedacht. Aber sieh, wie soll ich ihn, der ohnehin kein sanftes Herz hat, in diese Welt geben? Wird er nicht üppig werden, wird er nicht sich an Lust und Macht verlieren, wird er nicht alle Irrtümer seines Vaters wiederholen, wird er nicht vielleicht ganz und gar in Sansara verlorengehen?«

Hell strahlte des Fährmanns Lächeln auf; er berührte zart Siddharthas Arm und sagte: »Frage den Fluß darüber, Freund! Höre ihn darüber lachen! Glaubst du denn wirklich, daß du deine Torheiten begangen habest, um sie dem Sohn zu ersparen? Und kannst du denn deinen Sohn vor Sansara schützen? Wie denn? Durch Lehre, durch Gebet, durch Ermahnung? Lieber, hast du jene Geschichte denn ganz vergessen, jene lehrreiche Geschichte von Brahmanensohn Siddhartha, die du mir einst hier an dieser Stelle erzählt hast? Wer hat den Samana Siddhartha vor Sansara bewahrt, vor Sünde, vor

and I, where his vocation lies, to what path, to what deeds, to what sorrows his call will lead him? His suffering will not be small, for his heart is prideful and hard; people of that sort must suffer greatly, go far astray, do much injustice, burden themselves with much sin. Tell me, dear friend: are you not bringing up your son? Do you put no pressure on him? Do you not hit him? Do you not punish him?"

"No, Vasudeva, I do none of those things."

"I knew it. You put no pressure on him, you do not hit him, you give him no orders, because you know that softness is stronger than hardness, water is stronger than rock, love is stronger than physical force. Very good, I applaud you. But is it not a mistake on your part to believe that you are not putting pressure on him or punishing him? Are you not tying him hand and foot with your love? Are you not daily shaming him, and making things even harder for him, with your kindness and patience? Are you not compelling him, proud and spoiled boy that he is, to live in a hut with two old plantain eaters, for whom even rice is a delicacy, whose thoughts cannot be his, whose hearts are old and settled and move at a different pace from his? Does not all that constitute compulsion and punishment for him?"

Taken aback, Siddhartha looked down at the ground. Quietly he asked: "What do you think I should do?"

Vasudeva said: "Take him to town, take him to his mother's house; there will still be servants there, hand him over to them. And if there are no more, take him to a teacher, not for the sake of the instruction, but so he can be among other boys, and among girls, and enter his own world. Have your never thought about that?"

"You see into my heart," said Siddhartha mournfully. "I have thought about it frequently. But look, how can I turn him over to that world, seeing that his heart is not tender to begin with? Will he not become presumptuous, will he not give himself over to pleasure and power, will he not repeat all his father's mistakes, will he not perhaps become totally lost in *samsara*?"

The ferryman flashed a bright smile; he touched Siddhartha's arm gently, saying: "Question the river about it, friend! Hear it laugh over it! Do you really believe, then, that you committed your follies in order to save your son from them? And can you protect your son against *samsara*? How? Through instruction, through prayer, through admonition? Dear friend, have you, then, completely forgotten that story, that instructive story of the Brahman's son Siddhartha that you once told me on this very spot? Who saved the samana Siddhartha from *samsara*, from sin, from avarice, from

Habsucht, vor Torheit? Hat seines Vaters Frömmigkeit, seiner Lehrer
Ermahnung, hat sein eigenes Wissen, sein eigenes Suchen ihn be-
wahren können? Welcher Vater, welcher Lehrer hat ihn davor
schützen können, selbst das Leben zu leben, selbst sich mit dem
Leben zu beschmutzen, selbst Schuld auf sich zu laden, selbst den
bitteren Trank zu trinken, selber seinen Weg zu finden? Glaubst du
denn, Lieber, dieser Weg bleibe irgend jemandem vielleicht erspart?
Vielleicht deinem Söhnchen, weil du es liebst, weil du ihm gern Leid
und Schmerz und Enttäuschung ersparen möchtest? Aber auch wenn
du zehnmal für ihn stürbest, würdest du ihm nicht den kleinsten Teil
seines Schicksals damit abnehmen können.«

Noch niemals hatte Vasudeva so viele Worte gesprochen. Freundlich dankte ihm Siddhartha, ging bekümmert in die Hütte, fand lange
keinen Schlaf. Vasudeva hatte ihm nichts gesagt, das er nicht selbst
schon gedacht und gewußt hätte. Aber es war ein Wissen, das er nicht
tun konnte, stärker als das Wissen war seine Liebe zu dem Knaben,
stärker seine Zärtlichkeit, seine Angst, ihn zu verlieren. Hatte er denn
jemals an irgend etwas so sehr sein Herz verloren, hatte er je irgendeinen Menschen so geliebt, so blind, so leidend, so erfolglos und doch
so glücklich?

Siddhartha konnte seines Freundes Rat nicht befolgen, er konnte
den Sohn nicht hergeben. Er ließ sich von dem Knaben befehlen, er
ließ sich von ihm mißachten. Er schwieg und wartete, begann täglich
den stummen Kampf der Freundlichkeit, den lautlosen Krieg der
Geduld. Auch Vasudeva schwieg und wartete, freundlich, wissend,
langmütig. In der Geduld waren sie beide Meister.

Einst, als des Knaben Gesicht ihn sehr an Kamala erinnerte, mußte
Siddhartha plötzlich eines Wortes gedenken, das Kamala vor Zeiten,
in den Tagen der Jugend, einmal zu ihm gesagt hatte. »Du kannst
nicht lieben«, hatte sie ihm gesagt, und er hatte ihr recht gegeben und
hatte sich mit einem Stern, die Kindermenschen aber mit fallendem
Laub verglichen, und dennoch hatte er in jenem Wort auch einen
Vorwurf gespürt. In der Tat hatte er niemals sich an einen anderen
Menschen ganz verlieren und hingeben können, sich selbst vergessen,
Torheiten der Liebe eines anderen wegen begehen; nie hatte er das
gekonnt, und dies war, wie ihm damals schien, der große Unterschied
gewesen, der ihn von den Kindermenschen trennte. Nun aber, seit
sein Sohn da war, nun war auch er, Siddhartha, vollends ein

folly? Was his father's piety, were his teachers' admonitions, were his own knowledge and questing, able to save him? What father, what teacher, was able to protect him from living his own life, sullying himself with life on his own account, burdening himself with guilt on his own, drinking the bitter potion himself, finding his own path? Do you perhaps believe, dear friend, that anyone at all can be saved from that path? Your young son, perhaps, because you love him, because you would gladly spare him sorrow and pain and disappointment? But, even if you were to die for him ten times, you would not be able to abate even the tiniest part of his destiny by so doing."

Never before had Vasudeva made such a long speech.[13]

Siddhartha thanked him in a friendly way, entered the hut full of care, and was unable to sleep for some time. Vasudeva had told him nothing that he himself had not already thought and known. But it was a knowledge that he could not put into action; stronger than that knowledge was his love for the boy; his tenderness, his fear of losing him, were also stronger. For had he ever before lost his heart to anything more completely, had he ever so loved any human being, so blindly, so painfully, so unsuccessfully, and yet so happily?

Siddhartha was unable to follow his friend's advice, he was unable to give up his son. He let the boy order him around, he let the boy show disrespect for him. He remained silent and waited; daily he began all over again the unspoken battle of friendliness, the soundless war of patience. Vasudeva, too, was silent and waited, friendly, knowing, forbearing. When it came to patience, they were both past masters.

On one occasion, when the boy's face reminded him strongly of Kamala, Siddhartha suddenly recalled something Kamala had once told him, long before, in his youthful days. "You cannot love," she had told him, and he had agreed with her, comparing himself to a star, and the child-people to falling leaves; and yet he had also sensed a reproach in those words. In truth, he had never been able to lose himself completely in another person, to give himself completely, to forget himself, to commit loving follies for the sake of another; he had never been able to, and, as it seemed to him at the time, that had been the great difference between him and the child-people, setting him apart. But now, ever since his son had come, now he, too, Siddhartha, had totally become a child-person, suffering for some-

---

[13] It is only a few words longer than one of his speeches in the preceding chapter.

Kindermensch geworden, eines Menschen wegen leidend, einen Menschen liebend, an eine Liebe verloren, einer Liebe wegen ein Tor geworden. Nun fühlte auch er, spät, einmal im Leben diese stärkste und seltsamste Leidenschaft, litt an ihr, litt kläglich, und war doch beseligt, war doch um etwas erneuert, um etwas reicher.

Wohl spürte er, daß diese Liebe, diese blinde Liebe zu seinem Sohn eine Leidenschaft, etwas sehr Menschliches, daß sie Sansara sei, eine trübe Quelle, ein dunkles Wasser. Dennoch, so fühlte er gleichzeitig, war sie nicht wertlos, war sie notwendig, kam aus seinem eigenen Wesen. Auch diese Lust wollte gebüßt, auch diese Schmerzen wollten gekostet sein, auch diese Torheiten begangen.

Der Sohn indessen ließ ihn seine Torheiten begehen, ließ ihn werben, ließ ihn täglich sich vor seinen Launen demütigen. Dieser Vater hatte nichts, was ihn entzückt, und nichts, was er gefürchtet hätte. Er war ein guter Mann, dieser Vater, ein guter, gütiger, sanfter Mann, vielleicht ein sehr frommer Mann, vielleicht ein Heiliger – dies alles waren nicht Eigenschaften, welche den Knaben gewinnen konnten. Langweilig war ihm dieser Vater, der ihn da in seiner elenden Hütte gefangen hielt, langweilig war er ihm, und daß er jede Unart mit Lächeln, jeden Schimpf mit Freundlichkeit, jede Bosheit mit Güte beantwortete, das eben war die verhaßteste List dieses alten Schleichers. Viel lieber wäre der Knabe von ihm bedroht, von ihm mißhandelt worden.

Es kam ein Tag, an welchem des jungen Siddhartha Sinn zum Ausbruch kam und sich offen gegen seinen Vater wandte. Der hatte ihm einen Auftrag erteilt, er hatte ihn Reisig sammeln geheißen. Der Knabe ging aber nicht aus der Hütte, er blieb trotzig und wütend stehen, stampfte den Boden, ballte die Fäuste, und schrie in gewaltigem Ausbruch seinem Vater Haß und Verachtung ins Gesicht.

»Hole du selber dein Reisig!« rief er schäumend, »ich bin nicht dein Knecht. Ich weiß ja, daß du mich nicht schlägst, du wagst es ja nicht; ich weiß ja, daß du mich mit deiner Frömmigkeit und deiner Nachsicht beständig strafen und klein machen willst. Du willst, daß ich werden soll wie du, auch so fromm, auch so sanft, auch so weise! Ich aber, höre, ich will, dir zu Leide, lieber ein Straßenräuber und Mörder werden und zur Hölle fahren, als so werden wie du! Ich hasse dich, du bist nicht mein Vater, und wenn du zehnmal meiner Mutter Buhler gewesen bist!«

Zorn und Gram liefen in ihm über, schäumten in hundert wüsten und bösen Worten dem Vater entgegen. Dann lief der Knabe davon und kam erst spät am Abend wieder.

one's sake, loving someone, lost through love, a fool for the sake of love. Now he, too, felt belatedly for once in his life that strongest and strangest of passions; he suffered from it, suffered pitifully, and yet he was blessed, and yet he was in some way renewed, in some way richer.

To be sure, he sensed that this love, this blind love for his son, was a passion, something very human, that it was *samsara,* a muddied fountain, a dark water. Nevertheless, he felt at the same time that it was not without value; it was needful, it proceeded from his own nature. This pleasure, too, had to be atoned for; these pains, too, had to be experienced; these follies, too, had to be committed.

Meanwhile his son allowed him to commit his follies, allowed him to sue for his love, allowed him to be humbled daily by his moods and caprices. There was nothing in this father that could delight him and nothing to cause him any fear. He was a good man, this father, a good, kind, gentle man, perhaps a very pious man, perhaps a saint—but none of these were qualities that could win over the boy. This father bored him, keeping him a prisoner there in his wretched hut; he bored him, and his way of responding to any misbehavior with a smile, to any insult with friendly treatment, to any malice with kindness—that was precisely the most hateful ruse of that old sneak. The boy would much have preferred for him to threaten him, beat him.

There came a day on which young Siddhartha's feelings broke out and turned openly against his father. His father had assigned him a chore, ordering him to gather brushwood. But the boy did not leave the hut; he stood there in a defiant rage, stamping his feet, clenching his fists, and, in a mighty eruption, screaming out his hatred and contempt for his father.

"Go get your own brushwood," he cried, foaming at the mouth. "I am not your servant. I know that you do not strike me, you do not dare to; I know that you are constantly trying to punish me and belittle me with your piety and your considerateness. You want me to become like you, just as pious, just as gentle, just as wise! But, listen, to spite you, I prefer to become a highway robber and murderer and go to hell, rather than become like you! I hate you, you are not my father even if you were my mother's lover ten times over!"

His anger and grief overflowed, foaming over in hostility to his father in a hundred chaotic, vicious expressions. Then the boy ran away, not returning until late in the evening.

Am andern Morgen aber war er verschwunden. Verschwunden war auch ein kleiner, aus zweifarbigem Bast geflochtener Korb, in welchem die Fährleute jene Kupfer- und Silbermünzen aufbewahrten, welche sie als Fährlohn erhielten. Verschwunden war auch das Boot, Siddhartha sah es am jenseitigen Ufer liegen. Der Knabe war entlaufen.

»Ich muß ihm folgen«, sagte Siddhartha, der seit jenen gestrigen Schimpfreden des Knaben vor Jammer zitterte. »Ein Kind kann nicht allein durch den Wald gehen. Er wird umkommen. Wir müssen ein Floß bauen, Vasudeva, um übers Wasser zu kommen.«

»Wir werden ein Floß bauen«, sagte Vasudeva, »um unser Boot wieder zu holen, das der Junge entführt hat. Ihn aber solltest du laufen lassen, Freund, er ist kein Kind mehr, er weiß sich zu helfen. Er sucht den Weg nach der Stadt, und er hat recht, vergiß das nicht. Er tut das, was du selbst zu tun versäumt hast. Er sorgt für sich, er geht seine Bahn. Ach, Siddhartha, ich sehe dich leiden, aber du leidest Schmerzen, über die man lachen möchte, über die du selbst bald lachen wirst.«

Siddhartha antwortete nicht. Er hielt schon das Beil in Händen, und begann ein Floß aus Bambus zu machen, und Vasudeva half ihm, die Stämme mit Grasseilen zusammenzubinden. Dann fuhren sie hinüber, wurden weit abgetrieben, zogen das Floß am jenseitigen Ufer flußauf.

»Warum hast du das Beil mitgenommen?« fragte Siddhartha.

Vasudeva sagte: »Es könnte sein, daß das Ruder unsres Bootes verlorengegangen wäre.«

Siddhartha aber wußte, was sein Freund dachte. Er dachte, der Knabe werde das Ruder weggeworfen oder zerbrochen haben, um sich zu rächen und um sie an der Verfolgung zu hindern. Und wirklich war kein Ruder mehr im Boote. Vasudeva wies auf den Boden des Bootes und sah den Freund mit Lächeln an, als wollte er sagen: »Siehst du nicht, was dein Sohn dir sagen will? Siehst du nicht, daß er nicht verfolgt sein will?« Doch sagte er dies nicht mit Worten. Er machte sich daran, ein neues Ruder zu zimmern. Siddhartha aber nahm Abschied, um nach dem Entflohenen zu suchen. Vasudeva hinderte ihn nicht.

Als Siddhartha schon lange im Walde unterwegs war, kam ihm der Gedanke, daß sein Suchen nutzlos sei. Entweder, so dachte er, war der Knabe längst voraus und schon in der Stadt angelangt, oder, wenn er noch unterwegs sein sollte, würde er vor ihm, dem Verfolgenden, sich verborgen halten. Da er weiter dachte, fand er auch, daß er selbst nicht in Sorge um seinen Sohn war, daß er im Innersten wußte, er sei weder umgekommen, noch drohe ihm im Walde Gefahr. Dennoch lief er ohne Rast, nicht mehr, um ihn zu ret-

But the following morning he had disappeared. Also gone was a little basket woven out of palm fiber of two colors, in which the ferrymen kept the copper and silver coins that they received as fare. The boat was gone, too; Siddhartha saw it lying on the far bank. The boy had run away.

"I must follow him," said Siddhartha, who had been trembling with sadness ever since the boy's insults the day before. "A child cannot walk through the forest alone. He will perish. We must build a raft, Vasudeva, to get across the river."

"We shall build a raft," said Vasudeva, "so we can recover our boat, which the boy commandeered. But as for him, you should let him go, friend; he is no longer a child, he can help himself. He is seeking the way to town, and he is right, do not forget it. He is doing what you yourself put off doing. He is watching out for himself, he is going his own way. Oh, Siddhartha, I see you suffering, but you are suffering pains that are rather laughable, that you yourself will soon laugh over."

Siddhartha made no reply. He already held the ax in his hands and was beginning to build a raft of bamboo; and Vasudeva helped him to tie the stalks together with grass ropes. Then they sailed across, were carried far downstream by the current, and pulled the raft upstream along the opposite bank.

"Why did you take along the ax?" asked Siddhartha.

Vasudeva said: "It may be that the oar of our boat is lost."

But Siddhartha knew what his friend was thinking. He was thinking that the boy would have thrown away or smashed the oar to take revenge and to hinder them in their pursuit. And indeed there was no longer an oar in the boat. Vasudeva pointed to the bottom of the boat and looked at his friend with a smile, as if to say: "Do you not see what your son is trying to tell you? Do you not see that he does not want to be followed?" But he did not say it in words. He got busy fashioning a new oar. But Siddhartha took leave of him in quest of the runaway. Vasudeva did not stop him.

When Siddhartha had already been walking through the forest for some time, the thought occurred to him that his quest was useless. Either (as he thought) the boy was far ahead of him and already in town, or else, if he was still on the way, he would keep out of sight of his pursuer. As his thoughts evolved, he also discovered that he himself was not worried about his son, that he knew deep inside that he had neither perished nor was threatened by danger in the forest. And yet he pushed on without stopping, no longer to rescue him, but

ten, nur aus Verlangen, nur um ihn vielleicht nochmals zu sehen. Und er lief bis vor die Stadt.

Als er nahe bei der Stadt auf die breite Straße gelangte, blieb er stehen, am Eingang des schönen Lustgartens, der einst Kamala gehört hatte, wo er sie einst, in der Sänfte, zum erstenmal gesehen hatte. Das Damalige stand in seiner Seele auf, wieder sah er sich dort stehen, jung, ein bärtiger nackter Samana, das Haar voll Staub. Lange stand Siddhartha und blickte durch das offene Tor in den Garten, Mönche in gelben Kutten sah er unter den schönen Bäumen gehen.

Lange stand er, nachdenkend, Bilder sehend, der Geschichte seines Lebens lauschend. Lange stand er, blickte nach den Mönchen, sah statt ihrer den jungen Siddhartha, sah die junge Kamala unter den hohen Bäumen gehen. Deutlich sah er sich, wie er von Kamala bewirtet ward, wie er ihren ersten Kuß empfing, wie er stolz und verächtlich auf sein Brahmanentum zurückblickte, stolz und verlangend sein Weltleben begann. Er sah Kamaswami, sah die Diener, die Gelage, die Würfelspieler, die Musikanten, sah Kamalas Singvogel im Käfig, lebte dies alles nochmals, atmete Sansara, war nochmals alt und müde, fühlte nochmals den Ekel, fühlte nochmals den Wunsch, sich auszulöschen, genas nochmals am heiligen Om.

Nachdem er lange beim Tor des Gartens gestanden war, sah Siddhartha ein, daß das Verlangen töricht war, das ihn bis zu dieser Stätte getrieben hatte, daß er seinem Sohne nicht helfen konnte, daß er sich nicht an ihn hängen durfte. Tief fühlte er die Liebe zu dem Entflohenen im Herzen, wie eine Wunde, und fühlte zugleich, daß ihm die Wunde nicht gegeben war, um in ihr zu wühlen, daß sie zur Blüte werden und strahlen müsse.

Daß die Wunde zu dieser Stunde noch nicht blühte, noch nicht strahlte, machte ihn traurig. An der Stelle des Wunschzieles, das ihn hierher und dem entflohenen Sohne nachgezogen hatte, stand nun Leere. Traurig setzte er sich nieder, fühlte etwas in seinem Herzen sterben, empfand Leere, sah keine Freude mehr, kein Ziel. Er saß versunken und wartete. Dies hatte er am Flusse gelernt, dies eine: warten, Geduld haben, lauschen. Und er saß und lauschte, im Staub der Straße, lauschte seinem Herzen, wie es müd und traurig ging, wartete auf eine Stimme. Manche Stunde kauerte er lauschend, sah keine Bilder mehr, sank in die Leere, ließ sich sinken, ohne einen Weg zu sehen. Und wenn er die Wunde brennen fühlte, sprach er lautlos das Om, füllte sich mit Om. Die Mönche im Garten sahen ihn, und da er viele Stunden kauerte und auf seinen grauen Haaren der

merely out of longing, merely on the chance of seeing him again. And he proceeded onward into the outskirts of town.

When he came near town on the broad highway, he stopped short, at the entrance to the beautiful pleasure garden that had once belonged to Kamala, where one day he had seen her for the first time, in the sedan chair. The past loomed up in his soul; he saw himself standing there again, young, a bearded, naked samana, his hair full of dust. For a long while Siddhartha stood looking through the open gate into the garden; he saw monks in yellow robes walking beneath the beautiful trees.

For a long while he stood there, reflecting, seeing images, listening to the story of his life. For a long while he stood there, looking at the monks, seeing instead of them the young Siddhartha, seeing the young Kamala walking beneath the tall trees. He saw himself distinctly, being entertained by Kamala, receiving her first kiss, looking back pridefully and contemptuously at his Brahman days, pridefully and longingly beginning his worldly life. He saw Kamaswami, he saw the servants, the banquets, the dice players, the musicians; he saw Kamala's songbird in its cage; he relived all this, he breathed the air of *samsara*; again he was old and tired, again he felt the disgust, again he felt the wish to obliterate himself, again he recovered, thanks to the sacred *om*.

After he had stood for some time at the garden gate, Siddhartha realized that it had been a foolish longing that had driven him to that spot, that he could not help his son, that he ought not to attach himself to him. Deeply he felt love for the runaway in his heart, like a wound, and at the same time he felt that this wound had not been given to him so that he should keep reopening it, but that it must become a blossom and emit radiance.

That at this time the wound was not yet blossoming, not yet radiant, made him sad. In place of the wishful goal that had drawn him here, in pursuit of his runaway son, there was now emptiness. Sadly he sat down; he felt something in his heart dying, he experienced emptiness, he saw no more joy, no further goal. He sat in concentration and waited. This he had learned at the river, this one thing: to wait, to be patient, to listen. And he sat and listened, in the dust of the highway; he listened to his heart beating wearily and sadly, he waited for a voice. For many an hour he crouched there, listening; he saw no more images, he was immersed in emptiness, he let himself sink into it without seeing a way out. And whenever he felt the wound smarting, he silently spoke the *om*, filled himself with *om*. The monks in the garden saw him, and, since he crouched there many hours with the dust

Staub sich sammelte, kam einer gegangen und legte zwei Pisangfrüchte vor ihm nieder. Der Alte sah ihn nicht.

Aus dieser Erstarrung weckte ihn eine Hand, welche seine Schulter
berührte. Alsbald erkannte er diese Berührung, die zarte, schamhafte,
und kam zu sich. Er erhob sich und begrüßte Vasudeva, welcher ihm
nachgegangen war. Und da er in Vasudevas freundliches Gesicht
schaute, in die kleinen, wie mit lauter Lächeln ausgefüllten Falten, in
die heiteren Augen, da lächelte auch er. Er sah nun die Pisangfrüchte
vor sich liegen, hob sie auf, gab eine dem Fährmann, aß selbst die andere. Darauf ging er schweigend mit Vasudeva in den Wald zurück,
kehrte zur Fähre heim. Keiner sprach von dem, was heute geschehen
war, keiner nannte den Namen des Knaben, keiner sprach von seiner
Flucht, keiner sprach von der Wunde. In der Hütte legte sich Siddhartha auf sein Lager, und da nach einer Weile Vasudeva zu ihm trat,
um ihm eine Schale Kokosmilch anzubieten, fand er ihn schon
schlafend.

OM

Lange noch brannte die Wunde. Manchen Reisenden mußte Siddhartha über den Fluß setzen, der einen Sohn oder eine Tochter bei
sich hatte, und keinen von ihnen sah er, ohne daß er ihn beneidete,
ohne daß er dachte: »So viele, so viel Tausende besitzen dies holdeste
Glück – warum ich nicht? Auch böse Menschen, auch Diebe und
Räuber haben Kinder, und lieben sie, und werden von ihnen geliebt,
nur ich nicht.« So einfach, so ohne Verstand dachte er nun, so ähnlich
war er den Kindermenschen geworden.

Anders sah er jetzt die Menschen an als früher, weniger klug,
weniger stolz, dafür wärmer, dafür neugieriger, beteiligter. Wenn er
Reisende der gewöhnlichen Art übersetzte, Kindermenschen, Ge-
schäftsleute, Krieger, Weibervolk, so erschienen diese Leute ihm nicht
fremd wie einst: er verstand sie, er verstand und teilte ihr nicht von
Gedanken und Einsichten, sondern einzig von Trieben und Wünschen
geleitetes Leben, er fühlte sich wie sie. Obwohl er nahe der
Vollendung war, und an seiner letzten Wunde trug, schien ihm doch,
diese Kindermenschen seien seine Brüder, ihre Eitelkeiten, Begehrlichkeiten und Lächerlichkeiten verloren das Lächerliche für ihn,
wurden begreiflich, wurden liebenswert, wurden ihm sogar
verehrungswürdig. Die blinde Liebe einer Mutter zu ihrem Kind, den
dummen, blinden Stolz eines eingebildeten Vaters auf sein einziges

settling on his gray hair, one of them came over and placed two *pisang* fruit on the ground in front of him. The old man did not see him.

He was awakened from that stupor by a hand touching his shoulder. Immediately he recognized that touch, gentle and shy, and came to his senses. He arose and greeted Vasudeva, who had followed him. And when he looked into Vasudeva's friendly face, into the little wrinkles that seemed to be filled with nothing but smiles, into the serene eyes, then he, too, smiled. He now saw the *pisang* fruit lying in front of him, picked them up, gave one to the ferryman, and ate the other one himself. Then he silently went back into the forest with Vasudeva, returning home to the ferry. Neither one mentioned the events of that day, neither one mentioned the boy's name, neither one mentioned his running away, neither one mentioned the wound. In the hut Siddhartha lay down on his bed, and when Vasudeva came up to him a while later to offer him a bowl of coconut milk, he found him already asleep.

OM

The wound still smarted for a long time. Siddhartha had to take across the river many a passenger who had a son or daughter with him, and not one of them did he see whom he did not envy, thinking: "So many people, so many thousands, possess this sweetest happiness—why not I? Even wicked people, even thieves and highwaymen, have children and love them, and are loved by them, only I do not." That was how uncomplicated and unreasoning his thoughts now were; that was how much like the child-people he had become.

He now looked on people differently, not as before but with less cleverness, less pride; instead, he was warmer, more curious, more concerned. When he took passengers of the ordinary sort across the river, child-people, businessmen, soldiers, womenfolk, these people did not seem so foreign to him as in the past: he understood them, he understood and shared their life, guided as it was not by ideas or insights but solely by impulses and desires; he felt he was the same as they. Although he was close to perfection and was suffering from his final wound, he nevertheless felt that these child-people were his brothers; their vanities, desires, and laughable qualities lost their laughable side for him, becoming understandable, becoming lovable, even becoming worthy of respect for him. The blind love of a mother for her child; the foolish, blind pride taken by a conceited father in

Söhnlein, das blinde, wilde Streben nach Schmuck und nach bewundernden Männeraugen bei einem jungen, eitlen Weibe, alle diese Triebe, alle diese Kindereien, alle diese einfachen, törichten, aber ungeheuer starken, stark lebenden, stark sich durchsetzenden Triebe und Begehrlichkeiten waren für Siddhartha jetzt keine Kindereien mehr, er sah um ihretwillen die Menschen leben, sah sie um ihretwillen Unendliches leisten, Reisen tun, Kriege führen, Unendliches leiden, Unendliches ertragen, und er konnte sie dafür lieben, er sah das Leben, das Lebendige, das Unzerstörbare, das Brahman in jeder ihrer Leidenschaften, jeder ihrer Taten. Liebenswert und bewundernswert waren diese Menschen in ihrer blinden Treue, ihrer blinden Stärke und Zähigkeit. Nichts fehlte ihnen, nichts hatte der Wissende und Denker vor ihnen voraus als eine einzige Kleinigkeit, eine einzige winzige kleine Sache: das Bewußtsein, den bewußten Gedanken der Einheit alles Lebens. Und Siddhartha zweifelte sogar zu mancher Stunde, ob dies Wissen, dieser Gedanke so sehr hoch zu werten, ob nicht auch er vielleicht eine Kinderei der Denkmenschen, der Denk-Kindermenschen sein möchte. In allem andern waren die Weltmenschen dem Weisen ebenbürtig, waren ihm oft weit überlegen, wie ja auch Tiere in ihrem zähen, unbeirrten Tun des Notwendigen in manchen Augenblicken den Menschen überlegen scheinen können.

Langsam blühte, langsam reifte in Siddhartha die Erkenntnis, das Wissen darum, was eigentlich Weisheit sei, was seines langen Suchens Ziel sei. Es war nichts als eine Bereitschaft der Seele, eine Fähigkeit, eine geheime Kunst, jeden Augenblick, mitten im Leben, den Gedanken der Einheit denken, die Einheit fühlen und einatmen zu können. Langsam blühte dies in ihm auf, strahlte ihm aus Vasudevas altem Kindergesicht wider: Harmonie, Wissen um die ewige Vollkommenheit der Welt, Lächeln, Einheit.

Die Wunde aber brannte noch, sehnlich und bitter gedachte Siddhartha seines Sohnes, pflegte seine Liebe und Zärtlichkeit im Herzen, ließ den Schmerz an sich fressen, beging alle Torheiten der Liebe. Nicht von selbst erlosch diese Flamme.

Und eines Tages, als die Wunde heftig brannte, fuhr Siddhartha über den Fluß, gejagt von Sehnsucht, stieg aus und war willens, nach der Stadt zu gehen und seinen Sohn zu suchen. Der Fluß floß sanft und leise, es war in der trockenen Jahreszeit, aber seine Stimme klang son-

his only little boy; a vain young woman's blind, wild striving for jewelry and men's admiring eyes; all these impulses, all these childish actions, all these simple, foolish, but enormously strong impulses and desires—powerfully alive, powerfully forcing their way to fruition—were now for Siddhartha no longer childish actions;[14] he saw that people lived for their sake; for their sake he saw them accomplishing an infinity of things, traveling, waging war, suffering infinitely, enduring infinite burdens; and he was able to love them for that; he saw life, vitality, the indestructible, *Brahman,* in each of their passions, each of their deeds. These people were lovable and admirable in their blind loyalty, their blind strength and tenacity. They lacked nothing; the scholarly thinker was only superior to them in one detail, in one tiny way: he possessed the awareness, the conscious idea, of the oneness of all life. And at many times Siddhartha even doubted whether that knowledge, that idea, should be so highly valued, whether it, too, might not perhaps be a childish quality of thinking people, of the thinkers among the child-people. In every other way, worldly people were the equals of the sage, and were often far superior to him, just as animals in their dogged, relentless performance of necessary actions can at many moments appear to be superior to man.

Gradually there blossomed, gradually there ripened within Siddhartha the realization, the knowledge, of what wisdom really was, what the goal of his long quest was. It was nothing but a preparedness of the soul, a capability, a secret art of conceiving the idea of oneness at every moment, in the midst of life's activities: the ability to feel and absorb oneness. This blossomed within him slowly; he saw it reflected in Vasudeva's aged child's face: harmony, knowledge of the eternal perfection of the world, a smile, oneness.

But the wound still smarted; Siddhartha recalled his son yearningly and bitterly; he nurtured his love and tenderness in his heart; he allowed the pain to gnaw at him; he committed all the follies of love. This flame would not go out by itself.

And one day, when the wound was smarting violently, Siddhartha rowed across the river, hounded by longing; he stepped out of the boat, intending to go to town and look for his son. The river was flowing gently and quietly, it was in the dry season, but its voice had

---

[14] Hesse obviously rethought this sentence in midstream, leaving it grammatically incorrect in German: the nouns in the accusative (direct object) case at the beginning of the sentence turn out, after all the detours, to be the subject of the main verb!

derbar: sie lachte! Sie lachte deutlich. Der Fluß lachte, er lachte hell
und klar den alten Fährmann aus. Siddhartha blieb stehen, er beugte
sich übers Wasser, um noch besser zu hören, und im still ziehenden
Wasser sah er sein Gesicht gespiegelt, und in diesem gespiegelten
Gesicht war etwas, das ihn erinnerte, etwas Vergessenes, und da er sich
besann, fand er es: dies Gesicht glich einem andern, das er einst
gekannt und geliebt und auch gefürchtet hatte. Es glich dem Gesicht
seines Vaters, des Brahmanen. Und er erinnerte sich, wie er vor Zeiten,
ein Jüngling, seinen Vater gezwungen hatte, ihn zu den Büßern gehen
zu lassen, wie er Abschied von ihm genommen hatte, wie er gegangen
und nie mehr wiedergekommen war. Hatte nicht auch sein Vater um
ihn dasselbe Leid gelitten, wie er es nun um seinen Sohn litt? War nicht
sein Vater längst gestorben, allein, ohne seinen Sohn wiedergesehen zu
haben? Mußte er selbst nicht dies selbe Schicksal erwarten? War es
nicht eine Komödie, eine seltsame und dumme Sache, diese Wieder-
holung, dieses Laufen in einem verhängnisvollen Kreise?

Der Fluß lachte. Ja, es war so, es kam alles wieder, was nicht bis zu
Ende gelitten und gelöst ward, es wurden immer wieder dieselben
Leiden gelitten. Siddhartha aber stieg wieder in das Boot und fuhr zu
der Hütte zurück, seines Vaters gedenkend, seines Sohnes gedenkend, vom Flusse verlacht, mit sich selbst im Streit, geneigt zur
Verzweiflung, und nicht minder geneigt, über sich und die ganze Welt
laut mitzulachen. Ach, noch blühte die Wunde nicht, noch wehrte
sein Herz sich wider das Schicksal, noch strahlte nicht Heiterkeit und
Sieg aus seinem Leide. Doch fühlte er Hoffnung, und da er zur Hütte
zurückgekehrt war, spürte er ein unbesiegbares Verlangen, sich vor
Vasudeva zu öffnen, ihm alles zu zeigen, ihm, dem Meister des Zu-
hörens, alles zu sagen.

Vasudeva saß in der Hütte und flocht an einem Korbe. Er fuhr
nicht mehr mit dem Fährboot, seine Augen begannen schwach zu
werden, und nicht nur seine Augen, auch seine Arme und Hände.
Unverändert und blühend war nur die Freude und das heitere
Wohlwollen seines Gesichtes.

Siddhartha setzte sich zu dem Greise, langsam begann er zu
sprechen. Worüber sie niemals gesprochen hatten, davon erzählte er
jetzt, von seinem Gange zur Stadt, damals, von der brennenden
Wunde, von seinem Neid beim Anblick glücklicher Väter, von seinem
Wissen um die Torheit solcher Wünsche, von seinem vergeblichen
Kampf wider sie. Alles berichtete er, alles konnte er sagen, auch das
Peinlichste, alles ließ sich sagen, alles sich zeigen, alles konnte er
erzählen. Er zeigte seine Wunde dar, erzählte auch seine heutige

a peculiar sound: it was laughing! It was definitely laughing. The river was laughing; brightly and clearly it was laughing at the old ferryman. Siddhartha stood still, he bent over the water to hear it even better, and in the calmly moving water he saw his face reflected, and in that reflected face was something that jogged his memory, something forgotten; when he thought about it, he discovered what it was: that face resembled another that he had once known and loved and also feared. It resembled the face of his father, the Brahman. And he recollected how, long ago, as a youth, he had compelled his father to let him join the penitents, how he had taken leave of him, how he had left and never returned. Had not his father suffered the same sorrow over him that he was now suffering over his son? Had not his father died long ago, alone, without ever seeing his son again? Did not he, too, have to expect that same destiny? Was it not a comedy, a strange and stupid thing, this repetition, this running around in a disastrous circle?

The river was laughing. Yes, it was so, everything returned that had not been suffered through and untangled to the very end; the same sorrows were suffered over and over again. But Siddhartha stepped back into the boat and rowed back to the hut, recalling his father, recalling his son, laughed at by the river, at strife with himself, inclined toward despair, but no less inclined to laugh along at himself and the whole world. Ah, the wound had not yet become a blossom, his heart still resisted its fate, serenity and victory were not yet radiating from his sorrow. But he felt hope, and when he had reached the hut again, he sensed an unconquerable desire to bare his mind to Vasudeva, to show him everything, to tell all to him, that master of listening.

Vasudeva was sitting in the hut weaving a basket. He no longer went out with the ferryboat; his eyes were beginning to get weak, and not only his eyes but his arms and hands, as well. Only the joy and serene benevolence of his face were unchanged and blossoming.

Siddhartha sat down beside the old man; slowly he began to speak. He now told of things they had never discussed, his journey to town on that occasion, his smarting wound, his envy at the sight of happy fathers, his knowledge that such wishes were foolish, his futile struggle against them. He recounted everything, he was able to tell it all, even the most painful details, it became possible to say and show it all, he was able to relate it all. He openly displayed his wound, he recounted his escape of that day as well, how he had rowed across the

Flucht, wie er übers Wasser gefahren sei, kindischer Flüchtling, willens nach der Stadt zu wandern, wie der Fluß gelacht habe.

Während er sprach, lange sprach, während Vasudeva mit stillem Gesicht lauschte, empfand Siddhartha dies Zuhören Vasudevas stärker, als er es jemals gefühlt hatte, er spürte, wie seine Schmerzen, seine Beängstigungen hinüberflossen, wie seine heimliche Hoffnung hinüberfloß, ihm von drüben wieder entgegenkam. Diesem Zuhörer seine Wunde zu zeigen, war dasselbe wie sie im Flusse baden, bis sie kühl und mit dem Flusse eins wurde. Während er immer noch sprach, immer noch bekannte und beichtete, fühlte Siddhartha mehr und mehr, daß dies nicht mehr Vasudeva, nicht mehr ein Mensch war, der ihm zuhörte, daß dieser regungslos Lauschende seine Beichte in sich einsog wie ein Baum den Regen, daß dieser Regungslose der Fluß selbst, daß er Gott selbst, daß er das Ewige selbst war. Und während Siddhartha aufhörte, an sich und an seine Wunde zu denken, nahm diese Erkenntnis vom veränderten Wesen des Vasudeva von ihm Besitz, und je mehr er es empfand und darein eindrang, desto weniger wunderlich wurde es, desto mehr sah er ein, daß alles in Ordnung und natürlich war, daß Vasudeva schon lange, beinahe schon immer so gewesen sei, daß nur er selbst es nicht ganz erkannt hatte, ja daß er selbst von jenem kaum noch verschieden sei. Er empfand, daß er den alten Vasudeva nun so sehe, wie das Volk die Götter sieht, und daß dies nicht von Dauer sein könne; er begann im Herzen von Vasudeva Abschied zu nehmen. Dabei sprach er immerfort.

Als er zu Ende gesprochen hatte, richtete Vasudeva seinen freundlichen, etwas schwach gewordenen Blick auf ihn, sprach nicht, strahlte ihm schweigend Liebe und Heiterkeit entgegen, Verständnis und Wissen. Er nahm Siddharthas Hand, führte ihn zum Sitz am Ufer, setzte sich mit ihm nieder, lächelte dem Flusse zu.

»Du hast ihn lachen hören«, sagte er. »Aber du hast nicht alles gehört. Laß uns lauschen, du wirst mehr hören.«

Sie lauschten. Sanft klang der vielstimmige Gesang des Flusses. Siddhartha schaute ins Wasser, und im ziehenden Wasser erschienen ihm Bilder: sein Vater erschien, einsam, um den Sohn trauernd, er selbst erschien, einsam, auch er mit den Banden der Sehnsucht an den fernen Sohn gebunden; es erschien sein Sohn, einsam auch er, der Knabe, begehrlich auf der brennenden Bahn seiner jungen Wünsche stürmend, jeder auf sein Ziel gerichtet, jeder vom Ziel besessen, jeder leidend. Der Fluß sang mit einer Stimme des Leidens, sehnlich sang er, sehnlich floß er seinem Ziele zu, klagend klang seine Stimme.

river like a child running away, intending to walk to town, and how the
river had laughed.

While he spoke, spoke for a long while, while Vasudeva listened
with a calm face, Siddhartha perceived this listening of Vasudeva's
more strongly than ever before; he sensed how his pains and anxieties
flowed across, how his secret hope flowed across, and returned to
him from the other side. To show this listener his wound was the
same as bathing it in the river until it became cool and at one with
the river. While he still went on speaking, still went on making ad-
missions and making confession, Siddhartha felt more and more that
it was no longer Vasudeva, no longer a human being, who was listening to him; that this motionless listener was absorbing his confession
as a tree absorbs rain; that this motionless one was the river itself,
God Himself, the Eternal itself. And while Siddhartha ceased to
think about himself and his wound, this realization of Vasudeva's altered state took possession of him; and the more he felt and penetrated this, the less strange it became and the more he saw that
everything was in order and natural, that Vasudeva had been so for
some time now, almost always, but that he himself had not altogether
realized it; in fact, he saw that he himself was just barely different
from Vasudeva. He perceived that he now saw old Vasudeva the way
the common people see the gods, and that this could not last; he
began to take leave of Vasudeva in his heart. And all this while he
went on speaking.

When he had talked himself out, Vasudeva turned his friendly,
somewhat weakened eyes toward him; he did not speak, but silently
radiated love and serenity in his direction, understanding and knowledge. He took Siddhartha's hand, led him to the seat by the riverbank,
sat down with him, and smiled at the river.

"You have heard it laugh," he said. "But you have not heard everything. Let us listen, you will hear more."

They listened. The many-voiced song of the river resounded gently.
Siddhartha looked into the water, and in the moving water images appeared to him: his father appeared, lonely, lamenting for his son; he
himself appeared, lonely, he, too, bound to his faraway son with the
bonds of longing, his son appeared—he, too, the boy, lonely—raging
with desire on the fiery path of his youthful wishes. Each one had his
eyes on his own goal, each one was obsessed with the goal, each one
was suffering. The river sang with a voice of suffering, it sang yearningly, it flowed toward its goal longingly, its voice had a lamenting
sound.

»Hörst du?« fragte Vasudevas stummer Blick. Siddhartha nickte.

»Höre besser!« flüsterte Vasudeva.

Siddhartha bemühte sich, besser zu hören. Das Bild des Vaters, sein eigenes Bild, das Bild des Sohnes flossen ineinander, auch Kamalas Bild erschien und zerfloß, und das Bild Govindas, und andere Bilder, und flossen ineinander über, wurden alle zum Fluß, strebten alle als Fluß dem Ziele zu, sehnlich, begehrend, leidend, und des Flusses Stimme klang voll Sehnsucht, voll von brennendem Weh, voll von unstillbarem Verlangen. Zum Ziele strebte der Fluß, Siddhartha sah ihn eilen, den Fluß, der aus ihm und den Seinen und aus allen Menschen bestand, die er je gesehen hatte, alle die Wellen und Wasser eilten, leidend, Zielen zu, vielen Zielen, dem Wasserfall, dem See, der Stromschnelle, dem Meere, und alle Ziele wurden erreicht, und jedem folgte ein neues, und aus dem Wasser ward Dampf und stieg in den Himmel, ward Regen und stürzte aus dem Himmel herab, ward Quelle, ward Bach, ward Fluß, strebte aufs neue, floß aufs neue. Aber die sehnliche Stimme hatte sich verändert. Noch tönte sie, leidvoll, suchend, aber andre Stimmen gesellten sich zu ihr, Stimmen der Freude und des Leides, gute und böse Stimmen, lachende und trauernde, hundert Stimmen, tausend Stimmen.

Siddhartha lauschte. Er war nun ganz Lauscher, ganz ins Zuhören vertieft, ganz leer, ganz einsaugend, er fühlte, daß er nun das Lauschen zu Ende gelernt habe. Oft schon hatte er all dies gehört, diese vielen Stimmen im Fluß, heute klang es neu. Schon konnte er die vielen Stimmen nicht mehr unterscheiden, nicht frohe von weinenden, nicht kindliche von männlichen, sie gehörten alle zusammen, Klage der Sehnsucht und Lachen des Wissenden, Schrei des Zorns und Stöhnen der Sterbenden, alles war eins, alles war ineinander verwoben und verknüpft, tausendfach verschlungen. Und alles zusammen, alle Stimmen, alle Ziele, alles Sehnen, alle Leiden, alle Lust, alles Gute und Böse, alles zusammen war die Welt. Alles zusammen war der Fluß des Geschehens, war die Musik des Lebens. Und wenn Siddhartha aufmerksam diesem Fluß, diesem tausendstimmigen Liede lauschte, wenn er nicht auf das Leid noch auf das Lachen hörte, wenn er seine Seele nicht an irgendeine Stimme band und mit seinem Ich in sie einging, sondern alle hörte, das Ganze, die Einheit vernahm, dann bestand das große Lied der tausend Stimmen aus einem einzigen Worte, das hieß Om: die Vollendung.

»Hörst du?« fragte wieder Vasudevas Blick.

Hell glänzte Vasudevas Lächeln, über all den Runzeln seines alten Antlitzes schwebte es leuchtend, wie über all den Stimmen des

"Do you hear?" asked Vasudeva's silent eyes. Siddhartha nodded.

"Listen harder!" Vasudeva whispered.

Siddhartha strove to listen harder. His father's image, his own image, his son's image, dissolved into one another; Kamala's image, too, appeared and dissolved, and Govinda's image, and other images, and overflowed into one another; they all became part of the river, as river they all pressed toward their goal, yearningly, greedily, in suffering; and the river's voice was full of longing, full of smarting pain, full of unquenchable desire. The river pressed toward its goal, Siddhartha saw it hastening, that river composed of himself and his loved ones and all the people he had ever seen; all the waves and waters hastened in their suffering toward goals, many goals, the waterfall, the lake, the rapids, the sea; and all the goals were attained, and each was followed by a new one; and the water turned into vapor and rose into the sky, it turned into rain and poured down from the sky; it turned into a fountain, into a brook, into a river; it pressed onward again, it flowed again. But the yearning voice had changed. It was still resounding, full of sorrow, searchingly, but other voices were joining it, voices of joy and sorrow, good and evil voices, laughing and mournful ones, a hundred voices, a thousand voices.

Siddhartha listened. He was now all ears, completely absorbed in his listening, completely empty, completely receptive; he felt that he had now learned all that there was to learn about listening. He had often heard all this before, these many voices in the river, but today it sounded new. By this time he could no longer distinguish the many voices, could not tell the gleeful ones from the weeping ones, the children's voices from the grown men's; they all belonged together, the lament of longing and the knowing man's laughter, the cry of anger and the moans of the dying; it was all one, it was all interwoven and knotted together, interconnected in a thousand ways. And all of this together, all the voices, all the goals, all the longing, all the suffering, all the pleasure, all the good and evil, all of this together was the world. All of this together was the river of events, the music of life. And whenever Siddhartha listened attentively to that river, that song of a thousand voices, when he listened neither to the sorrow nor the laughter, when he tied his soul not to any individual voice, entering into it with his self, but instead heard them all, perceiving the totality, the oneness, then the great song of a thousand voices consisted of a single word, which was *om*, the absolute.

"Do you hear?" Vasudeva's eyes asked again.

Vasudeva's smile beamed brightly, a glow hovered over every wrinkle in his aged face, just as the *om* hovered over all the river's voices.

Flusses das Om schwebte. Hell glänzte sein Lächeln, als er den Freund anblickte, und hell glänzte nun auch auf Siddharthas Gesicht dasselbe Lächeln auf. Seine Wunde blühte, sein Leid strahlte, sein Ich war in die Einheit geflossen.

In dieser Stunde hörte Siddhartha auf, mit dem Schicksal zu kämpfen, hörte auf zu leiden. Auf seinem Gesicht blühte die Heiterkeit des Wissens, dem kein Wille mehr entgegensteht, das die Vollendung kennt, das einverstanden ist mit dem Fluß des Geschehens, mit dem Strom des Lebens, voll Mitleid, voll Mitlust, dem Strömen hingegeben, der Einheit zugehörig.

Als Vasudeva sich von dem Sitz am Ufer erhob, als er in Siddharthas Augen blickte und die Heiterkeit des Wissens darin strahlen sah, berührte er dessen Schulter leise mit der Hand, in seiner behutsamen und zarten Weise, und sagte: »Ich habe auf diese Stunde gewartet, Lieber. Nun sie gekommen ist, laß mich gehen. Lange habe ich auf diese Stunde gewartet, lange bin ich der Fährmann Vasudeva gewesen. Nun ist es genug. Lebe wohl, Hütte, lebe wohl, Fluß, lebe wohl, Siddhartha!«

Siddhartha verneigte sich tief vor dem Abschiednehmenden.

»Ich habe es gewußt«, sagte er leise. »Du wirst in die Wälder gehen?«

»Ich gehe in die Wälder, ich gehe in die Einheit«, sprach Vasudeva strahlend.

Strahlend ging er hinweg; Siddhartha blickte ihm nach. Mit tiefer Freude, mit tiefem Ernst blickte er ihm nach, sah seine Schritte voll Frieden, sah sein Haupt voll Glanz, sah seine Gestalt voll Licht.

GOVINDA

Mit anderen Mönchen weilte Govinda einst während einer Rastzeit in dem Lusthain, welchen die Kurtisane Kamala den Jüngern des Gotama geschenkt hatte. Er hörte von einem alten Fährmanne sprechen, welcher eine Tagereise entfernt am Flusse wohne, und der von vielen für einen Weisen gehalten werde. Als Govinda des Weges weiterzog, wählte er den Weg zur Fähre, begierig, diesen Fährmann zu sehen. Denn ob er wohl sein Leben lang nach der Regel gelebt hatte, auch von den jüngeren Mönchen seines Alters und seiner Bescheidenheit wegen mit Ehrfurcht angesehen wurde, war doch in seinem Herzen die Unruhe und das Suchen nicht erloschen.

Er kam zum Flusse, er bat den Alten um Überfahrt, und da sie drüben aus dem Boot stiegen, sagte er zum Alten: »Viel Gutes erweisest du uns Mönchen und Pilgern, viele von uns hast du schon

His smile beamed brightly as he looked at his friend, and now the same smile began to beam brightly on Siddhartha's face, too. His wound was blossoming, his sorrow was emitting rays, his self had flowed into the oneness.

In that hour Siddhartha ceased to struggle with his destiny, he ceased to suffer. On his face there blossomed the serenity of a knowledge that was no longer opposed by his will, a knowledge that knew perfection, that was in accord with the river of events, with the current of life, full of sympathy, full of shared pleasure, yielding to the current, part of the oneness.

When Vasudeva rose from the seat by the riverbank, when he looked into Siddhartha's eyes and saw the serenity of knowledge shining in them, he softly touched his shoulder with his hand, in his careful and gentle way, and said: "I have waited for this hour, dear friend. Now that it has come, let me depart. Long have I awaited this hour, long have I been the ferryman Vasudeva. Now it is enough. Farewell, hut; farewell, river; farewell, Siddhartha!"

Siddhartha made a low bow to the departing one.

"I knew it," he said quietly. "Will you go into the forests?"

"I go into the forests, I go into oneness," said Vasudeva radiantly.

Radiantly he made his departure; Siddhartha watched him go. With profound joy, with profound gravity, he watched him go, seeing his steps full of peace, seeing his head full of brightness, seeing his figure full of light.

GOVINDA

On one occasion, during a period of rest, Govinda was dwelling with other monks in the pleasure grove that the courtesan Kamala had given to Gotama's disciples. He heard reports about an old ferryman who lived a day's journey away by the river and whom many people regarded as a sage. When Govinda continued his journey, he chose the path to the ferry, desirous of seeing that ferryman. For, even though he had lived by the Buddhist rules all his life and was looked on with respect by the younger monks because of his age and his modesty, nevertheless the restlessness and seeking had never been extinguished in his heart.

He came to the river, he asked the old man to take him across, and when they were getting out of the boat on the other side, he said to the old man: "You are a great benefactor to us monks and pilgrims,

übergesetzt. Bist nicht auch du, Fährmann, ein Sucher nach dem rechten Pfade?«

Sprach Siddhartha, aus den alten Augen lächelnd: »Nennst du dich einen Sucher, o Ehrwürdiger, und bist doch schon hoch in den Jahren und trägst das Gewand der Mönche Gotamas?«

»Wohl bin ich alt«, sprach Govinda, »zu suchen aber habe ich nicht aufgehört. Nie werde ich aufhören zu suchen, dies scheint meine Bestimmung. Auch du, so scheint es mir, hast gesucht. Willst du mir ein Wort sagen, Verehrter?«

Sprach Siddhartha: »Was sollte ich dir, Ehrwürdiger, wohl zu sagen haben? Vielleicht das, daß du allzuviel suchst? Daß du vor Suchen nicht zum Finden kommst?«

»Wie denn?« fragte Govinda.

»Wenn jemand sucht«, sagte Siddhartha, »dann geschieht es leicht, daß sein Auge nur noch das Ding sieht, das er sucht, daß er nichts zu finden, nichts in sich einzulassen vermag, weil er nur immer an das Gesuchte denkt, weil er ein Ziel hat, weil er vom Ziel besessen ist. Suchen heißt: ein Ziel haben. Finden aber heißt: frei sein, offen stehen, kein Ziel haben. Du, Ehrwürdiger, bist vielleicht in der Tat ein Sucher, denn, deinem Ziel nachstrebend, siehst du manches nicht, was nah vor deinen Augen steht.«

»Noch verstehe ich nicht ganz«, bat Govinda, »wie meinst du das?«

Sprach Siddhartha: »Einst, o Ehrwürdiger, vor manchen Jahren, bist du schon einmal an diesem Flusse gewesen, und hast am Fluß einen Schlafenden gefunden, und hast dich zu ihm gesetzt, um seinen Schlaf zu behüten. Erkannt aber, o Govinda, hast du den Schlafenden nicht.«

Staunend, wie ein Bezauberter, blickte der Mönch in des Fährmanns Augen.

»Bist du Siddhartha?« fragte er mit scheuer Stimme. »Ich hätte dich auch dieses Mal nicht erkannt! Herzlich grüße ich dich, Siddhartha, herzlich freue ich mich, dich nochmals zu sehen! Du hast dich sehr verändert, Freund. – Und nun bist du also ein Fährmann geworden?«

Freundlich lachte Siddhartha. »Ein Fährmann, ja. Manche, Govinda, müssen sich viel verändern, müssen allerlei Gewand tragen, ihrer einer bin ich, Lieber. Sei willkommen, Govinda, und bleibe die Nacht in meiner Hütte.«

Govinda blieb die Nacht in der Hütte und schlief auf dem Lager, das einst Vasudevas Lager gewesen war. Viele Fragen richtete er an den Freund seiner Jugend, vieles mußte ihm Siddhartha aus seinem Leben erzählen.

you have already taken many of us across the river. Are not you, too, ferryman, one who seeks after the true path?"

Siddhartha said, with a smile in his old eyes: "Do you call yourself one who seeks, O venerable one, although you are already well advanced in years and you wear the robe of Gotama's monks?"

"To be sure, I am old," said Govinda, "but I have never ceased to seek. I shall never cease to seek; that seems to be my destiny. You, too, I believe, have sought. Will you tell me anything about it, honored sir?"

Siddhartha said: "What could I possibly have to tell you, venerable one? Perhaps that you are doing too much seeking? That your seeking prevents you from finding?"

"How is that?" Govinda asked.

"When someone seeks," Siddhartha said, "it is all too easy for his eyes to see nothing but the thing he seeks, so that he is unable to find anything or absorb anything because he is always thinking exclusively about what he seeks, because he has a goal, because he is obsessed by that goal. Seeking means having a goal. But finding means being free, remaining accessible, having no goal. You, venerable one, are perhaps really one who seeks, because, pressing after your goal, you fail to see many a thing that is right before your eyes."

"I still do not understand completely," said Govinda, and asked: "How do you mean that?"

Siddhartha said: "Once before, O venerable one, many years ago, you were at this river, and by the river you found a man asleep and sat down near him to guard him while he slept. But, O Govinda, you did not recognize the sleeper."

Astonished, like a man under a spell, the monk looked into the ferryman's eyes.

"Are you Siddhartha?" he asked timidly. "I would not have recognized you this time, either! I greet you warmly, Siddhartha; I am sincerely glad to see you again. You have changed a great deal, friend.— And so you have now become a ferryman?"

Siddhartha gave a friendly laugh. "A ferryman, yes. Govinda, many people must change a great deal and must wear all sorts of garments; I am one of those, my dear friend. Welcome, Govinda, please spend the night in my hut."

Govinda spent the night in the hut, sleeping on the bed that had once been Vasudeva's bed. He asked many questions of the friend of his youth; Siddhartha had to tell him many events of his life.

Als es am andern Morgen Zeit war, die Tageswanderung anzutreten, da sagte Govinda, nicht ohne Zögern, die Worte:»Ehe ich meinen Weg fortsetze, Siddhartha, erlaube mir noch eine Frage. Hast du eine Lehre? Hast du einen Glauben oder ein Wissen, dem du folgst, das dir leben und rechttun hilft?«

Sprach Siddhartha:»Du weißt, Lieber, daß ich schon als junger Mann, damals, als wir bei den Büßern im Walde lebten, dazu kam, den Lehren und Lehrern zu mißtrauen und ihnen den Rücken zu wenden. Ich bin dabei geblieben. Dennoch habe ich seither viele Lehrer gehabt. Eine schöne Kurtisane ist lange Zeit meine Lehrerin gewesen, und ein reicher Kaufmann war mein Lehrer, und einige Würfelspieler. Einmal ist auch ein wandernder Jünger Buddhas mein Lehrer gewesen; er saß bei mir, als ich im Walde eingeschlafen war, auf der Pilgerschaft. Auch von ihm habe ich gelernt, auch ihm bin ich dankbar, sehr dankbar. Am meisten aber habe ich hier von diesem Flusse gelernt, und von meinem Vorgänger, dem Fährmann Vasudeva. Er war ein sehr einfacher Mensch, Vasudeva, er war kein Denker, aber er wußte das Notwendige, so gut wie Gotama, er war ein Vollkommener, ein Heiliger.«

Govinda sagte:»Noch immer, o Siddhartha, liebst du ein wenig den Spott, wie mir scheint. Ich glaube dir und weiß es, daß du nicht einem Lehrer gefolgt bist. Aber hast nicht du selbst, wenn auch nicht eine Lehre, so doch gewisse Gedanken, gewisse Erkenntnisse gefunden, welche dein eigen sind und die dir leben helfen? Wenn du mir von diesen etwas sagen möchtest, würdest du mir das Herz erfreuen.«

Sprach Siddhartha:»Ich habe Gedanken gehabt, ja, und Erkenntnisse, je und je. Ich habe manchmal, für eine Stunde oder für einen Tag, Wissen in mir gefühlt, so wie man Leben in seinem Herzen fühlt. Manche Gedanken waren es, aber schwer wäre es für mich, sie dir mitzuteilen. Sieh, mein Govinda, dies ist einer meiner Gedanken, die ich gefunden habe: Weisheit ist nicht mitteilbar. Weisheit, welche ein Weiser mitzuteilen versucht, klingt immer wie Narrheit.«

»Scherzest du?« fragte Govinda.

»Ich scherze nicht. Ich sage, was ich gefunden habe. Wissen kann man mitteilen, Weisheit aber nicht. Man kann sie finden, man kann sie leben, man kann von ihr getragen werden, man kann mit ihr Wunder tun, aber sagen und lehren kann man sie nicht. Dies war es, was ich schon als Jüngling manchmal ahnte, was mich von den Lehrern fortgetrieben hat. Ich habe einen Gedanken gefunden, Govinda, den du wieder für Scherz oder für Narrheit halten wirst, der aber mein bester Gedanke ist. Er heißt: von jeder Wahrheit ist das

On the following morning, when it was time to set out on his day's journey, Govinda said, not without hesitation: "Before I continue my travels, Siddhartha, permit me one more question. Do you have a doctrine? Do you have a faith or a body of knowledge that you follow, that helps you live and act properly?"

Siddhartha said: "You know, my dear friend, that even as a young man, at the time when we were living with the penitents in the forest, I arrived at the point of distrusting teachings and teachers, and of turning my back on them. I have retained that attitude. And yet, since then I have had many teachers. For a long time a beautiful courtesan was my teacher, and a wealthy merchant was my teacher, and a few dice players. Once, a wandering disciple of the Buddha was also my teacher; he sat with me when I had fallen asleep in the forest, in the course of wandering. I learned from him, too; I am grateful to him, too, very grateful. But I have learned the most here, from this river and from my predecessor, the ferryman Vasudeva. He was a very simple man, was Vasudeva; he was no thinker, but he knew what was necessary as well as Gotama did; he was a perfected man, a saint."

Govinda said: "O Siddhartha, it seems to me you still enjoy making a little fun of people. I believe you and I know that you did not follow any particular teacher. But have you not yourself found, even if not a doctrine, then at least certain ideas, certain realizations, that are your own and help you to live? If you wished to tell me anything about them, you would gladden my heart."

Siddhartha said: "Yes, I have had ideas and realizations, from time to time. On occasions, for an hour or for a day, I have felt knowledge in myself, just as a man feels life in his heart. Those thoughts were numerous, but it would be hard for me to communicate them to you. Look, my dear Govinda, here is one of the thoughts I discovered: Wisdom cannot be imparted. Wisdom that a wise man attempts to impart always sounds like foolishness."

"Are you joking?" Govinda asked.

"I am not joking. I am telling you what I discovered. Knowledge can be imparted, but not wisdom. You can discover it, it can guide your life, it can bear you up, you can do miracles with it, but you cannot tell it or teach it. This was what I had several premonitions of, even as a youngster; it was this that drove me away from teachers. I have discovered an idea, Govinda, which you will once again consider to be a joke or foolishness, but which is my best idea. Namely: the opposite of every truth is equally true! What I mean is:

Gegenteil ebenso wahr! Nämlich so: eine Wahrheit läßt sich immer nur aussprechen und in Worte hüllen, wenn sie einseitig ist. Einseitig ist alles, was mit Gedanken gedacht und mit Worten gesagt werden kann, alles einseitig, alles halb, alles entbehrt der Ganzheit, des Runden, der Einheit. Wenn der erhabene Gotama lehrend von der Welt sprach, so mußte er sie teilen in Sansara und Nirwana, in Täuschung und Wahrheit, in Leid und Erlösung. Man kann nicht anders, es gibt keinen andern Weg für den, der lehren will. Die Welt selbst aber, das Seiende um uns her und in uns innen, ist nie einseitig. Nie ist ein Mensch oder eine Tat, ganz Sansara oder ganz Nirwana, nie ist ein Mensch ganz heilig oder ganz sündig. Es scheint ja so, weil wir der Täuschung unterworfen sind, daß Zeit etwas Wirkliches sei. Zeit ist nicht wirklich, Govinda, ich habe dies oft und oft erfahren. Und wenn Zeit nicht wirklich ist, so ist die Spanne, die zwischen Welt und Ewigkeit, zwischen Leid und Seligkeit, zwischen Böse und Gut zu liegen scheint, auch eine Täuschung.«

»Wie das?« fragte Govinda ängstlich.

»Höre gut, Lieber, höre gut! Der Sünder, der ich bin und der du bist, der ist Sünder, aber er wird einst wieder Brahma sein, er wird einst Nirwana erreichen, wird Buddha sein – und nun siehe: dies ›Einst‹ ist Täuschung, ist nur Gleichnis! Der Sünder ist nicht auf dem Weg zur Buddhaschaft unterwegs, er ist nicht in einer Entwicklung begriffen, obwohl unser Denken sich die Dinge nicht anders vorzustellen weiß. Nein, in dem Sünder ist, ist jetzt und heute schon der künftige Buddha, seine Zukunft ist alle schon da, du hast in ihm, in dir, in jedem den werdenden, den möglichen, den verborgenen Buddha zu verehren. Die Welt, Freund Govinda, ist nicht unvollkommen, oder auf einem langsamen Wege zur Vollkommenheit begriffen: nein, sie ist in jedem Augenblick vollkommen, alle Sünde trägt schon die Gnade in sich, alle kleinen Kinder haben schon den Greis in sich, alle Säuglinge den Tod, alle Sterbenden das ewige Leben. Es ist keinem Menschen möglich, vom anderen zu sehen, wie weit ⎪er auf seinem Wege sei, im Räuber und Würfelspieler wartet Buddha, im Brahmanen wartet der Räuber. Es gibt in der tiefen Meditation die Möglichkeit, die Zeit aufzuheben, alles gewesene, seiende und sein werdende Leben als gleichzeitig zu sehen, und da ist alles gut, alles vollkommen, alles ist Brahman. Darum scheint mir das, was ist, gut, es scheint mir Tod wie Leben, Sünde wie Heiligkeit, Klugheit wie Torheit, alles muß so sein, alles bedarf nur meiner Zustimmung, nur meiner Willigkeit, meines liebenden Einverständnisses, so ist es für mich gut, kann mir nie schaden. Ich habe an meinem

without fail, a truth can only be uttered and clothed in words if it is one-sided. Everything is one-sided if the mind can conceive it and words can express it; all of that is one-sided, all of that is a half-truth, all of that lacks completeness, roundedness, oneness. Whenever the sublime Gotama spoke about the world in his sermons, he had to divide it into *samsara* and *nirvana,* into illusion and truth, into suffering and salvation. You have no alternative, there is no other method for a man who wants to teach. But the world itself, what exists around us and inside us, is never one-sided. A person or an action is never totally *samsara* or totally *nirvana;* a person is never totally saintly or totally sinful. Because we are subject to illusion, it does actually look as if time were something real. Time is not real, Govinda; I have learned that over and over again. And, if time is not real, the span that seems to exist between world and eternity, between sorrow and bliss, between evil and good, is also an illusion."

"How so?" Govinda asked nervously.

"Pay close attention, dear friend, pay close attention! A sinner, such as you and I are, is a sinner, but some day he will be Brahma again, some day he will attain *nirvana,* he will be a Buddha—and now see: that 'some day' is an illusion, it is only a metaphor! The sinner is not journeying toward Buddhahood, he is not caught up in an evolution, even though our thought processes are unable to imagine things differently. No, the sinner contains the future Buddha, now and today he already is that Buddha; his future is already completely there; you must revere the becoming, the possible, the concealed Buddha in him, in yourself, in everyone. The world, friend Govinda, is not imperfect or on a slow journey toward perfection; no, it is perfect at every moment; all sin already bears its forgiveness within itself; every little boy already bears the old man within himself, every infant bears death, every dying man bears eternal life. No one is able to look at someone else and know how far along on his journey he is; in the highwayman and dice player lurks a Buddha, in the Brahman lurks the highwayman. In profound meditation there is the possibility of abolishing time, of seeing all past, present, and future life as being simultaneous; and there everything is good, everything is perfect, everything is *Brahman.* Therefore, whatever exists seems good to me; death is like life to me, sin like sanctity, cleverness like folly; everything must be as it is; everything needs only my consent, my willingness, my loving comprehension, and then it is good in my eyes, and can never harm

Leibe und an meiner Seele erfahren, daß ich der Sünde sehr bedurfte, ich bedurfte der Wollust, des Strebens nach Gütern, der Eitelkeit und bedurfte der schmählichsten Verzweiflung, um das Widerstreben aufgeben zu lernen, um die Welt lieben zu lernen, um sie nicht mehr mit irgendeiner von mir gewünschten, von mir eingebildeten Welt zu vergleichen, einer von mir ausgedachten Art der Vollkommenheit, sondern sie zu lassen, wie sie ist, und sie zu lieben, und ihr gerne anzugehören. – Dies, o Govinda, sind einige von den Gedanken, die mir in den Sinn gekommen sind.«

Siddhartha bückte sich, hob einen Stein von Erdboden auf und wog ihn in der Hand.

»Dies hier«, sagte er spielend, »ist ein Stein, und er wird in einer bestimmten Zeit vielleicht Erde sein, und wird aus Erde Pflanze werden, oder Tier oder Mensch. Früher nun hätte ich gesagt: ›Dieser Stein ist bloß ein Stein, er ist wertlos, er gehört der Welt der Maja an: aber weil er vielleicht im Kreislauf der Verwandlungen auch Mensch und Geist werden kann, darum schenke ich auch ihm Geltung.‹ So hätte ich früher vielleicht gedacht. Heute aber denke ich: dieser Stein ist Stein, er ist auch Tier, er ist auch Gott, er ist auch Buddha, ich verehre und liebe ihn nicht, weil er einstmals dies oder jenes werden könnte, sondern weil er alles längst und immer ist – und gerade dies, daß er Stein ist, daß er mir jetzt und heute als Stein erscheint, gerade darum liebe ich ihn, und sehe Wert und Sinn in jeder von seinen Adern und Höhlungen, in dem Gelb, in dem Grau, in der Härte, im Klang, den er von sich gibt, wenn ich ihn beklopfe, in der Trockenheit oder Feuchtigkeit seiner Oberfläche. Es gibt Steine, die fühlen sich wie Öl oder wie Seife an, und andre wie Blätter, andre wie Sand, und jeder ist besonders und betet das Om auf seine Weise, jeder ist Brahman, zugleich aber und ebensosehr ist er Stein, ist ölig oder seifig, und gerade das gefällt mir und scheint mir wunderbar und der Anbetung würdig. – Aber mehr laß mich davon nicht sagen. Die Worte tun dem geheimen Sinn nicht gut, es wird immer alles gleich ein wenig anders, wenn man es ausspricht, ein wenig verfälscht, ein wenig närrisch – ja, und auch das ist sehr gut und gefällt mir sehr, auch damit bin ich sehr einverstanden, daß das, was eines Menschen Schatz und Weisheit ist, dem andern immer wie Narrheit klingt.«

Schweigend lauschte Govinda.

»Warum hast du mir das von dem Steine gesagt?« fragte er nach einer Pause zögernd.

»Es geschah ohne Absicht. Oder vielleicht war es so gemeint, daß ich eben den Stein, und den Fluß, und alle diese Dinge, die wir betrachten

me. I learned from my body and my soul that I was in great need of
sin; I needed sensual pleasures, the ambition for possessions, van-
ity, and I needed the most humiliating despair in order to learn how
to give up my resistance, in order to learn how to love the world, in
order to cease comparing it with some world of my wishes or my
imagination, with some type of perfection that I had concocted, but
to leave it the way it is, to love it, and to be a part of it gladly.—
These, O Govinda, are a few of the ideas that have come into my
mind."

Siddhartha stooped down, picked up a stone from the ground, and
weighed it in his hand.

"This," he said effortlessly, as if at play, "is a stone, and within a certain time it will perhaps be earth, and from earth it will become a
plant or an animal or a person. Now, in the past I would have said:
'This stone is merely a stone, it is worthless, it belongs to the world
of *maya*; but, because in the cycle of transformations it may also become a person and an intellect, I assign some value even to it.' That
is how I might once have reasoned. But today I think: this stone is a
stone, it is also an animal, it is also a god, it is also Buddha; I do not
revere and love it because it may some day become one thing or another, but because it has for a long time, always, been everything—
and it is precisely the fact of its being a stone, of its appearing to me
as a stone now and today, that makes me love it and see value and
meaning in each of its veins and cavities, in the yellow, in the gray, in
its hardness, in the ring it emits when I strike it, in the dryness or
moistness of its surface. There are stones that feel like oil or soap to
the touch, and others like leaves, others like sand; and each one is
special and prays '*om*' in its own way, each one is *Brahman*; but, at
the same time and just as much, it is a stone, it is oily or soapy; and
that is precisely what I like and find marvelous and worthy of adora-
tion.—But do not let me say any more about this. Words do no good
to the secret meaning; everything always immediately becomes a little different when you express it, a little falsified, a little foolish—yes,
and that, too, is very good and pleases me greatly, I am also perfectly
contented that one person's treasure of wisdom always sounds like
foolishness to someone else."

Govinda listened in silence.

"Why did you tell me that about the stone?" he asked hesitantly
after a pause.

"I did it unintentionally. Or perhaps it was intended to show that
I love the stone, and the river, and all these things we look at and can

und von denen wir lernen können, liebe. Einen Stein kann ich lieben, Govinda, und auch einen Baum oder ein Stück Rinde. Das sind Dinge, und Dinge kann man lieben. Worte aber kann ich nicht lieben. Darum sind Lehren nichts für mich, sie haben keine Härte, keine Weiche, keine Farben, keine Kanten, keinen Geruch, keinen Geschmack, sie haben nichts als Worte. Vielleicht ist es dies, was dich hindert, den Frieden zu finden, vielleicht sind es die vielen Worte. Denn auch Erlösung und Tugend, auch Sansara und Nirwana sind bloße Worte, Govinda. Es gibt kein Ding, das Nirwana wäre; es gibt nur das Wort Nirwana.«

Sprach Govinda: »Nicht nur ein Wort, Freund, ist Nirwana. Es ist ein Gedanke.«

Siddhartha fuhr fort: »Ein Gedanke, es mag so sein. Ich muß dir gestehen, Lieber: ich unterscheide zwischen Gedanken und Worten nicht sehr. Offen gesagt, halte ich auch von Gedanken nicht viel. Ich halte von Dingen mehr. Hier auf diesem Fährboot zum Beispiel war ein Mann mein Vorgänger und Lehrer, ein heiliger Mann, der hat manche Jahre lang einfach an den Fluß geglaubt, sonst an nichts. Er hat gemerkt, daß des Flusses Stimme zu ihm sprach, von ihr lernte er, sie erzog und lehrte ihn, der Fluß schien ihm ein Gott, viele Jahre lang wußte er nicht, daß jeder Wind, jede Wolke, jeder Vogel, jeder Käfer genau so göttlich ist und ebensoviel weiß und lehren kann wie der verehrte Fluß. Als dieser Heilige aber in die Wälder ging, da wußte er alles, wußte mehr als du und ich, ohne Lehrer, ohne Bücher, nur weil er an den Fluß geglaubt hatte.«

Govinda sagte: »Aber ist das, was du ›Dinge‹ nennst, denn etwas Wirkliches, etwas Wesenhaftes? Ist das nicht nur Trug der Maja, nur Bild und Schein? Dein Stein, dein Baum, dein Fluß – sind sie denn Wirklichkeiten?«

»Auch dies«, sprach Siddhartha, »bekümmert mich nicht sehr. Mögen die Dinge Schein sein oder nicht, auch ich bin alsdann ja Schein, und so sind sie stets meinesgleichen. Das ist es, was sie mir so lieb und verehrenswert macht: sie sind meinesgleichen. Darum kann ich sie lieben. Und dies ist nun eine Lehre, über welche du lachen wirst: die Liebe, o Govinda, scheint mir von allem die Hauptsache zu sein. Die Welt zu durchschauen, sie zu erklären, sie zu verachten, mag großer Denker Sache sein. Mir aber liegt einzig daran, die Welt lieben zu können, sie nicht zu verachten, sie und mich nicht zu hassen, sie und mich und alle Wesen mit Liebe und Bewunderung und Ehrfurcht betrachten zu können.«

»Dies verstehe ich«, sprach Govinda. »Aber eben dies hat er, der Erhabene, als Trug erkannt. Er gebietet Wohlwollen, Schonung,

learn from. I can love a stone, Govinda, and also a tree or a piece of bark. They are physical things, and things can be loved. But words I cannot love. Therefore, teachings mean nothing to me; they possess neither hardness, nor softness, nor colors, nor edges, nor odor, nor taste; they possess nothing but words. Perhaps that is what prevents you from finding peace, perhaps it is all those words. For even salvation and virtue, even *samsara* and *nirvana,* are mere words, Govinda. There is no thing that is *nirvana,* there is only the word *nirvana.*"

Govinda said: "My friend, *nirvana* is not merely a word; it is a concept."

Siddhartha continued: "A concept, maybe so. I must confess to you, dear friend: I do not make a great distinction between concepts and words. To put it frankly, I have no high regard for concepts, either. I have a higher regard for physical things. Here on this ferryboat, for example, a man was my predecessor and teacher, a saintly man; for many years he simply believed in the river, and nothing else. He observed that the river's voice spoke to him; he learned from that voice, it educated and instructed him; the river was like a god to him; for many years he did not know that every wind, every cloud, every bird, every beetle, is just as godlike, knows just as much and can teach as much as the river he venerated. But when that saintly man left for the forests, he knew everything, he knew more than you and I, without teachers, without books, merely because he had believed in the river."

Govinda said: "But is that which you call 'physical things' something real, something substantial? Is that not merely a ruse of *maya,* merely an image and an illusion? Your stone, your tree, your river—are they realities?"

Siddhartha said: "That does not trouble me very much, either. The things may be illusory or not; if they are, I, too, am illusory, and so they continue to be of the same nature as myself. That is what makes them so dear and worthy of reverence to me: they share my nature. Therefore I can love them. And this now is a doctrine that you will laugh at: love, O Govinda, appears to me to be the chief thing of all. To penetrate the world's secrets, to explain its workings, and to despise it, may be the proper occupation of great thinkers. But my sole concern is to be able to love the world, not to despise it, not to hate it or myself, to be able to look at it and myself and all beings with love and admiration and respect."

"I understand that," said Govinda. "But it was just this that he, the Sublime One, recognized as illusion. He requires of us benevolence,

Mitleid, Duldung, nicht aber Liebe; er verbot uns, unser Herz in Liebe an Irdisches zu fesseln.«

»Ich weiß es«, sagte Siddhartha; sein Lächeln strahlte golden. »Ich weiß es, Govinda. Und siehe, da sind wir mitten im Dickicht der Meinungen drin, im Streit um Worte. Denn ich kann nicht leugnen, meine Worte von der Liebe stehen im Widerspruch, im scheinbaren Widerspruch zu Gotamas Worten. Eben darum mißtraue ich den Worten so sehr, denn ich weiß, dieser Widerspruch ist Täuschung. Ich weiß, daß ich mit Gotama einig bin. Wie sollte denn auch Er die Liebe nicht kennen. Er, der alles Menschensein in seiner Vergänglichkeit, in seiner Nichtigkeit erkannt hat, und dennoch die Menschen so sehr liebte, daß er ein langes, mühevolles Leben einzig darauf verwendet hat, ihnen zu helfen, sie zu lehren! Auch bei ihm, auch bei deinem großen Lehrer, ist mir das Ding lieber als die Worte, sein Tun und Leben wichtiger als sein Reden, die Gebärde seiner Hand wichtiger als seine Meinungen. Nicht im Reden, nicht im Denken sehe ich seine Größe, nur im Tun, im Leben.«

Lange schwiegen die beiden alten Männer. Dann sprach Govinda, indem er sich zum Abschied verneigte: »Ich danke dir, Siddhartha, daß du mir etwas von deinen Gedanken gesagt hast. Es sind zum Teil seltsame Gedanken, nicht alle sind mir sofort verständlich geworden. Dies möge sein, wie es wolle, ich danke dir, und ich wünsche dir ruhige Tage.«

(Heimlich bei sich aber dachte er: Dieser Siddhartha ist ein wunderlicher Mensch, wunderliche Gedanken spricht er aus, närrisch klingt seine Lehre. Anders klingt des Erhabenen reine Lehre, klarer, reiner, verständlicher, nichts Seltsames, Närrisches oder Lächerliches ist in ihr enthalten. Aber anders als seine Gedanken scheinen mir Siddharthas Hände und Füße, seine Augen, seine Stirn, sein Atmen, sein Lächeln, sein Gruß, sein Gang. Nie mehr, seit unser erhabener Gotama in Nirwana einging, nie mehr habe ich einen Menschen angetroffen, von dem ich fühlte: dies ist ein Heiliger! Einzig ihn, diesen Siddhartha, habe ich so gefunden. Mag seine Lehre seltsam sein, mögen seine Worte närrisch klingen, sein Blick und seine Hand, seine Haut und sein Haar, alles in ihm strahlt eine Reinheit, strahlt eine Ruhe, strahlt eine Heiterkeit und Milde und Heiligkeit aus, welche ich an keinem anderen Menschen seit dem letzten Tode unseres erhabenen Lehrers gesehen habe.) Indem Govinda also dachte, und ein Widerstreit in seinem Herzen war, neigte er sich nochmals zu Siddhartha, von Liebe gezogen. Tief verneigte er sich vor dem ruhig Sitzenden.

»Siddhartha«, sprach er, »wir sind alte Männer geworden. Schwerlich wird einer von uns den andern in dieser Gestalt wiedersehen. Ich sehe,

considerateness, sympathy, forbearance, but not love; he forbade us to tie our hearts in love to earthly things."

"I know," said Siddhartha; his smile was like golden beams. "I know, Govinda. And behold, here we are amid the jungle of opinions, quarreling over words. For I cannot deny it, my words about love contradict, or apparently contradict, Gotama's words. For that very reason I distrust words so much, for I know that that contradiction is illusory. I know that I agree with Gotama. How, then, could he, of all people, fail to be acquainted with love? He, who recognized the transitoriness and nothingness of all human existence, and yet loved people so much that he spent a long, laborious life doing nothing but helping them, teaching them! Even in his case, even in the case of your great teacher, the fact is dearer to me than words, his activities and life more important than his sermons, the gesture of his hands more important than his opinions. I see his greatness not in his sermons or his thoughts, but only in his activities, in his life."

For a long while the two old men were silent. Then Govinda said, as he bowed in farewell: "Thank you, Siddhartha, for telling me some of your ideas. They are partly strange ideas; I was not able to understand all of them immediately. Be that as it may, I thank you and I wish you peaceful days."

(But secretly he thought to himself: "This Siddhartha is a peculiar person, he expresses peculiar ideas, his doctrine sounds foolish. Not so the pure doctrine of the Sublime One, which is clearer, purer, more comprehensible, and which contains nothing strange, foolish, or laughable. But Siddhartha's ideas seem to me to be unlike his hands and feet, his eyes, his forehead, his breathing, his smile, his greeting, his way of walking. Never, since our sublime Gotama entered *nirvana*, never since then have I come across a person about whom I felt: this is a saint! Him alone, this Siddhartha, have I found to be so. Even if his doctrine is strange, even if his words sound foolish, nevertheless his eyes and his hands, his skin and his hair, everything about him radiates a purity, radiates a peace, radiates a serenity and mildness and sanctity that I have not seen in any other person since the final death of our sublime teacher.") While Govinda was thinking this and there was a contradiction in his heart, he bowed to Siddhartha again, attracted by love. He made a low bow to the one who sat there calmly.

"Siddhartha," he said, "we have become old men. We shall hardly meet again in our present forms. I see, beloved friend, that you have

Geliebter, daß du den Frieden gefunden hast. Ich bekenne, ihn nicht gefunden zu haben. Sage mir, Verehrter, noch ein Wort, gib mir etwas mit, das ich fassen, das ich verstehen kann! Gib mir etwas mit auf meinen Weg. Er ist oft beschwerlich, mein Weg, oft finster, Siddhartha.«

Siddhartha schwieg und blickte ihn mit dem immer gleichen, stillen Lächeln an. Starr blickte ihm Govinda ins Gesicht, mit Angst, mit Sehnsucht. Leid und ewiges Suchen stand in seinem Blick geschrieben, ewiges Nichtfinden.

Siddhartha sah es und lächelte.

»Neige dich zu mir!« flüsterte er leise in Govindas Ohr. »Neige dich zu mir her! So, noch näher! Ganz nahe! Küsse mich auf die Stirn, Govinda!«

Während aber Govinda verwundert, und dennoch von großer Liebe und Ahnung gezogen, seinen Worten gehorchte, sich nahe zu ihm neigte und seine Stirn mit den Lippen berührte, geschah ihm etwas Wunderbares. Während seine Gedanken noch bei Siddharthas wunderlichen Worten verweilten, während er sich noch vergeblich und mit Widerstreben bemühte, sich die Zeit hinwegzudenken, sich Nirwana und Sansara als Eines vorzustellen, während sogar eine gewisse Verachtung für die Worte des Freundes in ihm mit einer ungeheuren Liebe und Ehrfurcht stritt, geschah ihm dieses:

Er sah seines Freundes Siddhartha Gesicht nicht mehr, er sah statt dessen andre Gesichter, viele, eine lange Reihe, einen strömenden Fluß von Gesichtern, von Hunderten, von Tausenden, welche alle kamen und vergingen, und doch alle zugleich dazusein schienen, welche alle sich beständig veränderten und erneuerten, und welche doch alle Siddhartha waren. Er sah das Gesicht eines Fisches, eines Karpfens, mit unendlich schmerzvoll geöffnetem Maule, eines sterbenden Fisches, mit brechenden Augen – er sah das Gesicht eines neugeborenen Kindes, rot und voll Falten, zum Weinen verzogen – er sah das Gesicht eines Mörders, sah ihn ein Messer in den Leib eines Menschen stechen – er sah, zur selben Sekunde, diesen Verbrecher gefesselt knien und sein Haupt vom Henker mit einem Schwertschlag abgeschlagen werden – er sah die Körper von Männern und Frauen nackt in Stellungen und Kämpfen rasender Liebe – er sah Leichen ausgestreckt, still, kalt, leer – er sah Tierköpfe, von Ebern, von Krokodilen, von Elefanten, von Stieren, von Vögeln – er sah Götter, sah Krischna, sah Agni – er sah alle diese Gestalten und Gesichter in tausend Beziehungen zueinander, jede der andern helfend, sie liebend, sie hassend, sie vernichtend, sie neu gebärend, jede war ein Sterbenwollen, ein leidenschaftlich schmerzliches Bekenntnis der Vergänglichkeit, und keine starb doch, jede verwandelte sich nur, wurde stets neu geboren,

found peace. I confess that I have not. Tell me, honored one, one thing more; let me take away with me something that I can grasp, that I can understand! Give me something to accompany me on my path. My path is often wearisome, often gloomy, Siddhartha."

Siddhartha, remaining silent, looked at him with that unchanging, quiet smile. Govinda stared into his face, with anguish, with longing. Sorrow and eternal seeking were written in his gaze, eternal inability to find what he sought.

Siddhartha saw it and smiled.

"Lean over to me!" he whispered softly in Govinda's ear. "Lean over here to me! Like that, even closer! Very close! Kiss me on the forehead, Govinda!"

But while Govinda, amazed but impelled by great love and presentiment, obeyed his words, leaned over close to him, and touched his forehead with his lips, something miraculous happened to him. While his thoughts still lingered over Siddhartha's peculiar words, while he was still futilely and reluctantly struggling to think away time and imagine *nirvana* and *samsara* as one and the same thing, while a certain contempt for his friend's words was even fighting within him against a tremendous love and respect, this is what happened to him:

He no longer saw his friend Siddhartha's face; in its place he saw other faces, many of them, a long series, a flowing river of faces, hundreds, thousands, all of them arising and dissolving, and yet all seeming to be there at the same time; they all constantly changed and renewed themselves, and yet were all Siddhartha. He saw the face of a fish, a carp, its mouth opened in infinite pain, a dying fish with eyes glazing over—he saw the face of a newborn child, red and full of wrinkles, distorted in weeping—he saw the face of a murderer, saw him plunge a knife into someone's body—in the same second he saw that criminal bound and kneeling and his head being cut off by the executioner with the stroke of a sword—he saw the bodies of men and women naked in the positions and battles of furious love—he saw corpses stretched out, quiet, cold, empty—he saw heads of animals, of boars, of crocodiles, of elephants, of bulls, of birds—he saw gods, saw Krishna, saw Agni—he saw all these forms and faces interrelating in a thousand ways, each form helping the other, loving it, hating it, annihilating it, giving birth to it again; each one was a death wish, a passionately painful confession of mortality; and yet none of them died, each one was merely transformed, was constantly reborn, constantly received a new face, but without

bekam stets ein neues Gesicht, ohne daß doch zwischen einem und dem anderen Gesicht Zeit gelegen wäre – und alle diese Gestalten und Gesichter ruhten, flossen, erzeugten sich, schwammen dahin und strömten ineinander, und über alle war beständig etwas Dünnes, Wesenloses, dennoch Seiendes, wie ein dünnes Glas oder Eis gezogen, wie eine durchsichtige Haut, eine Schale oder Form oder Maske von Wasser, und diese Maske lächelte, und diese Maske war Siddharthas lächelndes Gesicht, das er, Govinda, in eben diesem selben Augenblick mit den Lippen berührte. Und, so sah Govinda, dies Lächeln der Maske, dies Lächeln der Einheit über den strömenden Gestaltungen, dies Lächeln der Gleichzeitigkeit über den tausend Geburten und Toden, dies Lächeln Siddharthas war genau dasselbe, war genau das gleiche, stille, feine, undurchdringliche, vielleicht gütige, vielleicht spöttische, weise, tausendfältige Lächeln Gotamas, des Buddha, wie er selbst es hundertmal mit Ehrfurcht gesehen hatte. So, das wußte Govinda, lächelten die Vollendeten.

Nicht mehr wissend, ob es Zeit gebe, ob diese Schauung eine Sekunde oder hundert Jahre gewährt habe, nicht mehr wissend, ob es einen Siddhartha, ob es einen Gotama, ob es Ich und Du gebe, im Innersten wie von einem göttlichen Pfeile verwundet, dessen Verwundung süß schmeckt, im Innersten verzaubert und aufgelöst, stand Govinda noch eine kleine Weile, über Siddharthas stilles Gesicht gebeugt, das er soeben geküßt hatte, das soeben Schauplatz aller Gestaltungen, alles Werdens, alles Seins gewesen war. Das Antlitz war unverändert, nachdem unter seiner Oberfläche die Tiefe der Tausendfältigkeit sich wieder geschlossen hatte, er lächelte still, lächelte leise und sanft, vielleicht sehr gütig, vielleicht sehr spöttisch, genau, wie er gelächelt hatte, der Erhabene.

Tief verneigte sich Govinda, Tränen liefen, von welchen er nichts wußte, über sein altes Gesicht, wie ein Feuer brannte das Gefühl der innigsten Liebe, der demütigsten Verehrung in seinem Herzen. Tief verneigte er sich, bis zur Erde, vor dem regungslos Sitzenden, dessen Lächeln ihn an alles erinnerte, was er in seinem Leben jemals geliebt hatte, was jemals in seinem Leben ihm wert und heilig gewesen war.

any time elapsing between one face and the next—and all these forms and faces were in repose, flowed, engendered themselves, drifted away and poured into one another; and all of them were constantly covered by something thin, insubstantial, yet existent, like a thin layer of glass or ice, like a transparent skin, a shell or mold or mask of water; and this mask smiled, and this mask was Siddhartha's smiling face, which he, Govinda, was touching with his lips at that very moment. And Govinda saw that this smile on the mask, this smile of oneness over the flowing shapes, this smile of simultaneity over the thousand births and deaths, this smile of Siddhartha's, was exactly the same, was exactly the same quiet, subtle, impenetrable, perhaps kindly, perhaps mocking, wise, thousandfold smile of Gotama, the Buddha, which he had seen with respect a hundred times. Thus, Govinda knew, do the perfect ones smile.

No longer knowing whether time existed, whether that vision had lasted a second or a hundred years; no longer knowing whether a Siddhartha, a Gotama, an "I" or a "you" existed; wounded in his inmost recesses as if by a divine arrow, the wound from which tastes sweet; enchanted and dissolved in his inmost being, Govinda stood there a little while longer, leaning over Siddhartha's quiet face, which he had just kissed, which had just been the theater of all formations, of all becoming, of all being. The countenance was unchanged, now that the depths of multiplicity beneath its surface had been shut away again; it was quietly smiling, softly and gently smiling, perhaps in a very kindly way, perhaps in a very mocking way, exactly as *he* had smiled, the Sublime One.

Govinda made a low bow; tears, of which he knew nothing, ran down his aged face; the sensation of the warmest love, of the most humble veneration, burned like a fire in his heart. He made a low bow, down to the ground, before the man sitting motionless there, whose smile reminded him of everything he had ever loved in his life, everything that had ever been valuable and sacred to him in his life.

A CATALOG OF SELECTED
DOVER BOOKS
IN ALL FIELDS OF INTEREST

A CATALOG OF SELECTED DOVER
BOOKS IN ALL FIELDS OF INTEREST

CONCERNING THE SPIRITUAL IN ART, Wassily Kandinsky. Pioneering work by father of abstract art. Thoughts on color theory, nature of art. Analysis of earlier masters. 12 illustrations. 80pp. of text. 5⅜ x 8½. 23411-8 Pa. $3.95

ANIMALS: 1,419 Copyright-Free Illustrations of Mammals, Birds, Fish, Insects, etc., Jim Harter (ed.). Clear wood engravings present, in extremely lifelike poses, over 1,000 species of animals. One of the most extensive pictorial sourcebooks of its kind. Captions. Index. 284pp. 9 x 12. 23766-4 Pa. $12.95

CELTIC ART: The Methods of Construction, George Bain. Simple geometric techniques for making Celtic interlacements, spirals, Kells-type initials, animals, humans, etc. Over 500 illustrations. 160pp. 9 x 12. (USO) 22923-8 Pa. $9.95

AN ATLAS OF ANATOMY FOR ARTISTS, Fritz Schider. Most thorough reference work on art anatomy in the world. Hundreds of illustrations, including selections from works by Vesalius, Leonardo, Goya, Ingres, Michelangelo, others. 593 illustrations. 192pp. 7⅛ x 10¼. 20241-0 Pa. $9.95

CELTIC HAND STROKE-BY-STROKE (Irish Half-Uncial from "The Book of Kells"): An Arthur Baker Calligraphy Manual, Arthur Baker. Complete guide to creating each letter of the alphabet in distinctive Celtic manner. Covers hand position, strokes, pens, inks, paper, more. Illustrated. 48pp. 8¼ x 11. 24336-2 Pa. $3.95

EASY ORIGAMI, John Montroll. Charming collection of 32 projects (hat, cup, pelican, piano, swan, many more) specially designed for the novice origami hobbyist. Clearly illustrated easy-to-follow instructions insure that even beginning papercrafters will achieve successful results. 48pp. 8¼ x 11. 27298-2 Pa. $3.50

THE COMPLETE BOOK OF BIRDHOUSE CONSTRUCTION FOR WOOD-WORKERS, Scott D. Campbell. Detailed instructions, illustrations, tables. Also data on bird habitat and instinct patterns. Bibliography. 3 tables. 63 illustrations in 15 figures. 48pp. 5¼ x 8½. 24407-5 Pa. $2.50

BLOOMINGDALE'S ILLUSTRATED 1886 CATALOG: Fashions, Dry Goods and Housewares, Bloomingdale Brothers. Famed merchants' extremely rare catalog depicting about 1,700 products: clothing, housewares, firearms, dry goods, jewelry, more. Invaluable for dating, identifying vintage items. Also, copyright-free graphics for artists, designers. Co-published with Henry Ford Museum & Greenfield Village. 160pp. 8¼ x 11. 25780-0 Pa. $10.95

HISTORIC COSTUME IN PICTURES, Braun & Schneider. Over 1,450 costumed figures in clearly detailed engravings–from dawn of civilization to end of 19th century. Captions. Many folk costumes. 256pp. 8⅜ x 11¾. 23150-X Pa. $12.95

STICKLEY CRAFTSMAN FURNITURE CATALOGS, Gustav Stickley and L. & J. G. Stickley. Beautiful, functional furniture in two authentic catalogs from 1910. 594 illustrations, including 277 photos, show settles, rockers, armchairs, reclining chairs, bookcases, desks, tables. 183pp. 6½ x 9¼. 23838-5 Pa. $9.95

AMERICAN LOCOMOTIVES IN HISTORIC PHOTOGRAPHS: 1858 to 1949, Ron Ziel (ed.). A rare collection of 126 meticulously detailed official photographs, called "builder portraits," of American locomotives that majestically chronicle the rise of steam locomotive power in America. Introduction. Detailed captions. xi + 129pp. 9 x 12. 27393-8 Pa. $12.95

AMERICA'S LIGHTHOUSES: An Illustrated History, Francis Ross Holland, Jr. Delightfully written, profusely illustrated fact-filled survey of over 200 American lighthouses since 1716. History, anecdotes, technological advances, more. 240pp. 8 x 10¾. 25576-X Pa. $12.95

TOWARDS A NEW ARCHITECTURE, Le Corbusier. Pioneering manifesto by founder of "International School." Technical and aesthetic theories, views of industry, economics, relation of form to function, "mass-production split" and much more. Profusely illustrated. 320pp. 6⅛ x 9¼. (USO) 25023-7 Pa. $9.95

HOW THE OTHER HALF LIVES, Jacob Riis. Famous journalistic record, exposing poverty and degradation of New York slums around 1900, by major social reformer. 100 striking and influential photographs. 233pp. 10 x 7⅞. 22012-5 Pa. $10.95

FRUIT KEY AND TWIG KEY TO TREES AND SHRUBS, William M. Harlow. One of the handiest and most widely used identification aids. Fruit key covers 120 deciduous and evergreen species; twig key 160 deciduous species. Easily used. Over 300 photographs. 126pp. 5⅜ x 8½. 20511-8 Pa. $3.95

COMMON BIRD SONGS, Dr. Donald J. Borror. Songs of 60 most common U.S. birds: robins, sparrows, cardinals, bluejays, finches, more—arranged in order of increasing complexity. Up to 9 variations of songs of each species. Cassette and manual 99911-4 $8.95

ORCHIDS AS HOUSE PLANTS, Rebecca Tyson Northen. Grow cattleyas and many other kinds of orchids—in a window, in a case, or under artificial light. 63 illustrations. 148pp. 5⅜ x 8½. 23261-1 Pa. $4.95

MONSTER MAZES, Dave Phillips. Masterful mazes at four levels of difficulty. Avoid deadly perils and evil creatures to find magical treasures. Solutions for all 32 exciting illustrated puzzles. 48pp. 8¼ x 11. 26005-4 Pa. $2.95

MOZART'S DON GIOVANNI (DOVER OPERA LIBRETTO SERIES), Wolfgang Amadeus Mozart. Introduced and translated by Ellen H. Bleiler. Standard Italian libretto, with complete English translation. Convenient and thoroughly portable—an ideal companion for reading along with a recording or the performance itself. Introduction. List of characters. Plot summary. 121pp. 5¼ x 8½. 24944-1 Pa. $2.95

TECHNICAL MANUAL AND DICTIONARY OF CLASSICAL BALLET, Gail Grant. Defines, explains, comments on steps, movements, poses and concepts. 15-page pictorial section. Basic book for student, viewer. 127pp. 5⅜ x 8½. 21843-0 Pa. $4.95

BRASS INSTRUMENTS: Their History and Development, Anthony Baines. Authoritative, updated survey of the evolution of trumpets, trombones, bugles, cornets, French horns, tubas and other brass wind instruments. Over 140 illustrations and 48 music examples. Corrected and updated by author. New preface. Bibliography. 320pp. 5⅜ x 8½. 27574-4 Pa. $9.95

HOLLYWOOD GLAMOR PORTRAITS, John Kobal (ed.). 145 photos from 1926-49. Harlow, Gable, Bogart, Bacall; 94 stars in all. Full background on photographers, technical aspects. 160pp. 8⅜ x 11¼. 23352-9 Pa. $12.95

MAX AND MORITZ, Wilhelm Busch. Great humor classic in both German and English. Also 10 other works: "Cat and Mouse," "Plisch and Plumm," etc. 216pp. 5⅜ x 8½. 20181-3 Pa. $6.95

THE RAVEN AND OTHER FAVORITE POEMS, Edgar Allan Poe. Over 40 of the author's most memorable poems: "The Bells," "Ulalume," "Israfel," "To Helen," "The Conqueror Worm," "Eldorado," "Annabel Lee," many more. Alphabetic lists of titles and first lines. 64pp. 5 3/16 x 8¼. 26685-0 Pa. $1.00

PERSONAL MEMOIRS OF U. S. GRANT, Ulysses Simpson Grant. Intelligent, deeply moving firsthand account of Civil War campaigns, considered by many the finest military memoirs ever written. Includes letters, historic photographs, maps and more. 528pp. 6⅛ x 9¼. 28587-1 Pa. $11.95

AMULETS AND SUPERSTITIONS, E. A. Wallis Budge. Comprehensive discourse on origin, powers of amulets in many ancient cultures: Arab, Persian Babylonian, Assyrian, Egyptian, Gnostic, Hebrew, Phoenician, Syriac, etc. Covers cross, swastika, crucifix, seals, rings, stones, etc. 584pp. 5⅜ x 8½. 23573-4 Pa. $12.95

RUSSIAN STORIES/PYCCKNE PACCKA3bl: A Dual-Language Book, edited by Gleb Struve. Twelve tales by such masters as Chekhov, Tolstoy, Dostoevsky, Pushkin, others. Excellent word-for-word English translations on facing pages, plus teaching and study aids, Russian/English vocabulary, biographical/critical introductions, more. 416pp. 5⅜ x 8½. 26244-8 Pa. $8.95

PHILADELPHIA THEN AND NOW: 60 Sites Photographed in the Past and Present, Kenneth Finkel and Susan Oyama. Rare photographs of City Hall, Logan Square, Independence Hall, Betsy Ross House, other landmarks juxtaposed with contemporary views. Captures changing face of historic city. Introduction. Captions. 128pp. 8¼ x 11. 25790-8 Pa. $9.95

AIA ARCHITECTURAL GUIDE TO NASSAU AND SUFFOLK COUNTIES, LONG ISLAND, The American Institute of Architects, Long Island Chapter, and the Society for the Preservation of Long Island Antiquities. Comprehensive, well-researched and generously illustrated volume brings to life over three centuries of Long Island's great architectural heritage. More than 240 photographs with authoritative, extensively detailed captions. 176pp. 8¼ x 11. 26946-9 Pa. $14.95

NORTH AMERICAN INDIAN LIFE: Customs and Traditions of 23 Tribes, Elsie Clews Parsons (ed.). 27 fictionalized essays by noted anthropologists examine religion, customs, government, additional facets of life among the Winnebago, Crow, Zuni, Eskimo, other tribes. 480pp. 6⅛ x 9¼. 27377-6 Pa. $10.95

FRANK LLOYD WRIGHT'S HOLLYHOCK HOUSE, Donald Hoffmann. Lavishly illustrated, carefully documented study of one of Wright's most controversial residential designs. Over 120 photographs, floor plans, elevations, etc. Detailed perceptive text by noted Wright scholar. Index. 128pp. 9¼ x 10¾. 27133-1 Pa. $11.95

THE MALE AND FEMALE FIGURE IN MOTION: 60 Classic Photographic Sequences, Eadweard Muybridge. 60 true-action photographs of men and women walking, running, climbing, bending, turning, etc., reproduced from rare 19th-century masterpiece. vi + 121pp. 9 x 12. 24745-7 Pa. $10.95

1001 QUESTIONS ANSWERED ABOUT THE SEASHORE, N. J. Berrill and Jacquelyn Berrill. Queries answered about dolphins, sea snails, sponges, starfish, fishes, shore birds, many others. Covers appearance, breeding, growth, feeding, much more. 305pp. 5¼ x 8¼. 23366-9 Pa. $8.95

GUIDE TO OWL WATCHING IN NORTH AMERICA, Donald S. Heintzelman. Superb guide offers complete data and descriptions of 19 species: barn owl, screech owl, snowy owl, many more. Expert coverage of owl-watching equipment, conservation, migrations and invasions, etc. Guide to observing sites. 84 illustrations. xiii + 193pp. 5⅜ x 8½. 27344-X Pa. $8.95

MEDICINAL AND OTHER USES OF NORTH AMERICAN PLANTS: A Historical Survey with Special Reference to the Eastern Indian Tribes, Charlotte Erichsen-Brown. Chronological historical citations document 500 years of usage of plants, trees, shrubs native to eastern Canada, northeastern U.S. Also complete identifying information. 343 illustrations. 544pp. 6½ x 9¼. 25951-X Pa. $12.95

STORYBOOK MAZES, Dave Phillips. 23 stories and mazes on two-page spreads: Wizard of Oz, Treasure Island, Robin Hood, etc. Solutions. 64pp. 8¼ x 11. 23628-5 Pa. $2.95

NEGRO FOLK MUSIC, U.S.A., Harold Courlander. Noted folklorist's scholarly yet readable analysis of rich and varied musical tradition. Includes authentic versions of over 40 folk songs. Valuable bibliography and discography. xi + 324pp. 5⅜ x 8½. 27350-4 Pa. $9.95

MOVIE-STAR PORTRAITS OF THE FORTIES, John Kobal (ed.). 163 glamor, studio photos of 106 stars of the 1940s: Rita Hayworth, Ava Gardner, Marlon Brando, Clark Gable, many more. 176pp. 8⅜ x 11¼. 23546-7 Pa. $12.95

BENCHLEY LOST AND FOUND, Robert Benchley. Finest humor from early 30s, about pet peeves, child psychologists, post office and others. Mostly unavailable elsewhere. 73 illustrations by Peter Arno and others. 183pp. 5⅜ x 8½. 22410-4 Pa. $6.95

YEKL and THE IMPORTED BRIDEGROOM AND OTHER STORIES OF YIDDISH NEW YORK, Abraham Cahan. Film Hester Street based on Yekl (1896). Novel, other stories among first about Jewish immigrants on N.Y.'s East Side. 240pp. 5⅜ x 8½. 22427-9 Pa. $6.95

SELECTED POEMS, Walt Whitman. Generous sampling from *Leaves of Grass*. Twenty-four poems include "I Hear America Singing," "Song of the Open Road," "I Sing the Body Electric," "When Lilacs Last in the Dooryard Bloom'd," "O Captain! My Captain!"—all reprinted from an authoritative edition. Lists of titles and first lines. 128pp. 5³⁄₁₆ x 8¼. 26878-0 Pa. $1.00

THE BEST TALES OF HOFFMANN, E. T. A. Hoffmann. 10 of Hoffmann's most important stories: "Nutcracker and the King of Mice," "The Golden Flowerpot," etc. 458pp. 5⅜ x 8½. 21793-0 Pa. $9.95

FROM FETISH TO GOD IN ANCIENT EGYPT, E. A. Wallis Budge. Rich detailed survey of Egyptian conception of "God" and gods, magic, cult of animals, Osiris, more. Also, superb English translations of hymns and legends. 240 illustrations. 545pp. 5⅜ x 8½. 25803-3 Pa. $13.95

FRENCH STORIES/CONTES FRANÇAIS: A Dual-Language Book, Wallace Fowlie. Ten stories by French masters, Voltaire to Camus: "Micromegas" by Voltaire; "The Atheist's Mass" by Balzac; "Minuet" by de Maupassant; "The Guest" by Camus, six more. Excellent English translations on facing pages. Also French-English vocabulary list, exercises, more. 352pp. 5⅜ x 8½. 26443-2 Pa. $8.95

CHICAGO AT THE TURN OF THE CENTURY IN PHOTOGRAPHS: 122 Historic Views from the Collections of the Chicago Historical Society, Larry A. Viskochil. Rare large-format prints offer detailed views of City Hall, State Street, the Loop, Hull House, Union Station, many other landmarks, circa 1904-1913. Introduction. Captions. Maps. 144pp. 9⅜ x 12¼. 24656-6 Pa. $12.95

OLD BROOKLYN IN EARLY PHOTOGRAPHS, 1865-1929, William Lee Younger. Luna Park, Gravesend race track, construction of Grand Army Plaza, moving of Hotel Brighton, etc. 157 previously unpublished photographs. 165pp. 8⅞ x 11¾. 23587-4 Pa. $13.95

THE MYTHS OF THE NORTH AMERICAN INDIANS, Lewis Spence. Rich anthology of the myths and legends of the Algonquins, Iroquois, Pawnees and Sioux, prefaced by an extensive historical and ethnological commentary. 36 illustrations. 480pp. 5⅜ x 8½. 25967-6 Pa. $8.95

AN ENCYCLOPEDIA OF BATTLES: Accounts of Over 1,560 Battles from 1479 B.C. to the Present, David Eggenberger. Essential details of every major battle in recorded history from the first battle of Megiddo in 1479 B.C. to Grenada in 1984. List of Battle Maps. New Appendix covering the years 1967-1984. Index. 99 illustrations. 544pp. 6½ x 9¼. 24913-1 Pa. $14.95

SAILING ALONE AROUND THE WORLD, Captain Joshua Slocum. First man to sail around the world, alone, in small boat. One of great feats of seamanship told in delightful manner. 67 illustrations. 294pp. 5⅜ x 8½. 20326-3 Pa. $5.95

ANARCHISM AND OTHER ESSAYS, Emma Goldman. Powerful, penetrating, prophetic essays on direct action, role of minorities, prison reform, puritan hypocrisy, violence, etc. 271pp. 5⅜ x 8½. 22484-8 Pa. $6.95

MYTHS OF THE HINDUS AND BUDDHISTS, Ananda K. Coomaraswamy and Sister Nivedita. Great stories of the epics; deeds of Krishna, Shiva, taken from puranas, Vedas, folk tales; etc. 32 illustrations. 400pp. 5⅜ x 8½. 21759-0 Pa. $10.95

BEYOND PSYCHOLOGY, Otto Rank. Fear of death, desire of immortality, nature of sexuality, social organization, creativity, according to Rankian system. 291pp. 5⅜ x 8½. 20485-5 Pa. $8.95

A THEOLOGICO-POLITICAL TREATISE, Benedict Spinoza. Also contains unfinished Political Treatise. Great classic on religious liberty, theory of government on common consent. R. Elwes translation. Total of 421pp. 5⅜ x 8½. 20249-6 Pa. $9.95

MY BONDAGE AND MY FREEDOM, Frederick Douglass. Born a slave, Douglass became outspoken force in antislavery movement. The best of Douglass' autobiographies. Graphic description of slave life. 464pp. 5⅜ x 8½. 22457-0 Pa. $8.95

FOLLOWING THE EQUATOR: A Journey Around the World, Mark Twain. Fascinating humorous account of 1897 voyage to Hawaii, Australia, India, New Zealand, etc. Ironic, bemused reports on peoples, customs, climate, flora and fauna, politics, much more. 197 illustrations. 720pp. 5⅜ x 8½. 26113-1 Pa. $15.95

THE PEOPLE CALLED SHAKERS, Edward D. Andrews. Definitive study of Shakers: origins, beliefs, practices, dances, social organization, furniture and crafts, etc. 33 illustrations. 351pp. 5⅜ x 8½. 21081-2 Pa. $8.95

THE MYTHS OF GREECE AND ROME, H. A. Guerber. A classic of mythology, generously illustrated, long prized for its simple, graphic, accurate retelling of the principal myths of Greece and Rome, and for its commentary on their origins and significance. With 64 illustrations by Michelangelo, Raphael, Titian, Rubens, Canova, Bernini and others. 480pp. 5⅜ x 8½. 27584-1 Pa. $9.95

PSYCHOLOGY OF MUSIC, Carl E. Seashore. Classic work discusses music as a medium from psychological viewpoint. Clear treatment of physical acoustics, auditory apparatus, sound perception, development of musical skills, nature of musical feeling, host of other topics. 88 figures. 408pp. 5⅜ x 8½. 21851-1 Pa. $10.95

THE PHILOSOPHY OF HISTORY, Georg W. Hegel. Great classic of Western thought develops concept that history is not chance but rational process, the evolution of freedom. 457pp. 5⅜ x 8½. 20112-0 Pa. $9.95

THE BOOK OF TEA, Kakuzo Okakura. Minor classic of the Orient: entertaining, charming explanation, interpretation of traditional Japanese culture in terms of tea ceremony. 94pp. 5⅜ x 8½. 20070-1 Pa. $3.95

LIFE IN ANCIENT EGYPT, Adolf Erman. Fullest, most thorough, detailed older account with much not in more recent books, domestic life, religion, magic, medicine, commerce, much more. Many illustrations reproduce tomb paintings, carvings, hieroglyphs, etc. 597pp. 5⅜ x 8½. 22632-8 Pa. $11.95

SUNDIALS, Their Theory and Construction, Albert Waugh. Far and away the best, most thorough coverage of ideas, mathematics concerned, types, construction, adjusting anywhere. Simple, nontechnical treatment allows even children to build several of these dials. Over 100 illustrations. 230pp. 5⅜ x 8½. 22947-5 Pa. $7.95

DYNAMICS OF FLUIDS IN POROUS MEDIA, Jacob Bear. For advanced students of ground water hydrology, soil mechanics and physics, drainage and irrigation engineering, and more. 335 illustrations. Exercises, with answers. 784pp. 6⅛ x 9¼. 65675-6 Pa. $19.95

SONGS OF EXPERIENCE: Facsimile Reproduction with 26 Plates in Full Color, William Blake. 26 full-color plates from a rare 1826 edition. Includes "The Tyger," "London," "Holy Thursday," and other poems. Printed text of poems. 48pp. 5¼ x 7. 24636-1 Pa. $4.95

OLD-TIME VIGNETTES IN FULL COLOR, Carol Belanger Grafton (ed.). Over 390 charming, often sentimental illustrations, selected from archives of Victorian graphics—pretty women posing, children playing, food, flowers, kittens and puppies, smiling cherubs, birds and butterflies, much more. All copyright-free. 48pp. 9¼ x 12¼. 27269-9 Pa. $7.95

PERSPECTIVE FOR ARTISTS, Rex Vicat Cole. Depth, perspective of sky and sea, shadows, much more, not usually covered. 391 diagrams, 81 reproductions of drawings and paintings. 279pp. 5⅜ x 8½. 22487-2 Pa. $7.95

DRAWING THE LIVING FIGURE, Joseph Sheppard. Innovative approach to artistic anatomy focuses on specifics of surface anatomy, rather than muscles and bones. Over 170 drawings of live models in front, back and side views, and in widely varying poses. Accompanying diagrams. 177 illustrations. Introduction. Index. 144pp. 8⅜ x11¼. 26723-7 Pa. $8.95

GOTHIC AND OLD ENGLISH ALPHABETS: 100 Complete Fonts, Dan X. Solo. Add power, elegance to posters, signs, other graphics with 100 stunning copyright-free alphabets: Blackstone, Dolbey, Germania, 97 more–including many lower-case, numerals, punctuation marks. 104pp. 8⅛ x 11. 24695-7 Pa. $8.95

HOW TO DO BEADWORK, Mary White. Fundamental book on craft from simple projects to five-bead chains and woven works. 106 illustrations. 142pp. 5⅜ x 8. 20697-1 Pa. $4.95

THE BOOK OF WOOD CARVING, Charles Marshall Sayers. Finest book for beginners discusses fundamentals and offers 34 designs. "Absolutely first rate . . . well thought out and well executed."–E. J. Tangerman. 118pp. 7¾ x 10⅝. 23654-4 Pa. $6.95

ILLUSTRATED CATALOG OF CIVIL WAR MILITARY GOODS: Union Army Weapons, Insignia, Uniform Accessories, and Other Equipment, Schuyler, Hartley, and Graham. Rare, profusely illustrated 1846 catalog includes Union Army uniform and dress regulations, arms and ammunition, coats, insignia, flags, swords, rifles, etc. 226 illustrations. 160pp. 9 x 12. 24939-5 Pa. $10.95

WOMEN'S FASHIONS OF THE EARLY 1900s: An Unabridged Republication of "New York Fashions, 1909," National Cloak & Suit Co. Rare catalog of mail-order fashions documents women's and children's clothing styles shortly after the turn of the century. Captions offer full descriptions, prices. Invaluable resource for fashion, costume historians. Approximately 725 illustrations. 128pp. 8⅜ x 11¼. 27276-1 Pa. $11.95

THE 1912 AND 1915 GUSTAV STICKLEY FURNITURE CATALOGS, Gustav Stickley. With over 200 detailed illustrations and descriptions, these two catalogs are essential reading and reference materials and identification guides for Stickley furniture. Captions cite materials, dimensions and prices. 112pp. 6½ x 9¼. 26676-1 Pa. $9.95

EARLY AMERICAN LOCOMOTIVES, John H. White, Jr. Finest locomotive engravings from early 19th century: historical (1804–74), main-line (after 1870), special, foreign, etc. 147 plates. 142pp. 11⅜ x 8¼. 22772-3 Pa. $10.95

THE TALL SHIPS OF TODAY IN PHOTOGRAPHS, Frank O. Braynard. Lavishly illustrated tribute to nearly 100 majestic contemporary sailing vessels: Amerigo Vespucci, Clearwater, Constitution, Eagle, Mayflower, Sea Cloud, Victory, many more. Authoritative captions provide statistics, background on each ship. 190 black-and-white photographs and illustrations. Introduction. 128pp. 8⅞ x 11¾. 27163-3 Pa. $13.95

EARLY NINETEENTH-CENTURY CRAFTS AND TRADES, Peter Stockham (ed.). Extremely rare 1807 volume describes to youngsters the crafts and trades of the day: brickmaker, weaver, dressmaker, bookbinder, ropemaker, saddler, many more. Quaint prose, charming illustrations for each craft. 20 black-and-white line illustrations. 192pp. 4⅝ x 6. 27293-1 Pa. $4.95

VICTORIAN FASHIONS AND COSTUMES FROM HARPER'S BAZAR, 1867–1898, Stella Blum (ed.). Day costumes, evening wear, sports clothes, shoes, hats, other accessories in over 1,000 detailed engravings. 320pp. 9⅜ x 12¼. 22990-4 Pa. $14.95

GUSTAV STICKLEY, THE CRAFTSMAN, Mary Ann Smith. Superb study surveys broad scope of Stickley's achievement, especially in architecture. Design philosophy, rise and fall of the Craftsman empire, descriptions and floor plans for many Craftsman houses, more. 86 black-and-white halftones. 31 line illustrations. Introduction 208pp. 6½ x 9¼. 27210-9 Pa. $9.95

THE LONG ISLAND RAIL ROAD IN EARLY PHOTOGRAPHS, Ron Ziel. Over 220 rare photos, informative text document origin (1844) and development of rail service on Long Island. Vintage views of early trains, locomotives, stations, passengers, crews, much more. Captions. 8⅞ x 11¾. 26301-0 Pa. $13.95

THE BOOK OF OLD SHIPS: From Egyptian Galleys to Clipper Ships, Henry B. Culver. Superb, authoritative history of sailing vessels, with 80 magnificent line illustrations. Galley, bark, caravel, longship, whaler, many more. Detailed, informative text on each vessel by noted naval historian. Introduction. 256pp. 5⅜ x 8½. 27332-6 Pa. $7.95

TEN BOOKS ON ARCHITECTURE, Vitruvius. The most important book ever written on architecture. Early Roman aesthetics, technology, classical orders, site selection, all other aspects. Morgan translation. 331pp. 5⅜ x 8½. 20645-9 Pa. $8.95

THE HUMAN FIGURE IN MOTION, Eadweard Muybridge. More than 4,500 stopped-action photos, in action series, showing undraped men, women, children jumping, lying down, throwing, sitting, wrestling, carrying, etc. 390pp. 7⅞ x 10⅝. 20204-6 Clothbd. $25.95

TREES OF THE EASTERN AND CENTRAL UNITED STATES AND CANADA, William M. Harlow. Best one-volume guide to 140 trees. Full descriptions, woodlore, range, etc. Over 600 illustrations. Handy size. 288pp. 4½ x 6⅜. 20395-6 Pa. $6.95

SONGS OF WESTERN BIRDS, Dr. Donald J. Borror. Complete song and call repertoire of 60 western species, including flycatchers, juncoes, cactus wrens, many more–includes fully illustrated booklet. Cassette and manual 99913-0 $8.95

GROWING AND USING HERBS AND SPICES, Milo Miloradovich. Versatile handbook provides all the information needed for cultivation and use of all the herbs and spices available in North America. 4 illustrations. Index. Glossary. 236pp. 5⅜ x 8½. 25058-X Pa. $6.95

BIG BOOK OF MAZES AND LABYRINTHS, Walter Shepherd. 50 mazes and labyrinths in all–classical, solid, ripple, and more–in one great volume. Perfect inexpensive puzzler for clever youngsters. Full solutions. 112pp. 8⅛ x 11. 22951-3 Pa. $4.95

PIANO TUNING, J. Cree Fischer. Clearest, best book for beginner, amateur. Simple repairs, raising dropped notes, tuning by easy method of flattened fifths. No previous skills needed. 4 illustrations. 201pp. 5⅜ x 8½. 23267-0 Pa. $6.95

A SOURCE BOOK IN THEATRICAL HISTORY, A. M. Nagler. Contemporary observers on acting, directing, make-up, costuming, stage props, machinery, scene design, from Ancient Greece to Chekhov. 611pp. 5⅜ x 8½. 20515-0 Pa. $12.95

THE COMPLETE NONSENSE OF EDWARD LEAR, Edward Lear. All nonsense limericks, zany alphabets, Owl and Pussycat, songs, nonsense botany, etc., illustrated by Lear. Total of 320pp. 5⅜ x 8½. (USO) 20167-8 Pa. $6.95

VICTORIAN PARLOUR POETRY: An Annotated Anthology, Michael R. Turner. 117 gems by Longfellow, Tennyson, Browning, many lesser-known poets. "The Village Blacksmith," "Curfew Must Not Ring Tonight," "Only a Baby Small," dozens more, often difficult to find elsewhere. Index of poets, titles, first lines. xxiii + 325pp. 5⅜ x 8¼. 27044-0 Pa. $8.95

DUBLINERS, James Joyce. Fifteen stories offer vivid, tightly focused observations of the lives of Dublin's poorer classes. At least one, "The Dead," is considered a masterpiece. Reprinted complete and unabridged from standard edition. 160pp. 5 3/16 x 8¼. 26870-5 Pa. $1.00

THE HAUNTED MONASTERY and THE CHINESE MAZE MURDERS, Robert van Gulik. Two full novels by van Gulik, set in 7th-century China, continue adventures of Judge Dee and his companions. An evil Taoist monastery, seemingly supernatural events; overgrown topiary maze hides strange crimes. 27 illustrations. 328pp. 5⅜ x 8½. 23502-5 Pa. $8.95

THE BOOK OF THE SACRED MAGIC OF ABRAMELIN THE MAGE, translated by S. MacGregor Mathers. Medieval manuscript of ceremonial magic. Basic document in Aleister Crowley, Golden Dawn groups. 268pp. 5⅜ x 8½. 23211-5 Pa. $8.95

NEW RUSSIAN-ENGLISH AND ENGLISH-RUSSIAN DICTIONARY, M. A. O'Brien. This is a remarkably handy Russian dictionary, containing a surprising amount of information, including over 70,000 entries. 366pp. 4½ x 6⅛. 20208-9 Pa. $9.95

HISTORIC HOMES OF THE AMERICAN PRESIDENTS, Second, Revised Edition, Irvin Haas. A traveler's guide to American Presidential homes, most open to the public, depicting and describing homes occupied by every American President from George Washington to George Bush. With visiting hours, admission charges, travel routes. 175 photographs. Index. 160pp. 8¼ x 11. 26751-2 Pa. $11.95

NEW YORK IN THE FORTIES, Andreas Feininger. 162 brilliant photographs by the well-known photographer, formerly with *Life* magazine. Commuters, shoppers, Times Square at night, much else from city at its peak. Captions by John von Hartz. 181pp. 9¼ x 10¾. 23585-8 Pa. $12.95

INDIAN SIGN LANGUAGE, William Tomkins. Over 525 signs developed by Sioux and other tribes. Written instructions and diagrams. Also 290 pictographs. 111pp. 6⅛ x 9¼. 22029-X Pa. $3.95

ANATOMY: A Complete Guide for Artists, Joseph Sheppard. A master of figure drawing shows artists how to render human anatomy convincingly. Over 460 illustrations. 224pp. 8⅜ x 11¼. 27279-6 Pa. $10.95

MEDIEVAL CALLIGRAPHY: Its History and Technique, Marc Drogin. Spirited history, comprehensive instruction manual covers 13 styles (ca. 4th century thru 15th). Excellent photographs; directions for duplicating medieval techniques with modern tools. 224pp. 8⅜ x 11¼. 26142-5 Pa. $12.95

DRIED FLOWERS: How to Prepare Them, Sarah Whitlock and Martha Rankin. Complete instructions on how to use silica gel, meal and borax, perlite aggregate, sand and borax, glycerine and water to create attractive permanent flower arrangements. 12 illustrations. 32pp. 5⅜ x 8½. 21802-3 Pa. $1.00

EASY-TO-MAKE BIRD FEEDERS FOR WOODWORKERS, Scott D. Campbell. Detailed, simple-to-use guide for designing, constructing, caring for and using feeders. Text, illustrations for 12 classic and contemporary designs. 96pp. 5⅜ x 8½.
25847-5 Pa. $2.95

SCOTTISH WONDER TALES FROM MYTH AND LEGEND, Donald A. Mackenzie. 16 lively tales tell of giants rumbling down mountainsides, of a magic wand that turns stone pillars into warriors, of gods and goddesses, evil hags, powerful forces and more. 240pp. 5⅜ x 8½. 29677-6 Pa. $6.95

THE HISTORY OF UNDERCLOTHES, C. Willett Cunnington and Phyllis Cunnington. Fascinating, well-documented survey covering six centuries of English undergarments, enhanced with over 100 illustrations: 12th-century laced-up bodice, footed long drawers (1795), 19th-century bustles, 19th-century corsets for men, Victorian "bust improvers," much more. 272pp. 5⅜ x 8¼. 27124-2 Pa. $9.95

ARTS AND CRAFTS FURNITURE: The Complete Brooks Catalog of 1912, Brooks Manufacturing Co. Photos and detailed descriptions of more than 150 now very collectible furniture designs from the Arts and Crafts movement depict davenports, settees, buffets, desks, tables, chairs, bedsteads, dressers and more, all built of solid, quarter-sawed oak. Invaluable for students and enthusiasts of antiques, Americana and the decorative arts. 80pp. 6½ x 9¼. 27471-3 Pa. $8.95

HOW WE INVENTED THE AIRPLANE: An Illustrated History, Orville Wright. Fascinating firsthand account covers early experiments, construction of planes and motors, first flights, much more. Introduction and commentary by Fred C. Kelly. 76 photographs. 96pp. 8¼ x 11. 25662-6 Pa. $8.95

THE ARTS OF THE SAILOR: Knotting, Splicing and Ropework, Hervey Garrett Smith. Indispensable shipboard reference covers tools, basic knots and useful hitches; handsewing and canvas work, more. Over 100 illustrations. Delightful reading for sea lovers. 256pp. 5⅜ x 8½. 26440-8 Pa. $7.95

FRANK LLOYD WRIGHT'S FALLINGWATER: The House and Its History, Second, Revised Edition, Donald Hoffmann. A total revision–both in text and illustrations–of the standard document on Fallingwater, the boldest, most personal architectural statement of Wright's mature years, updated with valuable new material from the recently opened Frank Lloyd Wright Archives. "Fascinating"–*The New York Times.* 116 illustrations. 128pp. 9¼ x 10¾. 27430-6 Pa. $11.95

PHOTOGRAPHIC SKETCHBOOK OF THE CIVIL WAR, Alexander Gardner. 100 photos taken on field during the Civil War. Famous shots of Manassas Harper's Ferry, Lincoln, Richmond, slave pens, etc. 244pp. 10⅝ x 8¼. 22731-6 Pa. $9.95

FIVE ACRES AND INDEPENDENCE, Maurice G. Kains. Great back-to-the-land classic explains basics of self-sufficient farming. The one book to get. 95 illustrations. 397pp. 5⅜ x 8½. 20974-1 Pa. $7.95

SONGS OF EASTERN BIRDS, Dr. Donald J. Borror. Songs and calls of 60 species most common to eastern U.S.: warblers, woodpeckers, flycatchers, thrushes, larks, many more in high-quality recording. Cassette and manual 99912-2 $9.95

A MODERN HERBAL, Margaret Grieve. Much the fullest, most exact, most useful compilation of herbal material. Gigantic alphabetical encyclopedia, from aconite to zedoary, gives botanical information, medical properties, folklore, economic uses, much else. Indispensable to serious reader. 161 illustrations. 888pp. 6½ x 9¼. 2-vol. set. (USO) Vol. I: 22798-7 Pa. $9.95
Vol. II: 22799-5 Pa. $9.95

HIDDEN TREASURE MAZE BOOK, Dave Phillips. Solve 34 challenging mazes accompanied by heroic tales of adventure. Evil dragons, people-eating plants, blood-thirsty giants, many more dangerous adversaries lurk at every twist and turn. 34 mazes, stories, solutions. 48pp. 8¼ x 11. 24566-7 Pa. $2.95

LETTERS OF W. A. MOZART, Wolfgang A. Mozart. Remarkable letters show bawdy wit, humor, imagination, musical insights, contemporary musical world; includes some letters from Leopold Mozart. 276pp. 5⅜ x 8½. 22859-2 Pa. $7.95

BASIC PRINCIPLES OF CLASSICAL BALLET, Agrippina Vaganova. Great Russian theoretician, teacher explains methods for teaching classical ballet. 118 illustrations. 175pp. 5⅜ x 8½. 22036-2 Pa. $5.95

THE JUMPING FROG, Mark Twain. Revenge edition. The original story of The Celebrated Jumping Frog of Calaveras County, a hapless French translation, and Twain's hilarious "retranslation" from the French. 12 illustrations. 66pp. 5⅜ x 8½. 22686-7 Pa. $3.95

BEST REMEMBERED POEMS, Martin Gardner (ed.). The 126 poems in this superb collection of 19th- and 20th-century British and American verse range from Shelley's "To a Skylark" to the impassioned "Renascence" of Edna St. Vincent Millay and to Edward Lear's whimsical "The Owl and the Pussycat." 224pp. 5⅜ x 8½. 27165-X Pa. $4.95

COMPLETE SONNETS, William Shakespeare. Over 150 exquisite poems deal with love, friendship, the tyranny of time, beauty's evanescence, death and other themes in language of remarkable power, precision and beauty. Glossary of archaic terms. 80pp. $5\frac{3}{16}$ x 8¼. 26686-9 Pa. $1.00

BODIES IN A BOOKSHOP, R. T. Campbell. Challenging mystery of blackmail and murder with ingenious plot and superbly drawn characters. In the best tradition of British suspense fiction. 192pp. 5⅜ x 8½. 24720-1 Pa. $6.95

THE WIT AND HUMOR OF OSCAR WILDE, Alvin Redman (ed.). More than 1,000 ripostes, paradoxes, wisecracks: Work is the curse of the drinking classes; I can resist everything except temptation; etc. 258pp. 5⅜ x 8½. 20602-5 Pa. $5.95

SHAKESPEARE LEXICON AND QUOTATION DICTIONARY, Alexander Schmidt. Full definitions, locations, shades of meaning in every word in plays and poems. More than 50,000 exact quotations. 1,485pp. 6½ x 9¼. 2-vol. set.
Vol. 1: 22726-X Pa. $16.95
Vol. 2: 22727-8 Pa. $16.95

SELECTED POEMS, Emily Dickinson. Over 100 best-known, best-loved poems by one of America's foremost poets, reprinted from authoritative early editions. No comparable edition at this price. Index of first lines. 64pp. 5³⁄₁₆ x 8¼.
26466-1 Pa. $1.00

CELEBRATED CASES OF JUDGE DEE (DEE GOONG AN), translated by Robert van Gulik. Authentic 18th-century Chinese detective novel; Dee and associates solve three interlocked cases. Led to van Gulik's own stories with same characters. Extensive introduction. 9 illustrations. 237pp. 5⅜ x 8½. 23337-5 Pa. $6.95

THE MALLEUS MALEFICARUM OF KRAMER AND SPRENGER, translated by Montague Summers. Full text of most important witchhunter's "bible," used by both Catholics and Protestants. 278pp. 6⅝ x 10. 22802-9 Pa. $12.95

SPANISH STORIES/CUENTOS ESPAÑOLES: A Dual-Language Book, Angel Flores (ed.). Unique format offers 13 great stories in Spanish by Cervantes, Borges, others. Faithful English translations on facing pages. 352pp. 5⅜ x 8½.
25399-6 Pa. $8.95

THE CHICAGO WORLD'S FAIR OF 1893: A Photographic Record, Stanley Appelbaum (ed.). 128 rare photos show 200 buildings, Beaux-Arts architecture, Midway, original Ferris Wheel, Edison's kinetoscope, more. Architectural emphasis; full text. 116pp. 8¼ x 11. 23990-X Pa. $9.95

OLD QUEENS, N.Y., IN EARLY PHOTOGRAPHS, Vincent F. Seyfried and William Asadorian. Over 160 rare photographs of Maspeth, Jamaica, Jackson Heights, and other areas. Vintage views of DeWitt Clinton mansion, 1939 World's Fair and more. Captions. 192pp. 8⅞ x 11. 26358-4 Pa. $12.95

CAPTURED BY THE INDIANS: 15 Firsthand Accounts, 1750-1870, Frederick Drimmer. Astounding true historical accounts of grisly torture, bloody conflicts, relentless pursuits, miraculous escapes and more, by people who lived to tell the tale. 384pp. 5⅜ x 8½. 24901-8 Pa. $8.95

THE WORLD'S GREAT SPEECHES, Lewis Copeland and Lawrence W. Lamm (eds.). Vast collection of 278 speeches of Greeks to 1970. Powerful and effective models; unique look at history. 842pp. 5⅜ x 8½. 20468-5 Pa. $14.95

THE BOOK OF THE SWORD, Sir Richard F. Burton. Great Victorian scholar/adventurer's eloquent, erudite history of the "queen of weapons"–from prehistory to early Roman Empire. Evolution and development of early swords, variations (sabre, broadsword, cutlass, scimitar, etc.), much more. 336pp. 6⅛ x 9¼.
25434-8 Pa. $9.95

AUTOBIOGRAPHY: The Story of My Experiments with Truth, Mohandas K. Gandhi. Boyhood, legal studies, purification, the growth of the Satyagraha (nonviolent protest) movement. Critical, inspiring work of the man responsible for the freedom of India. 480pp. 5⅜ x 8½. (USO) 24593-4 Pa. $8.95

CELTIC MYTHS AND LEGENDS, T. W. Rolleston. Masterful retelling of Irish and Welsh stories and tales. Cuchulain, King Arthur, Deirdre, the Grail, many more. First paperback edition. 58 full-page illustrations. 512pp. 5⅜ x 8½. 26507-2 Pa. $9.95

THE PRINCIPLES OF PSYCHOLOGY, William James. Famous long course complete, unabridged. Stream of thought, time perception, memory, experimental methods; great work decades ahead of its time. 94 figures. 1,391pp. 5⅜ x 8½. 2-vol. set.
Vol. I: 20381-6 Pa. $12.95
Vol. II: 20382-4 Pa. $12.95

THE WORLD AS WILL AND REPRESENTATION, Arthur Schopenhauer. Definitive English translation of Schopenhauer's life work, correcting more than 1,000 errors, omissions in earlier translations. Translated by E. F. J. Payne. Total of 1,269pp. 5⅜ x 8½. 2-vol. set.
Vol. 1: 21761-2 Pa. $11.95
Vol. 2: 21762-0 Pa. $12.95

MAGIC AND MYSTERY IN TIBET, Madame Alexandra David-Neel. Experiences among lamas, magicians, sages, sorcerers, Bonpa wizards. A true psychic discovery. 32 illustrations. 321pp. 5⅜ x 8½. (USO) 22682-4 Pa. $8.95

THE EGYPTIAN BOOK OF THE DEAD, E. A. Wallis Budge. Complete reproduction of Ani's papyrus, finest ever found. Full hieroglyphic text, interlinear transliteration, word-for-word translation, smooth translation. 533pp. 6½ x 9¼.
21866-X Pa. $10.95

MATHEMATICS FOR THE NONMATHEMATICIAN, Morris Kline. Detailed, college-level treatment of mathematics in cultural and historical context, with numerous exercises. Recommended Reading Lists. Tables. Numerous figures. 641pp. 5⅜ x 8½.
24823-2 Pa. $11.95

THEORY OF WING SECTIONS: Including a Summary of Airfoil Data, Ira H. Abbott and A. E. von Doenhoff. Concise compilation of subsonic aerodynamic characteristics of NACA wing sections, plus description of theory. 350pp. of tables. 693pp. 5⅜ x 8½. 60586-8 Pa. $14.95

THE RIME OF THE ANCIENT MARINER, Gustave Doré, S. T. Coleridge. Doré's finest work; 34 plates capture moods, subtleties of poem. Flawless full-size reproductions printed on facing pages with authoritative text of poem. "Beautiful. Simply beautiful."–*Publisher's Weekly.* 77pp. 9¼ x 12. 22305-1 Pa. $6.95

NORTH AMERICAN INDIAN DESIGNS FOR ARTISTS AND CRAFTSPEOPLE, Eva Wilson. Over 360 authentic copyright-free designs adapted from Navajo blankets, Hopi pottery, Sioux buffalo hides, more. Geometrics, symbolic figures, plant and animal motifs, etc. 128pp. 8⅜ x 11. (EUK) 25341-4 Pa. $8.95

SCULPTURE: Principles and Practice, Louis Slobodkin. Step-by-step approach to clay, plaster, metals, stone; classical and modern. 253 drawings, photos. 255pp. 8⅛ x 11.
22960-2 Pa. $11.95

THE INFLUENCE OF SEA POWER UPON HISTORY, 1660–1783, A. T. Mahan. Influential classic of naval history and tactics still used as text in war colleges. First paperback edition. 4 maps. 24 battle plans. 640pp. 5⅜ x 8½. 25509-3 Pa. $12.95

THE STORY OF THE TITANIC AS TOLD BY ITS SURVIVORS, Jack Winocour (ed.). What it was really like. Panic, despair, shocking inefficiency, and a little heroism. More thrilling than any fictional account. 26 illustrations. 320pp. 5⅜ x 8½. 20610-6 Pa. $8.95

FAIRY AND FOLK TALES OF THE IRISH PEASANTRY, William Butler Yeats (ed.). Treasury of 64 tales from the twilight world of Celtic myth and legend: "The Soul Cages," "The Kildare Pooka," "King O'Toole and his Goose," many more. Introduction and Notes by W. B. Yeats. 352pp. 5⅜ x 8½. 26941-8 Pa. $8.95

BUDDHIST MAHAYANA TEXTS, E. B. Cowell and Others (eds.). Superb, accurate translations of basic documents in Mahayana Buddhism, highly important in history of religions. The Buddha-karita of Asvaghosha, Larger Sukhavativyuha, more. 448pp. 5⅜ x 8½. 25552-2 Pa. $12.95

ONE TWO THREE . . . INFINITY: Facts and Speculations of Science, George Gamow. Great physicist's fascinating, readable overview of contemporary science: number theory, relativity, fourth dimension, entropy, genes, atomic structure, much more. 128 illustrations. Index. 352pp. 5⅜ x 8½. 25664-2 Pa. $8.95

ENGINEERING IN HISTORY, Richard Shelton Kirby, et al. Broad, nontechnical survey of history's major technological advances: birth of Greek science, industrial revolution, electricity and applied science, 20th-century automation, much more. 181 illustrations. ". . . excellent . . ."–*Isis.* Bibliography. vii + 530pp. 5⅜ x 8¼. 26412-2 Pa. $14.95

DALÍ ON MODERN ART: The Cuckolds of Antiquated Modern Art, Salvador Dalí. Influential painter skewers modern art and its practitioners. Outrageous evaluations of Picasso, Cézanne, Turner, more. 15 renderings of paintings discussed. 44 calligraphic decorations by Dalí. 96pp. 5⅜ x 8½. (USO) 29220-7 Pa. $4.95

ANTIQUE PLAYING CARDS: A Pictorial History, Henry René D'Allemagne. Over 900 elaborate, decorative images from rare playing cards (14th–20th centuries): Bacchus, death, dancing dogs, hunting scenes, royal coats of arms, players cheating, much more. 96pp. 9¼ x 12¼. 29265-7 Pa. $11.95

MAKING FURNITURE MASTERPIECES: 30 Projects with Measured Drawings, Franklin H. Gottshall. Step-by-step instructions, illustrations for constructing handsome, useful pieces, among them a Sheraton desk, Chippendale chair, Spanish desk, Queen Anne table and a William and Mary dressing mirror. 224pp. 8⅛ x 11¼. 29338-6 Pa. $13.95

THE FOSSIL BOOK: A Record of Prehistoric Life, Patricia V. Rich et al. Profusely illustrated definitive guide covers everything from single-celled organisms and dinosaurs to birds and mammals and the interplay between climate and man. Over 1,500 illustrations. 760pp. 7½ x 10⅛. 29371-8 Pa. $29.95

Prices subject to change without notice.

Available at your book dealer or write for free catalog to Dept. GI, Dover Publications, Inc., 31 East 2nd St., Mineola, N.Y. 11501. Dover publishes more than 500 books each year on science, elementary and advanced mathematics, biology, music, art, literary history, social sciences and other areas.